Hate To LOVE You

An Ellington U Novel

BY RAE QUINN

Hate To Love You
Copyright © 2024 Rae Quinn

Published by Rae Quinn
Cover Illustration by Maria Teressa
@essasketch
ISBN: 979-8-9913334-0-5

To my mom.
My best friend, my biggest supporter, and the strongest woman I know. I wouldn't be publishing my second book if it wasn't for you. Thank you for pushing me and making me feel like anything is possible.
I love you, always.

RYKER

The sound of my alarm blares in my ears as I lay in bed, refusing to open my eyes. I pull the pillow over my head and groan.

Fuck… it's too damn early.

Tossing the pillow on the ground and rolling over, I grab my phone off the nightstand and turn the alarm off. 7:00am. It should be a fucking crime to wake up this early.

The bed shifts as the naked woman beside me turns over to face me. Her eyes flutter open and she stretches, her perky tits flashing me causing my cock to stand up.

I don't normally do sleepovers, but I guess we fell asleep. I was drunk as fuck last night, and I barely remember even coming back to my room.

A tan arm lays on top of my waist as the girl kisses my neck. As much as I want to fuck right now, I have to get to class. I peel her arm off me and climb out of bed, grabbing my boxers off the floor and sliding them on. The girl groans and gives me the puppy dog eyes. Too bad that doesn't work on me.

"Stay in bed with me," she whimpers, tapping the empty space in my bed where I was laying ten seconds ago.

"Can't. I've got a meeting. I'm gonna shower. You can let yourself out." The girl pouts and doesn't make a move to get up.

"Well, will I see you again?" she asks, and I don't miss the hopefulness in her voice. No, probably not.

"Sure," I lie.

With that, I walk out of the room and head to the bathroom to shower, leaving the naked girl alone on my bed. Hopefully she'll be gone by the time I get back. I let the hot water fall down my body as I stare up at the ceiling thinking of all the ways I can get out of this meeting today.

Meeting with Robert Steele is the last thing I want to do today, or any day for that matter. My father texted me last night requesting that I meet him this morning to discuss an important matter. He probably wants to tell me what a shit son I am and how disappointed he is that I haven't chosen to follow in his footsteps no doubt. He could have just done that over the phone like he normally does.

My father and I have never gotten along. He's an asshole who only cares about two things, money and power. He's never given a shit about me, or my brother. He made that obvious when he chose his work over our family time and time again.

My mother begged him to spend time at home with us. She grew depressed as he distanced himself more and more and buried himself into work. I guess this was because my grandfather instilled in him that work was the most important thing a man has. Providing for his family was his duty, and if he could not do that, he was a failure.

Although, despite what my grandfather taught my father, he was the polar opposite. He was kind and loving, he treated my grandmother like a queen until the day she died. He never showed her anything but love and compassion, and even as a child, I recognized this.

My grandfather taught my brother and I more than my father ever could or was willing to. He would bring us to his office and let us run through the halls. He'd even chase us once in a while.

As we got older, he began teaching us about the business. The Steele Corporation was his baby, and he built it from the ground up to the multibillion dollar conglomerate it is today.

One day, as I sat in his office, the New York City skyline peeking through the huge windows and the scent of his cigars filling my senses, he told me I'd run the company someday.

"Someday, this whole corporation will be yours, Ryker. This is your legacy." I smiled because I thought my grandfather was the greatest man in the world, and I couldn't imagine doing anything different.

But when my grandfather fell ill, my father stepped up and took his place as CEO.

Growing up with my father was like trying to navigate my way through a long and winding maze of disappointment.

His words were constant reminders of everything I was doing wrong, and his actions were nothing short of cold. I longed for the loving dad I could have had, but all I got were cold stares and lectures on how I should try harder to be more like him.

His expectations were towering, impossible peaks that I could never climb. No matter how hard I tried, I was never good enough for him. Every achievement of mine was met with a dismissive wave, followed by a list of what I could have done better.

There were moments when I believed his fatherly love might break through the layers of bitterness, but they were fleeting. His love was conditional, a prize to be earned through constant flawless performance. But no matter how hard I tried, the goals kept shifting, and the prize always remained out of reach.

As I grew older, resentment settled in my gut like bad sushi. The pain of unmet expectations and constant criticism shaped me in ways I struggled to understand. I've carried the weight of his disapproval, questioning my worth at every turn.

Still now, twenty-two years later, I'm a disappointment, even though I'm going to this stupid school that he wanted me to go to, and have joined The Ellington Elite, despite my not wanting any part of it.

I let my shower run a little longer than I should have so I'm going to be late to our meeting which will only piss my father off and honestly, that's what I'm best at so why stop now?

I wrap my towel around my waist, brush my teeth, and comb my hair before walking back to my room and noticing the naked woman *still* in my bed, sleeping. For fucks sake, did she not get the fucking hint earlier?

I pick her bra and tiny dress up off my floor and toss them at her. They land right on her face as she startles awake.

I ignore her moan of protest as I walk to my closet, pulling out some black jeans and a black V-neck t-shirt. Pulling the shirt over my head, I walk out to see that the girl has finally gotten out of my bed and put her dress on.

She strolls over to me and slings a thin arm over my shoulder. I don't say a word which obviously irritates her because she pouts, her bottom lip jutting out so far, it's like she's begging me to grab it with my teeth. But I'm not in the mood anymore.

"I gotta go, you should've left while I was in the shower," I tell her, taking her arm off of my shoulder and side stepping her to walk to my door. She follows reluctantly.

"I wanted to see you before you left. Thanks for a great night, Ryker. We should totally do this again sometime," she bats her long black eyelashes at me, and I give her my best fake smile.

"Yeah, totally. See you around, Ashley," I say as I begin to close the door in her face. Her tiny palm slams on the door before it closes, and she looks upset. Shit, what now?

"It's Amy. My name is Amy," I stifle a laugh.

"Fuck, sorry. Right, see you around, Amy," With that, I close the door and lock it before she has the chance to say anything back.

God, I hate one-night stands.

Chapter 2

RYKER

I spot my father sitting at a small table outside the library on Ellington's campus about fifteen minutes later. Despite seeing him a few weeks ago, he looks like he's aged years. His black suit matches his jet black, slicked back hair and the black mustache that makes him look like a mob boss.

He doesn't look up from the newspaper he's reading as I take the seat across from him. My father emanates power and strength.

He clears his throat before speaking.

"Son," he says coldly. I watch him as he sips his drink and stares at his paper, not even giving me a glance.

"Father," I answer with the same coldness.

"It's been a while. How are things?" he doesn't actually care. He's only asking out of obligation so he can go back to my mom and report what I've told him.

"Same as always. Been busy," I tell him. My father huffs.

"Busy, huh? Dean Ashby called me the other day."

"Did he? And what did he have to say?"

My father went to Ellington University, as did my grandfather, and my great grandfather before him. Now, my brother and I attend.

My father has kept in contact with a lot of his peers from the university, especially Dean Ashby who he gets all of his intel on me from. He's not as concerned about my younger brother, Logan since he's the golden child and obviously can do no wrong.

"He mentioned your attendance is low," he still hasn't looked up from his paper, but I know exactly where he's going with this.

"Yeah, this one class has been proving to be a challenge. It's kept me up pretty late studying, so I've missed a few classes," I lie.

"…And that your GPA has fallen below average."

God damnit. I knew I wasn't doing well, but I didn't know it was that bad.

A warm breeze blows a stray piece of my dark hair away from my forehead as I stare at my father, waiting for him to continue his lecture. There's no doubt in my mind that he came here to talk about more than just my study habits.

"Just say what you came here to say, father," I grind my teeth so hard it hurts.

He finally puts down the paper to look at me, his eyes full of something unidentifiable. He taps his index finger on the table a few times before speaking.

"You know how hard I worked to get you into this school, Ryker. Do you know how embarrassing it is to get a call from the dean telling me my son, my legacy, is failing? It's unacceptable."

His face is bright red and the air outside which was warm before turns scalding as my skin starts to burn with heat. "If you want any chance at a successful future with The Steele Corporation, you need to start taking this seriously," I can't help but roll my eyes.

A successful future? Is he for real right now? It's one class. I'll get my grade up, graduate, and get the hell out of town right after. No one said anything about needing a 4.0 or anything.

"It's only the beginning of the semester. Don't worry, father. Your perfect reputation won't be tarnished. As long as I graduate, your legacy will live on," I say with a sardonic tone. My father lays both arms on the table as he leans in to get closer. He speaks in a low, harsh tone that only I can hear.

"That's the thing, *son*," he grits out the word like it's hard for him to even say aloud. "If you keep going down this path, you won't be graduating, and I will not use my power to help you."

As if I would even ask him to. I don't need his help. I never have.

"You haven't been to see your academic advisor in weeks. You've missed more than half of your classes doing God knows what."

He takes a deep breath, looking like he's trying not to strangle me in front of the crowd of students walking by. Sitting back in his chair, he straightens his tie and buttons his suit jacket.

"You need to get your shit together, and fast," he clears his throat. "You will attend your classes, *every* class, and you will get nothing short of a B plus in each of your courses, or so help me god, I will-"

"You'll what? What will you do, father?" I ask, pushing him to finish the sentence. There's nothing he *can* do. He glowers at me before standing and grabbing his coffee cup and paper off of the table.

"You don't want to find out, Ryker."

With that, he leaves me sitting there, watching him walk away, too stunned to move.

Chapter 3

RYKER

A few hours later, I'm sitting at the Ellington Elite mansion with Patrick, Holland, Logan, and Mason. We all share the house and mostly everything in it other than our rooms, thank God.

I never had to deal with that dorm shit since I'm part of the Ellington Elite and any member of the Elite stays in the house. There are a few other guys that live in the house on its third floor, but we don't really talk to them much unless we're having an Elite meeting which usually consists of fucking around and not getting anything done.

My brother Logan is one of them. We don't get along much, but I do try to look out for him. Logan has never experienced our father's disappointment or foul attitude. He's the golden child, and he can do no wrong. I'm the first born, I should be better.

Where I couldn't give a shit about what our father thinks of me, Logan lives to impress him. Logan didn't want anything to do with the Elite, but father didn't give him much of a choice, and Logan didn't argue. He attends meetings and participates in events and parties, but he doesn't get into trouble.

Holland and Mason sit on the couch, arguing over who should have won their last game of… whatever the fuck they're playing. I don't do video games.

Patrick sits at the small table in the corner of the room with Logan across from him on his phone. There are books spread out on the table and Patrick's head is crooked down, reading quietly while I sit in the chair diagonal from the couch scrolling through my phone.

Logan's only a year younger than I am, making him and Holland the same age, and the youngest of our group. Mason, Patrick, and I are seniors, and Logan and Holland are juniors.

I'd say Patrick is definitely the smartest of us all. He's studying to be a doctor, no, not just a doctor. A damn neurosurgeon. I don't get why because his family is even wealthier than mine and he could easily just get a job at his family's company. But he doesn't want to. He doesn't want to be stuck in an office all day, following orders from his father and not having a say in his life. That, I do understand.

Patrick and I have been friends since grade school. We grew up in the same circles and we hit it off pretty early on. Both of our fathers were part of the Ellington Elite, meaning we're both legacies, which is why we had no choice of any other school. We had to attend Ellington University or nothing at all.

Mason and Holland are cousins, so they came together. Holland's twin sister Ellie attends the university as well. She's cool, she goes out with us sometimes with her friend Lainey. Their dad's part of the fucking mafia or some shit like that. I never really cared enough to ask. Mason and Holland are chill, and we all get along pretty well which is a plus.

The Ellington Elite is like a secret society that isn't a secret, and everyone knows about it. Most of its members come from rich and important families. More than half are legacies, and the others earn their way in.

The Elite are the big men on campus. The ones every guy wants to be and every girl wants to fuck. We don't do anything illegal, just throw some big ass parties and mess with people a little when they deserve it.

We're pretty much untouchable due to how much money our families shovel into the university and the questionable positions some of our parents hold in society. Most professors let us skate by since a lot of them get paid off.

I guess one of my asshole professors didn't get the fucking memo, because I'm failing. Of course, I haven't really been to class in a bit. While I enjoy literature, I'd rather read stories that I enjoy, ones that interest me. Not ones I'm forced to read and then write eight-page essays on. That may be fun for some people, but it's not for me.

Professor Whitely has it out for me, I swear. Even when I do show up on occasion, she's a total bitch. She's hot though, and I don't doubt there's some blackmailing material to dig up on her.

Patrick looks up from his book to watch Holland and Mason's game, and his gaze slowly creeps over to me. I can feel his stare burning the side of my face.

"Can I help you?" I bite out. He shrugs, leaning back into his chair and crossing his arms over his chest.

"You're being unusually quiet over there," his eyes squint as if he's trying to search me for any hidden secrets.

"I'm always quiet," Holland and Mason shut their game off and put their controllers down on the coffee table, simultaneously looking at me and waiting for me to provide more of a response. Logan peeks over his phone slightly. God damnit.

"Not this quiet. Usually, you would have given one of us shit by now. You're not capable of sitting still this long," Patrick knows me too well, and he's not wrong about that. I get bored too easily. Another reason I hate sitting in those boring classes, listening to lectures about shit I don't even care about.

"Jesus, fine. I met with my dad today."

All three of their faces fall as concern takes over, and Logan looks back to his phone, no longer paying attention. It's no secret that my dad and I don't get along. They know the issues we have.

Patrick breaks the awkward silence that's taken over the room by clearing his throat. "Shit, man. You okay?" I nod.

"I'm fine. Can we drop it?" Mason and Holland exchange a look before turning their attention to their phones. Patrick gives me a salute and goes back to his book.

Fuck, I need a drink. But I have class soon, and now that my father's on my ass, I actually have to attend. Okay, class first, drinks after.

Chapter 4

GUINEVERE

The breeze feels amazing on my hot skin as I make my way across campus to my Literary Criticism class. This is one of my favorite classes so far this semester because I love reading and I enjoy talking about what I'm reading with people who are just as into it as I am. It makes the conversations so much better.

I stroll past Whittaker Hall and the library to get to Mallory Center where most of my classes take place since it's the creative arts building. All the buildings on campus are old, but not necessarily falling apart. They've done a lot of renovations and added some modern amenities, but the outside architecture is absolutely beautiful.

Ellington University was founded in the 1920s by Augustus Ellington. The story goes that Augustus was building his family a home, which was intended to be what is now known as Ellington House, or the administrative building. It was the only building standing before Augustus died and it was never finished. His wife and children moved away, and no one ever saw them again. Today, it is one of New England's grandest universities.

Many students who attend Ellington University are trust fund brats that come from families with more money than they know what to do with. I come from money, but I don't show it off like most kids here. The only reason I'm even here is because my dad was an Elite member, and his one wish was for me to attend his alma mater.

As I step into the building, my mother's name pops up on my phone screen. We talk every day, at least twice a day. Since my parents got their divorce when I was eighteen, my mom and I have gotten really close, but she's kind of been smothering me lately. I didn't want to leave her back home, but she insisted she would be okay.

It's only about a two-hour drive from where I am in Connecticut to Barrington, my hometown in Rhode Island. My father moved to California after the divorce, so I don't see him much, but he makes sure to give me updates about his life via his secretary sending me emails here and there. Him and mom are civil, but I don't see them talking much either.

Their divorce wasn't messy. It wasn't drawn out or dramatic. It was quick, painless. Like ripping off a Band-Aid. At least, it was for them.

I grew up with happy parents who were the picture of romance. They were always together, they never fought, and they loved me. My dad constantly brought home flowers for my mom, and sometimes he'd even buy me some.

"For my little princess," he'd say as he picked me up and twirled me around.

Up until I was about to leave for Ellington U, they were perfect. But the night before I left, they sat me down and told me they were getting a divorce. They admitted that they haven't been getting along for a while which was obviously a shock to me.

I didn't show them, but I was sick about it. I couldn't believe it; they were so happy.

I watched as my dad packed his things and tried not to cry. Honestly, I don't even think my mother cried.

My father left us loads of money, enough to live off of for the rest of our lives. He also set up an account for me for when I turned twenty-one, which was last year.

As soon as they signed the papers, my dad hopped on a one-way flight to California and hasn't been back since. He says he likes the weather and being close to LA.

Being a famous actor affords him many luxuries, but it also takes a lot of his time away from me. I haven't been out to visit him yet, and we rarely ever actually talk.

I answer the call and bring my phone to my ear. My mother's sweet voice speaks on the other end. "Gwenny?" The nickname makes me cringe, but I've gotten used to it.

"Hi, mom," I say with a small smile even though she can't see me.

"How are you? You didn't call me last night. I was worried. Are you okay?"

"I know, I'm sorry. I had a paper to write for my class this morning and it took a lot longer than I expected. I'm okay," I assure her. She worries so much, and I hate that she does.

I hear her let out a breath on the other end.

"Oh, okay. Good. When are you coming home?" she asks with hope in her voice. Honestly, I don't know. I don't mind my hometown, but when I'm there, it reminds me that my dad is no longer there which really brings down my mood.

"Soon, mom. I gotta get to class. I'll talk to you later," I tell her.

"Okay. Love you, sweetie."

"Love you, too," I hang up the phone and let out a small breath before continuing on my way up the stairs and to my lecture hall.

As I turn the corner toward the hall my classroom is in, I receive a text from my mother letting me know she forgot to inform me of the new dog she recently took in from our elderly neighbor. I chuckle as I begin to text back, but before I can, I run into someone, and my phone falls to the floor.

"Sorry, I-"

"Watch where you're going," the deep voice growls. What the hell? I pick my phone up off the floor, and as I stand back up, an unfamiliar face stares down at me. I don't think I've ever seen him around, but the campus is pretty big, so that makes sense.

"I'm sorry, I should have been looking-" he interrupts again.

"Yeah, you should have. Maybe don't look down at your phone while you're walking." Okay… why is this guy being so freaking rude? He was the one standing on the corner. I cross my arms over my chest and note the cell phone in his large hand.

"You were on your phone," I retort. His face is hard as stone, and if I knew better, I'd probably back down now. But there's no way I'm going to let him talk to me like that.

"I wasn't walking," he states.

"No, but you're standing right at the corner of a busy hallway, looking down at your phone. So, I should be saying that to you," I give myself a mental high five for the snark in my response.

The strangers' eyes narrow as they move up and down my body.

"Whatever. Just watch where you're going," he says again before proceeding to lean back against the wall and look down at his phone.

What a prick. If I were smarter, I would leave and forget this situation ever happened. But I'm not, so here I am. My hands land on my hips and I glare at the tall, muscular man standing in front of me.

"You know, you could be a little nicer. I said I was sorry."

His eyes roam over me once more and I'm suddenly aware of the goosebumps on my exposed arms.

The man pushes off the wall and stands in front of me. He's so close I can feel the heat emanating off his body. I can smell his musky cologne, and the slight mint in his breath. He looks me directly in the eyes before his gaze lowers to my lips, then back to my eyes. God, if he wasn't such an ass, I'd probably want him to kiss me.

"This is me being nice," he shakes his head and stalks off down the hall. I've met some assholes in my life, but he takes the freaking cake.

Chapter 5

GUINEVERE

The lecture room is big, yet stuffy since it's so old. The desks span each half of the room, with an aisle down the middle. There's a desk at the front of the room, and next to it stands a podium with a small microphone. The only thing in this room that's modern is the smart board behind the desk.

There's an old, musty smell that fills the air, and the large windows that overlook the west side of campus are smudged and slightly dirty from age.

The professor is almost always late but she's great at her job, and she loves me. I'm always one of the first ones here since I have a very particular ritual for when I arrive. I choose the same seat every single class. The end seat right near the aisle in the first row. This way I'm right in front and I can see everything without having to squint.

I take my seat and begin to empty my bag of everything I know I'll need. After a few moments, my laptop is in front of me, my pen and pencil are placed neatly on one side, my notebook and water bottle on the other.

I rub my hands on the jeans covering my thighs and adjust my blouse. My breasts sit nicely in my cotton push up bra, and the shirt definitely shows them off. The light sky-blue color makes my blue eyes pop.

My long brown hair is pulled back into a ponytail that lands at the middle of my back, and I didn't put on a ton of makeup this morning other than some mascara and blush, so I didn't look like I was dying.

As I begin typing my notes, more students file into the large room. This class isn't that popular, and most don't take it voluntarily like I did. Many people find it boring since it's just reading and then talking about it, but I find it thrilling to read new things all the time and I love debating with other points of view.

My best friend Lainey calls me a nerd because I can sit and talk for hours about a good book.

Everyone takes their seats in their typical spots, and my friend Damian takes his seat next to me, setting all of his things on the table.

His smile is contagious as he throws an arm around my shoulders, tucking me into his side.

"Hey Gwenny," he teases. He knows I hate that nickname, but he loves to annoy me. I've known Damian since we were in middle school. We met in seventh grade and have been inseparable ever since. His family moved into my neighborhood, and we hung out practically every day.

Everyone always thought we were dating, or we were going to get married one day. We did try to date once in high school, but we both decided that we were better off as friends.

When we graduated, we both applied to the same colleges, and when we were both accepted to Ellington, it made the decision easy. We take completely different classes since our majors are completely different.

Damian is a business major and I'm an education major. We wanted at least one class together so we'd always be able to see each other, even if we were too busy. So, when I suggested literary criticism, Damian agreed to enroll too.

"You know I hate it when you call me that. It's bad enough that my mom still does it," I roll my eyes at his smug expression. He loves to push my buttons. He pinches my cheek and I swat his hand away.

"What were you up to last night? You didn't answer my text," Damian pouts.

"I was working on the paper due today."

His eyes go wide.

"Shit," he mutters under his breath. Well, safe to say Damian forgot about the assignment. He's really very good at school, but since we got to college, he's been big on partying. I can't help the chuckle that escapes my mouth.

"Good morning, everyone. Sorry I'm late. Traffic was crazy this morning," Professor Whitely scurries down the steps and sets her belongings on her desk. She pulls out some stacks of paper and her laptop.

Professor Whitely is pretty young for a college professor. She can't be more than twenty-seven or twenty-eight. She's a small woman, probably around five foot one, and her dark brown hair makes her hazel eyes stand out.

She's almost always dressed in a long pencil skirt and a tight blouse which gives her this whole 'sexy librarian' look, and I'm sure that's why ninety percent of the men in this class are here.

"Alright. Let's talk. What did you all think about the book?" she pauses and looks around the room, waiting for someone to answer the questions. When no one responds, she continues. "Okay… who actually read it?" About less than half of the class raises their hands causing Professor Whitely to chuckle.

"Well, thanks for being honest, I guess. Okay, so someone who actually did the homework, tell me what you thought." Again, no one answers. I raise my hand since clearly no one is going to get this conversation started.

Professor Whitely smiles, relief taking over her features.

"Yes, Guinevere. What did you think? Romance, or tragedy?"

The book was a romantic tale about a young woman traveling the world on her own and finding the love of her life, but eventually she has to leave and go home.

Instead of going with her, the man who supposedly loved her decided to stay there and not go with her. She was heartbroken.

He ended up coming back to her, realizing she was more important than where he lived. But in the end, the woman dies, and the man is left alone in a place he doesn't know. It definitely wasn't a happy ending, and I sobbed like a baby.

"I believe it was a story of romance. A testament to what true love can overcome."

Professor Whitely smiles.

I hear a loud scoff come from somewhere behind me and my shoulders tighten. I whip around in my seat to find a face I recognize. It's the asshole from the hallway. "Is something funny?" I ask, my tone impertinent.

The guy brings a hand to his chest as if to say 'who, me?'. "I just think it's odd that you think this story is anything but a tragedy," he leans back in his seat, folding his arms across his broad chest.

"She finds the love of her life. He leaves his home to be with her. How is it not a romance?"

The guy rolls his eyes as if he's already over the conversation which only makes my annoyance with him grow.

Leaning forward and placing his forearms on the table in front of him, he steeples his fingers. I can already tell this guy is an arrogant dick.

"So, it's romantic that the woman dies in the end? It's romantic that the man moved away from his home and everything he ever knew to be with a woman who died soon after? That's not romantic, that's tragic," he argues.

I can partially see where he's coming from, but I don't want him to think that he's won.

His brows lift as if daring me to say something that contradicts his statement. A strand of his dark black hair falls into his face.

"Maybe you're just looking at it wrong. Maybe it's your cynicism that makes you think that this story is about anything other than love and devotion."

His eyes narrow and it seems like I struck a nerve.

"You don't know me," he growls.

"I don't need to know you to see how you view the world. Your pessimistic and bleak outlook on this story proves that you don't know anything about what it is to love or be loved."

It comes out so fast I can't even stop myself.

I don't think I meant to say it, but the way he was arguing with me made my blood boil. He just stares at me, no reply, nothing. Just a glare that causes a shiver to run down my spine.

Professor Whitely clears her throat. "Okay. Well, now we can see the story from different sides. Great job guys."

The rest of class goes by in a blur. After we turn in our essays, Professor Whitely dismisses us.

Damian and I pack up our things and head for the stairs, away from this nightmare of a situation I just caused.

GUINEVERE

As Damian and I head for the exit of Mallory Center, he grabs my upper arm and pulls me to the side and out of the way of oncoming students.

"Ow! What the hell?" I rub the spot on my arm he just assaulted. He lets go and looks around as if he's making sure no one is around to hear what he's about to say.

"Do you know who that was?" I shoot him a quizzical look.

"No?" Damian rolls his eyes.

"That was Ryker Steele. He's an Elite, and you just got on his bad side."

Now I roll my eyes.

Ah, yes. The Ellington Elite. The king pricks of Ellington University. The wealthiest men on campus and the most ruthless. I don't know much about their little club, but I know it's bad news. My dad didn't tell me much about his days as an Elite, but I do know to stay away from them.

Since most of them come from money, they think they're untouchable. They can pretty much do anything they want and get away with it since their parents have more money than God and can pay off any witnesses.

Girls beg for their attention and grovel at their feet to give them a chance. It's pathetic, honestly. They're nothing special. But in this life, money is power, and they have a lot of it.

"I'll be fine. He's just another douchebag with more money than brains."

Damian stifles a laugh.

I walk toward the exit with Damian trailing behind me. I turn back to make another comment on the situation at hand, but I'm interrupted as I run into something hard.

I look up, and up, and up. It's him again. Ryker Steele. God, he's tall. I take a step back and take him in. Why is he standing in my way? Again.

Damian steps up beside me as if he's ready to throw down with Ryker if he tries anything. Damian has never fought a day in his life, so he'd definitely get his ass kicked, but I appreciate the gesture.

Ryker glares down at me, his green eyes dark. He towers over me. He must be at least six foot two. His arms are crossed, and I can see the veins underneath his tan skin.

"You make a habit of running into people?" he asks. My body stiffens and I narrow my eyes.

"Do you make a habit of standing in the middle of walkways?" his jaw clenches as he crosses his arms over his chest, making the muscles ripple underneath his skin.

"So… Just another douchebag with more money than brains, huh? That's a new one," I should be embarrassed that he heard me, but part of me is actually glad he did.

"Really? You don't get that all the time?" I give him a sardonic smile, looking directly into his eyes. They're an unbelievable shade of green that I've never seen before, complete with a black ring around them. He has a bit of dark stubble around his jaw that matches the dark hair on his head.

His lips curl into an arrogant smirk. "Maybe, but never to my face. Words hurt ya know."

This guy is unbelievable.

My pointer finger taps on the side of my leg repeatedly as I try to calm myself. "I didn't say it to your face. You were eavesdropping. Now, can you please move out of my way now so I can go home?" I go to step around him, grabbing Damian's hand to follow, but Ryker follows, blocking us from leaving.

"Just hold on a minute," he studies my face for a moment, and I can feel my cheeks heat under his assessing gaze. "You don't like me very much, do you?" he asks, cocking a dark eyebrow. Is he kidding?

"I don't even know you," but if I did, I'd definitely hate him more than I already do. I cross my arms over my chest.

Ryker holds his hand out for me to shake. I don't take it. Instead, I just stand there glaring at him, hoping he'll get the hint that I want nothing to do with him. His arm falls and he chuckles.

"Okay, fine. I'm Ryker. And you are? Guinevere, was it?"

"Who I am doesn't concern you. Have a nice day," I grab Damian's hand again and begin to pull him with me and away from the asshole in front of me that is Ryker Steele, but I decide to say one more thing before I go. "Actually, no. Have a shit day."

I continue on my way, Damian in tow, but before we get far, Ryker grabs my forearm, halting my steps. Damian stops at my side, glaring at Ryker.

I stare at the spot on my arm that Ryker is holding, the heat from his hand scorching my skin. My eyes move from his hand to his face. His smug expression has turned into something darker as his gaze moves over my face.

"I think you owe me an apology, *Gwen*," the way he says my name sends a tingle down my spine.

An apology? I do feel kind of bad for what I said in class. I'm usually very calm and contained. But then I remembered how he treated me after I ran into him before class. He deserved every word.

"I don't owe you anything," I swipe my arm away from him and begin walking again. This time Ryker doesn't stop me.

Damian throws his arm around my shoulders as we walk down the sidewalk.

"You should really teach that girlfriend of yours some manners," Ryker calls after us. I flip him off without looking back.

Girlfriend? He thinks Damian and I are dating? Interesting.

———

My house off campus is only about a block away so I usually walk home after class. In the winter, I'll typically drive to campus to avoid freezing to death.

It doesn't take Damian and I long to arrive at my house, and when we do, I head straight for the couch in the living room while Damian heads to his self-proclaimed spot on the little chair in the corner.

Tossing my bag down on the ground, I slump next to Lainey and our other roommate, Ellie. We have one more roommate, Haley, but I'm pretty sure she's at class right now.

Letting out a loud groan, I fall forward, cradling my head in my hands. Out of the corner of my eye, I see Ellie and Lainey exchange a look of confusion.

"Gwen? You okay?" Lainey asks cautiously.

I peek up at her through my fingers and glare. "No."

"Okay…" she holds out the 'ay'. "What's going on?" she asks. Sitting up straighter, I pull a pillow onto my lap and play with the torn edge.

"She got into it with Ryker Steele in class today," Damian butts in. I send him a death glare, causing him to slouch down into his chair.

Lainey and Ellie jump out of their seats at the same time.

"*The* Ryker Steele?" Ellie replies, unimpressed.

"No freaking way. You got into it with an Elite?" Lainey squeals. She shakes her head, clearly in awe.

Lainey has this crazy obsession with the Elite, and I find it incredibly weird. Ellie knows who Ryker is because her twin brother is also an Elite member. I've met her brother Holland a few times and he's nice enough. Lainey and Ellie go to some of their parties once in a while, but I've chosen to opt out of those events.

The only thing I know about their group is their names. There's Holland, of course. Then Mason, who is Holland and Ellie's cousin and who I know from high school. We never really spoke, but we hung in the same circles, so I knew of him. Finally, Patrick, Logan, and worst of all, Ryker.

"Wait, why didn't we know he was in your class?" Lainey asks, looking offended that I've withheld this information from her for so long.

"Well, for starters, he's missed almost every single lecture. Also, I have no idea who he is. I didn't know his name until I ran into him outside Mallory after class," I shrug, plucking the loose strings on the pillow that I'm still holding in my lap. Lainey looks like she's about to combust.

Damian shifts in his seat, sitting up straighter with a mischievous grin on his face. "She literally *ran* into him. Like full on crashed into his chest," Damian chuckles and Lainey and Ellie's eyes widen.

I really don't know why they're making such a big deal out of this. The guy is a major prick. "She also called him a douchebag," Damian adds. Lainey spits out the water she just took a sip of, then pulls her long, curly brown hair up into a bun on top of her head.

"You called an Elite a douchebag? To his face?" Ellie asks at the same time Lainey asks,

"What did he feel like? Was he all muscly?" I roll my eyes.

"Technically I called him a douchebag with more money than brains, and it wasn't to his face, he overheard me. And Lainey, I'm not even going to acknowledge that question." Lainey pouts.

"Seriously?" Ellie leans back into the couch and laughs uncontrollably. Lainey shifts, turning her tiny body more toward me.

"Wait... did he say anything? After you called him a douchebag?"

"He told me to teach her some manners. Gwen really held her own. I was thoroughly impressed. Oh, he also thinks we're dating," Damian laughs.

Lainey throws her head back in a fit of laughter, as if me being Damian's girlfriend is hilarious. To be fair, it kind of is. Everyone knows Damian and I could never be anything more than best friends.

"That's fantastic. Why would he think that?" Lainey directs her question to Damian. He shrugs.

"Probably because I had my arm around her shoulders when we walked away."

"Low bar," Ellie says. Damian blows me a kiss and I pretend to catch it, smashing it on the floor and stomping it into the ground. His hand flies up over his heart, offended. Lainey looks back to me, her hand on my knee.

"Ryker Steele may be an ass, but did you even look at him? That man is fine as hell. That dark hair and those green eyes. I mean seriously, the man looks like a Greek god. There's no way you didn't notice," Lainey scoffs. Honestly, I didn't take a good look at him. I just wanted to punch his stupid face.

"I was too distracted by his arrogance to notice," I shrug. Lainey rolls her eyes as she lets out an exasperated sigh. Her way of saying she's given up on the conversation.

Ryker and I clearly have different views on things. Like how actually showing up to class is important. Or, how to be a human being.

Honestly, who does he think he is? Just because he's an Elite, and because he has money, he thinks he can demand things of me? Well, I have money too. But I don't go around demanding things from people or treating anyone poorly.

Ryker Steele has another thing coming if he thinks I'm one to bow down and give in to demands. Especially ones that come from his arrogant ass.

Chapter 7

GUINEVERE

When I arrived at class on Wednesday, I half expected Ryker to skip out again, but much to my dismay, he showed up. Torn jeans, a black t-shirt, and his black curls sitting messily on top of his head. I don't notice I'm staring until we make eye contact and Ryker smirks. I hate that smirk. I hate him.

Class seems to go by in the blink of an eye which is nice because the room feels a lot smaller and stuffier than usual.

Professor Whitely assigned a partner project and gave us until next class on Friday to choose. Obviously, Damian and I will be partners, there's no one else we know in this course.

As I pack my things into my bag, I can feel the heat of a stare on my back, and it causes a shiver to run down my spine, but I refuse to look behind me. I already know who it is.

"Gwen, Ryker, could you stay behind for a moment, please?" Damian nudges my arm. His eyes are wide as he shoots me a quizzical look.

I shrug, indicating that I have no idea what this is about. He mouths "good luck" and walks out of the lecture hall, leaving Ryker and I alone with Professor Whitely like the traitor he is.

I grasp the strap of my bag over my shoulder as I walk down to the Professor's desk. Ryker makes his way down slowly.

When he steps up beside me, I breathe in a whiff of his cologne, which smells like vanilla and sandalwood, creating a musky scent that reminds me of walking through a forest.

Professor Whitely leans back against her desk, her hands flat on the surface behind her. She clears her throat, her eyes moving from me to Ryker who looks extremely uncomfortable and slightly annoyed.

"So, I'll cut to the chase. I want you two to partner up for this project, and any future projects I assign."

My eyes go wide, and I can automatically feel my face getting red. What. The. Hell. This is the last thing I expected her to say. Why would she even suggest such a thing? I thought she liked me.

Professor Whitely crosses her arms over her chest, slightly pushing her breasts up and exposing more of her cleavage. My eyes dart to her chest, and quickly back to her face. I'm no better than a man. Jesus.

I look over to Ryker who hasn't said a word or moved a muscle. I don't even know if he's breathing.

"Professor, I don't think-" she holds up her hand, cutting me off.

"I understand you both may have reservations about this arrangement, but I believe this could be beneficial for you. You both have such different views, and I think that will be useful for this project."

"But-" This time it's not Professor Whitely who cuts me off. It's Ryker.

"I think you're right, Professor. This could be really beneficial for us both. Thank you. We'll get right to work."

What? No. No, this is not a good idea. It will not be beneficial. It will be catastrophic, like a category five hurricane.

"Ry-"

"Right, Rebel?" Rebel? What is happening right now?

"Perfect. I'm so glad you both feel that way. I can't wait to see what you come up with. See you on Friday."

With that, Professor Whitely gathers her things and walks between us and out of the lecture hall.

When she's gone and Ryker and I are completely alone, I turn to him slowly. He's already looking down at me with those mesmerizing green eyes, the muscles in his arms threatening to rip through the shirt he's wearing as he crosses his arms over his broad chest.

"What the hell was that? Why would you agree?"

He takes a step toward me, until he's so close I can smell the minty scent of his gum in his mouth.

My breath hitches and my body forgets how to move. He's intimidating when he's right in front of you. My grip on my bag's strap tightens, as if it can save me from the man two inches away from my face.

"Give me your phone," he demands. Again with the demands. I wonder if he's this demanding in the bedroom, the horny part of my brain overtaking the logical part. Wait, what? No. I'd never sleep with an Elite, especially not ones with green eyes and an ego the size of a whole planet.

Before I can tell him no, he grabs the wrist of the hand holding my phone and takes it from me.

I reach for it, but he holds it above his head which makes it impossible for me to reach, even if I jumped. I shove his chest, which does little to affect him at all. "Give me my phone!"

Ryker laughs at my futile attempts to get my phone back. He types something in, but when he's done, he doesn't immediately give it back. I pull on his arm, attempting to get my phone away from him.

"Ryker, give me-" Before I can finish my sentence, Ryker grabs my wrist and tugs me toward him causing me to crash into his hard chest. He holds my arm against him, gripping me hard enough to where I can't pull away, but it doesn't hurt.

His eyes bore into mine and his breathing shifts. My body reacts in a feral way, and I begin to attempt to pull back. His grip tightens on my wrist.

I'm so close to him, I can feel the heat of his body through our clothes. I can smell his aftershave, his shampoo. I can see the small black ring around the green of his eyes and the small freckle on his cheek.

"Calm down," he says in a low, gravelly voice. He looks over my face once more before releasing his hold on me and taking a step back, handing me my phone.

"I put my number in and texted myself so now I have yours. We'll make arrangements to get together to work on the project." I am so utterly confused right now. "See you soon, Rebel."

Ryker heads up the stairs and out of the lecture hall, leaving me standing here, completely stunned.

What the fuck just happened?

Chapter 8

RYKER

Later that night, the Elite house is filled with drunk people I don't know, blaring music, and utter chaos. It may be a Wednesday night, but I guess no one really cares.

I grab a beer from the kitchen and join Holland and Patrick in the living room where a couple is making out on the couch. Well, more like dry humping. I scan the room for Mason but he's not here, and Logan's at his girlfriend's dorm tonight according to the text I received about an hour ago. Him and Adrianna have been dating since they were in high school. They're practically inseparable.

The stench of cheap beer and sweat linger in the air as I walk through the crowded rooms and small hallways searching for Mason. He tends to get himself into trouble, *a lot*. Honestly, Holland should really be the one babysitting his cousin, but it seems like he might already be wasted.

I don't drink too much, but I'll have the occasional beer when we go to the bars or at a party, maybe do a shot or two, especially when I'm stressed. Like right now.

I've never been big on the feeling of being out of control. I enjoy being aware of my surroundings. I'd also rather not wake up feeling like I got hit by a bus.

Amidst the sea of dancing bodies and laughter, I spot Mason. He's got a girl pressed up against the wall, her head tilted to one side while he kisses and sucks on her neck. His hands are wandering all over her body and she looks like she's loving every second of it.

Mason's hand squeezes the girl's breast and then moves to the back of her head, pulling her hair so hard she yelps a little.

I make my way over to them and clear my throat loud enough so he'll hear me.

Mason pulls away from the girl, her face is flushed, and she looks slightly embarrassed. I would feel bad if not for the fact that they were literally just tongue fucking against a wall during a very crowded house party.

"Oh, hey man. I was just-" I look behind him to the girl who is slightly trembling.

"Can you give us a minute?" The girl looks to Mason, then back to me and nods, adjusting the strap of her top that had fallen down her arm. With one more look, she waves shyly, walking down the hall and disappearing around the corner.

"That's Candace. She's-" I don't let him finish because I don't give a fuck who she is.

"Dude, what did we talk about? No hooking up with girls at the parties. Especially when there's alcohol involved. If we get written up again, they'll shut us down."

Mason looks down at the ground, avoiding my gaze. He knows I'm pissed.

Last year, the Elite had a big scandal, and it hasn't quite been forgotten yet. One of the juniors hooked up with a girl at a party near Halloween. Apparently, the girl was really drunk, and the junior knew but still took advantage of her.

Turned out the girl was the Dean's stepdaughter. Needless to say, the situation didn't end well. The school took it really seriously, as they should, and threatened to shut us down if anything like that happened again.

Since then, all the guys have agreed that we can do whatever or whoever we want on our own time, but there would be no hooking up if there were drinks on the premises. Of course, some of the guys griped about it, but we can't risk getting the Elite shut down.

Mason nods, his face resembling a sad puppy. I pat his shoulder. "Come on, I think Austin and Teddy set up beer pong."

Austin and Teddy are freshmen. They're cool guys, much less annoying than most of the others.

Two rounds of beer pong later and I've had it. I'm more drunk than I've been in a while, and I hate it. I want to go to bed, but there's no way I'll be able to sleep with all the noise. It's not even midnight and I'm exhausted. I make my way over to the now empty couch and plop down, resting my head on the back.

Patrick lands next to me a few seconds later, draping his arm around my shoulders and disrupting my alone time.

"Done already?" he mocks.

"Yeah, I'm ready to call it a night," I say, running my hands down my face.

"You okay?"

"I'm good," I lie.

The room is starting to spin, and I know I need to lay down. I stand from the couch, slapping a hand on Pat's shoulder a few times before stalking up the stairs to my bedroom.

After my shower, I feel a lot better. I no longer feel like I'm on a boat, and my head feels less full. I yank on some athletic shorts and finally lay down.

My thoughts are racing, and oddly enough, I'm not thinking about my father and our talk. I'm not thinking about his disappointment or his veiled threats.

What I am thinking about is a feisty brunette who clearly despises my very being. I honestly don't know what possessed me to agree to such an asinine arrangement with her.

When Professor Whitely brought up the partnership, my first reaction was to tell her 'Fuck no'. But then I thought about it, and I came to the conclusion that this could work for me, and seeing how badly Gwen wanted to fight Professor Whitely made me want it even more.

Gwen's obviously smart, and she knows what she's doing. She might be able to help me get my grade up and get my father off my back.

When she argued with me in class on Monday, she ignited something in me. No one has ever talked to me like that, especially a woman. Most of them throw themselves at me. But

Gwen? She basically told me to fuck off, and it was the sexiest thing I've ever seen.

I hate to admit it, but Gwen is beautiful. She's all long tan legs, brown hair, and crystal blue eyes wrapped in this fiery personality. She's one of those girls that doesn't even have to try, she's just naturally gorgeous, and I bet she doesn't even know it.

An image of her wearing that light blue blouse that perfectly showed off her tits and the jeans that looked like they were painted on plays in my mind. Her bright blue eyes looking big and innocent. And that mouth. Fuck, why does her stubbornness and hatred toward me turn me on? My dick twitches in my pants, begging for release.

I shake my head, attempting to get rid of the image. No, I can't go there. Not with Gwen. She hates me, and I'm not so sure how fond I am of her.

I just want to get this project over with so I can pass this stupid fucking class and move on with my life, move on from my father. I can't afford to be distracted.

I'm really not a dick. I may be hardheaded, and I know I can be an ass sometimes, but I'm not evil. I respect women and yeah, I have the occasional one-night stand to let off some steam, but I always make sure the woman I'm with is satisfied. See, respect. I do admit I have a problem with authority due to my father and the emotional trauma he's caused me, but I'm pretty even tempered.

But when Gwen ran into me in the hallway, I was worked up about the meeting with my dad and I was in a shit mood. I could have reacted better, but it was too late. Plus, for some weird reason, I kind of like pissing her off. Her face gets all red and her nose scrunches up; it's pretty cute.

———————————

The next day goes by slow, and I haven't heard from Gwen yet, which I guess isn't surprising. The arrangement isn't ideal, and I know she doesn't understand why I even agreed to it. But this is the only way to get my dad to back the hell off. I just need to pass this class, and I need Gwen's help to do it.

I had a few boring classes this morning and now I'm sitting in the kitchen at the Elite house with Patrick, Mason, and Holland, as Pat, Holland, and I stare into a bowl of... honestly, I'm not even sure what this is. It smells putrid, and it looks even worse, but Mason made it, and I don't think any of us want to tell him it looks like puke.

Holland looks at me and I shrug, moving the sludge around with my fork. Mason looks like he's about to jump out of his seat with anticipation. He's clearly very proud of himself. Pat clears his throat before asking the question we all want the answer to.

"So... what is it?" Mason's face falls slightly, looking a bit confused.

"It's beef stew. What, you can't tell? Look," Mason points to a big block of something in Pat's bowl. "That's beef."

Pat picks it up with his fork and examines it before setting it back in his bowl. Mason looks around the table at Holland and I and then back to Pat.

"You're not gonna try it?"

"I'm really not that hungry. I actually have to uh... I have to study," Pat says, pushing away from the table and standing. Mason watches as Pat takes the bowl full of slop over to the fridge and sets it inside. Mason looks back at Holland and I expectantly.

"Yeah, I'm actually not that hungry either. But thanks for making dinner, bro," Holland stands from his seat next to me, pats Mason on the shoulder, and sets the bowl in the fridge. Those fuckers left me alone.

Mason watches me, seemingly waiting to hear what excuse I come up with. "And you? I assume you're not hungry either," he looks disappointed. I look down at the bowl one more time before ultimately deciding that I care more about my health than Mason's feelings.

"It was a great attempt, but I think we should let Pat do the cooking. Sorry, bud," I don't even bother putting the bowl in the fridge because I know I won't be eating it. I toss the contents in the trash and set the bowl in the sink.

As I make my way out of the kitchen, Mason calls after me.

"You guys are so ungrateful. I slaved over a hot stove all day to make you dicks dinner!" I shake my head and chuckle to myself. Such a drama queen.

Chapter 9

GUINEVERE

If the rain and gray skies are any indication as to how my day is going to go, I should probably just head back to the house now. Sinking back into bed and hiding under the covers while binging some terrible podcast sounds a lot better than what I actually have to do today.

As I stand in line at Cafe Grind, Ellington's one and only cafe on campus, I stare out the window at the rain pouring down from above, creating huge puddles on the walking paths. Some students walk by with umbrellas, some with only their hood up. Everyone has the same look though, dark and gloomy. I hate the rain.

"Last call for a coffee for Gwen," oh shoot.

My gaze darts from the window to the barista with long black hair that's up in a ponytail, a red bandana around her neck, and a scowl on her face.

I grab my coffee with a small smile.

"Sorry, thanks," the girl just walks away. Well okay then.

Taking a sip of the hot coffee, I immediately realize that there isn't any sugar in it, but I don't want to go back and complain. I guess I'll just drink it as is.

It's Friday morning, which means today's the day we begin our projects. I left the house before anyone was up, and I tossed and turned all night thinking of working with Ryker. I also haven't told Lainey or Ellie about this. I'm exhausted, my coffee's as bitter as my mood, and to top it all off, I forgot my umbrella.

To be fair, it wasn't raining when I left the house, and I didn't check the weather. Either way, now I'm going to get soaked walking to class. Mallory Center is only one building down from the cafe, but the rain is coming down pretty hard.

I take a deep breath and decide to make a run for it.

The rain pelts against my skin but I keep moving, and when I'm just about there, an arm moves in front of me, and the rain is suddenly not hitting me anymore.

"You looked like you needed this," Damian teases.

"Thanks," I mumble.

The dryer in the bathroom can only do so much. My white shirt is soaked, and my hair is dripping, but class is about to start, and I don't have time to do anything else.

I look into the mirror and run my fingers through my damp hair. My eyes move over my body and a small gasp leaves my lips as I realize my purple floral bra is completely visible through my top, and the sweater I was wearing is soaked, along with the rest of my clothes. Shit. Shit, shit, shit. Okay, Gwen. Don't panic.

I lean against the sink and take a deep breath. I'll call Damian. He might have something for me to wear.

Picking up my cell, I click on Damian's name and send him a quick text asking him to bring me a sweatshirt, so I don't have to humiliate myself further than I need to.

Five minutes later, I'm sitting next to Damian in the lecture hall, swimming in his large zip-up as Professor Whitely explains more about the project. My hair is still soaked, and I probably resemble a wet dog.

"Alright, here's the deal. The project is simple. Each team will come up with a comprehensive analysis of a novel of your choosing and explore themes within the novel," Professor Whitely looks around the room, probably making sure everyone is listening.

"You should have your novel chosen by class on Monday. You'll discuss everything together and agree on what themes are presented. At the end, you'll turn in a ten-page essay that you've written together and a full presentation. You have three weeks to complete this project. Any questions?"

No one raises a hand or makes a sound. I look over to Damian, but instead of paying attention to Professor Whitely, he's scrolling through his Instagram feed.

Something inside me forces me to look over my shoulder which was a mistake because I make eye contact with Ryker. I cannot work with him for three whole weeks, let alone the rest of the semester on other projects. I'm never going to make it. That, or he won't make it because I'm going to kill him.

I roll my eyes at him, and I see him smirk in response as I turn back around to face the front of the room.

"Alright. Get started." Professor says, rounding her desk and taking a seat behind it.

I filled Damian in on my situation with Ryker the night Professor Whitely decided to ruin my life. He laughed at my misfortune in true best friend fashion, and I slapped his arm so hard he yelped, which made me smile.

Damian looks at me and winks, giving me a teasing grin. "Have fun with your partner, Gwenny," I shoot him a lethal glare.

"I hate you."

I stand from my seat and walk toward the one person I don't want anything to do with. Ryker's stare makes me slightly uncomfortable as I get closer. His bright green eyes sweep over my body as I step up to his seat.

His jaw is tense, and his hands are steepled together on top of the table. Now that I'm really looking at him, I guess he is kind of attractive, in a cocky, 'I know I'm an asshole' kind of way.

The way his dark hair is a mess of curls on top of his head, one strand hanging down on his forehead. How his eyes look like emeralds, how his smirk is probably one of the hottest things I've ever seen, even though I hate it.

But he's a jerk. His attitude and personality are like a repellent, and I could never actually be into someone like him. He's exactly the kind of guy your parents warn you not to get involved with.

No matter how physically attractive he is on the outside, the inside is like black ice. Not to mention, I'm pretty positive he's fucked every girl attending Ellington U, and maybe even some girls in the neighboring colleges. He's probably got some kind of venereal disease. Gross.

Ryker stares up at me. "Hey, Rebel," he says, one side of his mouth slightly raised. I roll my eyes at the nickname.

"Don't call me that," I want to ask why he calls me that, but I don't want to speak to him longer than I have to.

His eyes shoot down to my chest and I look down to see what caught his eye.

Oh no. Oh my god. Damian's sweater is unzipped just enough to show off part of my bright purple bra through my still damp white shirt.

I hurriedly zip it back up all the way as my cheeks burn with embarrassment. Shit. Ryker Steele just saw my bra.

Looking up to see the look on his face, I find his gaze on mine, probably enjoying my embarrassment. Is it too late to go home and hide under my covers?

"You're a little wet," Ryker states in a patronizing tone, but there's also a hint of something I can't identify. "I like the purple. Brings out your eyes."

Shaking my head, I clear my throat and look to the ground.

"Shut up," I mutter. "Moving on…we need to choose a novel. Do you have any ideas?" I don't expect much from him, since he doesn't seem to care about-

"Wuthering Heights?" Okay…well that's a surprise. That's one of my favorite novels.

"You've read Wuthering Heights?"

I don't mean to sound so surprised, but the look on his face tells me he might be slightly offended by my question.

"I have. I am able to read, you know. I'm not an idiot."

"I never said you were," I argue. I may have thought it, and said it to myself, but I never said it to his face. "Okay, Wuthering Heights it is." Now Ryker's the one who sounds surprised.

"Wow, did we just agree on something?" I shake my head as a small grin crosses my lips.

"Don't get used to it."

Chapter 10

GUINEVERE

After we decided on the novel we are going to base our project on, Ryker and I begrudgingly made plans to start working on the project tomorrow since it's Saturday and neither of us have class. I know he was surprised when I agreed to the novel he suggested.

Honestly, I don't mind Wuthering Heights, but I also didn't want to stand there with him any longer, so agreeing with him was the best choice. On my walk home, I couldn't stop thinking about the way his gaze heated when he noticed my bra peeking through my shirt. I was so embarrassed, but he looked like he enjoyed the view.

I don't know why the thought of him enjoying what he sees sends butterflies flapping all around my stomach, but it does. Probably because I haven't had sex since well… since the summer when my ex and I called it quits.

Dawson was sweet and he really did care about me. We'd been friends since we were little, our parents were best friends. After Damian and I attempted to have a romantic relationship and it didn't work out, Dawson made it clear that he did feel a romantic attraction to me.

Damian convinced me to give Dawson a chance, so I did. He was perfect. Attentive, handsome, compassionate, and so many other things. He took my virginity. We were eighteen and we'd both just started college. He went to a different school, but we'd take turns visiting each other and our schools aren't that far away from one another.

It was his turn to visit, and we hung out in my dorm pretty much the whole weekend. Except when we decided to go on a picnic at this gorgeous overlook of the city.

We brought a blanket and food, and it was just like a movie. Our kissing turned into grinding, and the grinding turned into us being naked, and the nakedness, well that led to the loss of my virginity, I was in love. Dawson made me feel loved. He made me feel wanted and cherished and I was fully convinced I was going to marry him one day.

We dated for about three years, and one day, when it was his turn to visit, he texted me an hour before he was meant to arrive.

"I'm not coming. I'm sorry," the text read.

"What do you mean you're not coming?" I'd texted back.

"I think we should break up. This isn't working."

That was the last text I'd gotten from him, and I didn't bother responding. He broke up with me after three years over a text message and didn't even give me a reason. I mean, who does that?

I was heartbroken and I couldn't believe someone who'd treated me like a princess, someone who was so perfect for me would do such a thing. Damian and Lainey held me while I cried, and after a few months of crying and asking myself why I wasn't good enough, I decided to try and move on.

Ryker would probably ruin me. Physically and mentally, and I cannot take that. I am not even going to give that man the time of day, no matter what he makes me feel.

He is an Elite, he's a man whore, he's a jerk. I'm better than that, I know better than that, and I will not let another man ever make me feel like I'm not good enough.

When I arrive home, Lainey is lying on the couch with a book held in the air above her face.

Damian was supposed to walk home with me, but he and his partner, Allie Moore, decided to start work on their project tonight.

Lainey sits up and smiles at me from the couch. I haven't told her about my situation with Ryker, and I don't know if I want to considering the way she reacted when I had barely had an actual conversation with the man.

Making my way over to the couch, I pull my sneakers off my feet and sit on the opposite side of Lainey. She lifts her feet and sets them back down on my thighs as she sets the book down on the coffee table.

"How was class?" she asks, which she does almost every day if she's home when I arrive.

"Good, nothing exciting," I try not to sound nervous or annoyed so she doesn't ask me anything else, but I must fail because her eyes narrow and she sits up.

Lainey and I have known each other for so long now that we can easily tell when one of us isn't saying something, so I should have known she'd catch on.

I look down at my hands in my lap as I nervously twist the ring on my index finger. "What are you not telling me, Guinevere?" Lainey asks suspiciously.

I don't look her in the eye, I can't. She'll know I'm hiding something. "Nothing," I say, avoiding her dubious expression.

"Fine. I guess you don't want to know about my date tonight, then," Lainey shrugs her shoulders and begins to stand but I yank her back down.

She gives me a devious smile, as if knowing I couldn't refuse hearing about this date.

"Date? What date?" Lainey winks.

Before she can answer, the front door opens with Ellie and Haley trailing in, shutting it behind them.

"Ooo, what's going on here?" Haley wags her finger between Lainey and me.

"Gwen has something to share with us," Lainey says pointedly. I glower at her.

"Lainey has a date tonight!" I announce, hoping that will be enough to take the attention off of me and onto Lainey who's shooting me a death glare.

Lainey doesn't like not getting her way. She's really not used to having people tell her no. She's also a child of divorce, but her parents compensate by buying her things and essentially letting her do whatever she wants.

My parents? Well, they barely even communicate. I get calls from my dad here and there, mom calls every day, but that's about it. Don't get me wrong, I had a good childhood. I never wanted for anything, I always had everything I needed.

Ellie and Haley exchange a confused glance before setting their bags down and joining Lainey and I in the living room. Ellie takes a seat in the corner chair while Haley sits on the floor across from the couch, leaning her elbows on the coffee table in front of her.

"A date, huh? And when were you going to share this information with the group?" Ellie asks as if this were an interrogation. Lainey throws her hands up in exasperation.

"I was going to tell you guys when you got home, but *someone*," she darts her gaze back to me with the same scowl on her face as before, "beat me to it."

"Sooo…" Haley begins.

"So what?" Lainey asks.

"So, who is it? Your date," Haley asks with a smirk.

Haley is a really sweet girl. We're not as close to her since she only joined our house this year, but she's a good friend, and a great addition to our little team.

Lainey has been single for as long as I've known her. Sure, she's had her fun with some random flings, but she hasn't ever been in a serious relationship. She says she's 'allergic to commitment'. So, it's kind of surprising she has an actual date tonight.

"No one you'll know. Some guy from my chemistry class. His name is Evan, he's like six three, and absolutely hot as hell," Lainey swoons.

"Do you have a picture? Let me see," Haley asks, reaching over the coffee table and attempting to grab Lainey's phone. Lainey swipes the phone and holds it in the air.

"I don't have a picture! Gosh, Grabby, back down," Haley sits back on her feet and laughs. "Anyway, enough about me. Gwenny here still has something to tell us," I scowl at her, wishing with everything I have that I had laser vision to snipe her with.

"I do not," I lean back into the couch, crossing my arms over my chest. I can feel all of their eyes on me, waiting for me to speak.

As I debate on whether or not to tell them about the unfortunate predicament I've been forced into, the front door swings open again.

"Oh, Gwennyyyy! Allie cancelled. How was your discussion with Ellington's Most Eligible Elite?" Damian teases as he charges in as if he lives here. Well, I guess the debate is over. Ellie, Lainey, and Haley all turn to me at the same time.

I'm going to kill Damian.

Chapter 11

RYKER

Fuck.

I have not been able to close my eyes without seeing Gwen and that purple bra that peeked through her very wet white shirt. She tried to hide it with the sweatshirt, but it's like the universe wanted me to see her.

The bra perfectly fit her tits and pushed them up just the right amount to see enough but leave the rest to the imagination. She was so embarrassed, her cheeks turned a bright scarlet color, and it made me want to egg her on more.

The shock on her face when I mentioned we should do our project on Wuthering Heights would have been offensive, if not for the fact that I was still thinking about her impeccable tits.

I did however enjoy the way she blushed when I called her out on it. She automatically went on the defensive. I wonder if she does that often, tries to defend herself after everything she says or does.

I run my hand down my face as I lay on the couch in the living room where I've been laying since I got home from class. Patrick, Mason, and Holland haven't been home yet, and who the fuck knows where Logan is. Probably being daddy's good little boy and sitting in his room with a book in his face.

I roll my eyes and stare at the ceiling. My father is never going to let me have my own life. I don't really even know what I want to do when I leave Ellington in the spring, but I do know I want nothing to do with him while he runs the company.

Logan wants to be an engineer or something, but I don't even know why he's trying because our father will never let that happen. Honestly, why are we even wasting time in college if Robert already knows he wants us to work for him? What's the point? Why am I even trying so hard to impress him? Why do I care?

Even though I despise the man, he's still my father, and I feel some sort of sick loyalty to him. Robert Steele is no father, but I'm stuck with him. I may be twenty-two, but I'll be stuck under my father's thumb until he takes his last breath.

I hear the front door open in the distance and multiple pairs of footsteps ascending in the hallway.

Patrick, Holland, and Mason enter the living room looking exhausted and sweaty. Fuck, I forgot about practice. I've been too in my head about my father and Gwen and this project that I haven't even thought about it.

The boys finally notice me sitting on the couch, their laughter dying down and their faces twisting into a mix of confusion and concern.

"Where have you been, man?" Pat asks, setting his bag down on the ground and circling the couch to stand in front of me.

"Yeah, coach is pissed," Holland adds. Yeah well, coach will get over it. I'll just threaten his job and he'll back down.

I shouldn't use my last name for threats, that's something my father does, but sometimes it really can help.

I clear my throat and run my hand through my jet black, messy hair. "I forgot."

The guy's eyes go wide, and I hear Mason choke on the water he's just sipped on.

"You forgot?" Holland asks, the surprise clear in his voice. I stand from the couch and head to the connected kitchen, grab a water from the fridge, and take a long sip.

"Better not give coach that excuse. He'll kick your ass," Mason steals my spot on the couch, turning on his stupid game. I lean against the kitchen counter, watching the screen as guns and different characters pop up.

"What's going on?" Pat's eyes meet mine from across the room. He knows me better than anyone, and I can't keep much from him.

"Nothing. I had class this morning, and we were assigned a partner project."

"Dude, that sucks ass. Group projects are the worst," Mason says as he stares at the screen in front of him, causing me to roll my eyes. Yeah, no shit.

"Okay…" Pat draws out.

"Do any of you know a Gwen?" I realize now that I don't know her last name. We haven't gotten to that. It only occurs to me now that she knows exactly who I am, last name and all, but I barely know anything about her.

Holland looks back at me from the chair in the living room. "Guinevere Sharpe?" I shrug.

"I don't know. All I know is her first name."

"Well, my sister is roommates with a girl named Guinevere. Maybe that's her?" Holland questions. I shrug again.

"Yeah, maybe."

"Why?" Pat wonders.

"She's my partner," the guys look at me, waiting for me to continue. I roll my eyes. Nosey assholes. "We got into it one day during a debate and our professor seems to think our differing opinions will make for a great project."

I take another sip from the water bottle in my hand. I still can't see the logic in it. Our differing opinions are only going to hinder the process, but whatever.

"Is she hot?" Mason asks. Holland slaps the back of his head, causing Mason to rub the spot. "Ow! What the hell?"

Holland shakes his head. "You're an idiot."

"She's infuriating is what she is. She's got a big mouth and an even bigger attitude. I don't know whether to be pissed or turned on."

Pat snorts. "Dude, just tell her you're an Elite. She'll fall in line just like the rest of them."

Yeah, you would think. Except, Gwen isn't like the rest of them. She knows who I am, and she doesn't give a shit. Plus, I need her. I can't piss her off or make her run.

"Yeah, maybe," is all I say, ending this topic of conversation. "Anyway, I'll be at the next practice."

Most of us have been on the Ellington rugby team since freshman year. We needed something to let off steam and distract us from all the shit happening in our lives.

We were interested in hockey, but then we realized none of us can skate. Mason broke his wrist after he fell on it, and Pat left with a broken pinky finger. Suffice to say, we were not built for hockey. So, rugby it was.

Rugby's a tough sport, but at least it's on dry land and not on ice. We took to it pretty quickly, and we've been playing ever since.

Pat nods, acknowledging my statement. "Good," is all he says, effectively ending the conversation. Thank God.

Saturdays are the best. I get to sleep in, and I don't have to worry about shit. Except today, since I'm meeting with the she devil herself to start working on this project from hell.

I've already gone for my run, showered, shaved, eaten breakfast and it's only nine. The guys are still sleeping, leaving me to my thoughts.

It's only about eight weeks into the semester, and the weather here in Connecticut is starting to cool down quite a bit. I like the cooler weather. I think I run naturally hot, so the cold weather keeps me regulated.

It's beautiful here in the fall. The trees are all different colors, vibrant reds, greens, yellows, and oranges. The campus is decorated with Halloween decorations and all of the houses on our block are decked out with extravagant props.

Every year, the Elite throw a massive Halloween party that all the students come to, and every year we regret it the next day. The house is a mess, and there are random objects strewn around everywhere. Last year, I found a used condom and some chicks panties on my bed. I threw those sheets out immediately.

Since then, we've decided to lock our bedroom doors at every party so no one can mistake one of them as their own personal sex room.

Each year, we choose a group of freshmen to come up with a theme, get the decorations, send out invites, and basically take care of all the miniscule things while the elder members approve every move they make. It's a nice system.

Halloween is in two weeks, and I haven't heard anything from anyone which is causing me to be more on edge than usual. Not only am I thinking about the party, but I'm also thinking about the fact that my first actual session outside of the classroom with Gwen is in an hour.

I send a group text to Mason, Holland, and Pat about the party planning, and pack up to head to the library.

RYKER

The library is huge, with rows and rows of books of all genres. It's an old building, and the smell of old books and years of use is strong. There are circular tables scattered around the large space, a row of computers against the far wall, which seem out of place with how new they are.

The cathedral like ceiling is beautiful with old artwork spread across it. The tall windows let in some light, but not much because they are all stained with artwork.

I'm sitting at a table in the corner of the library by myself, waiting for a woman that I can't stand but also can't seem to get out of my head.

She's late. She'd texted earlier and told me to meet her in the library at ten. I was here at exactly nine forty-five, it's now ten fifteen and there's still no sign of her. I'll give her ten more minutes before I leave. I'm not one to be stood up, and Gwen would be the first woman to do it.

Just as I'm about to call it, a petite blonde woman strolls up to the table I'm sitting at. Amber, or Ashley, or was it Amy. Fuck, I don't remember. She holds a stack of books in her arms and her lips are curled up into a big smile.

"Ryker, hey. I didn't think I'd see you again," Amber/Amy says. I offer a small smile as to not be a complete dick.

"Hey…"

"Amy," she doesn't even look offended that I don't remember her name. Right, Amy. I knew it… kind of. Amy continues to smile; she looks slightly nervous which is something I'm used to when it comes to women.

Any woman that speaks to me usually seems a bit on edge, unless they're plastered. Then they're a lot more confident. I'd like to think it's because I look intimidating which could definitely be part of it, but mostly I think it's because I'm an Elite.

The only woman I know that hasn't acted like they were scared to talk to me is Gwen. She only ever looks at me like she's pissed off or like she wants to set me on fire. Clearly, I've made a great impression the few times we've actually spoken.

"You busy tonight?" Amy asks, shifting from one leg to the other as she looks anywhere but at me. I gesture to the table where Wuthering Heights sits in the middle.

"Studying," I say tersely. Amy nods, but she doesn't leave which is what I was hoping she'd do.

I don't normally sleep with the same woman twice; it makes them think we're more than we are. I'm not looking for anything serious, and I'm certainly not looking to be tied down to some chick right now. Most of the women I've slept with know this about me, but there's always a few that think they'll be the exception.

"Maybe when you're done, we can…" Amy begins, but she's interrupted by a familiar snarky brunette with long curls framing her face as Gwen steps up to the table. Amy looks from Gwen to my face, likely trying to gauge my reaction to some girl sitting at my table.

Gwen looks up at Amy, then to me, her face falling into an emotion that looks close to disgust.

"Am I interrupting?" Gwen asks sardonically.

"No."

I keep my gaze locked on Gwen who's looking at me with a bland expression on her face. Out of the corner of my eye, I see Amy look between the two of us before hiking the stack of books up in her arms and holding her head high.

"Right, well, see you around, Ryker," Amy says, almost in the form of a question. I don't even answer as she slowly slinks away.

Sure, Amy is hot. But she's clingy. I knew the morning after we fucked, and she wouldn't leave when I told her to. I figured that would be the last time I'd see her, but here we are.

Gwen finally peels her eyes away from my face, setting a copy of Wuthering Heights in front of her, along with a notebook and a pen. She sets her phone next to them, face up as she stares at the display, likely already counting down the minutes until we're done with this.

"Can we get this over with? I'd rather be," she pauses as if thinking of her next words carefully, "anywhere else."

Damn, if one things for sure, Gwen will always say exactly what she's thinking. No bullshit.

"You're the one that was late. I've been sitting here for a half hour," Gwen shoots me a glare.

"I'm here now, aren't I? So quit whining and let's just begin," she opens her notebook and clicks her pen, writing something on the paper before looking back at me, flipping her long brown hair behind her shoulder.

The thin strap of her tank top catches my attention as the cardigan she's wearing slips down her tan shoulder.

Her blue eyes stick out in contrast to the black tank top she's wearing, along with the brown of her long hair. Even though she looks like she wants to rip my eyes out of their sockets, she looks calm. Annoyed, but tough. Like nothing bothers her, except for me of course.

Setting the pen down, Gwen opens her mouth to speak but I interrupt her.

"Are you going to act like you hate me the whole time, or are you going to drop this little façade?" I ask, enjoying the rage that is so obviously building inside her.

"It's not a façade. I actually hate you," she states tersely, looking so sure of herself, and I don't know why it's so attractive.

"Really? Because-" she cuts me off.

"As much as I'd love to sit here and discuss the list of reasons I despise you, can we move on and start this stupid project?"

Her eyes don't leave mine, and a small smirk plays at my lips. I nod.

"Alright. Let's start with your view on the story, even though it's probably wrong," the red in her cheeks grows brighter at my comment. Her eyes narrow into tiny slits as she stares at me with annoyance.

"Fine. I believe it's a haunting tale of love and loss, with themes of passion, and revenge. Catherine and Heathcliff embody a tragic love story that eclipsed time and the societal norms of the time period."

I roll my eyes. "Figured."

Her head tilts slightly and the look on her face tells me she's not happy with my response.

"What's that supposed to mean?" she asks.

I lean back in my chair, crossing my arms over my chest, watching the way her shoulders rise and fall to the beat of her breathing.

"Just that I figured you'd see it like that," I shrug.

"And how do you see it?" Gwen asks, crossing her tiny arms over chest, attempting to look intimidating.

"I think it's a dark and twisted story with toxic relationships and destructive behavior. Heathcliff and Catherine's actions throughout the novel were all driven by selfishness and cruelty. They show the worst parts of what it means to be human. It's not romanticized. There is no real love. It's pure manipulation. Plain and simple," Gwen's narrowed gaze never leaves mine.

"Well, I find the raw emotion and deep intensity of Heathcliff's love compelling," her arms move from her chest as she folds them in front of her on the table. "Their love defies the societal expectations of their time."

"At what cost?" I ask. "Heathcliff's obsession borders on possessiveness, and Catherine's choices throughout prove to be selfish rather than genuine," I challenge.

"You would see it that way. You're such a pessimist. Were you not loved enough as a child? Did mommy and daddy not give you enough attention, so your outlook on love is tainted?" she questions.

I clench my fists at my sides, fighting the urge to lash out at her comment. She has no fucking clue what I've been through, no fucking idea what it was like for me growing up with a father who never thought I was good enough. Who never thought I was worthy of his love.

She probably grew up with a family that loved her. That supported her in everything she did. That loved her despite any mistakes she might have made. She knows nothing.

Taking a deep breath, I unclench my fists and lean in closer to Gwen's face. She backs up slightly, likely not expecting me to get in her face. I can see her pupils dilate, and the small freckle on the tip of her nose. I can smell her, the flowery scent of her shampoo and perfume.

"You shouldn't make assumptions about people's lives, Gwen," I say softly so only she can hear.

She looks like she wants to say something else, but she doesn't. She just stares at me.

I push my chair back and gather my things, shoving them into my bag and tossing it over my shoulder as Gwen watches me in surprise.

"We're done here."

I walk out of the library, the tension in my body palpable, leaving Gwen sitting alone.

Chapter 12

GUINEVERE

Well, that went about as well as I thought it would.

This arrangement is never going to work. Ryker is unbearable at best. I am never going to last. We're surely going to kill each other. His views on the novel are so jaded, and I don't foresee them changing. I mean, twisted? Toxic? Are you kidding me?

Clearly, he's projecting his own personality into the story. Has he even actually read the book? If he had, he wouldn't see this story as anything other than a classic romance.

Maybe I took it took far with my comment about his family. That probably was a bit unnecessary, but I couldn't help it. It's like I can't control what comes out of my mouth when I'm around him.

He's right. I don't know him; I don't know what his family is like or how he grew up. I just assumed because of his rich boy attitude and contemptuous outlook that he must have some deep, dark secret that's made him the way he is.

The way his face twisted when I said what I did, the way his muscles tensed and his breathing changed, the way he got so close to my face and the threat in his voice when he told me not to make assumptions about his life. I clearly struck a nerve, even though I was only saying it to piss him off a bit.

I definitely didn't think he would get up and leave. He didn't leave the last time I accused him of being cynical. I didn't mean to hurt him, even though I can't stand him. I'm not a mean person. I never have been, and I don't want to be. I care about people and their feelings. But I will not let people walk all over me, I refuse.

I decide to sit in the library a bit longer, rereading "Wuthering Heights", trying to see things from Ryker's perspective. Trying to see where he's coming from. I read the book so long ago, maybe I'm seeing it wrong. Maybe my perspective is the one that's jaded.

Maybe I'm naïve after growing up reading books, reading about men who love their woman unconditionally, irrevocably, completely. How they look at them with such love and want and need. The grand gestures, the way they look at their significant others as if they're the only woman in the world, the declarations of love.

I've never experienced a love like that myself. Dawson was a good boyfriend, but he didn't treat me like a book boyfriend would. I know they're just stories. I know they're not real, and real men don't act like that. Real life is not a romance novel. It's not love songs and perfection. Real life is raw, broken. It's imperfections and desperation.

But it must be out there, that kind of love. The passionate, exciting, obsessive kind of love. The happily ever afters. Even though I haven't seen it for myself, I know it's out there.

It has to be.

The sound of my phone vibrating against the table startles me awake. My eyes fly open, and I scan my surroundings, trying to figure out where I am.

The old library comes into focus as my body fully wakes up. I must have fallen asleep at some point, because I am hunched over the table in the empty, dark library with "Wuthering Heights" open and slightly damp from where I must have drooled.

Lainey's name is displayed on my phone, and I see I have several missed calls from her, Ellie, and Damian. Shit, it's late. They have to be wondering where I am.

I peal myself off the table and answer the call.

"Hel-"

"Where the hell are you? We've been calling you for over an hour," Lainey lectures into my ear. God, she's like my mother.

"I'm at the library. I fell asleep, I'm coming home now," Lainey repeats what I just said, assumingly to Ellie, Haley, and probably Damian.

"You've been there this whole time?" Lainey questions.

"Yes. I was working on my project with Ryker, he left, and I stayed. I must have passed out while I was reading."

Lainey, Ellie, and Haley flipped out on me when Damian dropped the Ryker and I being partners bomb. I was forced to tell them everything about our first discussion in class, and our plans to meet up tonight.

Of course, they were ecstatic. Well, Lainey and Haley were, Ellie really looked like she didn't care, which I appreciated. This isn't a big deal, and I don't want to make it one.

I pack my things into my bag, and as I stand, I can feel the strong ache in my neck from leaning over the table for so long. That's probably going to be worse by tomorrow.

Flinging my bag over my shoulder, I switch my phone from my right ear to my left.

"I'm on my way home now. I'll see you guys soon."

"You shouldn't walk, Gwen. It's late and it's dark," Lainey tells me. Now she really sounds like my mother. I roll my eyes.

"I'm on campus, I'll be fine, Lainey," I hear her sigh on the other end.

"Fine. Love you, bitch," Lainey teases. I shake my head and chuckle to myself.

"Love you too," I reply, hanging up as I head out of the library and walk toward home.

I don't usually walk at night. As a twenty-one-year-old woman, it's not really safe, even on a college campus. They tell you college campuses are safe since there's security. But the only thing campus security is good for is handing out stupid tickets and busting kids for smoking weed on campus.

Ellington University's campus is typically quiet, it's when you get closer to the off-campus housing that the quiet becomes louder and a bit rowdier.

Off campus housing consists of one street, literally right next to campus, with six houses on either side of it, a big mansion sitting on each end.

The big brick mansion on the right end is perfectly manicured, the landscaping is straight out of a magazine, and a large flag hangs on the tall flagpole in the center of the lawn. "The Ellington Elite" with the Elite crest under it is spread across the fabric.

Across the street, a home just as large houses the one sorority that Ellington U has. And then there's my house, the house Lainey, Haley, Ellie and I share, exactly three houses down from the sorority.

The sorority girls don't usually hold any parties, but the Elite mansion? There's a party there almost every weekend and sometimes weekdays.

Ellie and Lainey usually attend them, only for the sole purpose of pissing off Ellie's brother. Holland gets annoyed when Ellie crashes his parties. She says he 'feels like he's babysitting her', even though they're the same age. Haley never attends parties; she doesn't drink or do any recreational drugs since she's an athlete. I tend to hang back with her for the most part.

Holland is overprotective; I've seen it first-hand the last few years since I met Ellie. What's weird is that he always acts the same way with Lainey. Like he's watching out for her, or just *watching* her.

I don't think Lainey's notices the way Holland looks at her whenever they're in the same room. More importantly, I don't think Ellie's notices the way her brother watches her best friend.

Ellie and Holland have always been really close, from what I've been told. But when they got here, Holland told everyone in the Elite mansion to stay away from his sister. It pissed Ellie off so much, she walked up to some poor sap and made out with him right in front of Holland.

I say poor sap because Holland ended up punching him in the face, even though the guy didn't initiate the kiss.

When I enter my house, Lainey, Ellie, and Haley are sitting in the living room watching some movie about a one-night stand turned enemies to lovers.

Haley notices me first, jumping up from her perch on the floor, running over to hug me.

"Oh, thank God, you're alive!" she exclaims, pulling away, leaving her hands resting on my shoulders. "I was worried."

Her auburn hair falls over her shoulders and she gives me a frown.

"You're so dramatic. I'm fine," I chuckle.

Lainey and Ellie stay seated, but their expressions seem like they're waiting for me to explain further. I appreciate having friends who care about me this much, but in this case it's not necessary.

Walking into the living room, I cross my arms over my chest and stare down at Lainey and Ellie, while Haley comes back to take her seat on the floor.

"Okay, I'm sorry I was late tonight. But I'm here now," I shrug.

"Are you okay? Did something happen with Ryker?" Lainey asks, a slight twinge of concern in her voice.

"Nothing happened. I said something I probably shouldn't have, he got pissed, and then he left."

"What did you say?" Ellie asks, her eyebrows furrowing.

I shrug. "Nothing he didn't deserve."

I shouldn't feel bad. I shouldn't feel guilty. But here I am with a sour feeling in my gut and a heavy feeling in my chest.

Shit. Why do I have to be such a nice person?

Chapter 13
GUINEVERE

Ryker and I have met two more times since our last session in the library. He barely spoke to me, and our typical banter back and forth vanished. It's like he's actually mad at me, which makes me feel strangely guilty. I knew I pissed him off, but I thought he'd be over it by now.

The air is chilled as I walk through campus to the library to once again meet with Ryker. The coffee in my hand is helping keep me warm. I can't believe how fast the weather changed. I swear just a week ago or so there was at least still a warm breeze in the air.

Halloween is already next Friday, and I honestly can't believe how fast this semester has been going. I'm hopeful that Professor Whitely doesn't come up with any other partner projects before the end of the semester.

Someone has gone around and dressed up all of the buildings with small decorations such as pumpkins and little bats flying from the trees, small Halloween banners, and even some bigger stuff like the witch on her broomstick sticking out of the ground in front of Café Grind.

Leaves dance around the ground as the light breeze blows, causing the bats hanging from the tree branches to look as if they're going to fly off. The plaid scarf and beanie I'm wearing today are enough to keep me comfortable, but the lack of gloves is really doing me in.

The fresh scent of autumn and pumpkin spice fills my senses as I walk up to the library. I spot Ryker right away, sprawled out in one of the large study rooms. His dark hair is curlier than usual, and he has a bit more stubble on his chin than

I've ever seen him with. His green eyes meet mine as I enter the room, shutting the door behind me.

The twinge of guilt comes back full force as I watch his gaze lower back down to his book. He doesn't even say a word. No hello, no taunting remark, nothing. Damn, he really is pissed. God, Gwen. Why do you even care?

Ryker is a legacy member of the Ellington Elite; his family name drips with money and power. He's cruel and arrogant. He doesn't deserve my guilt, or an apology.

Gritting my teeth, I set my bag down on the ground, pulling out the chair across from Ryker. His eyes move up to my face and then wander down with my body as I sit.

"Well, if it isn't Ms. Guinevere Sharpe," his deep voice rumbles. How does he know my last name? I never said anything. I wonder if he told Holland about our partnership.

A flush of irritation mixed with a spark of awareness rips through my veins at the thought of Ryker Steele speaking about me to his housemates, but I push it away before it overtakes me.

At least he spoke to me. I guess he's breaking this whole silent streak. The guilt dissipates and it's replaced by annoyance at the tone of his voice.

I refuse to let this man get under my skin, no matter how annoyingly handsome he is with his tousled dark hair and smoldering green eyes.

Shit, no, don't think about him like that Guinevere.

Ryker raises an eyebrow, a glint of amusement shining in his eyes.

"I thought you'd give up by now. After all, I am Ellington University's most eligible asshole," he sits up, leaning forward, and I can't help but notice the way his muscles strain against his thin t-shirt.

I roll my eyes, ignoring the odd flutter in my stomach.

"What do you mean, give up?" I ask. This isn't something I can just give up on. We need to finish this project, and I am not failing because of him.

Ryker smirks. "Forget it, Rebel. Let's get this over with, shall we?"

For the next hour, we work in a strained silence, both refusing to back down or concede to the other's point of view.

I can feel my frustration grow as Ryker shoots down each of my ideas with that cocky, condescending smile of his, knowing he's pissing me off. It's like he enjoys it.

Finally, I've had enough. "What is your problem? Do you even care about passing this class?"

Ryker leans back in his chair, a lazy smile on his face. "Of course I do. I just think we need to take a different approach. You're so uptight. Does it hurt?" My eyes narrow into thin slits.

"Does what hurt?" I demand.

"Having that stick up your ass all the time," I can feel my temper flare. My nerve endings are on fire with how much I hate the man in front of me. I want nothing more than to take my pencil and shove it through his big, veiny hand.

And to think I was actually considering apologizing to this dick.

"Does that hurt?" I question, a smirk playing on my lips. Ryker's head tilts to the side and he leans closer to me over the table, anticipating what's going to come out of my mouth next.

"What?"

"The fact that you have to overcompensate for your small dick by being a total ass all the time?" Ryker guffaws and leans his torso even further over the table so he's right in my face.

I don't move. I don't lean back. I stay right where I am, with my eyes locked to his. Something wicked dances in them, and the anticipation in my body is palpable.

"Trust me, Rebel. There is nothing 'small' about me. I'd be more than happy to show you if you'd like," he winks.

My belly fills with a thousand butterflies at the visual of Ryker in front of me with his dick out, stroking it with one hand and staring at me as I play with my clit. Fuck.

"I'll pass," I force out. "Let's get back to the project."

Ten minutes later and we're back at each other's throats. I swear talking to him is like pulling teeth, and somehow, it's even worse not talking.

He's making it difficult to even concentrate as his leg bounces a million miles a minute under the table. The incessant clicking of his pen, and the way he's humming makes me want to throw a rock at him.

"Can you stop that?" I snap, finally having enough. Ryker cocks an eyebrow.

"Stop what?" he asks innocently.

"Everything that you're doing. Just stop," I look back down to my notebook where I was writing a few more thoughts on the book.

"Am I annoying you?" Ryker questions. Everything you do annoys me I think.

"Yes," is all I say. Ryker smirks, his green eyes glistening with mischief.

"Good."

I'm going to hit him with my car and feed his dead body to the wolves.

"Did you develop your personality in a car crash?" I ask with a snide smile.

Before he can say anything back, my phone begins to ring beside me on the table. Lainey's name pops up on the screen. I rush to answer the call so I can distract myself from wanting to stab Ryker in the eye.

"Hey, Lainey. What's up?"

Out of the corner of my eye, I see Ryker's smug expression. He thinks he's won this round, but he better buckle the hell up because I'm not backing down.

"You know how we were going to have a nice night in on Friday?" Lainey asks, a suspicious tone laces her soft voice. My eyebrows dip in question.

"Yes…" I answer carefully. I swear if she says we're-

"Well, we're going to a party instead," she says pointedly, as if I have no choice in the matter. "It's going to be so fun, and we get to dress up!" like that makes it any better.

"Lainey, I-"

"No. You're going. We'll go costume shopping later, kay? Okay, see you soon, bye!"

The call ends, leaving me a bit more irritated than I was before I answered it. I hate parties, especially Halloween parties. This is the last thing I want.

"Roommate trouble?" my head whips around to face Ryker, who is still sitting there with that stupid smug grin on his face, like he knows something I don't.

"Holland?" I ask, knowing that's the only way Ryker knows who I am, and that Lainey is my roommate. Ryker simply nods.

"Haven't seen you with your boyfriend in a while. What's up with that?"

"He's not my boyfriend."

Why does he even give a shit? It's none of his business. We shouldn't even be talking about that; we should be working on how to agree with each other on at least one thing for this damn project.

For the next hour or so, we stay on track, for the most part. Of course, it's not easy with all of Ryker's annoying habits and the fact that I am finding it really hard not to stare at him.

The way his muscles move under his shirt, the way his eyes gleam with danger and humor, the way the curls on the top of his head occasionally fall onto his face. And let's not forget those lips. They're so full and pink and I bet they'd feel really great on my pussy. Christ, Gwen. Get a grip.

Oh, shit. He definitely saw me staring at his lips.

Ryker's eyes fall to my lips and linger for a few seconds before coming up to meet my eyes. Those damn flutters in my stomach make me clench my thighs together under the table. As I do, my knee brushes Ryker's, and my face heats.

He opens his mouth to say something, but I speak before he can get the words out.

"Okay… well. This was so much fun," I say sardonically as I pack up my stuff. Ryker watches me as if I'm prey, and he's the hunter. His eyes follow my every movement and I'm suddenly very aware of the wetness in my panties from the thoughts of me being with him.

"But I have to go. We'll pick back up on Monday, yeah?" I don't even wait for him to reply. I hightail it out of the library. I don't have to look back to know Ryker is watching me leave, and for some reason, I like the thought of him watching me walk away.

Chapter 14

RYKER

Guinevere Sharpe is the most aggravating woman on this earth. I cannot wait until this damn project is over and I never have to speak to her again.

Only a week and a half left. A week and a half until I'm free of her.

But I swear, when she was looking at me, there was something other than pure hatred in them. I think it was lust. I think she doesn't hate me as much as she thinks.

She may annoy the living shit out of me, and she may make me wish I never stepped foot into that lecture hall, but as I watched her ass as she walked away from me, God. Her ass is perfect. It's round and plump in all the right places, and it makes me want to see more of her.

To see if her tits are just as plump and round as her ass. To hear her moans as I pound into her sweet little pussy so hard, she'd be ruined.

I never knew I could get this turned on by a woman who has no respect for who I am and thinks she can say and do whatever she wants around me. It's not something I'm used to, and if it were any other girl, I don't think I'd let it go so easily.

But Gwen? She's a whole other story. She's going to wreck me, and I'm going to let her. I'll let her do whatever she wants to me.

I imagine running my hands over her soft skin, tracing the curves of her body. My dick twitches in my pants at the thought of having her.

I wanted to know what Lainey had said to her. She looked less than pleased when they hung up, and I'm interested to know what her friend could have said to make her upset.

It doesn't matter. All that matters is that we have less than two weeks to come up with something and finish this project, or Professor Whitely is going to fail me, and my father? I don't even want to know what he'll do.

Speak of the mother fucking devil. My phone lights up as a call from none other than Robert Steele appears on the screen. I let out an exaggerated groan before pressing the button to accept the call. If I ignore it, he'll just keep calling.

"Father," I say in an abrasive tone.

"Son. I spoke with Dean Ashby today," he says casually. Great, what now? "He informed me that you've been attending all of your classes, and your grades have gone up. He's impressed at your turn around."

I don't hear it often, but it almost sounds like there's a hint of pride in his voice. Like he's genuinely proud of me. Except, I know it's all one big fat lie. He only wants me to do well so I don't tarnish his reputation with the Elite.

"Yeah. Everything's good," I tell him, unsure of what else to say.

"How is Logan? You're watching out for him, right?" I don't know dad, maybe you should ask him yourself.

I run my hands through my hair and sigh. "Yeah, dad. He's good."

"Good, well I have to get back to work. Bye, son," he says gruffly, hanging up the call before I can even say goodbye. Typical.

I really don't understand how my mother deals with that man every day. How could she love a man so cold and callous?

But she doesn't dare disappoint Robert. No one would. He'd bury you in the ground and make sure no one ever found you.

With all her good, my mother could be considered almost as bad as my father. She's been forced to sit idly by during punishments doled out by him, unable to defend her own children.

I know she can't leave him. It's not what Elite families do, and my father is all about status and appearances. He'd never allow her to leave, even if she could.

This life, it isn't something I asked for, and it's no longer something I want. I despise my father and his actions. I am thankful for the Elite because that's where I met Pat, Mason, and Holland. But if I could, I'd leave this life behind to start the one I want.

The now chilled breeze hits my face as I run through campus. I couldn't do my normal run this morning, so I had to wait until after class. Gwen was more tolerable today, but that might be because I wasn't paying attention to what she was saying.

I was distracted by the way the swells of her breasts sat above her tight purple shirt, and how her tongue poked out just a little while she was concentrating. Her intoxicating floral scent made me salivate and I had to fight the raging hard on that began to form in my pants.

So, here I am, running through campus, attempting to get rid of the thoughts of Gwen racing through my brain.

I'm fucking lost at the fact that I haven't been able to stop thinking about her. I've never had this problem before. I've never met a woman quite like Gwen.

She tough and resilient. She doesn't take my shit and she isn't afraid of me, which is a first. Even most of the professors are scared of me and what my father could do with just a call to Dean Ashby.

She hates me, but maybe I can change that.

I round a corner where some students are spread out on a blanket, having a small picnic, when I have to stop abruptly to avoid running into a small blonde standing right in my way.

I rip my headphones out of my ears, glaring down at the familiar face in front of me. Jesus Christ, can this girl not take a fucking hint? This is getting fucking old.

"Hey, Ryker," Amy says, tucking a piece of her curled blonde hair behind her ear. Her light hazel eyes are surrounded by black lashes, the tan on her skin making her look a bit too orange. I must have been really drunk when I slept with her.

My jaw clenches. "Amy," I say curtly. My arms fold across my chest, and Amy shifts from one leg to another, a nervous gesture.

She looks down and plays with her fingers.

"I heard you guys are having a party Friday. Costume party, right?" I nod, avoiding her eyes that are boring into my face.

"Maybe we could pick up where we left off," she says seductively, bringing her hand to my chest and batting her long, black lashes.

I grab her wrist tightly, ripping it away from my chest but keeping a hold of her so she can't back away. This is over.

Glaring down at her, I grip her wrist slightly tighter causing her to wince. She trembles slightly, and I kind of feel bad. But she obviously wasn't taking to the nice approach.

"I told you, it was one night. It's not happening again. What don't you understand?" I grit out. She shakes her head, trembling a bit more now. Her eyes gloss over as if she's about to cry.

"I- I just thought-" I cut her off.

"You thought wrong. Stay away from me." As soon as I release her wrist, she brings it up to her chest and rubs it with her other hand. I really wasn't holding her *that* tight. "Go."

Amy scurries off without another word or backwards glance.

God, that bitch was annoying.

RYKER

By the time I arrive to my block, the sky is grey, and it looks like it's about to rain. The air has cooled significantly, and the thin sweatshirt I'm wearing isn't really helping anymore now that I'm not running.

The sound of voices penetrates the air as I near the Elite mansion and finally see who the voices belong to and where they're coming from.

Holland and Ellie are in the front yard of Ellie's house, and from what I can hear, they're not having a happy brother and sister conversation. It sounds like an argument.

I stay put, trying to hear what they're saying.

"…I don't care, Holland. I can do what I want," Ellie says, raising her voice. Hollands eyes narrow and he takes a step closer to his sister.

"No, Ellie. You're not coming if you're going to bring that douchebag. He's not stepping foot in my house."

"It's not your house! It's the Elite's house. And you can't tell me who I can and can't be with," Ellie's small fists clench at her side.

"Ty fucking Manning is not coming. And you won't be either if he shows up. Got it?"

Ty Manning is an even bigger ass than I am. He's also on the rugby team, and I'm pretty sure none of the guys like him.

Since Pat's the captain, we've tried to convince him to go to coach, but Ty really hasn't done anything except be an annoying prick, and that's not enough to get him kicked off the team.

Ellie looks like she's about to punch Holland straight in the face and honestly, I'd pay good money to see that happen.

But instead, I make my way over to them in an attempt to distract them from wanting to rip each other's heads off.

Ellie sees me first, her bright blue eyes narrowing at the sight of me. God, she looks exactly like Holland. They have the exact same facial features, from the color of their eyes and the shape of their noses to the way their eyebrows sit. Same hair color and everything.

The only real differences between them are the fact that Holland is at least five inches taller, and very obviously a man. Ellie is small, probably five foot at the most. Her blonde hair goes to her shoulders, and she's almost concerningly thin.

I throw my arm over Holland's shoulder attempting to break the tension.

"What's going on, Monroe family?" I ask, a smirk playing on my lips. Ellie glares at me, and even though she's small, she's kind of scary. Not as scary as a certain brunette with big blue eyes and a strong dislike for me though.

"None of your damn business, Steele," Ellie grimaces.

I hold my arms up in mock surrender. "Okay, okay. Holland, tell your sister to calm down." Ellie's eyes narrow and now she looks like she wants to punch *me* in the face.

"You're both assholes. Don't be surprised if you find itching powder in your jock straps."

I attempt to tamp down the chuckle that's threatening to burst out of me, but the amusement dissipates when I see Gwen standing on the porch of the house, her dark hair up in a bun on the top of her head and a confused expression on her face.

She looks from Ellie to Holland, and then lands on me. My blood runs cold at the cold look in her eyes as she takes the few steps down to the yard.

"What's going on out here?" she asks, concern laced in her tone. "I heard yelling."

She looks between all of us once more, this time settling on Ellie, waiting for her explanation.

Ellie shakes her head. "Nothing. Everything's fine, except for the fact that my brother thinks he can tell me who I can and can't date. Despite us being the same exact age," she rolls her eyes before giving Holland a death glare.

Holland looks like he could scream right about now.

"Woah, you never said anything about dating. You only said you wanted to bring him to the party," he growls. Here we go again.

Ellie takes a step closer to Holland, but he stands his ground. I look to Gwen who stands silently, watching the situation unfold with unease.

"I gotta agree with Holland here, El. Ty Manning isn't the kind of guy you want," Ellie stares at me, unblinking.

"And how would you know what she wants?" Gwen asks pointedly, her hands flying to her hips.

Why must she always argue with me? Even when I'm trying to help her friend stay out of a toxic relationship, Gwen acts as if I'm the fucking devil.

I wonder if she's like this with everyone. But I've seen her with her friend in class, and she looks like she doesn't have a care in the world.

"Ty Manning is not a good guy. He's a prick, and I assume Ellie doesn't want that in a relationship," I shrug. If I had a sister, I wouldn't let her get within ten feet of Manning. I don't blame Holland for putting his foot down.

Gwen laughs, but there's no amusement in it.

"So, he's you."

"Ouch, Rebel. That one hurt," I taunt, setting my hand over my chest as if I'm in pain.

"Why do you call me that?" she demands. Because you're unlike any woman I've ever met. Because you challenge me when no one else would even think to. Because you don't back down or cower.

"That's for me to know, and you to… well, not."

"You know, the only time you're not as dumb as you look is when I close my eyes," she quips. I stifle a laugh at her comment.

Gwen's eyes narrow, her fists clenching on her hips as if she's holding back a punch. Not that a punch from her tiny fists would affect me much. She can't be more than one hundred forty pounds, and her head barely reaches my chest.

I wouldn't say I'm huge, but I'm bigger than a lot of the guys on the rugby team. I work out often to stay in shape and stay at the top of my game.

Gwen grabs Ellie's wrist, walking her back toward the house as she glares at me. Ellie lets Gwen pull her away, leaving Holland and I standing alone on the edge of their yard.

Ellie disappears inside the small house while Gwen stands on the porch staring at us.

"Get off our lawn. You're going to leave fire marks from your pitchforks," and then she's gone, slamming the front door shut. My dick is so hard, I have to discreetly move it so it doesn't stick straight out in my gym shorts.

If Ellie is talking about coming to the Halloween party Friday, I wonder if a sassy brunette will be there with her?

When I get home and into my room, I immediately head for the ensuite bathroom, turning on the shower. Leaning against the counter, I stare back at myself in the mirror. God, what is wrong with me?

Stepping out of my shorts and sweatshirt, I hop in the shower and let hot water and steam take over my senses. My muscles immediately relax, but my mind races with thoughts of Gwen. Imagining her naked and writhing under me, tasting every inch of her, watching her face as she comes all over my fingers.

Fuck.

I grab my hard cock in my hands and begin to stroke slowly. I let out a soft hiss of breath as my hand begins to move faster. Flashes of Gwen's lush lips, her perky tits, her round ass, and the scowl I see so often run through my mind.

My hand moves faster and faster until my balls tighten, and a familiar tingle runs at the bottom of my spine. I come so hard I have to hold myself up with my hand pressed against the shower wall.

By the time I finish my shower, I'm spent. I haven't come that hard in months. What is happening to me? I don't get hung up on women. They get hung up on me.

But knowing Gwen hates me, knowing she would never let herself admit to having any attraction to me, knowing she's fighting it only makes me want her more.

Christ, this woman is something else, and I don't know how long I can hold off.

Chapter 16

GUINEVERE

God, Ryker Steele is an enigma.

I don't know why he feels the need to antagonize me all the time. Why can't he understand that I will not allow him to rile me up?

Obviously, Ryker isn't used to a woman who isn't falling to his feet. I'm sure none of the Elite are used to woman not following their orders or speaking out of turn.

I may not know much about the Elite, but I know what people say about them around campus. They're pretty much just spoiled rich kids with control issues.

And Ryker is the worst of them all. But I think he's slowly learning that I'm not like the other girls on campus. I'm not going to bow, I'm not going to cower, I'm not going to hold my tongue.

No, that's not someone I'll ever be.

I can't tell how Ryker feels when it comes to me. He's infuriatingly hard to read; I can't seem to figure him out. One minute he's cold and calculated, the next he's looking at me like he wants me to be his next meal. For some reason, that thought makes my skin heat and my face flush.

Imagining Ryker's face between my legs has become a recurring dream, and I hate it. I hate him. I don't want to think about the way he would feel against me, how he would taste against my lips, how he could probably make me come without even a single touch.

But it's getting increasingly difficult when we are forced to work together, and we're locked in a room in the library at least three days a week. Being near him is making my mind go to places it hasn't been in a long time, and I can't stand it.

The last thing I want to do today is work with Ryker. We've gotten a lot done with the project, and surprisingly, we've agreed on a lot of things which has made the process a little less like pulling teeth.

We only have a week from today to finish, and I think we'll be done just on time. I think Ryker has been able to see where I'm coming from, and I've been able to try and understand his points of view, even though sometimes it really doesn't make sense.

He's actually been a bit more tolerable this week after the whole front yard fiasco on Monday. Like he knew I was about to blow up on him.

So, as he sits across the table from me in the basically empty library, I realize this is the first time I've looked at him and haven't wanted to strangle him.

Ryker looks down at his laptop, typing something intently. Every few seconds I find myself peeking over my book stealing glances at him. His eyebrows are pinched together in concentration and his green eyes are narrowed as he stares at the screen.

The dark stubble on his jaw contrasts with his olive skin tone, and his black inky hair is waved on the top and slightly curled at the base. His pale lips are slightly parted, and a small part of me wants to jump over the table and kiss them.

The sweatshirt he's wearing fits a bit too tight, accentuating his biceps and making me wonder what it would feel like to have them encase me. The logo for the Ellington Dodgers rugby team is spread across the middle.

Ryker's lips turn up slightly, but he doesn't look up from his laptop.

"See something you like, Rebel?" Shit. My cheeks flush as I try not to look too bothered by being caught watching him.

My eyes shoot back down to the book in my hands before Ryker glances over his computer to look at me. I can feel his patronizing gaze burning into my face, but I don't move, I don't look up.

"No," I say, trying to sound as confident as I can. Ryker's head tilts, and I finally look at him, seeing the self-satisfied smirk on his face.

His eyes fall to my lips, causing me to wet them out of instinct. Ryker's eyes darken and my thighs clench at the way they pierce into mine.

"If you want me, all you have to do is ask, Gwen," he taunts.

I roll my eyes. "There is no part of me that wants you," I lie.

Ryker shuts his laptop slowly, pushing it to the side. My body stiffens as he leans his elbows on the table and moves closer to me, but I don't back away.

The smell of his woodsy cologne hits my nose, and the look in his eyes has me panting internally. Keep it together, Gwen. You hate him, remember?

"You sure about that?" he looks back to my lips and then my eyes, waiting for me to admit that I want him. I can't do that. I won't do that. I gulp nervously and nod. Why am I so nervous all of a sudden? I'm never nervous, especially around Ryker Steele. My eyes narrow.

Ryker pushes back in his chair, stands, and sits on the table right in front of me. Wow, he's large. Everywhere. I can see the bulge sticking out in his grey sweatpants, and God, how does he carry that thing around all day?

Ryker's finger slips under my chin, bringing my head up to face him. He looks down to his cock, his lips turning up into a wide grin.

His finger lingers under my chin, and I don't make a move to remove it. His eyes search mine, likely waiting for me to swat him away.

"Take it out," Ryker demands huskily. My eyes widen. What did he just say?

"We're in the library." Ryker cocks a brow.

"So, if we weren't, you would?" he questions. He finally removes his finger from under my chin, but this time he pushes a stray hair behind my ear. The gesture sends tingles through my entire body.

"No," there's no way I'm giving this man the satisfaction of knowing I'm slightly attracted to him. But my body has other plans.

My breath quickens and Ryker notices.

"And here I thought you were just playing the good little student, studying hard, working day and night. But it seems there's more to you than that," Ryker's voice drops to a lower register, sending shivers down my spine despite myself.

Feeling flustered and annoyed at myself for the reactions I'm having, I stand up to face him, our bodies only inches apart.

"And what's that supposed to mean?"

Ryker's gaze flicks down to my lips before meeting my eyes again, a challenge flashing in them.

"It means, Gwen, that I think you're a tightly wound coil, just waiting to be unleashed. And I'd be happy to be the one to set you free."

My breath hitches, and I realize I've moved closer to him, standing between his parted legs.

I've completely forgotten how to breathe. This cocky, irritatingly attractive man in front of me has stolen the air from my lungs.

Ryker's hands find my hips and stay there while he watches my face. I imagine I look quite flushed and probably slightly nervous.

An idea forms in my mind as I stand there wondering what Ryker's next move is.

This could work for me. Making Ryker think that I'm going to give into him, knowing I never will. It's cruel, but so is he.

With a sultry laugh, I take a daring step forward, closing the small gap between us. I get so close to his face; I can feel his hot breath on my lips.

"And what makes you think I need to be set free?" My own gaze lingers on his lips, fighting the urge to close the gap completely.

Ryker's smirk returns as he reaches out to trail a finger along my jawline, sending sparks of electricity coursing through my veins.

"You can drop the hating game, Gwen. I see the want burning behind those eyes. I don't think you hate me as much as you think."

My heart pounds, desire taking over my usually practical mind.

"You're right," I lift my hand, gently stroking his stubbled cheek. He leans into my hand, and it's almost a sweet gesture.

When he closes his emerald green eyes, I lean in as if I'm going to kiss him but stop right as my lips begin to brush his.

"I hate you more," I whisper, backing away and grabbing my things off the table, leaving Ryker sitting there on the table completely stunned.

Did he really think it would be that easy to get me? He should really know better by now.

Chapter 17

GUINEVERE

I'm showered, my makeup is done, and the costume Lainey bought for me is on.

I stare at myself in the full-length mirror, already regretting letting Lainey and Ellie drag me to this Halloween party.

The much too small maid's costume shows off way too much skin. My tits are hiked up, my mid-section is showing, and the skirt is so short, it barely covers my ass. The tall white socks meet my knees, leaving my thighs exposed.

Ellie curled my long brown hair and did my makeup since I can't really do anything special with it myself.

I toss my hair behind my shoulder, taking one more look at the risqué costume before stepping out into the living room where Haley, Ellie, and Lainey sit. Lainey is dressed like a sexy pirate, and Ellie is a bunny which totally suits her. I'm not sure Holland will be happy when he sees her, but good thing he doesn't have a say.

Their eyes go wide as their gazes look over my appearance. I suddenly feel extremely self-conscious. Shit, I really don't want to go.

I run my hands over the soft material of my skirt, fidgeting slightly.

"Damn girl. You look hot as hell," Haley says, a book in her hands, her pajamas looking much comfier than this costume.

"Really? I feel a bit… exposed," I say, fighting the urge to tell them there is no way I am leaving the house like this.

Lainey jumps from her spot on the couch, her cute curly pigtails flying behind her. She grabs my hands and looks over my body again.

"That's the point," she says with a devious smile on her face. "Oh! I almost forgot. Stay here," Lainey drops my hands and runs into the kitchen, her stiletto type heels not even affecting her.

A few seconds later, Lainey comes out with a r, two candles on top, the number twenty-two lit with a flame. Her, Ellie, and Haley begin to sing happy birthday and my face lights up with emotion.

Lainey stops in front of me, my hands together in a praying position in front of my face.

She smiles brightly. "Happy birthday, Gwen. We love you," she gleams. I stare at my friends, standing in front of me with huge smiles on their faces. I can't believe they did this for me.

"Oh my God, you guys did not have to do this!"

Lainey shakes her head.

"Yes, we did. We're your best friends, and you deserve a cake on your birthday." My eyes well up with tears.

I never make a big deal about my birthday. It's not a significant day of the year for me, it's just another day. One where mom calls me and cries over how old I'm getting and sends me some gifts, and my father doesn't even remember. My birthday also falls on October thirty first, so it's often looked over anyway.

I can't even recall the last time he called to wish me a happy birthday. Probably the last year he decided he wanted be part of this family.

I usually don't tell anyone it's my birthday, but since I live with these three, they all knew when it was. And I'm kind of grateful they did, because this is seriously one of the nicest things anyone has ever done for me.

Ellie runs over to give me a giant hug, and then Haley does the same.

"Thank you guys so much. Seriously, this is amazing. I love you all," I beam.

"Blow out your candles!" Ellie jumps up and down, clapping her hands like a little kid.

With a chuckle, I blow out the candles, and the girls all clap.

"Okay, okay. Will you guys please tell me where this party is now?" They've been really secretive about the location of this party, and I don't know why. I hope it's not downtown; I hate going out there.

Lainey shrugs. "It's not far."

Ellie and Lainey exchange a suspicious look, while Haley slowly backs away to sit on the couch. Okay, now I'm a bit worried. Where could it be that they don't want-

Oh, no. No, no, no, no.

"Please don't tell me it's at the Elite house," I say warily.

Lainey sets the cake down on the coffee table and shrugs.

"Okay, I won't," she smiles. My eyes narrow and I slap her arm.

"Seriously? Lainey, what the hell?" I whine. The last thing I want to do is see Ryker after what happened in the library earlier.

My cheeks heat at the thought of being so close to him.

"It'll be fine!" she grabs my hand and starts to pull me to the door, but before we make it outside, my phone rings in my pocket.

The last thing I expect when I pull out my phone is to see my dad's name on the screen. I freeze, my breath catching in my throat. I don't remember the last time I heard from him. Did he actually remember my birthday? Is that why he's calling?

Lainey looks back at me with a concerned look on her face.

"Who is it?" Ellie asks from behind me. I shake my head in disbelief.

"It's my dad," I say, barely audible. I can feel Lainey and Ellie watching me as I stare down at my screen. It's like time has stopped.

At the last minute, I take a deep breath before deciding to answer the call, hoping I don't regret it.

"Hello?" I respond hoarsely.

"Guinevere?

Hearing my dad's voice for the first time in so long causes a shiver run down my spine.

"H… hi, dad," I stutter. I hear him clear his throat on the other end, like he's nervous.

"I have some news, and I wanted you to hear it from me first," the tone of his voice has switched to something more purposeful. A million things run through my mind. What could he possibly have to tell me?

"Okay…"

"I've just received a leading role in an upcoming film," he says proudly. A small smile curves on my lips. That's not exactly what I was expecting him to say.

A tiny party of me was hoping the news would be that he's coming home to see me. To wish me a happy birthday in person. To celebrate the birth of his only child.

"Wow, dad. That's great, congratulations," I try to sound as excited as I possibly can while simultaneously being disappointed.

"There's more. I will be moving to Germany to film. I'll be over there for a while, and I'll be quite busy, so I won't be able to call much," my heart drops. Germany? He's moving to Germany?

I don't even know what to say. How do I respond to that? He already barely calls me, and now he's moving to a different country? Does mom know? Of course, she's probably one of the first people he told.

"Oh. Uhm, okay. When do you leave?" I ask, my lip quivering as I try to hold back the tears building in my eyes. I don't know why I'm upset. It's not like we talk now, nothing's really changing.

"Monday. I just wanted to let you know in case you tried getting a hold of me," I hear him shuffling around in the background of the call, then I hear a woman call his name. He's with a woman? "Yes, Viv. Tell him I'll be there in a minute."

Who is he talking to? Who is Viv and who is my dad referring to when he says 'him'? The questions burn holes in my brain, but I'm too afraid to hear the answers.

"Guinevere, I have to go. But I'll try to get in touch with you once I get back. Bye, honey."

The phone hangs up before I even get a chance to say goodbye. A single tear runs down my cheek at the realization that my dad is leaving me, again, and he didn't even call to wish me a happy birthday.

He'd forgotten about me, again.

Chapter 18

GUINEVERE

The music thumps through my body, the bass vibrating in my chest as the alcohol I've consumed courses through my veins, clouding my thoughts and loosening the tension in my body.

As much as I hate drinking, I needed a drink after that phone call from my father, not to mention the fact that I am standing in my enemy's house.

So, I've been drowning my sorrows in alcohol and some very questionable drinks, attempting to forget the painful reality that my father has once again forgotten my birthday, and he is moving halfway across the world.

The skimpy French maid costume that pushes my cleavage together and my short skirt seemed like a bad idea before I left the house, but now I'm realizing I don't stand out at all. Every girl here is dressed in something similar, and just as revealing.

My curled hair tumbles messily around my shoulders, and my red lipstick stains the plastic cup I'm drinking from. I can feel sweat beading between my breasts and down my neck from all of the dancing I've done, and all of the bodies smashed into one room.

Lainey, Ellie, and Damian, who was already here when we arrived, dance with me, our laughter mixing with the loud sounds of people talking, screaming, and singing, the music loud enough for people in the next town to hear.

A guy wearing a fireman costume, or well, firemen's suspenders without a shirt on, and a hard hat enters our space, handing us each a shot. Normally I wouldn't accept a drink from a stranger, but I'm too intoxicated to care.

The guy hands me mine last, his stare lingering on me a bit longer than it did Lainey and Ellie. They down their shots and continue to dance, while I stare up at this attractive firefighter who still hasn't let go of my shot glass which is in my hand and his.

He's tall and tan, with blonde hair that's long on the top and shorter on the sides. His brown eyes look into mine before he shoots me an award-winning smile. Wow, this man is pretty. Not as pretty as Ryker though.

Wait, what? No, I didn't mean that. Or did I?

The guy finally lets go of my shot and runs a hand through his fluffy hair before stuffing his hands in his pockets.

"Hey, I'm Ashton. I don't think I've seen you around here before," the pretty boy says. Wow, what an original line. I stifle a laugh, smiling politely at the guy I now know as Ashton.

"Gwen. And yeah, I don't do parties much."

Ashton grins. "What brings you here tonight?" he asks.

"An asshole father who forgot my birthday," I tell him, unable to stop the words from tumbling out of my drunk mouth. Ashton nods understandingly.

"Damn, that sucks. I'm sorry," he shrugs as the grin on his face slightly morphs into something resembling pity.

"It's fine. Wanna dance?" I grab Ashton's hand and he laughs, dancing with me in the middle of the crowd.

The flashing lights and the loud music mixed with the abundance of alcohol running through me makes my adrenaline spike, and I feel like I could dance all night.

My eyes close as I move my hips to the beat of the song, my arms flying over my head as I run my hands through my curly hair slowly, feeling the long strands slide through my fingers.

Ashton's large hands find my hips, squeezing lightly, making me aware they're there. It feels good to be touched. I don't even tell him to get his hands off of me. I just continue to dance, and Ashton steps closer to me until our faces are inches away. His hands move off my hips slowly until I feel them hit my upper thigh behind me.

My eyes pop open when his hands cup my ass under my skirt. I attempt to back away, but Ashton's grip only tightens around me.

I look frantically around the room for a sign of my friends, but I can't find them. I have no idea where they went.

Ashton's face gets closer to mine as he whispers something in my ear, causing me to freeze completely.

"Let's head upstairs," he says.

I may be drunk, but I'm not that drunk.

"I think I'd rather stay down here with my friends. But thank you," I say politely, not trying to piss this guy off as I don't know him or how he'll react to being rejected.

He chuckles almost sinisterly. "Come on, let's have some fun. You know you want to."

The scent of whiskey mixed with weed hits my nose, and I have to keep my face from scrunching up at the smell. This guy is fucking gone, and he's not going to leave me alone, is he?

I place my hands on his hard chest, pushing myself away as much as I can with his grip still on me.

"Thank you for the dance, but I really have to find my friends," I plead, hoping he'll just let me go. But of course, he doesn't. Instead, his hands move slowly from my ass, up my back, and around to my face. He cups my cheeks and leans in.

"Don't be a fucking tease. Come upstairs with me," he demands. Adrenaline courses through me, a hint of fright hidden deep inside me. I begin to tremble slightly in his grasp as his face gets closer, his lips hovering over mine.

Before his lips meet mine however, his hands leave my cheeks as he's pulled back and thrown to the ground.

Ryker stands above Ashton's body on the ground. I'm too stunned to move. I'd forgotten all about Ryker and the fact that he lives in this house.

He looks down at Ashton, his face pulled into a furious expression, one I've never seen before. He looks like he wants to kill Ashton. Ashton looks up at Ryker with his arms up in surrender.

"What the fuck, man?" he asks. Ryker appears to be holding back his anger, but I can see it emanating off of his large body.

"She said no. Now get the fuck out of my house before I drag you out of here myself," Ryker threatens. Why am I finding this side of him so attractive?

Also, why is he protecting me? I've been such a bitch to him, and even though sometimes he deserves it, maybe I've been a little too harsh on him.

Maybe I've been so blinded by the rage I felt the first few times we spoke to realize that Ryker isn't that guy. Not all the time, at least not with me.

Ashton crawls backwards a bit until he's out of reach. Ryker watches him intently, fuming, as Ashton stumbles to his feet but doesn't seem to be making a move for the door.

Oh, you idiot. Just leave now before the situation escalates.

But Ashton doesn't leave. Instead, he steps closer to Ryker whose fists are clenched at his side.

"What, are you two fucking or something?" Ashton taunts. "We could share, ya know, she doesn't look like she'd mind."

My cheeks heat and my own hands ball into fists as I hold back the urge to punch this guy in the face. Who does he think he is? I step up to yell at him for his disgusting comment, but before I can, Ryker rears his fist back and punches Ashton in the face. The sound of something crunching and a splatter of blood let me know that Ashton's nose is likely broken.

Ashton's hands fly to his bleeding nose, blood sputtering out as he says, "Not into sharing, huh?"

This guy doesn't stop. If he had even a sliver of a brain cell, he'd turn around and walk away.

Ryker takes another step forward, raising his fist like he's ready to punch Ashton again, but I grab him before he can. As much as I want to see Ashton suffer, Ryker doesn't need to defend me. I don't want him to.

Ryker's eyes meet mine, then move down to look at my tiny hand on his massive arm. I feel his body relax a bit under my touch as he backs up to stand next to me.

Grabbing my hand, he begins to drag me to the exit. I'm still so intoxicated I can barely walk in a straight line, and I do want to leave. But I have to find my friends to tell them I'm going home. I wonder if they saw what just happened.

As we come up to the door, I tug my arm away from him and stop in my tracks. My mind is foggy and the room around me seems to be spinning more than it was a few minutes ago. The adrenaline I felt mere moments ago has begun to dissipate, and my inhibitions are questionable at best.

I don't know how I feel about Ryker stepping in and saving me. I'm pissed that he thought I needed saving. I'm thankful because I did need saving. I don't know what would have happened if Ryker didn't step in, but I'd never admit that to him.

But the reaction that has me questioning what the hell is wrong with me is the way my heart feels like it'll fly out of my chest at any moment, the way my nipples pebbled under my small top, the pressure building low in my belly.

Am I seriously turned on by Ryker Steele?

Chapter 19

RYKER

The house is packed wall to wall with people in costumes, screaming, drinking, and dancing wildly. The party is a raging success, which isn't a surprise since Holland, Mason, Pat, and I were in charge.

The group of freshmen consisted of Austin, Teddy, a kid I've never spoken a word to, and one of Logan's friends, Max. They did well with the set up and nothing seems to be going wrong, so I'd say they did a good job this year.

There are fake spider webs all over the large spiral banister, some hang from the chandeliers, and more are spread out over various countertops. The lights are dimmed, and flashing orange and purple beams fill the large space.

The DJ in the corner blasts music as people surround the space, grinding and dancing with each other without a care in the world.

The Elite parties are usually wild, but the Halloween party is the most anticipated event of the year, and it looks like this year will be no different than the past.

I stand in a small opening in the corner of the large living area with Holland, Logan, and Pat. Who knows where the fuck Mason went. Probably hitting on some freshman who doesn't know any better.

As my eyes scan the room, I notice a lot of the girls are wearing similar costumes and most of the guys aren't really dressed up. Some have random masks on, some have full costumes, but the majority look like they didn't even try. Much like me and the guys.

We're all wearing black jeans, a black t-shirt, and black boots that make our white and red masks stand out on our faces.

The guys and I don't usually dress up for these things, so we decided on something small this year and masks took the win.

Logan lifts his fifth beer of the night to his lips and takes a long swig.

"Well done, boys. Well done," Logan nods in the direction of the mass of people in front of us.

"Hey, where's Adrianna tonight?" Pat asks elbowing Logan in the arm softly and lifting his own beer bottle to his mouth and taking a sip.

Logan shrugs. "Who knows. Probably out fucking some other guy," he says coldly. Logan mutters something under his breath that I can't make out before he sulk away.

Patrick and I share a look of confusion, while Holland blows out a breath of air.

"Shit, that sucks."

I hand Pat my beer after deciding that I should probably go find my brother. We don't talk much, and we definitely don't share our feelings with one another, but something's wrong with him, and I need to find out what.

As I make my way through the crowd, I'm run into by several drunk students milling about. I swerve around a couple groping each other in the middle of the room and stop when I see familiar faces.

Ellie, Lainey, and the guy from class stand together as they laugh and drink, but Gwen is not with them. Did she know the party was here, so she decided not to come? Was she okay? Why wouldn't she come with her friends?

Why am I so concerned? Jesus Christ, I shouldn't care this much about her.

But even my thoughts don't hold me back from walking up to the group to ask where she is.

"Hey," I begin, making them all whip their heads around to look at me. Ellie glares my way, and Lainey smiles. The guy from class, who I still haven't figured out his name, stands with his arms over his chest.

"Hey, Ryker. What's up?" Lainey says brightly. Her coiled brown hair is in pigtails and her tan skin makes the makeup on her face stand out. I wonder if Holland's seen Ellie yet. Her skimpy bunny costume is definitely going to piss him off, and I want to be there when shit goes down.

"Did Gwen come with you guys?" Fuck, I sound like a desperate teenager. I don't do this shit. I don't chase. I don't get hooked on one girl, ever. This is not me. And yet, I don't care.

"Yeah, she's right over there," Lainey points in the direction of the dance floor, where I spot a curly haired brunette in a sexy maid costume that leaves little to the imagination. She's dancing like she doesn't have a care in the world, and I don't think I've ever seen her this happy.

Gwen has a genuine smile on her face. She sways her hips to the music as her hands run through her long hair, her long toned legs accentuated by her white knee length socks. God, she looks like a fucking wet dream.

But then I see she's not alone. Some stupid fucker in a fireman's costume sets his grubby hands on her hips and I see red as they move around to cup her ass.

Her body stiffens and I can see she's clearly uncomfortable, but the guy keeps going. Before I know it, the guy's stupid suspenders are in my fist and I'm throwing him to the ground.

The rest of the encounter is a blur, and then I'm pulling Gwen away from the prick who put his hands on her. She stumbles behind me, trying to keep up with my long strides to the front door.

My breathing is rapid, and my heartbeat is pounding in my chest, adrenaline coursing through my veins. I've never gotten into a fight over a girl. I've never wanted to crush another man for touching something that doesn't belong to him. But Gwen doesn't belong to me either.

I don't even give myself time to dwell on that fact as I begin to open the door. But before I can, Gwen rips her hand out of my grasp and stares at me as if I'm insane.

All I want to do is get her out of here. Get her away from me, because when she's around me, my thoughts aren't rational. I don't want to be having these feelings about her. The need to protect her. The need to make sure she's okay. I shouldn't care.

"What are you doing?" Gwen snaps, crossing her tiny arms over her chest, making her cleavage even more prominent.

Part of me wants to yell at her for wearing that costume, if you can even call it that. There's practically nothing there, and I know every guy in there was watching her. That thought alone almost makes me turn around and punch anyone that even glanced in her direction.

"We're leaving," I tell her. I'm going to bring her home and make sure she stays there. I don't exactly know how, but if I have to tie her down, I will. Jesus, who the hell am I?

"I'm not leaving," Gwen's hands land on her hips, and maybe she'd be more intimidating if she wasn't in a maid's costume and wasn't the size of my pinky finger.

I release a sharp breath. "Yes, you are. Come on," I demand, reaching for her hand once again, but she backs away, almost tripping over herself. I eye her suspiciously. Her eyes are glazed over, and her cheeks are flushed. "Are you drunk?"

"Yeah, and? It's a party, Ryker," she throws her hands up in the air, gesturing to the chaos around us, a small chuckle leaving her bright red lips. My anger rises, and this time, it's not at the fireman. It's at her. Why would she let herself get this bad?

I open the door and grab Gwen's wrist, pulling her out of the house with me. She stumbles and almost falls into me before steadying herself.

"I'm not going anywhere with you!" she yells, stomping one foot on the ground like a toddler throwing a tantrum. I stifle a laugh at the sight, because even though she's mad, and even though I'm mad, she looks adorable. My fists clench as I try to keep my temper in check.

Why does she insist on being difficult literally all of the time?

RYKER

As we stand in the front yard of the Elite mansion, the cool autumn air whips around us, and I imagine Gwen is freezing due to the lack of clothes on her body, but she doesn't show it.

She stands in front of me with a glare, arms crossed, and being as stubborn as ever. I want to take her home. She's drunk, she was almost taken advantage of by some fucking creep, and there's something behind her eyes that makes her look damaged.

Was something bothering her? Is that why she got so drunk tonight?

I take a step closer to her, but only slightly so she doesn't back away from me.

"Please, let me take you home," I plead, attempting to sound less demanding in hopes it will make her more inclined to do what I say. But no such luck.

"No. I'm staying," she says defiantly. Oh, I want to strangle her right now. I close the gap between us, and Gwen doesn't even flinch.

"No, you're not," Gwen's breath quickens, her chest rising and falling rapidly. She looks fucking beautiful as her blue eyes narrow, searching mine.

"I can do whatever I want, Ryker," she practically slurs. Fuck, she is wasted.

I move in close to her face, our lips almost touching.

"You are insufferable," I whisper, watching goosebumps form on Gwen's arms and chest as her cheeks turn a bright shade of pink. Her arms fall to her sides, and she licks her perfect red lips.

"And you're a dick," she says simply. I hold back a laugh, bringing my hand to her pink cheek, sweeping my thumb over it a few times. I can smell her perfume and the copious amounts of alcohol on her breath.

"If I'm such a dick, why does your breath hitch whenever I get close?" I move even closer, so we are chest to chest. "Why do you get goosebumps every time I touch you?" I move my hand from her cheek, down to her bare side, causing her to intake a sharp breath.

And then, I slowly trace my fingers down her taut stomach, past her naval, and down to the spot between her legs. I cup her pussy above the thin shorts under her skirt and her breath ceases. "And why are you so wet?" I search her eyes for any argument, but nothing comes. God, what I wouldn't give to be inside her, to feel her wetness, to smell her arousal.

I brush my lips against hers, not enough to qualify as a real kiss. Just enough to be a tease and leave her wanting more. My dick twitches in my jeans, and if we weren't standing in my front yard surrounded by drunk partygoers, and if Gwen wasn't so drunk, I'd rip her pants off right here and devour her.

Backing away slowly, I watch as Gwen's eyes open slowly, finding mine.

"I'm taking you home. Now," I say, hoping that she'll surrender and just do as she's told.

"I'm. Staying," she enunciates each word, baring her teeth. I growl, having had enough of this incessant game she's playing. I'm annoyed, very fucking pissed off, and she's being a stubborn bitch.

An unamused laugh flies out of me.

"For what? So you can drink yourself into oblivion instead of talking about what's wrong with you? So you can find some random guy to fuck?" I spit. I have no idea where that came from, but it's out there now and I can't take it back.

Gwen's eyes narrow and her lips purse before a sinister grin overtakes her features.

"And so what if I did?" My blood runs cold. My fists clench, and a low snarl begins in my throat.

"Watch it, Gwen," I grit my teeth, my jaw hardening. Gwen steps closer, but we're not quite as close as before.

"Or what?" she challenged.

"Don't."

Is she trying to piss me the fuck off? Her arms cross again.

"What are you going to do about it?" her words remind me of the ones I said to my father at our last encounter after his empty threats.

But one thing about me, I always keep my word.

I grab Gwen's arm roughly, causing her to let out a small squeak.

"We're leaving," I tell her, dragging her behind me since she's not moving much on her own. "Guinevere… don't make me carry you out," I threaten. This catches Gwen's attention. Her eyes widen and she stops completely.

"You wouldn't dare."

"You want to bet?" I don't even give her a chance to answer. I fling her over my shoulder like she weighs nothing, because she doesn't really. Gwen squeals as she hits her tiny fists against my back. I slap her ass, causing her to yelp.

"Can you stop? That tickles," I taunt. I hear her growl from behind me.

"You asshole! What is your problem?"

I walk in the direction of her house, aware that several pairs of eyes are now on us from the scene we just created. But I don't care. Let them watch, let them talk.

"You need to sleep it off," I call back to her.

As I approach Gwen's house, she seems to have given up on fighting me. I set her down once we're on her porch. She no longer looks like she's angry. Instead, her eyes are glossy, and she looks like she's about to cry.

Gwen looks down at her feet, her long hair falling in front of her face, avoiding my gaze which has turned from anger to concern.

Fuck. Something pulls in my chest and before I can stop myself, my hand reaches out. I place my finger under her chin, lifting softly for her to look at me.

A tear streams down her cheek and her bottom lip quivers. Shit, this girl is going to ruin me. I want to help her, I want to hurt whoever made her cry, make them suffer.

"Gwen, what's wrong? What happened?" I don't even recognize my own voice. I've never cared this much about anything before. Why is Gwen any different?

She swipes the tear away with a fist, clearly frustrated that she's crying.

"I'm fine," she says softly. "I just need to sleep. You can go back to your party."

Gwen turns around and reaches for the door handle, but I grab her arm before she can open it. How could she even think I'm worried about the party right now?

"I don't care about the fucking party, Rebel. What's wrong?"

Gwen's ocean blue eyes meet mine, and for a second, I forget how to breathe. The sadness in her eyes makes my heart fucking break. I need to know what's causing it. But Gwen wouldn't be Gwen if she didn't give a little push back.

"I'm fine, Ryker. Just go," she demands. I grip her arm a bit tighter, letting her know I'm not ready to go.

"I'm not going anywhere until you tell me why you're crying."

Gwen rolls her eyes in exasperation. I don't care that she thinks she hates me, she can hate me all she wants, but I will not leave her alone until she lets me in.

Gwen sighs and sits down on the porch. She doesn't seem as drunk anymore, probably from the adrenaline, but she's definitely still a bit wobbly.

I follow suit, sitting down next to her, hoping she's ready to talk. She stares blankly out at the street, the sound of partygoers screaming and talking fills the air. There's a cold breeze, and I'm honestly surprised Gwen would want to stay out here longer. Even I'm getting a little cold.

Her tiny hands wring as she lets out a shaky breath.

"My father called," she says, a hint of resentment in her voice. My brow cocks, and I tilt my head to look at her.

"Okay…" Did she and her father not get along? Did he say something to her to make her upset? Gwen shakes her head, looking down at the ground. She lets out a harsh laugh.

"I'm so stupid. I actually thought he'd remembered," her hands run down her face, and she groans. "God, I'm such an idiot." What is she talking about? I gently grab her hands and pull them away from her face. I want to kiss her. I want to make everything better.

"What do you mean? Remember what?" I pry. Gwen searches my face, her eyes full of sadness. She looks like she's about to retreat into herself, but I won't let her. This is clearly weighing on her, and she needs to talk about it.

"It's…" she sighs. "He forgot my birthday. My own father forgot my birthday. I don't even know why I'm surprised. Honestly, I'd have been more surprised if he'd remembered. How sad is that?" she lets out a breath.

Birthday?

I grab both sides of her face, forcing her to look at me. I search her expression, trying to make out what emotions she's feeling right now, but I can't make it out.

"Gwen, is today your birthday…?" I ask hesitantly. She nods slowly.

Oh, for Christ's sake. It's her fucking birthday? Why the hell wouldn't she tell me? We spent half the day together working on that stupid fucking project and she never even mentioned it.

"Shit, Gwen. Why didn't you tell me?"

"It's not a big deal. It's just another day," she shrugs, completely defeated. I want to be mad at her for keeping this from me. I want to yell at her for being so stubborn, but she doesn't need that right now.

"Your dad is an asshole. Trust me, I know a thing or two about asshole dads." Gwen looks like she wants to question what I mean, but I appreciate that she doesn't ask. I don't want to explain my fucked-up relationship with my father right now.

"I'm guessing you and your dad don't get along much, huh?" I ask, hoping she'll share a little more of her life with me.

Gwen shakes her head. "Not really. Him and my mom got divorced when I was nineteen, and he moved to California. He's an actor, so he doesn't have much time to talk to me."

That's bullshit. Everyone can make time to talk to someone they love. She's making excuses for him, and from the sound of it, he doesn't deserve that.

"We haven't really spoken in a while, and when he called out of the blue tonight, I really thought he was calling to wish me a happy birthday," she chuckles. "I'm such an idiot."

"Stop that."

Gwen's eyes narrow in question. "Stop what?"

I turn so that my body is fully facing hers. Our knees touch, and my cock grows, the stupid bastard.

"Putting yourself down. You aren't an idiot, you're one of the smartest people I know. Your dad is the idiot. You deserve so much better than that," I sound like a sappy chick flick. God, how the mighty have fallen.

Gwen reaches for my hand and squeezes, sending a spark of need down to my groin. I keep my eyes on hers as she licks her lips. I want to bite that lip. I want to know what it would feel like around my-

"Will you come in with me?" My eyes widen before they narrow in question. Did she just ask me to come inside her house with her? She must still be drunk. There's no way sober Gwen would invite me in.

She stands and walks toward the door. I stand and watch as she opens the front door, then turns around to meet my gaze which had landed on her perfect ass.

"You coming?" I am so going to regret this. Against my better judgement, against everything I thought I knew of myself, I follow her inside, shutting the door behind us.

Gwen's bedroom looks exactly like what I thought it would. Floral décor, pictures of her with an older woman who must be her mother, a light purple bed spread, a small desk under the window, and a full-length mirror in the corner.

I sit on the edge of Gwen's bed as the water runs in the ensuite bathroom. I don't know why she wanted me to come in. But her thoughts seem to be a bit scattered at the moment with the amount of liquor she drank tonight and the emotions running through her head.

She steps out of the bathroom in nothing but an oversized t-shirt, her hair up in a bun on the top of her head, and her makeup completely washed off. Holy shit, she's perfect.

Climbing onto the bed, the shirt rides up an inch revealing the light blue thong she's wearing and if I thought I was hard before, it's unbearable now.

Gwen pulls the covers up over her and relaxes into the bed. I watch as she closes her eyes, and it's taking everything in me not to crawl on top of her and smash my lips to hers.

"Stay until I fall asleep?" she asks softly. Jesus. I run my hands down my jean covered thighs and clear my throat.

"Okay."

Several minutes later, Gwen's breathing slowed, and her face softened. She looks so peaceful; so unafraid, so fucking sexy.

Happy birthday, my little Rebel.

Chapter 21

GUINEVERE

The aroma of coffee beans and baked goods fills my senses as I wait for my latte. Café Grind is always packed on a Monday, but today is particularly freezing outside, so everyone is here waiting for their warm drinks before heading to class.

This past weekend was… interesting, to say the least.

When I woke up Saturday morning, I had six missed calls from Damian, and several texts from Lainey and Ellie wondering where I went and if I was part of the fight earlier in the night.

When I walked into the kitchen, they were all sitting there drinking coffee, and giving me a stern look. I told them everything, including the fact that I had Ryker stay with me until I fell sleep.

Why the hell I did that, I have no freaking clue. I don't know why I even told him anything about my dad and my family drama.

I don't know if Ryker stayed until I fell asleep, considering I don't even remember going to bed. But when I woke up in the morning, he was gone. I haven't heard from him since, and honestly, I don't even care.

Okay, maybe I care a little bit. But why? Sure, he punched a guy for me, and sure, he listened to my sob story. But he only did that because I cried like a fucking idiot in front of him. He doesn't actually care about me.

The barista calls my name, and I grab my latte, saying thank you before walking away. My phone rings in my pocket, and when I pull it out, my mother's face is on the screen. I take a deep breath before answering.

"Gwenny?" Mom says as soon as the line connects. She sounds concerned. I set down my latte and my bag on the table to my side and take a seat in the accompanying chair.

"Mom? Is everything okay?" I ask. My mother sighs, making my eyes narrow as curiosity runs through me.

"Are you okay? Did your father call?" My father must have told her he called me the other night. But why is she just calling me now when this happened three days ago?

"I'm fine, mom. Why are you just calling me about it now?" I don't mean to sound rude, but I'm over thinking about my dad. I just want to move on. He doesn't deserve my tears.

"He just called me. He told me he called Friday to tell you about his move," she says softly. "I asked him if he'd wished you a happy birthday, but he said he'd forgotten. I know you must be hurt, so I wanted to call to check in."

He'd obviously called my mom to tell her about his upcoming move. He said he wanted me to hear the news from him, which meant he couldn't tell my mom before me because she would have told me.

"I'm so sorry, honey. But I hope you still had a wonderful day. Did you get my gifts?" I smile. Mom sent me a few outfits, a new watch, and a couple gift cards.

"I did, thank you. I really love them."

"Good. Are you coming home for Thanksgiving?" she asks, a bit of hope in her voice. I haven't really even thought about Thanksgiving let alone what I'll be doing. Of course I'll probably go home, I don't really have another option.

"Yeah," I say. I hear my mom's soft squeal of excitement on the other end which makes me chuckle.

"Oh, perfect! I can't wait to see you, Gwenny. It feels like it's been forever."

It has. I haven't been home since the beginning of the semester. I haven't really had a reason to go back, and honestly, I hate driving. I know it's a pretty short drive, but it's a drive, nonetheless. I check the new golden watch on my wrist for the time.

"Shit. Mom, I have to go to class. I'll talk to you tomorrow. Love you!"

I shove my phone in my pocket, grab my bag and latte, and practically sprint out of the café to Mallory Center. I have never been late, and I can't believe I let myself get so distracted.

As I round the corner down the hall from the classroom, I bump into a hard body. Thankfully, my latte doesn't spill all over my new blouse and scarf.

I look up to see Ryker standing in front of me, a huge smirk on his face. Rolling my eyes, I let out a groan.

"Haven't learned your lesson yet, huh Rebel?" I narrow my eyes at him as he guffaws.

"You're the one standing in the middle of the hallway!" I glance around the empty hall and into the classroom, noting that Professor Whitely is not yet in the room. Good, I'm not entirely late.

"What are you doing out here anyway?"

Ryker's smirk turns into something softer, more serious.

"Waiting for you. I haven't heard from you since Friday night," he explains. My heart skips and my stomach flutters.

My arms fold over my chest, and I quickly look down at my feet, hoping he didn't see the way my cheeks blushed at the thought of him waiting for me.

"I've been busy," I lie. In reality, I've been avoiding him, because the feelings I'm having regarding him are damn confusing.

I hate him. At least, I want to hate him. But every time we're together, I feel this pull, this need to be close to him, and I really despise not having control over my feelings.

Ryker doesn't look like he believes me one bit. His brow cocks and his head tilts slightly as he takes a step closer to me. My breath catches in my throat. A dark piece of hair falls across his forehead as his green eyes bore into mine.

"Well, our project is due Friday. We should probably finish everything up, yeah?" he asks. How can he look so casual yet so intimidating at the same time? I nod.

"Yeah. Yes. We should…do that," shit. Who the hell am I right now? I don't stutter. I don't fawn over men. Especially one that I hated not even two weeks ago.

"You can come to the Elite house. The guys have a meeting on campus tonight, so they won't be there," Ryker winks suggestively. Did I say hated? I meant very much still hate.

I roll my eyes. "In your dreams."

Something flashes behind Ryker's stare, and I can't pinpoint what it is. Challenge? Lust?

"You're coming to the rugby game tonight," Ryker demands. Hell no I'm not. I've never been to one of those games, and I'm not starting now. Especially since he's the one that asked. I shake my head as I begin walking to the lecture hall.

"That wasn't a question, Gwen. You're coming!" he calls after me, and I flip him off behind my back. I can almost feel his smirk burning into the back of my head, and for some reason, that send a warm feeling through me.

Ryker Steele, what are you doing to me?

Chapter 22

GUINEVERE

The crowd roars to life as the Ellington Dodgers take the field. My heart races with anticipation as I watch Ryker stretch. Honestly, part of me wants to see him get tackled, but another part, a newer, more intriguing part, wants to tackle him myself.

The stands are packed with students, mainly girls who are dressed like it isn't only fifty degrees outside, screaming the guy's names and completely embarrassing themselves over guys that most likely have no clue they even exist.

Lainey and Ellie sit beside me screaming their heads off. I don't think they even really know what's going on. I wanted Haley to come because she's so much more levelheaded. She'd tell me to pull my head out of my vagina and start thinking with my brain. If Damian wasn't working on his project tonight, he'd be here too. But he'd join Lainey in telling me to 'fuck Ryker Steele's brains out' as they like to say.

Ryker Steele isn't a guy that dates. He isn't a guy that brings you flowers, he isn't the guy that opens car doors for you or makes you feel like you're the only girl in the world.

No, Ryker is the type of guy to screw you over in the blink of an eye. He'll push you off the cliff and laugh while you fall. He is not the type of guy that settles down, and that's precisely why, among many other reasons, I cannot let myself go there. No matter how attractive I find him in that jersey. Holy Hell, that man is fucking sexy as sin.

Lainey elbows my arm, reminding me she's there. She gives me a knowing grin, following my line of sight and then looking back to me.

"For someone that didn't want to come, you sure look like you're enjoying it," she teases. I roll my eyes at her, trying not to give myself away.

The game begins and Ryker's team dominates from the start. He's seriously a force to be reckoned with on and off the field. He's agile, strong, and really hard not to watch as his muscles flex beneath his green Ellington Dodgers jersey. I find myself watching his every move, my breath quickening as he runs across the field, passing and tackling with skill and precision.

Ryker looks like he was made for this. Made to play this game and lead a team, even if he's not the captain. The guys seem to follow his directions and listen to his cues. He's a natural leader, encouraging and strategizing the whole time.

His muscles move and flex, and his face drips with sweat. I wonder what it would be like to feel those powerful arms around me, to taste his sweat-dampened skin, to feel his nimble fingers between my legs.

The ball moves back and forth, the players running, tackling, and pushing their way towards the goal line. The other team is putting up a fight, but they're flailing.

Groverland University is a good school, only about twenty miles from Ellington. I guess their skill isn't rugby.

The crowd roars as Ryker runs down toward the goal line, determination written all over his handsome features, and then everyone jumps to their feet as the ball soars through the goal post, earning Ellington three points, making it a three to zero game.

"I have to pee," Lainey shouts over the crowd, distracting me from the confusing thoughts running through my brain.

"Me too!" Ellie shouts. "Gwen, do you have to go?"

"No, I'm good," I tell them as they stand from their seats. Ellie grabs Lainey's hand, pulling her toward the exit.

"Okay, we'll be right back!"

I watch as they fight through the crowd of students that are still screaming and jumping around the stands before turning my attention back to the game. Ryker looks tired, sweat pouring off his beat red face as he sits on the bench.

"Hey there," a slightly familiar voice says from beside me, the sound making my hairs stand on the back of my neck. I turn to meet the gaze of the firefighter from the party on Halloween, Ashton.

Wonderful, just what I needed.

"You know, it wasn't really nice of your boyfriend there to put me on my ass just for dancing with you," he sneers. God, if he wasn't such an ass, he'd be really attractive. His floppy blonde hair and brown eyes along with his chiseled jaw and perfect nose make him look like a model.

"He's not my boyfriend," I say sternly. This guy gives me the creeps, especially because he tried to force me to go upstairs with him at the party, despite my drunken state.

Ashton shrugs. "Doesn't matter. I think you should make it up to me," he suggests, bringing his finger to my neck and drawing a line down to my shoulder which is covered by my heavy coat.

I shiver at his touch, and not in a good way. Suddenly, the autumn air feels a lot colder.

Pulling away, I glare at him. Why do all the guys at this school feel entitled to everything?

"I'm not the one who touched you. Take it up with Ryker," I tell him, focusing on the field in front of me. The game is heating up and from the looks of it, Groverland's team is sinking.

"I'd rather take it up with you," his hand skims my thigh and inches closer to the inside hem. I freeze, my heart pounding in my chest and my breathing accelerating. He wouldn't do anything here, right? We're in the middle of a huge crowd.

I don't think anyone would be stupid enough to do something such as touch someone against their will in the middle of college rugby game, surrounded by peers, faculty, and parents. But I've been wrong before.

I look down to Ashton's hand resting on my thigh, my jaw tensing as I fight the bile rising in my throat. Where are Lainey and Ellie? They should be back by now.

"You're a little tease, you know that? Acting like you don't want me when I can clearly see you do. Come on, baby.

Let's ditch this game, and you can come back to my place. I'll make it worth your while," Ashton's evil smirk makes my blood run cold. Christ, this guy just can't take a fucking hint. I grimace.

"Not a chance, asshole. Now go away, I'm trying to watch the game."

Ashton laughs snidely, rolling his eyes as his hand grows tighter on my leg. I hold back a wince. I don't want him to see me rattled.

"We'll see about that," he says, his tone threatening.

Lainey and Ellie will be back any moment. But for some reason, I kind of want Ryker to notice so he can put Ashton in his place.

Why does the thought of Ryker beating Ashton's ass turn me on?

RYKER

My head is throbbing as sweat drips down my face, burning my eyes. The cold fall air does nothing to cool me down as I run up and down the field, trying to end this damn game.

We've played Groverland before, and as much as I hate to admit it, they're a good team. They beat us last game, but we're not going to make it easy for them today. We're playing great, and Pat is making some great calls.

Coach looks like he's about to explode, his wrinkled face is bright red as he fists a clipboard and runs a hand through his grey hair. We're six to three Ellington right now, and there's only five minutes left.

As I take a seat on the bench for a shift change, I look into the stands, finding myself looking for the one girl that isn't cheering for me. It's easy to spot her, since she's one of the only fans sitting. "Fan" is a loose term, considering she's never been to a game, and she hates my guts.

My veins ice over after my eyes focus in on who she's sitting with. Where are Lainey and Ellie? Why is Ashton fucking Davis sitting next to her with his hand on her thigh?

Did Gwen want him there? Was she okay with him touching her? My glare deepens when I see something flash on her face. She looks scared, and that causes my blood to boil.

Gwen peaks down, presumably questioning why Ashton's hand is still on her thigh. But otherwise, she's frozen. Until Lainey and Ellie make their way back to their seats. I watch as Ashton leans down once more, seemingly whispering something into Gwen's ear. Her face pales as Ashton saunters away with a malevolent smile on his face.

God, did this guy not learn his lesson that last time I knocked him on his ass? The fucker must have a death sentence.

The whistle blows, indicating the end of the game. Ellington won six to three and my teammates are gathered on the middle of the field, screaming and hugging. Coach hooks his arm around Holland's neck, congratulating him for making the winning goal.

Instead of wanting to celebrate our win with my teammates, my jaw is tight, and my body is on fire. Seeing another man touch Gwen, watching the way her body tensed at his touch, the way fear danced in her eyes. I want to grab the guy by the neck, shove him against a wall, and watch as blood spews from his smug fucking face.

I hurriedly get dressed in the locker room after all the celebration, not bothering to shower right now. I need to find Gwen.

The guys talk about the game and how some guy tackled Ty Manning a bit too hard for absolutely no reason. Honestly, he probably deserved it.

"Dude was out of line," I hear one of the guys say. Some huff in agreement, while I roll my eyes. Pat, Holland, and Mason meet me at my locker as I shove everything in and slam it shut.

"He's gonna fucking pay for that," Manning threatens. This guy thinks he's a lot tougher than he actually is. Since I can't help myself, and I'm a dick, I laugh. Ty's head whips around to me, glaring.

"What's funny, Steele?" he asks. I shake my head, letting out another guffaw.

"Nothing, just that you think you'll be able to fight a guy twice your size," I shrug. Pat, Holland, and Mason chuckle at my sides.

Manning moves closer to me, almost in my face as he grimaces, his face red.

"Do you want to test it?" God, yes. What I wouldn't give to punch Manning in the face, but I have more important things to worry about right now.

"You know what? Yeah, I'd actually really love to put you on your ass, but I have shit to do," I say, my face falling into a stern scowl. I get in his face, looking him directly in the eye. "If you so much as get within ten feet of Groverland, I'll know about it. You won't be the reason our team goes down."

Ty backs away slowly, watching my face as he walks back to his spot next to his cronies.

Pat stands straight before pinning Ty with a threatening stare.

"I'll have your ass kicked off this team faster than you can say Dodgers, got me?" Ty nods slowly. "Good."

With that, all four of us walk out of the dank locker room and toward the stands. I'm still fuming about seeing Gwen with that prick Davis. My fists clench at my sides as I attempt to tamp down the rage burning inside me.

The stands are still emptying as students and faculty make their way to the parking lot. The clouds in the sky have opened up letting cold rain drops fall and land on my burning skin.

"Dude, you good?" Pat asks, grabbing my arm and stopping me in my tracks. I growl and rip my arm away.

"I'm fine. I just… I have to find Gwen."

Holland's eyebrows shoot up in question. "Why? Doesn't she hate you?" My eyes narrow in his direction.

"I saw her in the stands. That stupid dickhead Ashton Davis had his hands on her. She didn't want it. I could see it on her face, she was uncomfortable," I seethe. These guys have always been there for me. They've understood all the ups and downs with my father, with Logan, everything. I know they'll understand this.

Pat nods. "Got it, okay. So, we're going to kick his ass?"

"Yeah, let's kick his ass!" Mason chimes in. I shoot him a warning glare and he steps back.

"We will. But first, I need to make sure Gwen's okay," I say, looking around the packed parking lot to find the tiny brunette in question.

I don't understand the feelings I'm having right now. I've never been more frustrated and confused. This girl has made me crazy; she's made me question myself and question the things I do. She's infuriating and obstinate. She's tough and she knows what she wants.

I'm weak. I can't stand up to my own father, I have no idea what I want, and worst of all, I'm jealous over a girl I find absolutely exasperating.

I'm honestly surprised she even came to the game at all. But Ellie wanted to come for Ty, and lord knows that made Holland livid.

According to Ellie, Lainey wanted to come because she couldn't stand sitting at home doing nothing, so Gwen was dragged along. I'm sure she put up a good fight though. There's no way they got her here without push back.

From what I could see from the field, Gwen looked good. Her long hair was pulled back in a braid, her giant coat a bit overkill for the chilly weather, but it'll come in handy once December comes around.

As the parking lot chaos dwindles down, a pink puffy coat catches my eye, and I automatically know it's Lainey. I head off in her direction, the guys trailing behind me.

"Where's Gwen?" I ask, trying not to sound too rattled. *She's not your girlfriend Ryker, remember? She doesn't even like you.* I shake off the annoying thoughts, even though they couldn't be truer.

Lainey eyes me curiously. "Hello to you too. She's with Ellie in the bathroom. Why?" she places her tiny hands on her hips.

Lainey is tall, taller than Gwen and Ellie. She must be five ten. She has the look of a supermodel and the attitude of a cat. Sweet when she wants to be but will scratch if provoked.

I don't answer her. Instead, I stand watching the bathrooms waiting until Gwen appears.

"Hello? I asked you a question," Lainey pokes my shoulder.

I look down at her, her arms crossed over her chest and her eyes narrowed.

"I heard," I deadpan. Lainey huffs.

"Hey Barkley," Holland nods in Lainey's direction. Her glare moves from me to my friend. "Enjoy the game?"

I send Holland a curious look. Why is he making small talk with her?

"Holland," she nods, her cheeks slightly pinking up. "Yeah, I did. I especially loved the part where the guy from the other team knocked you on your ass," she smiles snarkily. Wow, I like her.

Hollands hand flies to his chest. "Ouch, Barkley."

Lainey keeps the smile on her face as she looks at Holland up and down, and then she shrugs.

"Maybe rugby just isn't for you. You should try something less physical, like golf," she mocks, and I have to stifle a laugh.

"Funny, coming from someone who's never played a sport in her life," Holland taunts.

Just then, Ellie and Gwen walk out of the bathroom and toward our group. Gwen's eyes find mine instantly, and I wonder what she's thinking.

"Holland, what are you doing here?" Ellie asks, clearly not happy to see her brother. Holland rolls his eyes. They start to argue about something, but I completely drown them out as I stare down at Gwen, attempting to read the expression on her face.

My eyes fly to her soft lips as her tongue darts out lick them. God, I want to know what that tongue feels like when it's in my mouth.

Her blue eyes rake over me before she opens her mouth to say something.

"Good game, I guess. I don't know much about Rugby," she shrugs casually. My eyebrow raises and a smirk forms on my lips.

"Was that a compliment, Rebel?" Gwen rolls her eyes.

"Barely. Are you ever going to tell me why you call me that?"

"Maybe," my face falls back into a scowl as I think about Davis touching her. "What did Davis want?" it comes out a bit harsher than I meant it to.

Gwen blinks a few times and her lips part before slamming shut again, her eyes narrowing with suspicion.

"Were you watching me?" she asks as she squares her shoulders. I don't even hesitate.

"Yes."

"Why do you care?" she challenges. I step an inch closer and for a moment, I forget we're not alone.

"Just tell me what he wanted," I demand.

"Me," Gwen looks down at the ground before looking back into my eyes. My blood runs hot and a rage builds inside me. Her?

Over my dead fucking body.

Chapter 24

GUINEVERE

Ryker looks like he's about to blow a fuse.

After I explained what was said between Ashton and me, Ryker was ready to find him and kill him. I don't know why he even cares. He's made it his life's mission to annoy the fuck out of me every chance he gets. He doesn't like me. Sure, he's made some sexual comments, but he doesn't care about me.

I wonder if he has a personal vendetta when it comes to Ashton. That must be the reason he's so bothered by him, right?

Honestly, I was kind of bothered by Ashton and his unwelcomed touches and threats. I'm not sure why he's chosen to bother me. There are hundreds of girls on campus he could torment. Why me?

All I did was dance with him at a party when I was drunk. I don't remember giving any indication that I wanted to sleep with him. Did I?

Ryker paces back and forth across the space of our living room. I don't know how I ended up here, having Ryker Steele in my living room, angrily spewing out threats while I sit on the couch with my roommates and three other Elites.

This was certainly not on my bingo card for this semester.

I clear my throat, effectively halting Ryker in his tracks. He looks at me, his green eyes boring into me.

"I don't know why you're so worried. He's just a stupid guy that can't take a hint. He'll get bored eventually," I try to sound as confident as possible. Truth is, I'm not sure if Ashton will give up, but eventually he has to, right?

Ryker's eyes narrow with anger. "Gwen, the guy said he wants to use you to get back at me. He's not going to stop until he does just that, and I'm not letting that happen," he states in a gravelly tone.

I watch as Lainey raises her hand, looking a bit nervous. Ryker's head twists in her direction.

"What?" he snaps. Lainey doesn't even flinch at his harsh tone.

"So, what are we supposed to do about him? We can't exactly get rid of him," she points out. Holland chuckles under his breath.

"You let us deal with that, Barkley. Nothing to worry your pretty little head over," he gives her a condescending smile. Her blue eyes narrow in his direction.

"Why are you even here? Shouldn't you be out finding some poor girl to fuck over?" she taunts. Ellie and I exchange a questioning glance. What the hell is going on between them? I make a mental note to ask Lainey about it later.

"Will you two shut the fuck up?" Ryker demands, more than he asks. The two continue to glare at each other without speaking.

Ryker's gaze moves back to me, his eyes serious as they move over my body, then land on my face.

"I don't want him anywhere near you. You should have one of us with you at all times," he insists. Is he serious? He thinks I need a bodyguard now? This is ridiculous.

I stand from my seat on the couch, holding my hands at my side so I don't punch Ryker in his stupidly attractive face.

"I don't need a fucking bodyguard, Ryker. For one thing, I can take care of myself, I don't need you. Two, Ashton is going to forget all about this in a week. There's no reason to get this worked up about it."

Ryker takes a step closer to me, the smell of his shampoo and soap swirling around me.

"Why can't you just listen to me for once?" he spits.

"Because you're not always right, Ryker!"

"Well, I'm right about this," he declares, as if he can see the future and knows for a fact that he is absolutely sure about this.

"How do you know?" I challenge. "There's no way you can know for sure that Ashton is going to be a problem," I inch closer until I'm right in his face. Ryker's eyes don't leave mine.

"Trust me," is all he says. Trust him? Why should I?

"I don't need you to save me. I can handle it," I say in a low voice, now aware that my friends are watching this entire scene. I look around the room at the confused expressions carefully watching us and shake my head.

"I'm going to bed. Let yourselves out."

With that, I stalk off to my room, slamming the door in frustration.

Tonight took a turn that I truly did not expect. I didn't want to go to that stupid game in the first place. Now I'm stuck dealing with a creep who's decided that he needs me to get back at the guy that confuses and pisses me off to no end.

I can't for the life of me understand why Ryker is going to such lengths to protect me when he's done nothing but try to make my life harder since we started this damn project.

We have four days left to be forced together to finish our presentation. Why can't he just focus on that?

I don't know if I could handle this whole Ashton situation by myself if it were to take a turn, but I do know I don't need Ryker to be my knight in shining armor.

But did I want him to be? The thought of Ryker defending me, protecting me, causes my entire body to heat. The spot between my legs pulses, and my breath quickens.

I know I shouldn't think about him like that. I know he's probably slept with other girls since we met, I'm not stupid. I know if I let myself go there with him, I won't be able to go back, and he'll break me.

Yet, I can't stop the ache in my core and the way my thighs clench under my covers.

I shouldn't do this; I know I shouldn't. But the way Ryker looked at me tonight, like he would burn the world down if something tried to hurt me, the way the smell of him made my mouth water, the look of frustration in his eyes when I refused his help. I need a release. Just this once, and then I'll never think about it or him again. Not like this.

I relax back into my pillow and make myself comfortable as I reach for the waistband of my pajama pants, pulling them down to my knees.

I run my fingers along the dampness of my panties. The cold air in my room makes me shiver, causing goosebumps to rise on my skin.

Pulling my panties down to meet my pajama pants at my knees, I gently run my finger between the wetness of my pussy. As I begin to rub my sensitive clit, I imagine Ryker's strong hands on my body.

My breath quickens as I think about Ryker's hard cock, how it would feel inside me, stretching my walls and making me feel full.

My eyes close and I picture Ryker's face, his intense gaze locking with mine as he pushes me against a wall, kissing me passionately with his warm, plush lips.

I whimper softly as I continue to circle my clit with my wet finger, wishing it was Ryker's tongue teasing me, making me beg for more. I want him to take control, to fuck me senseless until I can't remember my own name.

Images of Ryker and I entwined, Ryker's muscular body pressing against me, his hands gripping my hips as he thrusts into me over and over.

I can feel the intensity building inside me, the pleasure coiling tighter and tighter with each stroke of my fingers. I quicken my pace, desperate to reach the climax I crave so much.

My mind imagines Ryker whispering dirty things into my ear, telling me how wet and tight I feel, how he wants to make me come all over his cock.

Trying to stifle my moans, I quickly put my other hand over my mouth as I imagine him fucking me harder, our sweat-soaked bodies slamming together. I can feel my orgasm building, and as much as I don't want the fantasy to end, I need to come.

As I near the edge, I picture Ryker's hand around his thick cock, stroking himself as he watches me finger my pussy.

That's it, that's all it takes to make me come so hard, my body convulses and shakes with pleasure. I continue moving my hand as I ride the waves of my orgasm.

Fuck that was intense.

My eyes open slowly as I catch my breath and come down from my high. I'm sensitive and satisfied, and even more confused than I was before.

Would it feel that good in real life? Maybe I should find out.

RYKER

I wanted to work on finishing our project right after class today, but Gwen has plans with her friend Damian who I now know is the guy I thought was her boyfriend.

Apparently, they've known each other since like middle school or some shit. Whatever, I still don't like him. He may not look at Gwen like I do, but there's no way he hasn't at one point, and that makes me want to rip his eyes out.

My phone buzzes in my pocket, and when I pull it out to look at the caller ID, I audibly groan, earning a few annoyed glances from students walking by.

Against my better judgement, I answer my mother's call. I haven't heard from my mother in weeks, and she only calls when she needs help with my father.

"Hello?" I say, trying to hold back my distaste.

"Hi sweetie, how are you?" my mother's sugary voice asks. I roll my eyes, because I know she doesn't really care.

"I'm fine, mom. What's up?" I hear some rustling in the background, and then what sounds like a door shutting. Mom lets out a long sigh.

"Nothing, I just wanted to hear your voice," she sniffs. "I miss you and your brother. I'm all alone in this big house since your father's always at work."

I sigh. My mom calls every once in a while to complain about how lonely she is, and how my father isn't paying enough attention to her.

I mean, I do feel bad for the woman. She married a heartless bastard without a family bone in his body. One that would rather be at work and away from home than spending time with his wife and kids. Honestly, I think he only got married to have heirs for The Steele Corporation.

I know Logan is okay with taking over the company one day. He has absolutely no problem working for our father, but that seems like the worst thing that could possibly happen to me. I can't stand my father, and being forced to work with him every day would lead to me killing him.

I let out a deep sigh. "I'm sorry, mom. I'll come and visit soon," I lie. I won't be going home until Thanksgiving break. I need my time away from that place. Next year, when I'm fully graduated, I'll be getting my own place, but for now, I'm stuck at home.

Mom goes out of her way to smother us while we're there. Making sure we're eating, making sure we have everything we want or need, making us play games with her, and she only does it because my fathers not there.

That's the only time she's ever a real mother.

I hear her small sigh of relief on the other end of the phone.

"Oh, good. I'll have Tatia make those cookies you like. The ones with the cream cheese and the frosting," she coos.

Tatia, our home chef makes the best desserts, and when I was little, she'd make these ricotta cookies that were absolute heaven. She'd make them for me when I was upset over my father, when I was scared, or just to surprise me.

One night when I was eleven, my father had screamed at me for getting a low grade on a math quiz. He was so angry that I didn't do a better job.

He'd said, "I didn't raise you to be fucking stupid, Ryker. You're a disappointment to me, and your mother."

My mother just sat there, not even saying a fucking word. She watched as my father made me feel like a failure of a son, and she didn't try to stop him.

I ran to my room and cried for hours. Eventually, Tatia showed up with a tray of those cookies, and I was hooked ever since. She'd make them every time I cried.

"Okay, mom. Thanks. I have to go now, okay? I'll call soon."

"Okay, sweet boy. I love you."

I hang up the phone without another word, shoving it in my pocket. I do love my mother, but I'm so disappointed that she couldn't step in and defend us against our father.

I just can't seem to forgive her for that.

Instead of thinking about that, I turn my attention over to yet another thing that's been bugging me lately.

Logan hasn't spoken to me since the Halloween party when he made that dramatic exit after being questioned about Adrianna. I went to go find him, but I got a bit distracted, what, with throwing Ashton Davis to the ground for touching my rebel.

She's not yours, Ryker.

Anyway, now that I have nothing to pull my attention away, I need to figure out what's going on with my little brother. We don't talk about girls or feelings, or even our father. But he seemed really upset the other night, and he is my brother after all.

I sit outside of Café Grind, waiting for Logan to show up and hoping he isn't ditching me. I pull out my phone to send him another text asking where he is, but before I hit send, he's walking up to me with his backpack slung over his shoulder and an unreadable expression on his face.

He pulls out the chair across from me and sits down, setting his bag on the ground. I push the coffee I bought him across the table, and he grabs it, taking a sip. He doesn't make a face, so I assume I got it right this time.

"So, why'd you want to meet?" he asks cautiously. Honestly, I hate that we've let it get this bad between us.

"What, I can't just want to hang out with my brother?" I ask in mock offense. Logan's eyes narrow suspiciously.

"No," he says flatly. Okay, then. This is going to be harder than I thought.

Taking another sip of my coffee, I clear my throat and make eye contact with Logan.

"I just wanted to make sure you were okay," I tell him honestly. No need to beat around the bush. I guess this is a bit uncomfortable for both of us. Logan grimaces.

"Never been better. Can I go now?" he goes to stand but I grab his wrist, forcing him to sit back down. Christ, he's just as stubborn as Gwen.

"Logan, come on. What's going on with you and Adrianna?" I ask. Logan looks down at his coffee cup, swirling it around a few times before setting it back down on the table.

Logan and Adrianna have always been inseparable. I thought they would get married and pop out a bunch of kids, and move far away from here, far away from me, far away from our father.

Adrianna was always a sweet girl. She's sweet and innocent, exactly like my brother. Honestly, they are perfect for each other. I can't see her cheating on Logan, it doesn't even seem possible. I'm pretty sure they were each other's firsts.

Logan takes a deep breath. "She slept with someone else," he says simply. Shit. It's always the innocent looking ones. "I went to her dorm the other night to hang out, and she was naked in bed with someone else. How could she do this to me? After everything we've been through," he sounds defeated, and it causes a pang of empathy to run through my chest.

"Did you see the dude's face?" I ask. A cold breeze causes my dark hair to fall into my face and I brush it away before taking a long sip of my coffee. Logan looks up to meet my gaze, his face pale. He nods slowly, causing my brow to furrow in question.

"Well, did you know him? We can beat his ass if you want," I say casually, knowing Pat, Mason, and Holland would have absolutely no problem wreaking a little havoc on some douchebag that slept with a girl who was in a releationship.

Logan shakes his head.

"Yeah, I knew him. And no, it's fine. I don't care, she can do whatever she wants. I'm done," he shrugs. I cock my head to side, recognizing the tactic he's using right now since I'm the fucking king of it. He's avoiding. Avoiding what? I don't know. But I'm going to find out.

"Logan, spit it out before your tongue falls out." He looks confused.

"What do you mean?" he asks.

"You're not telling me something. What is it? Do I know the guy? Is that why you won't tell me?" I accuse. My patience is wearing thin, and I don't have time to sit here with him all day going back and forth.

"It doesn't matter, Ryker. Leave it alone," he demands, his eyes boring into mine, challenging me. What aren't you telling me, little brother?

"Fine. I'll just pay Adrianna a little visit and get the information from-"

"No! Jesus fuck, Ryker. You don't need to know everything. It's my life, not yours." I laugh at that, because he doesn't know how wrong he is.

"Tell that to dad," I say, knowing Logan has no idea what I'm talking about. He doesn't know our father calls me every other day to ask about his favorite son. He doesn't know dad avoids calling him because he doesn't want to push him too hard. That dad doesn't want him to turn out like me.

"What is that supposed to mean?" Logan seethes. I shake my head, not answering his question.

"Who was the guy, Logan?" I ask again, hoping he understands that I'm done fucking around. I wasn't kidding when I said I'd go find Adrianna myself and force her to tell me.

Logan looks around as if he wants to make sure no one is listening. Then, he looks me in the eyes and says,

"It was Ashton Davis."

Chapter 26

RYKER

About two hours after my meeting with Logan, I'm sitting on the couch in my living room sending a group text to Pat, Mason, and Holland. I shake my head at the ridiculous name Mason gave the chat before sending the message.

The Elite Four

Me

Elite meeting asap.

Mason Howard

Miss me already?

Patrick Samuelson

What's going on? You okay?

Mason Howard

You baby him too much.

Patrick Samuelson

Fuck off, Howard.

Holland Monroe

Be home in ten.

Also, fuck off, Howard.

Mason Howard

You guys always gang up on me.

Holland Monroe

That's because you're an idiot

Me

Can you guys shut the fuck up and get here already?

Mason Howard

Aye aye, Captain.

Patrick Samuelson

Pulling in now.

Holland Monroe

Be there soon.

Tossing my phone on the coffee table, I take a deep, calming breath as I try to talk myself down and think logically. Except, thinking logically doesn't seem to be in the cards for me right now.

My nerve endings feel like they're on fire, my heart is racing, and my whole body is shaking with anger and adrenaline. I want to pound someone's face in, that face being Ashton's for fucking with my brother and Gwen.

That's why I need the guys here. They'll be able to see the situation from the outside and give me rational advice. Because if I acted on my instinct right now, Ashton would probably be in a hospital, and I'd be in jail.

Logan made me promise to not do anything stupid when it comes to Ashton. He told me it would just make things worse, which is kind of like what Gwen told me. Why won't they let me help them?

Well, I don't care. I'm going to do what I see fit, and right now, beating Ashton Davis to a pulp seems pretty fit. It's not like he doesn't deserve it. I'm sure he's tried to force himself on more than half the girls at Ellington. The thought of that has me grinding my teeth and clenching my fists.

There is no way I'm letting him get away with the shit he's done. I don't care what Gwen thinks, I don't care what

Logan says, Ashton Davis needs to learn a fucking lesson, and I'll gladly be the one to teach him.

Gwen thinks she can take care of him herself. I know she's strong, I know she can handle herself, that I've seen first-hand. But she can't stop Davis from pursuing her. But I sure as hell can.

I hear the front door open and shut, followed by the sound of three sets of footsteps climbing the stairs. Mason, Pat, and Holland stroll into the living room looking ready for business as usual.

Immediately, Pat and Holland meet me in the living room, Pat taking a seat next to me while Holland takes the corner chair. Mason heads to the fridge and grabs a bottle of water for each of us, handing them to us before taking his seat in the chair opposite Holland.

They look at me, waiting to hear what's going on. I only called the three of them for an Elite meeting, which is unusual and technically not allowed, but the other guys don't need to get involved in this, and I don't trust them as much as I do Holland, Mason, and Patrick. I know they'll get behind me, minimal questions asked.

I lean over, resting my elbows on my knees as my eyes wander to each of them.

"We have a fucking problem," I seethe. The guys exchange a quick look of confusion and then focus their attention back on me.

"What's going on?" Pat asks, always the one to get to the point.

"Ashton fucking Davis. He needs to be dealt with."

"Because of what happened with Gwen?" Holland asks. I know they're all confused as fuck about what's going on between Gwen and me, and honestly so am I. I can feel the tension between us every time we're together. I can see the ways I affect her when I'm close, and I know she's struggling just like me.

I don't know if she'll ever give in though. She's fucking stubborn as hell, and she won't admit defeat. And the worst defeat for her would be accepting that she wants me just as much as I want her.

"That, and Logan," this makes their eyes shoot up.

"What about Logan?" Pat asks, already more defensive. Even though I don't get along with my brother much, he's still one of us, and we look out for our own. The guys would take a bullet for him just as soon as they'd take one for me.

"You know that comment Logan made at the Halloween party? About Adrianna cheating on him," Pat and Holland nod, Mason looks confused since he was off doing God knows what during the conversation. "Davis was the guy Adrianna cheated with."

Holland lets out a woosh of air as Pat rakes a hand through his jet-black hair. Mason leans forward, resting his chin on his had.

"Shit, man," Holland comments. Yeah, tell me about it.

"So, when are we beating his ass?" Mason asks. This kid is always ready to fuck someone up. I don't know if it's because of the way he grew up, or just because he enjoys the adrenaline high.

Mason's dad, Holland's uncle, is worse than mine. He's abusive and mean. Mason never really talks about his dad, and everything I know about him came from Holland. Apparently, Mason's dad would beat him if he ever did the slightest thing wrong. He wouldn't even give him a chance to explain.

Holland says him and Ellie haven't seen their uncle in years. Their parents wouldn't allow it. Their uncle is their dad's brother, and apparently, he's always been ruthless. I feel bad for Mason, growing up with a father like that. But I guess we all have shitty fathers, don't we.

We have to think this through. We can't just show up to his place guns blazing. We can't get caught either, or Dean Ashby's gonna have my ass, and so will my father.

We have to be careful, calculated, smart.

"Tonight. We'll do it tonight. I just… I don't know how to do this without getting caught," I say honestly.

"That's not gonna be a problem," Holland's confident voice says. My eyebrow cocks, wondering where he's going with this.

"What do you mean?"

Holland shrugs. "Davis always goes to the gym late on Wednesdays. I know because I'm usually there too," he explains casually, like we aren't discussing jumping a guy. "We wear masks, and we meet him in the parking lot. He'll never see it coming, and he won't be able to prove it was us if he decides to squeal."

I've never been more thankful for Holland in my life. That's perfect. It's secluded, he'll be alone, and he won't know it was us. Sure, he'll assume, but like Holland said, he won't be able to prove it.

"Alright. Remember, we're not trying to kill the guy. We're in and we're out. Don't let emotions control your fists," Pat says, looking directly at me. I scowl at him, but I know he's right, he always is. The practical one, the strategic one, the one that has a plan for everything. That's one thing that hasn't changed since we were kids.

"I got it," I mumble.

Mason claps his hands before rubbing them together and slapping them on his thighs.

"Great, let's go," he says excitedly, rising from his chair.

Holland shoots his cousin a glare. I don't know how Holland is more mature than his older cousin, but someone needed the brains in that family.

"He doesn't get to the gym until around nine thirty. We'll get there as he's leaving. Less time for error. Pump the fucking breaks, dude," Holland chastises. Mason rolls his eyes and sits back in the chair.

"You guys are no fun," he mumbles under his breath.

I have so much to think about right now, and my stress levels are high as hell. Thinking about my mother, my father, the project with Gwen that's due in two days.

The thought of not having a reason to see or spend time with Gwen anymore makes my stomach clench. I'm not ready to be done yet.

When this whole thing started, I couldn't wait for the three weeks to be over. I couldn't stand the way she defied me, the way she argued and challenged me at every turn, the way she looked at me with contempt.

But now, I think I kind of like it. I like being challenged, I like that she doesn't let me do or say whatever I want, I like the way her face scrunches up when she's angry and she's holding herself back from punching me in the face.

Gwen has slowly crept her way into my life, making me crave her touch, her kiss, the feeling of her soft skin on mine, the way she says my name.

I want to feel her lips on mine, feel her warm mouth as it wraps around my cock, feel her hair as I pull it back, forcing her to look at me as I fuck her mouth.

Fuck.

She'll never give it to me though. She'll keep denying the attraction between us until I explode. And after this project is over, she'll never talk to me again.

It's ten thirty, and Patrick, Holland, Mason, and I are sitting in my escalade waiting for Ashton to come out of the gym. He looks to be finishing up his last set from what we can see through the floor to ceiling windows of Ellington's gym.

The school invested a shit ton of money into the gym facility since we're pretty big on sports. They wanted a place where the athletes could go and train that wasn't old and decrepit like the rest of the buildings on campus.

My dad provided most of the funding for the facility, knowing it would make him look like a supportive father who approves of his son playing Rugby for the school. In reality, he told me to grow the fuck up and stop dicking around playing a silly little game.

His name is now on the doors of the big athletic facility.

"The Robert Steele Athletic Department." Isn't that nice? Being reminded of my father every time I step foot into this place makes bile rise in my throat. I hate him. For what he did to my mother, for what he's done to me all these years, for loving Logan more than me. I hate him.

I stare out the windshield, watching as Ashton grabs his things and makes his way out of the gym. He enters the parking lot, swinging his keys around casually and whistling. He has no idea his world's about to get rocked.

"Let's go," I say, reaching for the door handle.

The guys follow suit, pulling our masks down over our faces. Mason grabs a baseball bat from the trunk, and then we make our way over to Ashton who is now shoving his gym bag in his car.

We have the advantage, considering he's alone and had no idea we were here. So, when he turns around to see the four of us standing in front of him, he jumps.

"Fuck! Jesus, you guys scared the shit out of me," Ashton says, scanning the group before shutting his car door. "What the hell's going on?" he asks, his voice slightly shaky. I have a feeling he's not quite as tough as he tries to make himself seem.

"You think it's cool to force yourself on girls that don't want you?" Pat spits. Ashton takes a step back.

"What the hell are you talking about, man?" Yeah, what the hell man? We agreed not to say anything to him that would make him suspicious.

I shoot Pat a glare through my mask, not even sure if he can see it, but he backs up an inch and doesn't open his mouth again.

I take a step toward Ashton, who hasn't even made a move to leave yet. He's even stupider than I thought.

Without saying a word, I clench my fist and let it fly into Ashton's face. Ashton falls to the pavement, clutching his nose. I thought I'd broken it the night of the party, but I guess not. If I didn't, it's broken now.

Ashton spits before wiping his nose on the back of his hand. He stumbles to his feet looking ready to fight back. Before he can even get a punch in, my fist hits his jaw, knocking his head back before hitting him in the stomach. Back on the ground, I kick him in the stomach while Pat, Mason, and Holland stand back and watch.

When I've had enough, I lean over him, grasping his shirt in my fist. Ashton's face is bloody and bruised, making a sly smile creep onto my lips.

"Watch your fucking back, Davis," I seethe.

The guys and I watch Ashton on the ground writhing in pain before walking away. Hopping in my car and driving away without a word.

I shouldn't have said anything, but I wanted Ashton to see how serious I am. If he goes near Gwen again, I'll kill him.

Chapter 27

GUINEVERE

The library is empty aside from the old librarian sitting at her desk, practically asleep. I sit in the private room that Ryker and I typically work in, alone, attempting to finish my half of the presentation.

I'm finding it hard to concentrate on what I'm doing since I haven't been able to get the other night out of my mind. The night I came to the thought of Ryker touching me, tasting me, teasing me. I came harder than I have in a long time, and I can't believe it was because of him.

I haven't seen Ryker since class yesterday. I ended up getting lunch with Damian since he had been blowing up my phone wondering why he hasn't seen me outside of class lately. I told him everything about what happened on my birthday, about what happened after my birthday, the tension between Ryker and me.

Of course, Damian told me to go for it, but I don't even know how to do that. It's obvious that I have some sort of feelings for Ryker, and I'm pretty sure that feeling is lust. But can I allow myself to forget how it'll affect me in the future so I can enjoy the present?

I don't know. Would Ryker even want to? I know he feels the tension between us when we're together. I know he's made comments here and there about me and us, but does he mean them?

Ryker should be here any minute now to finish his side of the presentation, and I don't know if I can think straight with him in this small space. I should leave now; tell him I'm not feeling well and that he'll have to finish on his own. But something inside me makes me stay in my seat.

I shouldn't be thinking about this, shouldn't be thinking about him. This project is so important, and Professor Whitely will be so upset with me if it's not perfect. I can't be distracted right now. Yet, Ryker Steele has been consuming almost every thought I've had since my birthday.

The sound of the door creaking open catches my attention and makes my nerves skyrocket. I don't turn around, instead deciding to keep my focus on my laptop screen.

When he passes me, I can smell his cologne and a hint of his aftershave. His face is clear of the stubble that had been there just the other day. His green eyes look intense and stormy, like they're hiding a lifetimes worth of stress and secrets. The dark bags under his eyes make me think he hasn't really slept much lately, eliciting a pang of sadness through me.

I don't know how I got here. Caring about a guy I hate, but maybe… maybe I don't hate him anymore. I don't know when it happened. I don't know how it happened. But here I am, craving the touch of a man I no longer seem to hate.

Ryker sits in the chair across the table from me, sets his laptop on the table in front of him and doesn't say a word to me as he begins to work. He hasn't even looked at me.

Okay… what's his problem?

I peer at him over my laptop, and this time I don't try to hide it. I blatantly stare at him until he clears his throat and fidgets in his chair.

"Do you need something?" he says with a sharp edge. My eyes search his face, wondering why he's being like this.

"N…no, I was just-" he finally looks up from his laptop.

"Just what?" Ryker shuts the laptop as his eyes bore into mine. His tone makes me shiver. My eyes catch on his hand which is covered in cuts and bruises. My eyes narrow, and then they widen. What the hell happened?

"What happened to your hand?" I ask. Ryker quickly pulls his hand under the table.

"Nothing," he tells me, never taking his eyes off of me.

Did he go after Ashton after I told him not to? "Ryker, what happened to your hand?" I ask more sternly.

Ryker watches me, studies me for what feels like forever, before he slowly rises from his chair and leans on his hands as he stands above the table. He looks angry, frustrated, but I don't know why. Why won't he tell me about his hand?

"You don't need to know everything, Guinevere."

"Why won't you just tell me? Did you go after Ashton?" I ask in an accusatory tone. Ryker's eyes flash with something that reminds me of guilt but also a bit of something I don't recognize.

He steps around the table, and its reminiscent of one of the first nights we worked together. I don't move or back away when he gets so close I can feel his body heat. I stay in my seat and watch as his forearms cord as he sits on the table and leans back.

"And if I did?" he challenges. Jesus, what is wrong with him? Why is he acting like this?

Ryker leans closer to my face like he has many times before, his long, strong arms landing on the chair at either side of my head, and my breathing quickens.

"What would you do about it, Gwen?" his head tilts in question. What could I do about it? I can't control what he does. I can't make him do anything. Ryker's the kind of guy that will do whatever he wants, no matter the consequences.

His eyes travel from my face down to my chest as it heaves up and down in a fast rhythm, my cleavage noticeable at the top of my green Ellington U tank top. Slowly, he peels his gaze away and lands back on my burning face.

He's so close, I can smell him. I can feel his heat. I can see the large bulge in his pants as it seems to grow harder. I swallow hard, looking back up to see his glazed over eyes.

One of his hands traces up my neck softly, gently sliding over my cheek and staying there for a brief moment as I relax into it. His touch feels so good, and I want more. I need more. There's no doubt my panties aren't completely soaked through at this point.

The ache between my legs becomes more prominent as his thumb tenderly caresses my cheek, sending goosebumps all over my body. When his hand moves, I almost want to pout. But instead of leaving me completely, he cups the back of my head, lacing his fingers through my hair.

And then, without warning, Ryker fists my hair and pulls my head back, forcing me to look him in the eye. The dull soreness in my head isn't even noticeable when Ryker stands to straddle me over my chair, pushing it and me away from the table.

Even though there's no one here in the library right now, this feels so wrong. This feels like a disaster waiting to happen.

"What, no more questions?" he asks derisively, a smug smirk crossing his pink lips.

My eyes narrow because I know he's realized his little plan to distract me worked. But I haven't forgotten what began this game that he's started.

Here's the thing, Ryker. Something you don't know about me is I'm competitive as hell, and I always win.

"Fuck. You," I smirk, and I can see the challenge flash behind Rykers bright green eyes.

I'm sure he's not used to hearing that coming from a woman, or anyone really. But I don't care. If he's going to be an ass, I can be bitch right back. I am not afraid of him.

Ryker's other hand comes around to cup my chin, putting slight pressure on it to hold me still. My clit pulses at the sudden movement, and I can feel my nipple pebbling under my bra.

Flashes of the other night float through my mind. Touching myself, orgasming so hard I saw stars.

"Oh, Rebel. You have such a dirty little mouth. What should we do about that?" he tsks. The brat in me wants to push him off of me, but the horny, desperate part of me wouldn't dare.

I shrug.

The rough pad of Ryker's thumb skates over my bottom lip, causing me to intake a sharp breath.

Ryker's eyes search mine for a moment, his expression laces with so many different emotions. Hate, lust, anger, confusion. He's fighting himself, wondering what his next move should be, and the deranged part of me wants him to smash his lips against mine. Another part of me wants to challenge him a bit more, see how far I can go.

"I can't stand you," I tell him, partly the truth and partly a lie. His smirk causes a giddy feeling in my chest. Does he want me to hate him?

"Ms. Sharpe is that a lie?" he cocks a brow. I shake attempt to shake my head, but his grip on my chin has only gotten tighter. "I don't like liars."

His grip finally loosens enough for me to rip my face out of his calloused hand. I glare at him, because that's what got us into this whole thing. The fact that he wasn't telling me whether he went after Ashton or not. Though not technically a lie, he is withholding the truth. And in my book, that's the same thing.

"Maybe you should look in the mirror, Mr. Steele." The contempt in my voice surprises me.

Ryker is still in my face, our breathing mixing together as we each get a little more riled up. His eyes are wild, and it looks like he's losing the battle in his head. I refuse to be the first one to break.

"You're infuriating," he spits.

"What? The big bad Ryker Steele can't handle little ole me?" I challenge.

I don't know when I got so angry, but the mix of him refusing to tell me something I want to know, and him being so cold earlier makes me want to hurt him.

Ryker's eyes darken with rage, and I can see I've hit a nerve.

"I hate you," he fumes. The words hurt only slightly, since I'm feeling them a bit too right now. But for some reason, I'm still throbbing with need. The need to feel something. To feel anything. To feel him.

"I hate you, too," I practically pant as his face grows closer to mine, his lips lightly grazing mine.

Without moving, he says, "Show me how much you hate me."

Before I know it, Ryker picks me up out of my chair, and my arms and legs instinctively wrap around him. He lets out a low growl before pulling me roughly against him, his lips crushing mine.

I've never been kissed like this before. So rough, so wild, so needy. It feels good.

I melt into him, parting my lips, allowing Ryker to explore my mouth with hungry strokes of his tongue against mine.

He places me on the table, my laptop and books pushed to ground with our frantic movements. His hands roam my body, cupping my breasts, his thumbs grazing my sensitive nipples through my tank top.

Fuck, this is better than I thought it would be, kissing Ryker. He's not gentle, he's demanding.

Moaning into his mouth, I respond eagerly to his touch, my hands tangling in his hair as I try to pull him closer, craving more.

Breaking the kiss, Ryker trails hot, open-mouthed kisses along my jawline and down my neck, nibbling and sucking at the sensitive skin.

"You have no idea how long I've wanted to do this, Rebel," he growls, his voice husky with desire. My stomach flutters. He's right, I don't know how long he's wanted to do this, but the way he's kissing me seems like it's been a while.

I let out a gasp as Ryker continues his path downward, his tongue tracing my cleavage. I should tell him to stop, right? This is crazy, and if we get caught, we'll both be expelled. Well, at least I will. He'd probably get off scot free since he's an Elite.

"Ryker," I pant, my back arching into him, encouraging his actions as I fight with the thoughts in my brain.

Ryker cups both my breasts over my shirt, and my head falls back as pleasure coils tightly within me.

I've never felt this way before, so wanton and unrestrained. It's as if Ryker has unleashed a side of me I never knew existed; a side that wants to be touched, tasted, and taken by this captivatingly arrogant man.

He continues his exploration, his hands sliding down my body to grasp my thighs, pulling me closer to him on the edge of the table. His hard erection presses against my pussy through our clothing.

I let out a soft whimper as he grinds against me, the friction sending shocks of pleasure to my core.

With nimble fingers, Ryker pulls my shirt over my head, exposing my lace-covered breasts. Unclasping my bra, he moves it slowly down my shoulders, so my chest is bare to him. My cheeks redden at the thought of Ryker standing in front of me, seeing my naked breasts.

His gaze lingers there for a few seconds before lowering his head to take one aching peak into his mouth, his tongue swirling and sucking until I'm squirming and moaning his name.

"Ryker, please," I pant, my hands still tangled through his hair, as he sucks on my nipple.

His eyes shoot to mine, a devious smile playing on his lips.

"Please what?" he asks innocently. I roll my eyes.

"Please don't make me say it," I beg, my cheeks flushing.

Ryker chuckles and halts his movements, making me squirm as the agonizing ache between my legs grows.

"Tell me what you want, Guinevere," he orders. He's really not going to do anything until I say it, is he? I groan.

"Ryker, please… please make me come," I beg. His lips quirk up into a devilish grin before he kisses a path down my stomach, his breath hot against the damp fabric of my panties.

With deft fingers, he hooks his thumbs into the waistband of my jeans, pulling them down along with my panties to reveal my soaking wet pussy.

"So beautiful," Ryker murmurs, his fingers tracing my sensitive lips.

I cry out as he touches me, my hips bucking involuntarily as he glides his thumb over my clit in fast strokes.

Ryker falls to his knees, pulling me so my ass is partially off the table. I feel his hot breath as his mouth lands on my opening, his tongue flicking my clit in a painstaking rhythm. I feel the familiar pressure building in my core as he continues his assault on my clit, moving faster and harder.

"Ryker, I need-"

"I know what you need, Rebel" he growls, capturing my mouth in another searing kiss as he slides a finger deep inside me, curling it to find that magic spot that has me crying out for more.

I'm lost in a maelstrom of sensation as Ryker works his magic, his fingers skillfully stroking me, his mouth devouring mine. I'm aware of the risk, the possibility of being caught, but the rush of adrenaline only adds to my arousal.

As my orgasm builds, I keep my mouth locked with his as I surrender to the pleasure consuming me.

"Ryker, I'm gonna-"

Ryker doesn't let me finish, adding another finger and increasing the pressure on my clit.

"Come for me, Gwen," he commands, his voice thick with his own need.

I shatter, crying out as waves of pleasure pulse through me, my body convulsing uncontrollably. I ride out my orgasm, my breath coming in ragged gasps as Ryker continues to stroke me gently, drawing out my ecstasy.

Slowly, I open my eyes, a sated smile on my lips as I look at Ryker. He's watching me, his eyes dark with desire, his breath coming in sharp bursts.

"That was…" I can't even finish my sentence. There isn't just one word to describe what just happened.

Ryker smiles slyly, looking so proud of himself. His dick looks like it wants to spring out of his jeans, and I want nothing more than to feel him inside me.

I sit up slightly, leaning on my elbows. I'm suddenly very aware that I'm fully naked, while Ryker is fully dressed, and that we're still in the small private room of the library. Goosebumps rise on my skin, and I shudder.

Ryker grabs my discarded clothes and hands them to me. I take them, quickly pulling them on and giving Ryker a shy smile.

He smiles softly, tucking a piece of hair behind my ear.

"Come back to my place?" he asks.

Something tells me to flee. To go home and forget this even happened. But my god, the look on Ryker's face has my inhibitions out the window. Except, we really do need to finish this project. The presentation is tomorrow, and we haven't practiced what we're going to say.

But right now, looking at him with desire in his eyes, I don't even care. As much as I hate to admit this, I want more of Ryker Steele.

Chapter 28

RYKER

I've never claimed to be a saint.

That would be complete bullshit. I know I'm not the kind of guy moms like or dads accept. I know what people say about me around campus. I've heard the comments from both guys and girls, although none of it is ever to my face.

People are afraid of me. They don't want to piss me off in fear of my last name and what it means to this university. My father has gotten many professors fired for stupid things like giving me bad grades or speaking to me wrong. The kind of pull he has at Ellington is astounding. And everyone knows that.

No one questions me, women throw themselves at me, and all that should make me feel good. Shouldn't it?

So I don't understand the empty pit in my stomach that is there every single day, and it never goes away.

Except when I'm with *her*. Guinevere Sharpe. The feisty five four brunette with those bright blue eyes and a natural affinity to pissing me the fuck off.

Gwen is unlike any woman I've ever met.

She's spirited, independent, and unafraid to speak her mind. She's bold, assertive, and confident, with a strong sense of self and a willingness to stand up for what she believes in.

I knew she was attractive the day she ran into me in the hallway. Her petite frame, the way tits looked in the blouse, the way her jeans highlighted her toned legs and round ass underneath. She caught my attention immediately, and I knew she was far different than the rest of them.

I know she thinks I'm an asshole. I know she thinks I'm this terrible person that she should stay far away from. And maybe I am. But I know I can't stay away from her, and I'm done trying. Fuck what anyone else will say.

Now that I've had a taste of Gwen, I'm not letting her go. No matter what she says. I know she'll fight it, she's as stubborn as a mule. She'll never truly accept her feelings, but I am going to make it so damn difficult for her to get away.

She finally gave into me today. Gave into the feelings I knew she was having and failing to fight. She really shouldn't try to fight this connection between us, because I'm determined now to keep her, and I always get what I want.

Gwen, my beautiful, perfect rebel, sits on my bed, watching me as I lock my door behind me. No one's home, and I've never been more thankful to have the floor to myself. The things I'm going to do to Gwen, the way she's going to be screaming my name, I don't want anyone else to hear her moans of pleasure.

Guinevere Sharpe is mine, even if she doesn't know it yet. But she will soon enough. And when this project is over, she'll know that isn't the end of us, it's only the beginning.

Her legs hang off the end of the bed, and I can't help but think about the way my face was just between them, savouring the taste of her delicious pussy. God, she tasted good. I could do that all day if she'd let me.

The strap of her green Ellington U tank top has fallen slightly down her arm, and her long, espresso coloured hair falls against her back as her eyes, like deep blue pools, stare at me as I walk toward her, landing between her legs.

I reach down, putting my finger under her chin, gently bringing her head up to look at me. Her eyes are filled with lust and desire, and my cock twitches knowing it's all for me.

Gwen might be strong and hardheaded, but I've already gathered that she isn't that way in the bedroom, which is perfect for me because I am a control freak.

Many of the women I've been with haven't been able to handle that side of me, but something tells me that my little rebel isn't going to mind one bit.

My heart is racing, and my breathing is shallow. I'm pretty sure I'm actually fucking nervous right now. I don't get nervous for sex, ever. But looking down at this girl who I never even thought would be a possibility sitting in front of me, wanting me, I don't even recognize myself.

The air crackles with anticipation and excitement. It's been weeks of this pent-up anger and tension and desire, and we're finally about to act on it.

"Take your shirt off," I demand. Gwen watches my face for a long second before reaching down to grab the hem of her shirt, pulling it off over her head.

I keep my face neutral as I take in that lacey bra covering those perfectly peeked nipples of hers that I so enjoyed not twenty minutes ago.

"Bra," I say in the same demanding tone. Gwen unclasps her bra and tosses it on the floor with her shirt.

Her tits are beautiful. The best tits I've ever seen.

Grabbing one in my hand, I squeeze lightly on her nipple, making her head fall back and a soft moan leave her lips. I need to hear more of her moans.

Leaning down and placing my hands on the bed on either side of her, I linger in front of her face for a moment, revelling in the way her breathing quickens and her lashes flutter rapidly. Then, I lean in and smash my lips against hers.

She kisses me with fervour, opening her mouth to allow me full access. Kissing Gwen is like lighting a spark in the dark, a sudden burst of warmth and light, and I never want to pull away.

Gwen moans again, melting into my touch as she reaches out for my belt, beginning to undo it without ever breaking the kiss. My heart speeds up and it suddenly feels like I've just run a marathon.

This girl is about to see me, all of me. Vulnerable and exposed. Two things I don't want to ever be. But looking at her and the way her breasts bounce while she kisses me and pulls my pants down so they land around my ankles, I don't even care about being vulnerable.

I reluctantly break the kiss, staring down at her.

"Get on your knees, Gwen," I whisper hoarsely.

Gwen's eyes light up before slowly sinking off the bed and landing on her knees in front of me.

She looks so beautiful kneeling in front of me, ready and waiting for my cock to push into her mouth. Her eyes fill with a mix of anticipation and apprehension.

Hooking her fingers in the elastic of my boxers, she pulls them down slowly, revealing my erection. Her breath catches in her throat at the sight. She licks her lips involuntarily, unable to tear her gaze away.

"Suck it," I order, my voice laced with desire.

Gwen leans forward without hesitation, extending her tongue to lick the precum off the tip of my dick.

A soft groan escapes my lips, and that seems to encourage her to take me deeper. She opens her mouth wide, wrapping her lips around my shaft and taking me in inch by inch.

My hands tangle in Gwen's hair, guiding her movements as her head bobs back and forth. She hollows her cheeks, sucking eagerly and sending a tingle to the base of my spine. Her hands roam over my thighs, gripping tightly as she works me with growing enthusiasm.

Gwen moans softly, the vibrations sending shudders through my body. Holy shit, this girl is fucking perfect. The sounds she's making, the feeling of her tongue as I hit the back of her throat. I make a mental note that Gwen has no gag reflex.

She moves her tongue in a way that has me gripping her head a bit harder.

"Fuck, Gwen... just like that," I grit my teeth, my hips beginning to thrust gently in time with her motions.

Gwen's skill and eagerness are about to send me over the edge. I feel the heat building, my balls drawing up tight as the need to come intensifies. But I don't want to come yet. I don't want this to be over. I need to feel her, to feel what it's like to be inside her.

Reaching down, I gently pull Gwen away, my cock glistening with her saliva. Jesus, I've never been so turned on in my life.

"That's enough, baby," I say in a strained voice. "I don't want to come yet."

Gwen's eyes sparkle with mischief as I pull her to stand and push her back on the bed.

"Lay back," I order, and she does so without question. My eyes scan her perfect body, raking over her nipples, already hard and erect, down to her tight stomach.

My eyes darken with lust as I step forward, cupping her breasts in my large hands and bending down to take a hard nipple into my mouth.

Sucking greedily, I flick my tongue over the sensitive peak, causing Gwen to cry out as she threads her fingers through my hair.

Releasing one breast, I trail hot kisses down her abdomen, pausing only to hook my thumbs into the waistband of her jeans and panties before tugging them downward. They fall in a heap onto the ground, leaving Gwen completely naked and fucking stunning in front of me.

I kneel before her, pulling her closer to the edge of the bed. Gwen props herself up on her elbows to watch me as my tongue laps against her.

I run a finger through her glistening folds, collecting her arousal before bringing it to my mouth and tasting her, letting out a low groan as I look in her eyes. Gwen whimpers and squirms impatiently. I grin, chuckling lowly.

"Patience is a virtue, Guinevere," I tease. Gwen's eyes narrow, clearly unamused. I run my finger over her swollen clit a few times causing her head to fall back as she pants and moans. My finger rubs slow circles, and I can feel Gwen getting restless, which only makes me want to keep going.

"Fuck you," she says. My head cocks and I raise an eyebrow.

"Now Guinevere, that's not very polite," I swipe over her clit once with my tongue. She cries out before looking down at me as I pull away.

"Ryker..." she practically growls in warning. God, she's beautiful when she's pissed and naked. Her chest heaves up and down, making her perky breasts move with the motion.

"Yeah, Rebel?" another lick.

"Make me come," she pants, and as much as I want my tongue on her again, I really want to see how far I can take this.

"You want to come?" I ask in a patronizing tone, earning another glare. She only nods. "Beg me."

Gwen's face is a scowl. I know her stubborn ass won't ever beg for a thing. But if she wants to come, she's going to have to do as I say.

"I'll never beg you," she states. Looking up to her face, I smirk and shrug, standing up. I begin to pull my boxers and jeans back on as Gwen's face twists with confusion.

"What the hell are you doing?" she asks, sitting up fully to watch me. My dick is throbbing, and I need to come, but I have no intention of letting her win this game.

"Getting dressed," I say simply.

"Ryker…" she says, her voice trembling. She's breaking, I can see it. She needs to come, and she knows now that I won't let her until she's begging for me to fuck her. I walk over slowly, crawling over her naked form, making her lay back on the bed. Her breath hitches and her eyes widen.

I bring my finger to her mouth. "Suck," I demand.

Gwen gives me a slightly suspicious look before opening her mouth and taking my finger, swirling her tongue around it.

I pull it out and trail my finger down her stomach and then down to her pussy. There's a quick intake of breath when she believes I'm going to touch her.

"Beg for it, Gwen," I command. Her eyes roll, making my lips twitch as I try not to smile.

"Please…" she says, but it's not good enough. She can do better than that.

"Come on, Rebel," I urge, slowly beginning to rub her again. Her eyes close, and I grip the back of her head to pull her hair. "Open your eyes."

Gwen's eyes fly open.

"I want you to look at me when you beg for my cock," I tell her, moving my finger faster.

"Please, Ryker… I'm…" she's almost there, she's really going to beg me. My dick swells at the thought of this stubborn girl begging for me.

"You're what?"

"I'm begging you, please make me come," she finally says, desperately writhing under me.

"That's a good girl," I praise, and that seems to make her even more wet.

I take that as my sign to descend on her clit, my tongue flicking and teasing until she's squirming and moaning incoherently.

"Ryker... please... oh fuck!" Gwen cries out, her hands grasping my hair as pleasure washes over her. I pull away.

"You're such a good fucking girl, aren't you Gwen?" I ask, desire burning me from the inside out. Gwen nods frantically, and I can tell she's about to come.

"Yes!" she cries.

I continue my oral assault, revelling in the sweet taste of her pussy as I drive her closer to the edge. Her juices flow freely, coating my face as her cries fill the room, and with a few more swipes of my tongue, she tumbles over the precipice.

Gwen's body shakes uncontrollably as a powerful orgasm claims her, and I watch in amazement at this girl in front me who claims to hate me.

As her tremors subside, I stand, my cock throbbing with urgent need, and I can't wait another minute to be inside her.

I climb up over her to her face, claiming her lips. My tongue finds hers as her long legs wrap around my waist. I take both of her hands and pin them over her head with one of mine while I use the other to rip my pants and boxers down. My dick teases her swollen pussy, causing her to whimper and arch her back, seeking friction. I chuckle darkly.

"You want it?" I growl. Gwen nods desperately.

"Yes... please, Ryker," Gwen begs. I lean down to kiss her again as I slowly push forward, filling her with my thick length.

"Are you on birth control?" I ask, realizing I probably should have asked that before I was inside her. She nods.

"I have an IUD," she says breathlessly.

That's all I need before I begin to move. Gwen gasps, her eyes rolling back as I begin to stretch her. I can't help but groan at the sensation.

"Fuck, Gwen…" I growl, my hips snapping forward as I set a relentless pace.

Gwen meets my thrusts, her nails digging into my back as she urges me on.

"Harder," she cries out. God damn.

I oblige, slamming into her with fierce abandon. The bed creaks with the force, the sound of our flesh slapping together filling the room. Gwen's tits bounce wildly with each thrust, her cries mingling with my grunts of pleasure.

I can feel Gwen's walls begin to clench around me, signaling her impending orgasm.

"Come for me, Gwen," I demand, lifting her hips off the bed and driving into her with renewed vigor.

Gwen's body tenses.

"Ryker! Oh fuc-" her words cut off as she screams, her orgasm causing her to pulse around my cock.

Continuing to thrust through her orgasm, my own builds with each squeeze of her pulsing walls. With a final, powerful surge, I bury myself deep within her and come hard, filling her completely.

Spent, I collapse onto the bed beside Gwen, our chests heaving as we struggle to catch our breath.

A satisfied smile plays on Gwen's lips as she leans on her side next to me, her head resting on her hand. My own smirk plays on my lips.

"What?" I ask, my hand reaching up to push a strand of hair behind Gwen's ear.

"I can't believe that just happened," she laughs, causing me to chuckle.

"Do you regret it?" I ask, hoping she doesn't say yes because I really don't want her to regret this.

Gwen shakes her head. "No, I think I liked it," she watches my face for my reaction. I grab her hip and squeeze.

"Oh, I know you liked it," I tease. Gwen rolls her eyes and pushes my shoulder playfully. She is so God damn pretty.

"It wasn't the worst sex I've ever had," she shrugs, a smug grin on her face.

"Careful, Rebel. I might actually think you like me," I wink, and Gwen makes a mock face of disgust.

"No way in hell," she chuckles, falling to her back on the bed.

I can't tell what I'm feeling right now as I stare down at Gwen, naked and sated and stunning. When we started this partnership, I was just using her as a means to an end. As something to help me get my father off my back.

I don't know when that changed. But I do know I definitely want to do that again. And again.

Chapter 29

GUINEVERE

"No, you have to put it into different words. You can't read right off the PowerPoint," Ryker stares at me, looking as clueless as ever. Our project is due in less than twenty-four hours, and I am exhausted.

"Why not? Isn't that why we made it?" he asks. I involuntarily roll my eyes. Has he never given a presentation before? Who am I kidding? He's probably never had to.

"We made it so everyone can visualize what we're saying, and to use it as a guide as to what to discuss next."

Ryker looks like he's about to fall asleep as he sits on the floor at the end of his bed while I pace his room. There's no way we're going to be ready for tomorrow. Ryker is unteachable.

"Ryker! Wake up, we need to practice!" I chastise.

Ryker jerks, his body sitting up straighter and looking a bit less like it's about to fall over in exhaustion. He stretches his long, strong arms over his head and yawns obnoxiously.

"Hey Rebel, why don't you just do all the talking? That's what you do best," he mocks.

I scowl at him, grabbing the rugby ball off of his dresser and throwing it at him. He holds his arms up in front of him, effectively blocking it.

"Funny," I say with the fakest of smiles. Ryker shrugs.

"I wasn't being funny; you talk a lot."

"I despise you."

Ryker blows me a kiss and winks, making me roll my eyes in annoyance.

"Can you be serious for like, one minute? We really need to get this down," I ask, practically begging. Ryker sits up, crossing his legs and setting his hands in his lap.

"Fine," he says earnestly, his lips forming a straight line. My eyes narrow suspiciously, but I turn my back to pull up the next slide on my laptop.

"Thank you. Okay, so do you want to-" I'm cut off by a thump on my back, turning around to see the rugby ball fall to the floor in front of me.

I whip around to Ryker, who's leaning his back against the end of the bed, his hands behind his head and his legs outstretched in front of him with a cocky smile on his face.

"Seriously?" I yell, completely exasperated. It's like dealing with a toddler. Ryker holds his hands up in the air in mock surrender. "We have shit to do, Ryker. If you're not going to take this seriously, I'm just going to-" Ryker stands from his spot on the ground, walking over to stand in front of me. I look up at him, his green eyes hooded and laced with desire.

"Okay, okay. I'll be serious now. Show me what I have to do."

———————————

My eyes flutter as they adjust to the sunlight pouring into the small space. Once they're finally not fighting for their life, my gaze sweeps over a strong tan arm draped over my waist. I follow the arm up to the face and see Ryker sleeping peacefully.

"Shit!" I say, a bit too loudly. We must have fallen asleep while working on the PowerPoint. We have class in a few hours.

Jumping off the bed, I look around for my phone which I find on the ground at the end of the bed. I check for any missed calls or messages and find that our group chat has blown up overnight.

Four Hot Girls & Damian

Ellie Monroe

Gwen, are you alive?

Lainey (BFF) Barkley

Gwen, if you're not alive, can I have your room?

Ellie Monroe

Omg, Lainey!

Lainey (BFF) Barkley

I'm just kidding! Gwen, please be alive.

I'll miss you too much.

Haley Caldwell

Guys, if anyone's getting her room it's me.

Damian Cole

Absolutely not. It'd be me. She loves me the most.

Me

You guys are ridiculous. I'm at Ryker's. We fell asleep.

Ellie Monroe

What!?

Lainey (BFF) Barkley

Is it big? Ya know, his

Oh my god.

I lock my phone and shove into my back pocket before picking up a pillow and hitting Ryker with it.

He groans and turns to lay on his back, the defined muscles on his abdomen flexing as he stretches. I hold back the urge to climb back on top of him because we have to get ready for class, but wow is this man sculpted by the lord himself.

Lainey wasn't wrong. Ryker is all muscle, and I assume it's from playing rugby and working out constantly. I can kind of see the appeal now that I've had a taste of him, but I'd never tell him that. His ego can't afford to grow any bigger.

He was kind, the perfect mix of gentle and dominating, and that cock… I've never been one to compliment a penis, but Ryker's? That thing should be in the Hall of Fame. I mean, I didn't know sex could be like that. And coming from penetration? I thought that was a myth. But it's not; it's real and I've experienced it first-hand. Now that it has, I don't want it to stop.

After, we didn't discuss it at all. Instead, we, or well, I jumped right into the project again. Ryker actually gave me and the project his full attention for the rest of the night. He accepted his part in it and did a really great job with explanations.

Of course, it was hard for me to concentrate because I was watching his mouth as he talked, remembering how it felt while he ate me out and made me come, twice, with his tongue. I shudder at the thought of how many women he's had to sleep with to perfect that.

Not that I care who he's slept with. Or do I? I told myself that last night was going to be a one-time thing, just to get rid of the pent-up frustration and stress. But I don't know if I'm going to be able to stick to that, because that was the best sex I've had like, ever.

I won't admit it to Ryker just yet. He'll know he was right. I don't hate him as much as I thought I did or wanted to. Somewhere along the way, the hatred turned into lust, and lust turned into a night of Ryker completely ruining any other guy for me.

With another groan, Ryker grabs his phone of the nightstand, squinting at it as his eyes get used to the shine of the screen.

"Fuck, we slept late," he says, not even sounding concerned that we have less than an hour to get ready for class.

"I didn't mean to fall asleep. Why did you let me fall asleep?" I accuse. I should have been home, getting a good night's rest and setting an alarm for an appropriate time to wake up.

Ryker shrugs as he sits up in bed, running a hand through his tousled hair. God, he looks sexy in the morning.

Knock it off, Gwen. Focus.

Ryker stands, the sheet falling as he walks away from the bed, buck naked. My head tilts as I watch him walk to the bathroom, his taut ass moving with each step. Then, he's walking out, and his dick is standing at full attention.

He wipes his hands on a towel and smirks.

"Bite that lip any harder and you're going to bleed," he comments. I hadn't even realized I was biting my lip.

I shake my head, attempting to focus on what needs to be done.

"I have to go. I have to get ready," I tell him as I hurriedly grab my things and shove them into my bag, throwing it over my shoulder. As my hand touches the door handle, I turn around to find Ryker watching me. "Please don't be late," I plead.

"Wouldn't dream of it," he says, giving me a salute.

I roll my eyes and run out of the room. On my way down the stairs, I run into a tall, muscular figure.

"Shit, I'm sorry," I begin as I look up, seeing a face I recognize.

"Gwen? What are you doing here?" Holland asks with an inquiring gaze. Wow, he really does look like Ellie, just with facial hair and muscles.

I straighten, smiling shyly because I was just caught leaving Ryker's room at eight in the morning. I feel my cheeks heat, and there's no doubt they're bright pink right now.

"I was just… I'm just leaving," I point down the stairs.

"Did you stay the night?" Holland's eyes sweep me from head to toe. I nod.

"Um… yeah. Ryker and I were working on our project, and we fell asleep," I tucks a strand of hair behind my ear, shifting from one leg to the other. Holland nods slowly in understanding, still looking a bit skeptical. But I don't have time for questions, I need to get ready for class.

"Listen, I gotta go get ready, but I'll see you later? K, great. Bye!" I run past a stunned Holland and out the front door of the Elite mansion, straight to my house.

After taking a quick shower to rinse off the smell of sex, I throw on an old pink floral blouse I've had since high school and pair it with some black jeans. I don't even bother drying my hair, opting for tying it up on the top of my head.

I top off the look with a bit of mascara, grab my bag, and run out the door.

No one was in the living room or the kitchen when I got home, so I didn't have to deal with being interrogated by my crazy, lovable roommates. But I'm sure I'll get bombarded later.

I feel good about today and the work we did on this project. I think Professor Whitely will be thoroughly impressed.

It's funny, how just a few weeks ago I thought my life was going to implode after being forced to work with Ryker Steele, but here we are, actually getting along.

Oh yeah, you're getting along really well, Gwen, my thoughts say.

As long as Ryker shows up, we should be totally fine. I just saw him less than an hour ago, and I assume he doesn't need that much time to get ready.

Walking down the path to get to Mallory Center, I change the song I'm listening to on my phone and look back up to see I've been joined by a shaggy blonde with blue eyes.

I pull my headphones out of my ear, shutting them back in their case.

"So, a sleepover with *the* Ryker Steele, huh?" Damian mocks. I elbow him playfully as I roll my eyes. Damian grabs his arm as if I'd actually hurt him.

"I didn't mean to fall asleep. It was late and we had to finish up the PowerPoint," I defend. Damian shoots me a knowing glance.

"And then you fell into his bed. Tell me, is he as good as all the girls on campus say he is?" Damian chuckles to himself.

"Why are you the way that you are?" I ask as we walk up the stairs to our classroom.

"Gwen," a deep, familiar voice says. The sound send's shivers down my spine, causing me to stop dead in my tracks. Damian and I turn around to meet the gaze of Ashton Davis. The prick that wants to use me as part of his revenge plan with Ryker.

My blood runs cold at the sight of his battered face. A big purple and yellow bruise covers the right side of his jaw, and his nose looks out of place, like it'd been broken.

Ashton stares at me, but his eyes look empty. He looks like he hasn't slept in days, and if I wasn't standing here with Damian in front of our crowded lecture hall, I might be afraid.

"What do you want, Ashton?" I ask in a repulsed tone, finally working up the courage to respond.

I watch him carefully as he takes a small step forward, leaving only a few inches between us. I can feel Damian tense beside me, but I do my best to stand tall and look unaffected.

"Just wanted you to see your boyfriend's handywork," he grimaces. My brows furrow. What the hell is he-

And then it hits me. Last night in the library, Ryker's cut up hand, the way he pulled it away from me and ignored my questions about where it came from. I asked him if he went after Ashton, and he wouldn't give me a straight answer.

Ryker did go after him. My stomach clenches, and I don't know whether to feel thankful or appalled at the fact that Ryker actually beat Ashton's ass.

Damian watches me carefully and I give him a curt nod, letting him know he can head into class. He gives me a wary look before glaring at Ashton and making his way inside the room.

My gaze settles on Ashton as his lip curls slightly.

"I have no clue what you're talking about," I say casually. It's not a complete lie, since I don't really have any proof that Ryker did anything.

Ashton shakes his head and chuckles, but it's not an amused chuckle, it one of disbelief.

"You're not a very good liar, Gwen," he replies with malice, making the hair rise on the back of my neck. "He told me to watch my back... now tell him to watch yours."

With that, he pats my shoulder with his big hand and stalks away, as if he didn't just threaten me.

Rage boils inside me as I watch him leave, thinking about how Ryker told me he wouldn't go after him, and he did anyway. How maybe if Ryker had listened to me and just let it go, we wouldn't be in this mess.

But no, Ryker Steele does whatever he wants, whenever he wants. And now I'm the one that's screwed.

Chapter 30

RYKER

Gwen told me not to be late, and here I am, but where the hell is she?

One thing I know about her is Guinevere Sharpe is never late. So she must be sick or in trouble because there's no way she's-

I watch as Gwen strolls into the lecture hall looking like she's seen a ghost, while simultaneously looking like she wants to rip someone's head off. I didn't know that was possible, to show both emotions at the same time.

For once, I don't think I'm the one on the other end of that pissed off expression, and honestly, that feels good. I think we've finally hit a point where both of us can coexist and maybe even like each other.

Last night was fucking incredible. I didn't mean to have her sleep over, but we were working so late, and she dozed off while I was in the bathroom. She looked so peaceful, and for selfish reasons, I didn't want her to go. So, I let her sleep.

I know she wasn't entirely thrilled about it when she woke up this morning, but I got a kick out of watching her rush out of my house.

Holland told me he caught her on her way out. He said she looked flustered and left in a hurry. That made me laugh.

Gwen flustered? I haven't seen that happen very often. She's independent and controlling, but last night? She let me take control of everything, and seeing her let go of herself, even for a little while, made me want to do it over and over again.

Gwen takes her seat next to Damian, setting her bag down on the ground. He leans in to whisper something in her ear, and my blood boils as I watch how close he is to her. How he touches her.

I'm realizing now that I really do want all of her, every day and every night, all to myself.

Gwen shakes her head at whatever Damian said, and now I'm wondering what he said to her.

Professor Whitely rushes down the stairs to her desk, late, as usual. Her tight pencil skirt hits her knees and the blouse she wears opens slightly at the top, revealing her cleavage. Her hair is curled and in a half up, half down style, and her glasses sit on the bridge of nose.

She looks like she should be on set for a shitty porno instead of teaching a college literary criticism course.

I look back down to Gwen, who is sitting a bit straighter than she was before, watching and waiting intently for the professor to begin class.

There's barely anyone here, which I assume is due to the fact that many people hate presenting or didn't even finish the project.

I thought I'd feel relieved when this project ended, but now, I'm not sure how I feel. I know Gwen and I will still see each other, but I wonder if our dynamic will change if we're not forced to be together all the time. And I hate that I care this much.

Professor Whitely claps her hands together once, breaking me out of my thoughts and turning my attention to the front of the room.

"Okay, here's what's going to happen," she begins. "I've put all of your names in this hat," she holds up a small blue baseball cap with tiny sheets of paper inside.

"I'm going to pick a name, and your team will come up to present. When you're done presenting, you may leave."

I let out a sigh of relief because I did not want to be stuck here listening to a bunch of boring ass presentations that I couldn't care less about.

After three presentations, I'm about to fall asleep in my seat. This shit is reminding me why I skipped out on so many classes. I'm impatient, and impulsive. I cannot stand staying still.

"Gwen and Ryker, let's see what you got," Professor Whitely says in a giddy tone. I roll my eyes. No one person is that happy, it's not possible.

Gwen slowly rises from her seat, bringing her laptop with her and walking down to Professor Whitely's desk, without looking back at me, I notice.

When I meet her down there, she doesn't even look at me. My eyes narrow in confusion at her coldness. She was fine when she left this morning. Did something happen between then and now? Does she regret what we did?

"Hey, what's wrong?" I whisper as Gwen pulls up the slideshow.

Keeping her eyes locked on the screen, she says, "Nothing."

Okay…

After I've presented my half, Gwen finishes hers, shutting the laptop as Professor Whitely and the few students in the room clap. She gives a shy smile before grabbing her things, saying goodbye to Damian, and rushing out of the room, leaving me standing there, utterly confused.

What the fuck just happened?

I don't even wait for Professor Whitely's feedback. I grab my bag and chase after Gwen to make sure she's alright.

She's sitting on a bench just down the hall from the classroom, looking flushed and out of breath. What the hell is going on with her?

I take a step closer to where she sits, making her look up, her crystal blue eyes meeting mine. Fuck, she's gorgeous.

Taking a seat next to her, she doesn't flinch or move away. She simply stays there, her hands wringing in her lap as she stares down at the ground.

I clear my throat. "What was that about?" I ask softly. Gwen looks at me, and I expect to see tears or fear in her eyes, but that's not what I see.

"You went after Ashton Davis after I ask you not to, didn't you," she accuses. My blood turns to ice. How the fuck did she find out? I know she saw my hand the other day, but I didn't answer when she'd asked about Ashton.

As if reading my mind, she continues.

"He came to see me. He told me what you did," I see red. My entire body freezes and I have the sudden urge to punch a fucking wall. My jaw tenses.

"What do you mean he came to see you? When? Why didn't you tell me?"

"Just before class. He stopped me outside of the lecture hall. Told me you're the one that fucked up his face," she looks at me as if she's challenging me to deny it. I don't.

"He told me to tell you to watch my back," she says softly. "He threatened me."

I'm going to fucking kill the bastard. I'm going to rip his skin off of his pathetic body and burn him alive. He's not going to get away with threatening Gwen. I'm not going to let him think he can fuck with either of us.

But first, I need to make sure Gwen hasn't gone back to hating my guts, because to be honest, I like it a lot more whe she doesn't.

"Gwen, look. I'm not going to apologize for beating the guy's ass. He had it coming. But I-" she cuts me off with a heart stopping kiss, kissing me rough and hard, needy. The roughness of the kiss contrasts with her soft, plump lips as they move against mine. Her tongue finds mine and our breaths tangle together.

I have no fucking clue what's going on right now. Is she mad at me? Is she turned on?

Gwen pulls away, her eyes moving from my face, down to my crotch. My dick swells in my pants, picturing the things we did just last night.

She reaches down and grabs my hand, pulling me toward an empty room and locking the door behind us.

I stand in the middle of the room, crossing my arms over my chest while Gwen walks slowly toward me, her expression unreadable.

"Why would you go after Ashton?" she asks, as if it isn't obvious.

"The guy's a major prick, Gwen," I shrug. Gwen takes a step closer until we're about three inches away from one another. The lights are off, but I can still see a hint of her lips as she speaks.

"I know. But why did you go after him at the party?" she asks again. I run my hands through my hair, beginning to get a bit frustrated.

"Because he deserved it."

Gwen takes another step, and now we're face to face, and I can see her eyes as they bore into mine, waiting for an answer that I don't know.

"Why?" I stand up straighter, making Gwen flinch, but she recovers quickly.

"Because he had his hands all over you, and you looked like you didn't want anything to do with him," I explain, hoping that's the answer she's looking for.

Her hands ball into fists at her side.

"Why do you care what he was doing to me? You don't even like me." My body fills with anger at her words. How could she not realize that that isn't exactly true anymore? Especially after the other night?

I know it doesn't make us best friends or even boyfriend and girlfriend, but it does mean we have a connection.

"I hit him because I saw him grinding all over you and grabbing your ass and I could tell you were uncomfortable from across the room," I grab her arms, holding her in front of me.

"When I got closer, I heard him ask you to go upstairs and then I heard you tell him no. He kept pushing and I... I saw red. I couldn't help it. He was trying to take advantage of you, trying to take what's mine. And I don't fucking share," I watch her expression carefully as I try to catch my breath from my confession.

Her brows furrow in confusion and frustration. She pulls out of my grasp and backs away slightly.

"What's yours? I am not yours, Ryker," she crosses her arms defiantly.

I walk forward, effectively backing Gwen into a table so she can't go anywhere. She is mine, and I'm about to show her just how wrong she is.

"Yes, you are," I tell her, my tone dark and demanding. "I've had a taste of you, Gwen. And I am not letting you go."

"I can't stand you, Ryker," she says, trying, and failing to sound confident in her statement. I roll my eyes, a knowing grin spreading on my lips.

"Not what you were saying last night, when my tongue was on your clit, making you come while screaming my name. When my cock was buried inside you, driving you to the edge," I can hear her sharp intake of breath. She opens her mouth to say something but closes it before anything comes out.

Something in her expression changes, and I can't tell what she's thinking. Is she going to bolt? Is she going to hit me?

No, she's not. Instead, her lips smash against mine again and I'm overtaken by everything about her.

Chapter 31

GUINEVERE

My lips move with Ryker's in a passionate, tension filled kiss as we stand together in the middle of the dark, empty classroom. There are six tables and one long desk in the front of the room. From the looks of the counters covered in beakers and scales, this looks like a chemistry room.

I didn't really pay attention to what kind of room it was before dragging Ryker in here. I don't know what I was thinking, I just knew I wanted to scream at him, ask him why he would go through the trouble of beating some guy up over me. Does he actually have some sort of feelings for me?

I can't imagine why he would. I've been a total bitch to him since the day we met. Granted, he was a total ass since the day we met, and arguably still kind of is. But I never did anything to try to impress him.

There's no denying that I don't look like the girls people would expect a guy like Ryker Steele to be with. The girls Ryker's been with are like super models, and I'm just me. Plain and boring. Simple.

I get good grades, I listen to my mom, I don't party too much, I rarely do my hair or makeup. I'm nothing like someone Ryker would go after. So why me? Why is he so caught up with me?

Honestly, I can't even believe what happened last night. I mean, I definitely don't regret it or whatever, but seriously? Ryker Steele, Ellington University's most eligible asshole wanted me. Three weeks ago, if someone would have told me that, I would have laughed in their face.

But here we are, standing in this room, our mouths linked together as we move against one another.

Ryker's hands find my hips before he effortlessly picks me up and puts me on the table in front of him. His hands run up my thighs and up to the hem of my shirt, staying there.

I can taste the sweetness of Ryker's mouth as our tongues dance together, my hands roaming over his muscular body. I can feel his desire, and it only makes me want him more. But we're in a classroom, and I don't want to get caught.

It doesn't seem like Ryker cares much about being caught though as he slowly lifts my shirt over my head.

"Ryker, we're going to get in trouble," he chuckles deeply against my lips.

"You forgot who you're with, Rebel."

I roll my eyes, because yeah, I did forget who I was with. The guy that can literally get away with murder on this campus. Okay, maybe not murder, but whatever.

I really didn't plan for this to happen. I mean yeah, I made out with him in the hallway, but that was a moment of weakness.

But after he explained why he went after Ashton, something bubbled up inside me. It's not just the fact that he defended my honor; it's the raw, animalistic nature of the act. The thought of Ryker being so possessive and protective of me makes my pussy drip with anticipation.

I pull away from our kiss for a moment, breathless and eager, looking into his eyes and seeing the desire burning there, causing me to smile mischievously. I want to make him feel good. I want to feel his dick moving in and out of my mouth as I suck eagerly. But that'll have to wait. I need him inside me, right now.

With one quick movement, I unbuckle his belt, tugging his pants and boxers down, releasing his thick, hard cock. It springs free, and I waste no time in wrapping my fingers around it, pumping it with ardor.

Ryker groans, tangling his fingers in my hair as I begin to pump faster. I can't help the soft moan that leaves my lips as I feel him and continue my assault on his lips. He feels so big in my tiny hands, and I honestly can't believe that thing was inside me.

I grab his hand and move it to the button on my jeans. His hand begins to fumble with the button and zipper without breaking our kiss. I lift myself off the table so he can drag the jeans and panties down my legs, throwing my shoes off in the process. I can't believe we're about to do this, in public, again. The risk of getting caught sends thrills through my body, anticipation coiling in my veins.

Ryker reaches down to the floor, grabbing his wallet and pulling out a small foil packet.

He grabs both sides of my face and kisses me hard. Ryker takes a small step closer, and I can feel the head of his dick at my entrance. Before he pushes in, he glides a finger through my wetness.

"So, fucking ready for me," he practically growls. I whimper, desperate to feel him, and before I can say anything, he's pushing into me fast and hard. He doesn't give me any time to adjust to his length or thickness. Instead, he pounds into me unforgivingly.

He grips my hips, thrusting into me, and my eyes lock with his dark ones. A tingling feeling swirls in my core as I watch his intense gaze move from mine to the spot where our bodies are joined.

The slick sound of Ryker moving in and out of me fills the empty room, along with our heavy breathing and moans. I throw my head back, my breasts heaving as Ryker picks up the pace.

Holy shit. I'm not going to last much longer. The need to cry out overtaking my senses. My nails dig into his shoulders as I feel the familiar wave of my orgasm building.

"Ryker, I'm going to come," I pant. Ryker smirks, grabbing my waist and pulling out of me. I let out a loud groan in protest. What the hell is he doing?

Grabbing my arm, Ryker twists me around, shoving my upper body on the table I was just sitting on. In one smooth motion, he enters me from behind with a rough thrust that makes us both groan loudly. The new position brings new waves of pleasure and I'm even closer to the edge now.

Ryker pounds into my pussy with abandon, spanking my ass cheek hard. The unexpected gesture makes me scream out, the pain mixing with pleasure as my sensitive flesh tingles under his rough treatment. I've never been slapped during sex before, and if you'd asked me twenty minutes ago if I'd enjoy it, I probably would have said no. But now?

"You like that, don't you, Gwen?" Ryker growls in my ear, his hot breath causing goosebumps to rise on my skin. "You like being fucked like this, with the chance of anyone walking in on us at any moment. You're not as innocent as people think you are, are you, Rebel?"

"Ryker!" I cry out, my face pressed against the cool surface of the table, contrasting with the heat of our bodies. "Oh God, Ryker, don't stop!"

Ryker chuckles to himself.

"Not a chance, baby."

Ryker grips my hips tightly, slamming into me with all his strength. The force of his thrusts shakes the desk, making it scrape against the floor slightly. A loud moan escapes my lips, and Ryker's hand slips over my mouth gently, keeping me quiet.

"Shh, Guinevere. Someone will hear you. And I'm the only one that gets to hear you moan."

My nerve endings feel like I'm on fire, my whole body tingling with pleasure at his dirty words and almost painful thrusts. I have never been fucked like this before, so roughly, so passionately. It's Ryker claiming me, marking me his, and I love every second of it.

As Ryker continues slamming into my pussy, he reaches around, his finger rubbing my swollen clit. A few circles over it, and I'm so close to coming. My body trembles as a powerful orgasm begins to rip through me, my pussy starting to clench tightly around Ryker's cock.

"That's it, come for me, Gwen," Ryker grunts. "Let me feel that tight pussy milk my cock. Yes, just like that. That's my good fucking girl."

His words push me over the edge, and I cry out loudly, my body shaking uncontrollably. Ryker follows right behind me. With a few more thrusts, he buries himself deep inside me, and I can feel his dick pulsing inside me.

We stay like this for a moment, breathless and spent, our bodies still connected. Then, slowly, Ryker pulls out, looking down at my dripping pussy.

He helps me up and puts his hands on both sides of my face, pulling me in for a long, passionate kiss. God, this is not what I thought was going to happen today. But I really don't regret that it did.

Ryker pulls away, a smirk playing on his lips as he pulls up his pants and hands me my clothes. He looks satisfied, yet still lustful as he watches me get dressed.

"We should probably go before a class starts and see's us in here," Ryker says. He's right. I cannot get caught in an empty room with him. I'd never hear the end of it. I'd probably be the talk of campus for weeks.

I know people are already talking about us since we've been seen on campus together working on our project, and because of the way Ryker defended me against Ashton at the Halloween party.

I guess a lot more people saw what happened than I originally thought. Ryker's been there twice to defend me, and even though we couldn't stand each other not too long ago, I still believe he would have been there to save me.

Something tells me that when Ryker Steele gets something in his head, he doesn't let it go easily. I wonder if he claimed me before we even really started getting to know each other.

That girl in the library the first time Ryker and I met up seemed like she was waiting for him to get up and leave with her. She looked like she was upset when he blew her off. I wondered who she was back then, but it didn't really matter at that point. I'm not stupid. I know it had to be a girl he'd fucked or that wanted to fuck him. But I didn't care because all I wanted to do was get out of there.

I know Ryker doesn't do relationships. I can't expect that a guy like him will want to be together just because we've had sex a couple times.

But he seems so possessive over me, so protective. I can't help but think, is he that way with all of the girls he sleeps with?

"Gwen?" Ryker's voice distracts me from my thoughts. I look down to see his hand stretched in front of me to help me off the table. I take it hesitantly, and he helps me jump down. I could have gotten down on my own, but I didn't want to. Not with the offer of his help.

We walk to the door, and Ryker opens it slightly, peaking around the hallway to see if anyone's around. When he decides the coast is clear, he lets me leave the room before him, him following after.

I don't know why this feels awkward. Like I don't know what to say to him now that we're not in the heat of the moment. Where do we go from here? We don't have a project to work on anymore, and we have no real reason to hang out.

Ryker stands in front of me, his hands tucked in the pockets of his jeans. His thick, dark hair mussed from the sinful activates that just occurred. He looks effortlessly sexy in his dark maroon colored shirt and black pants. My core aches at the thought of him fucking me again.

I open my mouth to say something, but the sound of a cellphone cuts me off before I can.

Rolling his eyes, Ryker pulls his phone out of his back pocket, groaning when he looks at the screen.

"I have to take this," he says, almost regretfully. "I'll call you, okay?" he looks into my eyes, as if making a promise.

I nod. "Okay, yeah," I reply softly, a dull ache swirling in my chest as I watch him leave.

Chapter 32

GUINEVERE

"**Y**ou really slept with him?!" Lainey squeals as we sit in the courtyard, sipping on hot coffees from Café Grind.

The fall air has now turned into the beginning of a cold winter chill, and the trees are pretty much empty. No one really sits out here this time of year, but there's always a few people milling about.

"Shh! Keep your voice down," I scold. Lainey rolls her eyes and looks around the vast space, seeing only four people scattered around.

"No one's here! Besides, no one would know who we're talking about anyway," she swats my arm playfully.

I tug my black winter coat, wrapping it around me tighter as a cold breeze passes. This is really not the ideal place to be talking about this, but we both have a class in ten minutes, so we didn't want to walk home.

"So, how was it?" Lainey asks, curiosity and a bit of jealousy swirl in her eyes. Rolling mine, I take a minute to answer. How was it? It was… it was earth shattering. It was mind blowing. It was like scratching an itch I didn't even know I had. And I hate him for it. I hate that he's made me feel this way about him. Like I want him, need him.

I don't need anyone. I'm fine on my own. Although, I do want someone to share things with. Like when I have an awful day and need to rant, or when I'm upset and need someone to hold me. Could Ryker be that person?

No. He couldn't. Ryker Steele could never.

"It was fine," I tell her. I know she's not going to accept that for an answer, but it was worth a try.

"Come on! Give me more than that! I need to live vicariously through you," she begs. She's acting like she isn't constantly fucking a new guy like every week.

I love Lainey, and she can do whatever she wants, but why would she need to live vicariously through *my* sex life? Just because it's Ryker?

I chuckle at her outburst. "I'm not giving you details! I shouldn't have even told you. It's not like it matters," I huff as I watch Lainey's smile fall. God damnit, I want off this topic. "He was good. Better than good, he was great. He made me…" I trail off. Lainey adjusts herself in the spot next to me, angling herself so that her knee is now touching mine.

"Made you what? Come? Well I'd hope so," she teases.

I roll my eyes. "Of course, yeah. But… he also made me feel good. Like, he made me feel beautiful and wanted."

Lainey's face turns from a grin to a look of adoration.

"Omg! That's so cute," she squeals, clapping her hands together in excitement. "Okay, I need to know. Is it pierced?"

I almost spit out to coffee I just drank. Did she just ask what I think she did?

A few people walk by us, talking to themselves and not paying any attention the scene Lainey is creating with her laughter. She just loves making me uncomfortable.

"Lainey! What the hell?" I cry.

"What?" she asks innocently, as if she didn't just ask if Ryker Steele's dick is pierced. "I just wanna know if it's true! There's a rumor going around that he has three piercings on his-" oh my god.

"No, he's not pierced. He has no piercings at all. Anywhere," I say tersely. Lainey's face falls in disappointment.

"Well, I also heard that he has a small mole right on his-"

"Okay, conversation over!" I hold both my hands up to stop her from continuing. If I hadn't stopped her, she would go on and on about the rumors she's heard from all the women Ryker has or hasn't slept with.

I know he's had sex with a lot of the girls on campus, but I'd rather not think about it.

Lainey chortles. "Okay, okay," she swats her hand dismissively. "Ellie and Ty Manning fucked," Lainey shrugs casually, as if she didn't just drop a bomb about our friend. My eyes widen.

Holland is so not going to be happy. He was pissed about her even going to the party with him. Obviously, none of us are going to tell him, so there's no way he'll even find out. As long as Ty Manning doesn't decide to be a fucking idiot and brag about it in the locker room.

Ty is a moron, but he's sweet and Ellie seems to really like him. I don't know if he's exactly the boyfriend type, and Ellie is so innocent and traditional, she'll want him to be.

Holland will kill him if he breaks her heart.

"Seriously? When?" I ask.

"The night you were with Ryker. I didn't know he was there, but I ran into him on his way out. It was super awkward," she explains, a smirk on her delicate features. "I made Ellie tell me everything once he left."

Taking another sip of coffee, I try to imagine Lainey pouncing on Ellie for details like she's currently doing to me.

"Wow. I mean, good for her."

Lainey shrugs. If Holland ever finds out, he's going to beat Ty's ass. It'll definitely be a sight to see."

It's Saturday night, which means I'm being dragged out with Ellie and Lainey to a dance club about twenty miles away from campus against my will.

Lainey has already done my makeup and given me a tight black dress that barely covers my ass with a pair of heels that I'm probably going to take off at some point of the night.

I took the liberty of curling my hair, leaving it down so the long curls cascade down my back. Lainey gave me a smokey eye kind of look and put on some false eyelashes. I look like a completely different person, and I hate wearing this much makeup. But it made Lainey happy, so I didn't argue.

With one last spray of perfume and a quick glance in the mirror, I strut into the living room where Ellie and Lainey stand, looking deep in conversation. My eyes narrow. Whenever they're like this, there's usually something they're not telling me, or something they don't want me to know.

Lainey turns around to look at me, her curly brown hair up in a bun on top of her head, two curly strands hanging out in the front. Her makeup is flawless, and she looks stunning in her dark green tank top that shows off her breasts, and the tight black skirt that makes her ass look perfectly round and perky.

"Oh good, you ready?" she singsongs, grabbing her clutch off of the coffee table and walking passed me to the front door. Ellie hasn't moved from her spot.

"What aren't you guys telling me?" I ask accusingly.

Ellie's eyes shoot behind me to Lainey who now has the front door open and one foot out.

"Nothing," Lainey shrugs suspiciously. "Let's go, I want to get a good table!"

Lainey casually strolls out of the house, hopping into the passenger seat of my old beetle. I look back to Ellie who just shrugs her shoulders, hooking her arm through mine and leading me out of the house.

What they're up to, I have no idea. But I have a feeling I'm not going to be too happy about it if they're being so secretive about it.

The parking lot of Party Glowers is packed, which is to be expected on a Saturday night. The building is a large two story with an exclusive upstairs area and a huge dancefloor with a stage on the lower level.

They provide glow sticks, glow necklaces and bracelets, and glow paint for their patrons. There are colorful flashing lights that shoot across the space, and the dancefloor lights up with different colors while people dance.

It's a pretty cool concept, and it's right between the colleges, so both Groverland and Ellington U students congregate here.

The nice thing about the club is that Holland and Ellie's father owns it, so we get free entry and free drinks when we come.

I'm usually the DD since I don't drink too much if and when I do go out. Lainey and Ellie typically get shitfaced, and I end up having to drag their asses out of whatever club or party they've dragged me to.

I can usually get out of it since a lot of the parties they go to are over at the Elite mansion. I'm not really sure why they wanted to come here tonight.

Lainey heads straight to the bar, Ellie and I following close behind. With a swift wave of her hand, a handsome bartender with tattoos up his arms and muscles that make your jaw drop comes over to take her order. She orders her signature drink of choice, a whiskey sour, and Ellie gets a gin and tonic.

I of course opt for a water.

Lainey leads us over to a corner booth, away from the huge throngs of drunk patrons.

Taking a sip of her drink, Lainey leans in to yell something in my ear over the thumping of the bass.

"You should get a drink! One won't kill you," she urges. I shake my head.

"I'm good for now, maybe later."

Lainey rolls her eyes and takes another sip. I catch a glimpse of Ellie staring up toward the exclusive area above us and notice a few familiar faces. My stomach flips and my nerves skyrocket. My eyes catch with emerald green ones that I've come to know over the last few weeks.

He cocks his head, narrowing his eyes as he takes me in.

I avert my gaze quickly, feeling my cheeks burn. I turn slowly to see Lainey watching me for a reaction. So this is what they were hiding.

"What are they doing here?" I seethe. I was not planning on running into Ryker tonight. Lainey shrugs.

"Holland texted and said they'd be here. I figured it would give you and Ryker a chance to talk," Lainey explains simply. I try to tamp down the annoyance that's boiling deep in chest, but it's proving to be rather difficult.

"We don't need to talk, Lainey. There's nothing to talk about," I explain.

That's a lie. There are some things we should probably talk about. Like, I don't know what Ryker and I even are. Are we friends? Are we fuck buddies? Do we even actually like each other?

But I'm not about to be the one to bring that up. I don't need him thinking I want a label on us or anything. Because I don't. Do I?

"You should ask him if his brother is single. He's like, really freaking hot, in an 'innocent rich boy' kind of way. I could teach him a thing or two," Lainey winks.

"Teach who what?" a male voice asks. Our heads turn to see Holland, Ryker, Mason, and a guy that looks vaguely familiar, standing at the edge of our table.

Ryker's green eyes watch me as I take a sip of my water.

Ellie glares at Holland and he just smirks, knowing his presence bothers her. Holland's gaze skips over to Lainey, who is looking at him over the rim of her glass.

"Hey, Barkley," Holland nods toward Lainey. Lainey rolls her eyes, looking seductive and bored all at the same time.

"I knew you were going to be here, but I was still hoping you wouldn't show," she says cooly.

"What'd they put in that drink? You're bitchier than usual," Holland comments, rolling his eyes.

"Why don't you crawl back down to Hell where you belong?" Lainey questions sarcastically, glaring at him.

I shift uncomfortably in my seat as the tension at the table shifts to borderline sexual.

"Meet you there, Satan," Holland muses.

I've never noticed it before, but Holland and Lainey argue like an old married couple.

Ellie doesn't even seem bothered by it anymore. She just sits back and lets it go. I think she finds it entertaining honestly, and most of the time it is.

But right now, it feels a bit like I'm interrupting something.

Lainey sets her drink down and sighs.

"I'm going to dance. El, Gwen, you coming?" she asks with a hopeful expression. Usually I'd say no, but right now there's a little too much happening at this table.

I nod, taking one last sip of my water before walking passed the guys. I can feel Ryker's stare as we make our way onto the dance floor.

The song changes to something with more of a techno vibe, and Ellie, Lainey, and I dance together shamelessly. I'm not as sensual as they are, and I'm definitely not a dancer, but I've always liked having little dance parties just us girls.

As we dance and the songs change, I periodically find myself looking back to the booth to see if Ryker and his friends are still standing there.

They've taken up residence at our booth as they watch us carefully from their seats. I'm suddenly very aware of the short dress and tall heels I'm wearing, and the way the dress is riding up, almost revealing my thong to everyone in the club.

"Who's that guy sitting next to Mason?" I ask, leaning into Lainey so she can hear me over the music. She looks back to the table to see who I'm referring to.

"Oh, that's Logan, Ryker's brother. He's my year, and the total opposite of Ryker," Oh Lainey, the perpetual gossip. Thank God for her or I wouldn't know shit that happens on campus.

That explains why he looks familiar. He's got Ryker's eyes, and the same scowl that I'm pretty sure is permanently engraved into Ryker's face. Seriously, does the guy ever actually smile?

"I heard they don't really get along, and their dad is like, a total jackass."

I look back to the table, but this time Ryker isn't there. I look around the dark but colorfully lit space, landing on the bar, where I see Ryker and some tall, leggy blonde with her hands all over him.

My stomach sinks, and the dancing mood I was in just minutes ago vanishes, now replaced with a sour, bitter feeling that I most definitely do not like.

I glance around me and pluck someone's shot out of their hand, downing it. The burn in my throat distracts me from the unfamiliar feeling in my chest. Am I jealous?

Chapter 33

RYKER

Amy's tits are in my face as I lean against the bar waiting for my beer.

Her blonde hair is pulled back into a sleek bun and her makeup is completely over the top. I know we're at a club, but no one needs that much makeup on their face.

The perfume she wears reminds me of summer. Her dress is skintight, leaving very little to the imagination as her tits pour over the top. There's a large diamond shaped hole right in the middle, showing off her taut stomach and belly ring.

She flutters her eyelashes flirtatiously. I just want her to go away. I guess she didn't get the fucking message the last time I had to tell her to leave me the fuck alone.

Amy takes a step forward, placing herself between my legs. Her hands slide up my chest seductively as she wraps her thin, tanned arms around my neck. I have to stifle the urge to throw her off of me as to not create a scene in the very crowded club.

Leaning in, Amy uses her tongue to trace the shell of my ear before whispering, "You look reallyyy sexy tonight," she says, the stench of tequila on her breath.

I reach around, slowly peeling her arms off of me and pushing them away. She pouts, her dark red bottom lip jutting out in a way that would be sexy as fuck if I wasn't obsessed with a girl that can't decide whether she hates me or wants to fuck me.

"I thought I told you to stay away from me," I say curtly, as the bartender finally hands me my beer. Amy has the nerve to look hurt, but she recovers quickly, pasting a fake as fuck smile on her face.

"Come on, Ryker. Don't be like that," she reaches out to me again. I catch her wrist, grabbing it tightly. I say the only thing I can to let her know I'm serious. I'd never actually do it, but the threat should be good enough.

I look her dead in the eyes. "Touch me again, and I'll have you kicked out of this school so fast you won't even have time to pack," I spit. Amy's eyes go wide, and then she backs away slowly. She smiles awkwardly, looking around us to see if anyone had been listening.

I straighten up and head straight back to the booth the guys and I stole from the girls when they got up to dance.

Pat stayed home tonight, he said he had a big exam he had to study for. So Mason, Logan, Holland, and I are here tonight without him. Mason has been gone since the girls hit the dancefloor. He's probably found some drunk chick to grind up against.

I've been watching Gwen dance with Lainey and Ellie for twenty minutes straight. She looked slightly out of place, like she wasn't totally sure what she was doing, which is completely different from the way she carries herself around campus.

I slide in next to Holland, following his gaze to the dancefloor where Lainey and Ellie dance provocatively. An alarm bell goes off in my head when I notice that Gwen is not with them.

My mind automatically thinks about Ashton and that he'd threatened her. Was he here? I hadn't seen him when I scanned the room from the top floor, nor had I seen him as I watched the crowded dancefloor.

My blood runs cold and my jaw tenses. If that mother fucker touches her, he's fucking dead. I let him off easy with that beating, but I swear to God I'll-

My thoughts are cut short when I catch a glimpse of the five four brunette dancing a few feet away from her friends. I wonder if she's even noticed she'd drifted.

When the area around her clears a bit, I notice that she in fact, not dancing alone. A tall guy holds her hips as she grinds her ass all over him. Gwen's thin arms slide up the stranger's chest and back around his neck.

What the fuck is she doing? Does she know I'm watching her? Does she care?

My blood boils as I try to tamp down the raging jealousy attempting crawl its way out of me.

I stay seated, watching and waiting to see how this plays out.

Gwen turns around, keeping her hands locked around the guys' neck as she sways her hips to the music. Then, she removes her arms from the guy and begins running her hands up her thighs and through her hair, making direct eye contact with me.

She doesn't look embarrassed or upset that she's been caught. In fact, a small seductive smirk crosses her lips, and she winks at me. The stranger presses against her again, his hands roaming possessively over her hips, but she ignores him, keeping her eyes locked on mine.

I clench my jaw so hard I'm surprised I haven't broken a tooth. So, she is doing this shit on purpose. Why?

The guy moves his hand to the small diamond shaped hole on Gwen's stomach, and I watch as two of his grubby fingers disappear beneath her dress. She hasn't taken her eyes off of me, even as I stand from the booth.

"I'll be back," I tell Holland as I begin to weave my way through the crowd toward Gwen, her eyes burning with challenge.

I come to a stop, standing in front of her, clenching my fists at my side to keep from punching this fucking guy in the face for touching what's mine. All while Gwen keeps up with her movements.

My eyes narrow in frustration as I try my best to look unaffected by her little show, but I'm really fucking struggling. I'm so pissed she's messing with my head, and I'm fucking turned on imaging her dancing on me like that. This woman drives me crazy.

I clear my throat, but it's unnecessary since Gwen's eyes are already on mine.

"Having fun?" I ask cooly.

"Yes," Gwen says, finally stopping her production. She stands with her hands on her hips as she glares at me.

"What are you doing?" Gwen looks at me as if I'm stupid while glancing around the crowded dancefloor.

"What does it look like? I'm dancing," she says pointedly. Fuck, how can someone this cute be so damn frustrating?

"No. What are you doing with *him*?" I seethe. The guy at least has the decency to back up a bit to give us some semblance of privacy.

Gwen looks over her shoulder at the stranger.

"Who, Matt? We were just-"

I step into her, watching as her entire demeanor changes, and I can hear the sharp intake of breath getting caught in her throat.

"I know what you were doing, Gwen. And now you're done," I say sharply as I grab her tiny wrist and begin to drag her through the crowd.

We turn a corner and I drag Gwen up the spiral staircase that leads to the VIP area. I shove her into the bathroom, locking the door behind us.

The harsh lights in the bathroom make her beautiful tan skin look flushed, her hair is slightly frizzy from the humidity in the packed club, and the dress she wears barely covers her perky ass. Her legs look long and toned, and the heels she's wearing make her at least two inches taller than she is.

My cock stands at attention when Gwen takes a step toward me, and I want nothing more than to bend her over the sink and fuck her until she's begging me to let her come. But I need to hold off until she explains what this was about.

"That was quite the little show you put on for me, Guinevere," I say smoothly. Gwen scoffs.

"I don't know what you're-" I cut her off, pushing her against the wall, wrapping a hand around her neck just enough to apply a bit of pressure. Her eyes widen and I have to stop myself from unloading right here and now as her perky tits rub against my hard chest.

She looks down to my hand on her throat, then back at my face to search my eyes.

"Don't play dumb, Rebel. It doesn't suit you," I seethe in a low, husky tone. "Why were you grinding your ass on a man that wasn't me?"

"I… I don't know," she says timidly. She's hiding something from me, something she doesn't want me to know.

My eyes narrow with curiosity.

"Guinevere, tell me why you were dancing against another man's dick?"

I remove my hand from her neck and slide it down slowly to the hem of her tight black dress. Gwen's breath hitches, and I can feel the small tremble in her body as she tries to control herself.

"I saw you," she begins. My head tilts to the side in question. Saw me? What the hell was I doing? What did she see? I didn't touch another woman all night.

Gwen looks down at the ground, her cheeks brightening.

"With that girl, at the bar. I saw her all over you," her voice practically a whisper. Shit. Amy.

That fucking girl is like a bad case of herpes that keeps coming back.

I laugh, knowing that the interaction with Amy was nothing for Gwen to be upset over.

"Are you jealous?"

"No," she answers almost immediately, but I can hear the uncertainty in her voice. My eyebrows raise and I smirk.

I lean in closer to whisper my next word into her ear. "Liar."

My hand moves to push up the end of Gwen's dress, feeling the inside of her thigh as I go. My heart pounds in my ears and my breathing picks up. My dick is rock hard, and I don't know if I can restrain myself much longer.

My fingers trace over the wet spot of Gwen's lace panties and I let out a groan. Her head falls back against the wall as her eyes close. She whimpers softly, making my cock twitch.

God, I need to be inside her right now.

"You're soaked, baby girl. Why?" Gwen shakes her head, her red lips parting slightly. I reach up to grip her chin with my free hand, forcing her to look at me. "Look at me, Rebel. Tell me why you're dripping all over my hand right now," I demand.

I move her panties to the side, rubbing a finger through her wet slit before bringing it back to her pretty clit. She squirms slightly in my grasp, letting out a delicate moan.

"Tell me Guinevere, do you like it when I'm rough with you?" I ask, sliding a long finger into her tight hole.

"God, yes," she cries as she grinds ever so slightly on my finger.

My lips twitch as I shoot her a cocky smile. I pull the finger out, using her wetness to slide over her most sensitive spot with ease. I can tell she's already close by the way her breathing speeds up and the way her heart pounds so rapidly.

"Do you want to come, baby girl?" I ask, already knowing the answer, but desperate to hear her say it.

"Yes, God Ryker, yes," she pleads, and it's literally the hottest thing I've ever heard.

As much as I want to watch Gwen come apart by my hand, I want to teach her a lesson.

Pulling my hand away from her clit, I bring my finger to my mouth and taste her. Fuck, she tastes so fucking good.

Gwen pouts. "What are you doing? Why did you stop?"

I push a strand of hair behind her ear, keeping my hand splayed on her cheek in a gentle gesture. Her chest rises and falls with each pant, and I notice her puckered nipples under the thin layer of her dress. I really want to rip it off of her, but I'd rather not have her walk out of here naked.

My eyes lock with hers, hers searching mine for any reasoning behind why I wouldn't let her finish.

"Oh, sweet Rebel, you've been teasing me all night," I growl, my voice hoarse with desire. "Using that body of yours to drive me crazy. Don't you think it's only fair I do the same to you?" she shakes her head, her eyes on fire.

"I'm sorry, Ryker. Please, make me come," Gwen whines and the sound goes straight to my dick. Suddenly, I can't hold back. I need my mouth on hers.

My mouth crashes against hers in a hungry kiss. Gwen moans into my mouth, her hands tangling in my hair as she kisses me back with equal fervor. I lift her up, her legs wrapping around my waist as I bring her to the sink and set her on the counter.

I stand between her open legs, kissing her, feeling her. My hands skate up her thighs, my fingers linking on to her panties and pulling them down to reveal the sweet pink pussy I've come to be obsessed with.

I trail hot, open-mouthed kisses down her neck, nibbling and sucking on the sensitive skin knowing it drives her wild.

Gwen throws her head back, closing her eyes in pleasure as I leave a path of wet, greedy kisses along her collarbone and down to the swell of her breasts.

"Say it again," I demand, moving back up to her shoulder to pull the straps of her dress down. She pants, her anticipation palpable.

"Make me come," she purrs, her breath coming in short gasps as I pull the dress down, exposing her stunning tits.

I groan loudly at the sight and the desperate tone of her voice. I was supposed to be teaching her a lesson, but I can't even control myself when I'm around her. I don't know how I thought I'd be able to hold out.

Without another word, my hand reaches to squeeze one of her breasts, my mouth moving to her other nipple as I bite and suck. Gwen's moans spur me on. I rub my finger through her arousal before sticking one finger inside, watching as her body tenses around me.

She sits straighter, reaching for my belt. Her small hands fumble with the buckle, and I can tell that she's trying really hard to concentrate on her task but failing with my finger pumping in and out of her.

The bathroom is nice, but it's small and kind of stuffy. With our body heat and energy we're giving off, the air in here is too warm for my liking. It's not the most ideal place to fuck, but I'm not waiting any longer.

Gwen finally gets the buckle undone, undoing my button and then my zipper before shoving my jeans down my legs. She looks down to my erection which is now tenting my boxers.

I swear I see the heat and want in her eyes as she lets out a small moan. God she's gorgeous like this. All naked and spread out on the sink like the good fucking girl she is.

Her hands reach for the waistband of my boxers, pushing them down over my hips. Her eyes take in my rock-hard cock before reaching for it and grasping it in her hands.
I let out a pained groan as her fingers brush against the tip, collecting the small drop of precum onto her thumb before licking it off.

Holy fucking shit. Jesus Christ, this girl.

She begins to pump harder, faster, and I pull my finger out of her wet pussy to grab her wrist.

Her ocean blue eyes look at me with confusion, and I hate myself for making her stop because it felt so good. But I don't want her to make me come yet.

"I want to come inside of you," I tell her in a low, husky tone. I push her back toward the mirror and pull her hips forward until her ass is practically hanging off of the counter. She bends her legs, holding them in the air above her giving me better access.

"I'm going to devour you," I growl. Gwen whimpers in anticipation, watching my every move. My heart rate accelerates even more as I take in the sight of her spread legs, her pussy soaked with arousal.

"Please," Gwen begs, threading her hands through my hair as I fall to my knees in front of her, the counter the perfect height for me to kneel and still reach her.

Before letting myself taste her, I decide to try something. Gwen is stubborn. She doesn't like being told what to do, and she doesn't listen. When she gets caught up on something, she will see to it that it's done to her liking. She thrives on control, which is why she fights me at every turn.

But I have a feeling she'll like this.

My gaze hardens. "Put your hands behind your back. Keep them there," I demand. Gwen shoots me a wary look before doing as she's told, and fucking hell, she looks perfect like this.

I look up at her from my spot beneath her, meeting her eyes, making her squirm. A tingle runs down my spine and stays in abdomen.

Christ, this girl is going to end me.

Chapter 34

GUINEVERE

My heart hammers in my chest as I feel the cold damp air in the bathroom against my bare skin. Ryker's hot breath ghosts over my sex, making me squirm with anticipation.

He nips at my inner thighs as he works his way up. I can't hold back my whimpers, my hands grasping together as I feel his hot tongue trace the slick folds of my pussy. He teases me, licking and sucking gently, avoiding my swollen clit, and driving me wild with need.

God, I need his mouth on me right now. He's been teasing me this whole time, and I'm about to explode.

"Please," I beg, my voice hoarse with longing. I feel like I'm always begging him.

With a low chuckle, Ryker finally grants me mercy swirling his tongue around my sensitive bud before sucking it firmly into his mouth. I cry out, my hips bucking against his face as the long-awaited pleasure rips through me.

I can feel his tongue fucking me in time with the relentless circling of my clit, and within moments, I'm climaxing, my body shaking uncontrollably as wave after wave of pleasure washes over me.

As the intense sensations begin to subside, Ryker stands, pressing his hard length against my core. I can feel his cock twitching against me, waiting to plunge deep inside. My body shivers involuntarily. My eyes meet his, darkened with desire and heat.

"What do you want, Rebel?" he asks in a husky tone, making me crave him even more.

"I want you" I tell him as I unabashedly grind my wet, slick pussy against his hardon. "Fuck me."

Ryker groans, angling my pelvis slightly for easier access.

I lean in, leaving a soft kiss on his lips. He deepens it, and I can feel his tongue slide over mine as we begin a rhythm.

"Fuck, Rebel," Ryker closes his eyes briefly, and when he opens them, they're darker than before.

My heart pounds and my breath catches in my throat as Ryker kisses me again, this time much rougher as he begins to press into me.

I can't help the cry that comes out as my body adjusts to him inside me. This feeling has easily become the best feeling in the world, and I don't know how I ever lived without it.

Ryker pulls out slowly, and then pushes in again, hitting a deeper spot inside of me. I cry out, my nails digging into his shoulders as she begins to thrust harder. His hands grip my thighs as he drives into me with fierce abandon.

The sound of skin against skin echoes off the bathroom walls, mingling with our heated groans and gasps.

I don't know how he manages to bring me to the edge so fast each time. It's unlike anything I've ever experienced. I need him to fuck me harder. I need more.

"Harder, please," I pant, wanting to feel him deeper, wilder.

Ryker lets out a predatory growl as he grasps my ass cheeks, lifting me higher as he pounds into me. The rough treatment sends sparks of pleasure shooting through my core and I tighten my legs around his waist, urging him on.

Our bodies glisten with sweat under the harsh lights in the small bathroom, and I feel like I could scream.

I meet each of Ryker's thrusts with one of my own, our pelvises slamming together in a frantic rhythm. I moan loudly, and Ryker does the same.

"Come again for me, baby," Ryker grunts, his eyes screwed shut in concentration. "I need to feel you coming on my cock."

My breath hitches as another orgasm builds within me. He feels fucking incredible, rubbing all the right spots inside me and even though I need to come, I don't want this to end.

My heels dig into Ryker's ass, urging him deeper as I chase my release.

Then, with a loud cry, I shatter, my body convulsing around his thick length.

"Atta girl," he says gruffly. "That's it, Rebel."

Ryker thrusts a few more times before he stiffens, groaning loudly as he chases his own release. I feel him pulsing inside me, and it's the most erotic thing I've ever felt.

Our pants mix together as we come down from our high. We stay together for a few silent moments, Ryker slumping forward so his forehead meets mine.

Then, gently, he lowers my legs and slowly pulls out of me, gazing at me with dark, satisfied eyes.

I smile up at him, my hair tumbling around my flushed face, pieces sticking to my cheeks and forehead.

"I think we can call it even," I tease, reaching up to tug playfully at his hair. He chuckles softly, shaking his head.

"How do we always find ourselves in this situation?" he asks with a grin.

"In what situation?" I ask, my head cocking to the side.

He looks around the bathroom and chuckles to himself.

"Fucking in public places," he smirks. "Is it like, our thing?" he asks teasingly.

I shake my head, unable to keep a giant grin from taking over my face.

"We don't have a thing," I state. Ryker's grin widens.

"I think it's our thing," he says, leaving a few small kisses along my neck and nipping my ear before setting a soft peck on my lips. "Get dressed. I'm taking you home."

I hop off the sink and get dressed quickly.

Ryker isn't wrong. It does seem to be a recurring thing for us now, having sex in public spaces. Something I have never done and never even thought about doing until I met Ryker.

This is not the way I saw tonight going, mostly because I had no idea Ryker would even be here.

Honestly, I was kind of looking for a reprieve so I could think. I can't believe I let him rattle me so much, completely distracting me during our presentation.

I've never been distracted during class. I worked so hard on that project, and I barely remember even saying anything. I rushed out of the room so quickly; I didn't even get to hear what Professor Whitely had to say about it.

Did we pass? There's no way we didn't. We both spent so much time on it, and something tells me Ryker didn't really have a choice but to pass.

When we started working together, I thought there was absolutely no way I wouldn't kill him. I didn't think I'd get through one day, let alone three whole weeks with him. He was mean, he was callous, he was arrogant. Okay, well, that hasn't really changed. But the rest?

He's different. He's kinder, gentler, and I'd like to hope it's because of me.

A small part of me wondered if it was all bullshit. I'm letting this man who just three-ish weeks ago hated me and treated me like shit use me for sex. I guess I'm using him for sex too, but this time, it felt like more than that.

I know we were in a bathroom, but the way he looked at me, the way his eyes met mine with desire and lust, it almost felt like he wanted more. Which is ridiculous right?

Ryker Steele has never had a girlfriend, so why would I think I'd be the first?

I'm nothing special, but Ryker makes me feel like the most beautiful woman on earth, and I haven't felt that way in a long time. He feels good, warm, safe, and I find myself hoping to God that nothing ruins this. That nothing ruins us before we even get a chance to explore what we can be.

―――――――――――

My leg moves rapidly, up and down and up and down. My pointer finger taps my outer thigh repeatedly. I feel clammy and uneasy as I look around the small office space.

There's a one window facing main campus, a desk and chair that look like they've been there since the school opened its doors, two chairs sitting across the desk, and a large bookshelf against the wall.

There are a few pictures on the wall of the beach and the school, but other than that, there is nothing in here other than the nameplate on the desk that reads Aurora Whitely.

I've never been called into an office by a teacher. I've always done as I was told, followed the rules, and kept to myself. School is a means to an end.

All I need to do is get my degree and then I'll be a teacher and my life here at Ellington will be nothing but a distant memory.

But sitting in this stuffy office with Professor Whitely sitting in front of me feels like I'm in some sort of trouble.

We've been sitting here for fifteen minutes now making small talk and for a moment, I thought that might be all she wanted to do. We do get along great in class, and she can't be much older than me. But it would still be odd for her to ask me to come to her office just to chat.

My hair stands on my arms and a tingle of anticipation shoots down my spine, just like it always does when Ryker's around now. It's like my body can sense him.

Professor Whitely's face lights up as she looks passed me to the door. I don't even turn around.

Ryker strolls into the office looking as drop dead gorgeous as he always does in black joggers and an Ellington Dodgers sweatshirt. A strand of his black hair hangs down on his forehead and when his green eyes land on me, they soften just a bit. He takes the seat next to me, dropping his bag on the floor beside him.

My heart pounds and I have to remind myself that we're not alone and I can't crawl on top of him.

"Well, let's get to it then," Professor Whitely says, a small smile on her face. "You guys ran out before I could give you a grade."

My cheeks heat, remembering why I ran out so quickly. Ashton had just threatened me for Ryker beating his ass, and I was so consumed with anger toward Ryker that I didn't even want to look at him.

Then, Ryker fucked me until I came in the chemistry classroom. The memory causes a shiver to run down my spine and my thighs to clench. Jesus, get it together, Gwen.

"Honestly, I had my doubts that this would work. Of course, I wanted it to work out. But with the way you two argued, I wasn't sure either of you would last," she shrugs, an amused look on her face.

"But you surprised me. Your presentation was flawless, you should be proud of yourselves. I've given you both an A. Great job."

This isn't exactly what I was expecting when Professor Whitely emailed me this morning for a meeting. I thought she was going to lecture me about running out.

I'm honestly just as surprised as she is. I thought for sure Ryker and I would give up and we'd fail the project because we couldn't get past our own shit. But we did it. We survived, and we freaking passed.

Not that I really need to worry about my grades. I have straight A's and a 4.0 GPA. I was a bit afraid that if Ryker couldn't get his shit together, he'd make us fail and my GPA would drop.

My mother would have been understanding. She's never really been the type of mom to tell me I need to pass every one of my classes with an A. My father on the other hand, he's a perfectionist.

He always wanted the best for me and thought that since he got good grades and a perfect GPA at Ellington that I had to do the same. He'd turned from the playful, fun dad, to the meticulous, strict parent by the time I hit seventh grade.

My mom is a smart woman, she went to college and got her bachelor's in writing. When I was little, she'd always be writing, and I thought that it was the coolest thing in the world. But her parents weren't as strict as dads. They didn't push her to get perfect grades and participate in extracurriculars, and she turned out just fine.

Because of my father's high expectations, I was always under so much pressure to be perfect, to never let my grades slip. I missed out on a lot of my teenage years due to studying which is probably why I'm not like a normal college kid who loves to party.

I wipe my clammy palms on my thighs and let out a breath I didn't even realize I was holding.

A small chuckle leaves my lips as I look to Ryker who is already staring at me with a wide grin. I want to jump out of my seat and hug him. I want to kiss him and feel his strong body against mine.

Something flashes in Ryker's eyes. A mix of lust and yearning, and I feel it too. The need to feel him courses through my veins like a wildfire.

My phone begins to ring in my bag causing me to jump and pulling me out of my thoughts.

"I'm sorry," I start, pulling the cellphone out of my bag, seeing my mother's name on the screen. I let it go to voicemail, but then I see she's tried to call five times already.

My stomach drops and my heartbeat accelerates. She never calls me this many times in a row just to say hi. Something's wrong.

Looking up from my phone, I see Ryker's and Professor Whitely's gazes set on me. I'm sure my face has turned a ghostly white and they're probably wondering what happened in between our conversation and me looking at my phone.

I don't have time to explain. I need to call mom back to make sure she's okay. She'd only blow up my phone during the day for an emergency. Is she okay? Did something happen to her? My head starts going through all of the worst-case scenarios.

Ryker watches me intensely as I stand up from my seat slowly, grabbing my bag off the floor and slinging it over my shoulder. I feel like I'm moving at the pace of a snail.

"I'm sorry, I have to take this. Thank you, Professor Whitely."

She smiles politely and nods. I give one last look to Ryker, his brows are pulled together in curiosity, and somehow that look makes him even hotter, if that's possible.

I have to force myself to look away and walk out of the room on shaky legs.

Chapter 35

GUINEVERE

There's a light dusting of snow on the ground, and the cold November air burns my cheeks as I make my way out of Mallory Center and toward Café Grind.

A few students sit at the small tables against the windows. I find an open table in the corner and when I take a seat, I immediately look at my phone, noticing a text from my mother.

Mom <3

Mom

Guinevere, please call me!

Mom never texts. In fact, she hates it. She says it's less personal and you can misconstrue what people are saying since you can't actually hear them. I guess she's not wrong, but it's so much more convenient than calling, especially when you don't love talking to people in general.

I stare at mom's contact name for a few moments before taking a deep breath and pressing the call button. It only rings once before my mother's panicked voice fills my ear.

"Gwen? Honey, finally. I've been calling you. Where have you been?" she asks, her voice laced with worry.

"I'm at school, mom. I was in a meeting with my professor," I take a breath before asking, "What's wrong?"

I can usually tell how my mom's feeling by her tone. She has very specific tones for each mood she's in. When she's angry, her voice goes down at least two octaves. When she's happy, her voice goes up to an annoyingly high pitch. When she's sad, she speaks slower and it's a pitch higher than when she's angry, but lower than when she's happy.

But right now, I can't tell if she's pissed off or devastated, and that's slightly concerning.

Mom lets out a shaky breath. "It's your father."

My heart sinks. My father? Did something happen to him in Germany? Is he okay? How would I feel if he were gone?

"Is… is he okay?" I ask as nervousness takes over my entire body. My mom laughs sardonically.

"Oh, he's fantastic. He married his twenty-seven-year-old assistant in Germany. Oh, and somehow we completely missed the fact that they had a child two years ago."

Her tone is bitter and if I didn't know any better, I'd say she sounds jealous. But that's not possible because they really haven't spoken much in years. So why does she sound so upset about it?

My blood runs cold at the memory of the phone call I had with my dad on my birthday. How he'd spoken to someone named Viv, and then he had told her to tell 'him" he'd be there in a minute.

He must have been talking about their son. My brother. A brother I didn't even know existed until just moments ago.

I guess I knew there was a chance of my parents moving on and one day marrying someone new. But what I didn't expect was not being invited to my own father's wedding and not knowing he had a freaking kid.

"I didn't even know he was seeing anyone," my voice is barely a whisper as I digest the news I've just received.

I shouldn't even be surprised, but a small part of me really thought that even though he's practically been absent since I was nineteen, that he'd at least tell me, his only daughter, that he was getting married.

My father married a woman only a few years older than me. Bile rises in my throat just thinking about it. I never pictured my dad being that kind of guy. I think that's the biggest shock of all.

"Neither did I. I knew he had a new assistant, but I had no idea they were actually together. I wanted you to hear it from me before you heard it from the news outlets," she explains, her voice soft.

"Are you okay?" I wonder. My mom is strong, but this is some next level shit.

I hear a deep sigh on the other end of the phone.

"I'm okay. I just can't believe he didn't say anything. I can't believe he didn't even mention it to you. I'm so sorry, honey. I… I don't even know who he is anymore," she sounds like she's on the verge of tears, her voice wavering.

I hate when my mom's upset. She's always been my rock and to see her breaking, it fucking hurts. I would do anything to take the pain away from her. She doesn't deserve this.

"You're still coming home in a few weeks, right?" she asks, hope clear in her gentle voice. I've already told her I'd be coming home, but she always needs reassurance. Thanksgiving break is coming up, and then there's only a week and a half left of classes when we come back.

I nod, even though she can't see me. "Yes, mom. I'll be home."

Mom lets out a breath of relief, and when she speaks again, her entire demeanor has changed.

"Good. I can't wait to see you, Gwenny. I've missed you," she tells me, and my eyes suddenly feel the burn from unshed tears.

"I miss you too, mom. I have to go, I've got class," I lie. I don't have a class for the rest of the day, but I need to get out of here. I need to go home and curl up in a ball and cry. "I love you," I tell her, my voice as soft as a whisper.

"I love you, too, honey."

My eyes squeeze shut as I attempt to tamp down the tears threatening to spill out, but it's too late. A single tear falls from my eye as I press the end call button.

Taking a look around the café, I realize that it has become more packed with students trying to avoid the cold weather outside and warming up with hot chocolate and coffee.

I wipe my cheek quickly, grabbing my things and heading out of the warmth and into the brisk cold winter air. It's cold enough to where you can see your breath, but I have so much pent-up sadness, so much rage, so much confusion building up inside me that I don't even feel the chill.

My heart is beating a million miles per minute, my thoughts are jumbled and racing, and my legs feel numb as I run toward home.

I hurriedly unlock the front door, toss my boots off and run to my room, passing Haley on the couch in the living room. I dive onto my bed, bringing a pillow to place under my face as I let out a scream. The muffled sound doesn't take the pain away, but it certainly helped get some of the anger out.

There's a small knock on my door, and then Haley is peeking her auburn head in. Her face is etched with concern as she takes in my position on the bed.

"Gwen… you okay?" Haley asks cautiously.

"No…" I mumble as I switch to sit up, holding the pillow in my lap. I hate admitting that I'm not okay. I try so hard to be strong. To not let things affect me. But this? This is messing with my head. My own father.

Haley pushes the door open wider before slowly making her way over to my bed and climbing on to sit across from me. She crosses her legs and sets her hands in her lap as she plays nervously with her fingers.

"Do you wanna talk about it?" she asks hesitantly, keeping her eyes focused on her hands. She seems nervous, like I'm a bomb that could go off at any moment. We've never really done this before, talked about our feelings with each other. Lainey is usually the one I complain to and she either tells me to suck it up and move on or holds me while I cry.

Haley also doesn't know anything about my relationship with my dad, so she won't fully understand what I tell her, but I need to talk to someone.

"My dad got remarried and had a kid he never told me about," the words spill out of me. I peek up through my lashes to assess Haley's reaction.

Her eyes are wide and she's no longer playing with her fingers.

She gulps. "Wow," she wipes her hands on her thighs before looking at me. "That's really messed up. I'm sorry. I-"

I cut her off because she looks like she'd rather be anywhere but here.

"Yeah, it's fine," it's not fine, but whatever.

Haley shifts uncomfortably. "Do you… do you need anything?" I shake my head. I don't know what I need. I don't know if anything will make this better. I feel betrayed, forgotten, insignificant. Is there anything anyone could do or say to fix that? Probably not.

"I'm just gonna take a nap. But thank you for talking with me," I say with genuine appreciation. I know this made her uncomfortable, and it was probably the last thing she wanted to be doing. So it means a lot that she still came to try to help.

Haley nods in understanding. "Okay. Well, let me know if I can get you anything," her lips turn up into a sad smile.

"I will," I flash the best smile I can muster as Haley walks out of my room, shutting the door behind her.

I throw myself back onto my pillows, completely wrecked and exasperated. It's only noon and I'm already spent.

If I'm being honest with myself, a small part of me always hoped that my parents would get back together. That dad would come to his senses and get over his midlife crisis and realize that he loved my mom so much he couldn't be apart from her.

That he loved me so much he couldn't bear being so far away.

Sometimes I think it would have been easier if they got the divorce when I was younger, so I'd be able to get used to it. But by the time they split, I had grown up watching them love each other. I'd based any relationship I had or wanted on them. I wouldn't settle for less than the kind of love my dad showed my mom.

I'd gotten used to having my parents together. To seeing them happy and in love. And then at nineteen, I had to just accept that all of it was fake? That they'd actually been fighting for years.

The sound of my phone vibrating against my nightstand pulls me out of my pity party.

Arrogant Asshole (Ryker Steele)

Arrogant Asshole (Ryker Steele)

You okay? You looked upset when you left.

My stomach flutters and my heart immediately speeds up. This reaction must be unhealthy, right? I wasn't expecting him to check in. I know he says I'm his, whatever that means, but we're not officially together, and he probably thinks this whole thing is just sex.

But if he thought it was just sex, would he text to make sure I was okay? That seems like something you do for someone you actually care about, right?

I'm not good with casual releationships. I'm a hopeless romantic. I believe in love and happily ever after's and Ryker Steele? He's the king of casual relationships. What if that's all he wants from me? I don't think I can do that. No, I know I can't. I was jealous over some woman talking to him at a bar.

If I knew he was having sex with other women while he was also sleeping with me? I couldn't handle that.

Rolling my eyes, I type out a response.

Arrogant Asshole (Ryker Steele)

Me

Dad drama. I'll be fine.

Arrogant Asshole (Ryker Steele)

Do you want to talk about it?

My heart skips a beat. He actually wants to talk to me about it? Shit, what is happening right now?

Ryker Steele doesn't do feelings. He doesn't care about anyone but himself. But no matter how much I tell myself these things, I can't help wanting to tell him everything.

However, I don't feel like going over it again right now. I just want to sleep and forget everything for a while.

Me

No.

I lock my phone before Ryker can answer. I know he'll probably argue, and I don't have the energy to fight with him. After setting the phone on the nightstand, I roll over and close my eyes, drifting off quickly as sleep takes over.

Chapter 36

GUINEVERE

BANG!
BANG!
BANG!

My eyes fly open and my heart stops for a moment. How long have I been sleeping?

I feel frozen in place as I think of who could be knocking on the front door. All of us have keys, and I even made one for Damian so it wouldn't be them.

The blood in my veins turns to ice as the thought of Ashton knowing where I live and showing up at my house creeps into my brain.

He couldn't know where I live, right? No one but Lainey, Ellie, Haley, Damian, Ryker, and Ellie's brother know where I live, and I know none of them told him.

"She's asleep!" I hear Haley say from the living room. "You can't just barge in here!"

A second later, my bedroom door flies open and Ryker storms in. His gaze softens when he finally sees me curled up on the bed. He walks over slowly, the bed moving as he takes a seat on the edge.

I don't move. I just stare at him, dumbfounded. Why is he here?

Ryker's green eyes search mine as his hand caresses my cheek, pushing my hair back behind my ear. He lets his hand rest there as his thumb moves slowly up and down.

My eyes close instinctively at his touch. At the way he makes me feel when he touches me.

When I open my eyes, Ryker is watching me intently, a sorrowful expression on his face. He hasn't spoken, so I decide to be the one to break the silence.

"What are you doing here?" the question sounded kind of rude, but I genuinely want to know why he's in my bedroom right now. Something flashes behind Ryker's eyes, and I wonder if maybe I'd hurt his feelings.

"I needed to make sure you were alright," he says simply, as if that statement wasn't completely out of character for him. My eyes soften a bit at the thought of Ryker being so worried about me that he showed up at my house to make sure I was okay.

"I told you I was fine," I sigh. Ryker's brow furrows slightly.

"You said you'd *be* fine. Which means you are not fine right now," he says, his voice deep and serious. "Tell me what's wrong," he demands.

I roll my eyes because of how demanding he is.

I remember thinking it back when we were first working on the project. I also remember thinking about if he was just as demanding in the bedroom. He is in fact, even more demanding in the bedroom and it is the sexiest thing in the world, hands down.

"What if I don't want to tell you?" I try, knowing he's going to make me tell him one way or another. There's no way I'm getting out of this.

Ryker's jaw ticks as he grips my chin to make me look at him. It's not hard or forceful, but it's enough to hold me in place.

"Tell me, Rebel," he says through gritted teeth. God, why does he want to know so badly?

"Ryker, it's nothing."

The grip on my chin tightens just a bit as Ryker's patience with me begins to wither. His roughness stirs something inside me, and my once dry panties are now wet. *Ugh*, he's so hot.

"Guinevere Lane Sharpe, I'm not playing with you," he growls. The use of my middle names takes me off guard and he can clearly see that. "I looked you up when I found out who you were," he says casually, as if that isn't super creepy.

"What the hell, Ryker! Why would you do that?" I try to pull out of his grasp, but it's no use.

"I needed to see who I was going to be working with. I can't take any chances," he explains. This is insane.

"What are you talking about? Take any chances?"

Ryker shakes his head, a small knowing smirk crossing his lips.

"Nice try, Rebel. We're talking about you," his eyes turn serious, and I can tell he's done messing around. "Now talk."

I groan exaggeratedly as I pull myself up into a sitting position, bringing my knees to my chest and wrapping my arms around them.

"My mom called today. She told me some things about my dad that I just… I wasn't expecting," my voice is low, barely a whisper as I begin to recall everything my mother said.

Ryker's eyes move between mine, waiting for me to continue. My heart tightens and I can feel myself shutting down, but I know Ryker won't let me.

"She told me my dad had another kid. A two-year-old son," I begin, trying to hold back tears. I don't want to cry in front of him. I don't want to look like a weak little girl.

But my tear ducts betray me, the fuckers.

A tear flows freely down my cheek, and I have to turn away to hide it. But it's too late.

Ryker reaches up to brush it away with his thumb. My lower lip wobbles at the gesture. Why is he being so gentle with me?

"Keep going," Ryker urges, and I take a deep breath before continuing.

"He got married. He got married and didn't even invite me to the wedding. I mean, that's messed up right?" I sniff as Ryker watches me with furrowed brows.

"I don't get it. He was so different when I was growing up. We laughed, we played… it was good. Normal. Now he can't even remember I exist," I say through gritted teeth, throwing my pillow across the room. It hits the wall softly before tumbling to the ground.

I bring my hands to my face and groan loudly.

"Wow, Rebel. What'd that pillow do to you?" Ryker teases, probably trying to lighten the mood but there's no way to make this situation any less shitty. I scoff.

My thoughts are all over the place and tears sting the back of my eyes.

"Why wasn't I enough?" I ask, not really looking for answer. I hate being this vulnerable, especially in front of Ryker. I never wanted him to see this side of me. The side that shows I have actual feelings. When you have feelings, they're easy to hurt. People see you as an easy target to screw over.

For some reason though, I don't think Ryker will.

Ryker's eyes darken slightly, and then soften when they meet mine which are now full of tears. He brings his hands up to cup my face, forcing me to look at him.

"Don't ever say that again," he demands, looking like he wants to punch something. His eyes are on fire, and I've only seen him look like this one other time. The time he found out Ashton threatened me.

"You are more than enough. Gwen, you are…" Ryker rolls his lips, his eyes darting around the room as if he's searching for his next words. "You are everything. And anyone who can't see how fucking perfect you are doesn't deserve you. Your dad is a fucking dick, and I'm sorry he made you feel like you're anything less than amazing."

My breath catches as Ryker's words wash over me. The tears have subsided, thank God, and all I can do now is stare at Ryker in awe because what the fuck?

His eyes dart down to my bottom lip before running the pad of his thumb across it. When his eyes land on mine, there's a fire in them. Desire, lust, and longing begin to cloud my thought, and I can't believe I'm going to say this, but I think I'm actually starting to fall for him, which is incredibly dangerous.

"Because, Gwen, you are extraordinary," he seems desperate for me to believe him, and I want to so badly.

"You may be infuriatingly frustrating, stubborn as hell, and a total brat more than like, eighty percent of the time, but you are also the smartest, most beautiful woman I've ever met.

And I've met a lot of women," he winks. I elbow his side and he has the decency to at least act like it hurt.

My heart is pounding, and adrenaline is taking over my body as I watch Ryker, this sexy, arrogant man, sitting in front of me after just telling me that he thinks I'm the most beautiful woman he's ever met. A genuine smile crosses my face for the first time in a while, and Ryker's eyes focus in on it.

"Fuck, Rebel," he growls under his breath.

"What?"

"That smile. You're perfect."

Butterflies let loose in my stomach and suddenly, I don't feel so sad anymore. I just want him.

Sitting up a bit straighter, I reach up to pull Ryker's hands away from my face, holding them in my lap as I look down at them, embarrassed since I've just cried and spilled my drama to him.

Ryker's grip on my hands tightens, causing me to look up. His eyes darken with desire.

"I'm going to show you just how fucking perfect you are, baby."

Before I know it, Ryker's lips are crashing against mine in a breathtaking kind of kiss.

Our tongues dance together, and Ryker's hands begin to roam over my body, gently caressing every inch of me. He pushes me back and my head hits the pillow below me as he spreads my legs and leans over me, deepening the kiss.

His hands slide down my side and over my hip to grip my ass, and I'm silently thanking myself that I changed into a baggy t-shirt and no pants. I think Ryker is too because he growls and says something incoherent under his breath.

Ryker's teeth sink into my bottom lip lightly causing me to let out a moan. My hands tangle in his hair, and I can feel his hard erection pressing against me sending a thrill through my body and making me ache with need. Breaking the kiss, Ryker trails hot kisses down my neck, sucking gently as he reaches the sensitive spot below my ear, eliciting a gasp from me.

"You have no idea what you do to me, Guinevere," Ryker murmurs against my skin, his breath hot and sending shivers down my spine. "I want all of you, right now. I'm going to worship this incredible body and make you feel so good you won't ever question if you're enough again."

I whimper at his words. I'm not completely sure what they mean for us. I don't know if this is how he talks to every girl he's with, or if it's just me.

I really hope it's just me.

Ryker smiles against my neck before pulling my shirt over my head and gently kissing a path down my body, pausing to pay attention to my breasts, circling my already pebbled nipples with his tongue before taking them into his mouth and sucking gently.

My back arches as the feeling of his tongue and teeth against my nipples makes me cry out. After a few minutes, he continues his way down, kissing and nipping at my soft skin as he goes.

When he reaches just above the waistband of my panties, he grabs it between his teeth and begins to pull down. I lift my hips for him to slide them under me and down my legs. Hell, that was hot.

Ryker doesn't even have to freaking try to be attractive. He just is, and I find that incredibly unfair.

He makes his way back up my legs, leaving kisses all the way up until he's right in front of my pussy. His hot breath skates across my flesh causing me to shiver.

His fingers lightly side through my slickness, making me squirm. Then, his finger is inside me and I have to bite my fist to quiet the moan I let out.

"You're always so ready for me, Rebel. Who knew all I had to do to get that stick out of your ass was make you come," he teases. I send him a death glare and he just chuckles to himself. His expression turns serious again as he sticks another finger inside me, pumping faster now. Oh my god.

My eyes squeeze shut as I focus on the feeling of his fingers curling inside me, hitting the spot that always drives me over the edge. Pulling his fingers out, I feel the heat from his mouth before his tongue begins to lick my clit, causing me to buck against him.

"Oh, God," I groan. I feel Ryker tremble against me.

"Yes?" he pulls his face away to look at me, a cocky smirk on his unfairly handsome face.

"Shut up," I demand, pushing his head back down to continue. He laughs but continues his magic on my clit.

As he licks and sucks, I feel his finger push inside me again before it moves down to... what is he doing?

His finger begins to circle my other hole, putting slight pressure on it but not going in. I crane my neck to watch him.

"I've never..." I shake my head as I try to catch my breath. "I've never done that."

Ryker cocks his head to the side, but he doesn't stop rubbing. It kind of feels good. Unusual, but good.

"Do you want to try?" he inquires, his eyes lit with mirth. I don't know, do I? I've never really thought about it, but I trust Ryker.

I nod, and a small grin lifts on Ryker's lips. "Good. Lie back."

I do as he says, lying back and waiting to see what comes next.

Ryker's tongue goes back to my clit, and then down, and down even further until he's on my other hole. He pulls my ass cheeks apart as he assaults my hole with his warm tongue, and I can't believe I like this.

Moving back up to my face, he kisses me hungrily. His tongue finds mine and we're kissing so hard our teeth clash, but I don't even care. I can't because Ryker's finger and slowly pushing into my asshole and the feeling is unlike any other.

My breath hitches as he inches in slowly and stops, breaking our kiss to look at my face.

"Are you okay?" he asks, and I have to hide the huge grin that's about to break out on my face from the fact that he's making sure I'm okay as he's shoving a finger in my ass.

I nod, urging him to continue. He obliges, and when he's all the way in, he places a finger on my clit as well and circles it gently.

Holy shit, this is intense. Oh my...

"Yes, yes, yes. Please don't stop," I cry out as the telltale feeling of my orgasm begins to build. I tingle shoots down my spine and my core clenches as I begin to tremble. I don't want to come yet; I want him to keep going.

"That's my girl," Ryker's raspy voice says, and that pushes me to my climax. I come so hard I swear I see stars.

Holy fucking shit, what the hell was that?

Chapter 37

RYKER

This fucking girl.

How can she not see how perfect she is? I don't know how her father could ever want to give her up.

I could kill him for making her feel like she's not good enough. I could kill anyone who has ever made her feel like she isn't worthy. I would never make her feel like she isn't the most important person on the planet. Because she is, to me.

As she lays below me, naked and spent, I can't even remember a time that I didn't know her. This thing with her feels natural, like it was always meant to be her and I, and I will do whatever it takes to prove that to her. To make her trust me.

Gwen's blue eyes search my face and her lips purse.

"What?" I ask.

"You didn't come," she says with a gentle lilt in her voice. There's a loud groan and it takes me a moment to realize it's coming from me.

Before I can say anything, Gwen sits up and pushes my chest so I fall onto my back on the mattress. Her eyes are filled with need as she straddles me, kissing me like she's desperate for my taste, and fuck, I know I am for her.

She bites my lower lip and begins to kiss down my neck, causing a shiver to run down my spine. My cock twitches and I have to force myself to think of anything else before I come in my pants like a horny teenager.

"Take this off," she pleads, gripping the hem of my t-shirt and shoving it up impatiently. I chuckle at her eagerness before sitting up slightly to pull the shirt over my head.

The smile on Gwen's face is incredible. She doesn't smile often I've noticed, at least, she hasn't smiled much with me up until recently. But it always seemed distant and fake.

The smile I see in front of me right now is real, and I vow in this moment to continue making her smile just like this.

Gwen kisses me again before moving down to my neck and nipping my ear. She giggles and it's the most enthralling sound I've ever heard.

She continues kissing down my chest, all the way to my navel before she licks a path back up and kisses me again.

Oh my holy hell. I don't know how much more of this I can take. She's driving me wild, and she knows it.

Her dainty hand moves down my torso, stopping at the waistband of my joggers. Then, she dips her hand inside, finding my hard length and stroking softly. I groan with pleasure at the feel of her warm hand moving over my erection.

My grip on her hips tightens as she finally moves under the thin fabric to grasp my dick, wiping the precum off the tip before stroking.

Gwen lets out a soft moan and I swear I'm going to explode.

She pulls her hand out before sitting up and moving to pull my pants and boxers down my legs, my erection springing free. Her eyes gloss over with admiration before lowering her head and licking me from root to tip. A hiss of air leaves my clenched teeth as the sensations roll through me.

I let her have her fun for a few more minutes before grabbing her head and pulling her away from me. I want to be inside her when I come.

Gwen's bottom lip juts out in a pout, her eyes wide with concern.

"What? Did I do something wrong?" I chuckle, because she absolutely did nothing wrong. I shake my head.

"No, baby. You were doing everything right. That's why I had to stop you immediately before I came from your mouth," I tell her. She tilts her head a bit, looking even more confused. "I want to be inside you when I come, Rebel."

I see the goosebumps raise on her arms before I feel them. Gwen's breath quickens as I pull her up to my face. The feel of her wet pussy sliding against my cock as her tongue moves with mine makes me feral.

She positions herself over me before slowly sinking down, pulling a hiss from my throat. From this angle, I can see all of her, and I'm in awe.

Her eyes close as she tilts her back and her tits bounce as she begins to ride me.

"Yesss…" I rasp. Her pants and moans send a surge of pleasure through me.

Looking up at her, I savor the sight of her pussy, glistening and taking my cock so well.

"You're unreal, Gwen," I tell her through breaths, gripping her hips as she moves up and down. Her crystal-like eyes meet mine and a wide grin spreads across her face. "And you're all," thrust, "fucking," thrust, "mine."

"Oh my, Ryker, don't stop…right there…oh God!" Gwen chants, her breath coming in short gasps as her orgasm begins to build.

"Don't come yet, baby," I tell her.

She falls forward, her head finding the crook of my neck and her hands weaving through my hair. I reach for her ass, squeezing tightly, eliciting another loud moan.

I pull out of her and quickly flip her over to her back. Her face is flushed, and her pupils are dilated. She's desperate for release, and I'll give it to her. But first, I need to make sure she knows she's the only girl in my life that can make me feel the way she does.

Before sliding back into her, I lean down, kissing her gently. It's not rushed, it's not messy. It's a slow, deliberate kiss, and it suddenly feels a lot more serious.

Something in the air shifts between us, and when I pull away to look at her face, I can tell she feels it too. My heart is skipping beats, and my breathing is shallow as I let the feelings settle in my brain. These unfamiliar feelings that I never thought I'd have toward another person.

Positioning myself at her entrance, I watch her face as I slowly bury myself inside her. Her lips part slightly as she gasps at the intrusion.

I move in and out of her slowly as I intertwine our fingers above her head. I'm so deep inside her that I can feel my balls as they hit her skin, and the sound makes me want to pound into her faster. But that's not what I want this to be.

We've fucked, that's what I'm good at. But Gwen isn't just any other girl that I find at a party and screw to forget about my shitty father or my impending future. Gwen is important, she's the kind of girl you keep around because you'd be a fucking idiot if you let her go, and she's exactly what I need.

I bring my face back to hers and kiss her passionately, pouring all of my feelings into it and hoping she can feel them without me having to say anything just yet.

Chapter 38

RYKER

I rub my temples with my hand in attempt to alleviate some of the stress as my father's grating voice seeps through the speaker of my Escalade. We've been on the phone for less than ten minutes and he's already managed to piss me the hell off.

I don't know what he doesn't understand. I don't want anything to do with The Steele Corporation while he's in charge. I don't want to work for him or under him, I want to run it. I want to bring it back to what my grandfather envisioned because it surely isn't what my father's turned it into.

As long as my father is CEO, he will keep running it to the ground until my grandfather's legacy is completely tarnished, and I can't let that happen. I don't know how, but I will take over the company one day, and my father won't have a say.

"Who is Guinevere Sharpe?" my father's accusatory voice barrels through the car speaker. My jaw tenses and a shiver runs down my spine. How the fuck does he know about Gwen?

My finger taps against the steering wheel repeatedly as I think of something to tell him since I can't really tell him she's the girl I'm slowly beginning to realize might just be my entire life.

"No one. Why?" I ask, hoping I sound as nonchalant as I meant to. I don't need my father to have any more reasons to bitch at me. A girl would certainly be a means for his bitching. Especially because he wants me to marry someone from another Elite family.

Slow down, Ryker. No one said anything about marriage yet. It's way too early to even think that about that as a possibility. Except, I'm realizing now that Gwen is the only woman I've ever even considered marrying.

"Dean Ashby notified me that you've been seen with her quite often around campus," his rough voice sounds irritated. "You need to be focusing on school and the Elite, Ryker. Not some gold-digging whore who's only with you for your money."

My blood boils at his dig against Gwen. He doesn't even know her. How could he make assumptions about a woman he's never even met?

I want to defend her. To tell my dad to fuck off and to never talk about her like that again. But I have to play this smart. If he knows Gwen and I are involved in any capacity, he'll try to get rid of her. I won't let that happen.

"I'm focused, Father. Everything is under control," I assure him through gritted teeth.

"Good," he says gruffly. "Your mother is looking forward to seeing you boys for Thanksgiving. You'll be there, yes?" he asks as if I even have a choice. If I did, I'd stay at the Elite Mansion and avoid home at all costs.

I sigh. "Yes, Father. I'll be there."

"Alright. See you soon, Son," he says, hanging up the phone quickly.

My head falls forward and hits the horn on my steering wheel causing it to blare loudly, but I don't have the will to move.

A knock on my window brings me out of my post-father phone call funk. I hoped it would be Gwen, but Mason's face peers in at me instead.

He points in a downward motion indicating for me to roll the window down. Rolling my eyes, I do so reluctantly.

Looking him over, his hair is disheveled, and he appears like he just woke up, even though its one in the afternoon, but our game isn't until later, so I guess he doesn't have a reason to be up.

"Dude, do you mind? You're waking up the entire block," Mason groans as he runs a hand through his hair.

"It's one. The only person still sleeping was you," I grumble.

"Not anymore," Mason mumbles under his breath. "What are you doing laying on your horn like that?" he asks.

I grunt as I close the window before opening the door, causing Mason to jump back. He holds his hands up as if surrendering.

"My father called," is all the explanation I give him before storming passed and entering the mansion.

Mason's footsteps follow close behind me as we make our way to the second floor. Pat, Holland, and Logan sit in the living room watching football, and their heads turn when they hear Mason and I enter.

"What jackass was laying on their horn out there?" Holland leans his head back over the couch to look behind him while I grab a water from the fridge.

Mason throws a thumb over his shoulder at me, a small grin tugging at his lips. I'm glad he finds this amusing. Holland's gaze moves over to me, and Pat finally looks away from the TV long enough to assess me.

Pat's eyes move over me, and his eyes narrow in question.

"You good?" he asks, his voice gruff and slightly concerned. He's a good guy, he always has been. He's been there for me through a lot of my dad's bullshit, and I've been there for him when his dad is being an ass.

He understands where I'm coming from more than Logan does, since Logan is completely okay with the way dad talks to him and with what's expected of him.

Logan hasn't even looked away from the game to glance at me, even though I'm sure he knows why I'd be pissed off. It's not hard to guess. Not much gets me riled up, but my father knows how to really get under my skin.

I nod. I don't really need to rehash everything that was said. It's all the same every time. Him calling me a disappointment and telling me everything I'm doing is wrong, telling me he wishes I was more like my brother, that I should respect him more for everything he's done for me.

I'm aware I grew up quite well. I'm aware that there are people out there that would kill to have what I have. But I'd give it all up if I could just have a normal relationship with my father.

My grandfather would be incredibly disappointed in who my father has become, I know he would.

Dad is selfish, he's cruel, and he's always one step ahead of everything. When I was eighteen, I thought I'd go away to college and be free of him, but it only got worse. He got more demanding of my responsibilities as a Steele. He started watching my every move, making sure I was keeping out of trouble.

He'd even visit the campus under the guise of visiting old Elite brothers or Dean Ashby. But I know he was checking up on me. Even if he never made it obvious, it was obvious to me.

The fact that he mentioned Gwen by name has my nerve endings on fire. I can't believe he'd have Dean Ashby watching me that closely. I mean, I can believe it, but I don't want to. I bet he doesn't have him watching Logan. My eyes roll involuntarily.

He called Gwen a whore. He referred to her as a gold digger. How fucking dare he talk about her like that. He knows nothing about her.

"You don't look good," Holland says, his brow raised.

"I'm fine," I snap. This makes Logan finally look back at me, his brows furrowed, and his lips pulled into a frown.

Holland and Pat exchange a glance before turning back around to the TV. Logan keeps his curious eye on me though, no doubt trying to figure out what my father could have said to piss me off so much.

I take a long sip of water before Mason speaks up again. This time, not about my phone call or why I'm pissed.

"Weston U's fullback told Teddy that Walsh is gunning for you tonight, man," he grins wildly at me. Shit.

Weston U has a good team. We've played them several times before, and they play rough. They're dirty and they love to shit talk. I also have issues with their fly-half.

Connor Walsh is a dick. He's an asshole who loves to get in my face because I slept with his girlfriend last semester.

To be fair, I didn't know they were dating. She'd told me she was single, and I'd never seen them together, so the thought never even crossed my mind.

Even if it did, I probably wouldn't have cared. Their relationship is their business, not mine. The girl came to me for a good time, and I gave her one. That's it. It's not my fault she wasn't satisfied with her boyfriend.

The difference between Connor Walsh and I is that I can put the past in the past, for the most part, and focus on the game. He can't, and that might give our team the advantage. He'll be so focused on taking me down that he'll screw over his own team.

I shrug cooly, brushing it off.

"Walsh doesn't scare me," I tell Mason.

"He's a pussy. He won't try anything," Holland calls from over the back of the couch.

"Even if he did," Pat chimes in as he stands from his spot on the couch. He walks over to me and his hand lands on my shoulder. "We've got your back."

I swallow hard. I honestly don't know what I'd do without these guys.

"Thanks."

"Ellie says Gwen will be at the game tonight," Holland tells me with a wink. My heart pounds in my chest and the familiar feeling of electricity buzzes through me at the sound of her name.

She's coming to the game? The last time she game to a game, that dickhead Davis tried to threaten her, and I swear to God if I see him again, I'm going to fucking kill him.

Would he be dumb enough to show up to one of my games to talk to Gwen? I don't know, probably. But if he knows what's good for him, he'll stay the hell away.

I have to keep my head in the game. I can't be distracted by douchebags like Walsh and Davis. I already have to deal with Ty Manning, and honestly, he's an even bigger douchebag than them.

"Will she?" I ask noncommittally. The guys know somewhat how I feel about Gwen. I haven't told them much, but I know they can tell how my mood shifts after I've hung out with her. I'm not sure if Gwen has told her roommates about us, or what she'd even tell them.

I haven't made anything official, there is no label, but I feel like the other night we both felt a shift. We know this isn't just simply fucking anymore. This thing between us is more. I know she feels it. She wants me just as badly as I want her.

"Yeah, her, El, and Barkley. Sounds like it was actually Gwen's idea. Any idea why?" Holland asks tauntingly. I roll my eyes and flip him off.

Logan looks up from his phone, making eye contact with me.

"Are you two a thing now?" he asks, and he seems genuinely curious. I hop onto one of the barstools at the counter, leaning my back against the edge and propping my forearms on the surface.

I shrug. "Yeah," I say confidently, making the decision for the both of us. Pat chuckles to himself.

"Does Gwen know that?" he asks, and Mason guffaws, giving Pat a fist bump.

"Funny, Samuelson. Real funny."

No, she doesn't. But she will. After the game tonight, I'm going to make it official.

Gwen's the type of girl who likes tradition. And I'm certain that includes putting a label on what we are. It's not something I would have ever considered before meeting her, but I would do anything for Gwen.

I decided Gwen was mine a long time ago, even if I wasn't ready to admit it to myself. Fuck what my dad thinks, and fuck what anyone else says.

No one is going to stop me from having her.

Chapter 39

GUINEVERE

———

I don't know why I decided it would be a good idea to come to the rugby game tonight. It's so cold out I actually think I might freeze to the stands.

I'm wearing my thick winter jacket, a scarf, a hat, and gloves along with my thickest Ellington U sweatshirt and I'm still shivering. Ellie and Lainey were smart and brought a blanket to huddle under, but it's difficult to fit all three of us under it, so we keep taking turns.

Damian doesn't seem to be bothered by the cold as he sits next to me sipping on a large soda and popping m&m's into his mouth.

The stadium lights illuminate the field and stands where faculty and students are chatting and laughing, waiting for the teams to take the field. The energy is charged, and my adrenaline is running high.

Last time I was here, I didn't really understand much of what was going on, but this time I know a bit more, so it'll be easier to follow. Plus, Ryker looks hot as hell in his jersey.

Lainey wanted to paint his number on my cheek, but I shut that down quickly since I'm not even sure what Ryker wants. He's been confusing as of late. We fuck, we talk, and it's great. But the other night, it was more than just fucking.

It was something else entirely. More intense, heated. Something I wasn't even sure Ryker was capable of. Actually, I was fully convinced it wasn't something he'd be capable of. But it felt like a lot more than hate sex, or pent-up tension, or jealousy. It felt real… and that kind of scares me.

———

I know Ryker already believes I'm his, and knowing his possessive streak, he might've been happy to see his number on my face. But I'm not sure *I'm* ready for the whole campus to know. Because trust me, when one person finds out, that shit will spread around campus like a bad STD.

The rumors and the attention will drive me insane. Ryker is one of the most popular and feared guys on this campus, and anyone in his circle is up for judgement and ridicule.

I don't think I could ever willingly put myself in the spotlight. I like being alone too much to be bothered by stupid people who only want to be near you to gain something for themselves. But I would do it for Ryker. I'm learning that I'd do just about anything for him.

"Damian, be a doll and go grab us some popcorn," Lainey demands, giving Damian her best puppy dog eyes. He rolls his and scoffs as he pops a brown m&m into his mouth.

"Go get it yourself, Princess," he mocks. Lainey huffs and leans back in her seat, crossing her arms.

"Fine, then you don't get to share the blanket with us. Good luck when your legs start to freeze off," Lainey's snarky tone makes me giggle.

"I don't need your blanket. It's not even that cold. You guys are just babies."

I elbow him in the side, making him drop some of his snack on the ground.

"Hey! What was that for? M&m's are expensive you know," he whines.

Shaking my head, I laugh and turn back to the field. The crowds' cheers get louder, and the stadium lights flash as both teams rush the field. Weston U in their purple and black jerseys and Ellington U in their green and white.

I've overheard a few people say that Weston U is a hard team to beat, and that they can get pretty violent. I've also heard a lot of people talking about some guy on Weston U's team named Connor Walsh. They've said he's a monster on the field, and a few even said they heard he was going after Ryker tonight.

I'm not sure why, and I didn't feel the need to ask. I know Ryker can handle himself and I'm sure it's all just gossip anyway.

My eyes follow Ryker as he runs to his position. After I left the last game, I did some research. Ryker's position is called the fly-half. It's a weird name, but then again, all of them kind of are.

Ryker's job is to lead his team's defense and attacks on the other team. According to Google, the fly-halves have to be aggressive, they have the best kicks, and they have to be aware of everything going on at all times to make the right calls.

It seems like a really stressful job, and apparently, it's one of the most important positions. I can see how Ryker could be the best fit for it.

When he's in position, I see his head turn to search the crowd, and when his green eyes land on mine, my heart stutters, and I can feel my cheeks heat. His smile makes me clench my thighs because holy shit balls, he's so freaking sexy.

Jesus, who am I?

"Your man looks mighty happy to see you," Damian nudges me lightly, winking. A small laugh leaves my lips.

"Shut up," I say, not even correcting him for calling Ryker 'my man'.

Ryker turns back to focus on the start of the game, and when the whistle blows, the crowd goes nuts. Two girls behind me stand and scream as they jump up and down. One cheers for Holland, and the other cheers for Ryker.

To my surprise, my blood boils and jealously rages through my veins. I know he has fans, and I know most of them are girls, but it doesn't mean I have to like it.

I know being with Ryker is going to be challenging. Girls throw themselves at him, and that's just something I'll have to get used to. It's not really something he can help.

Watching the guys run across the field, my heart pounds and my hands tap against my thighs nervously. Rugby is a contact sport. It's kind of scary to see the way these guys get tackled, and seeing Ryker get hit is making me cringe.

The last game I went to, I was hoping he'd get thrown to the ground. Now, I can't stand to see him hurt.

My eyes follow him up and down the field, every so often landing on his roommates. I believe Pat is the team's captain, and according to my rugby research, Holland is the hooker, and Mason is a fullback.

I really didn't look into those positions much, but it seems like each of them has an important job, and they're all doing really well.

"You hungry?" Lainey leans into my side, yelling in my ear so I can hear her over the loud voices. My stomach growls at the thought of food. I hadn't realized I was hungry until she mentioned it.

I nod, yelling back, "Yeah."

"What do you want? I can go get us food from concessions," Lainey offers. I feel the need to stretch my legs, so I offer to go instead. I have to pee too, so I might as well.

Standing up, I tug my coat on tighter and begin to make my way down the aisle. Ellie's hand shoots out to grab my wrist, her blue eyes peering up at me.

"Can you grab me a slushie? The red one?" she smiles sweetly. I nod, chuckling.

"Yeah. Lainey, cheese fries?" Lainey nods enthusiastically without looking away from the field. I follow her gaze and find it landing on Holland. My eyes narrow with suspicion, but I keep heading for the concession stands, shoving away my curiosity.

The line for the bathroom was surprisingly short, but most people are still watching the game, so I guess it makes sense.

Unfortunately, the concession stands are all outdoors, so I have to wait in the cold for our food and drinks. I only ordered some popcorn for myself, Lainey's cheese fries, and Ellie's slushie, so it doesn't take too long to before everything's in my hands and I'm walking back to my seat.

My phone buzzes in my coat pocket but I can't reach for it with the food in my hands. Setting everything down on one of the empty concession booths, I pull my phone out and see my mom's name on the screen. I decide to call her back in the morning, hanging up and shoving my phone back in my pocket.

"Hi Gwen," the familiar throaty male voice sends a feeling of dread down my spine. "Enjoying the game?"

Reluctantly, I look up slowly to see Ashton Davis standing in front of me with his hands in his pockets. His blonde hair is falls in his eyes, and his soft brown eyes look harder, more focused.

My fists clench at my sides and my jaw tenses. I feel my nerves beginning to take over as the last time I saw him replays in my head over and over again. He threatened me.

I don't really know him, and I don't know what he's capable of, but I did find out he's on the hockey team. I don't think he'd be stupid enough to risk getting caught doing anything to harm me.

All Ashton wants is to get back at Ryker for embarrassing him at the Halloween party. I'm not sure why he's decided that targeting me would be his best bet, but here we are.

"I am, thanks for asking," I say sardonically. Ashton quirks an eyebrow and smirks.

"Good, I'm glad," his rough voice sounds like nails on a chalkboard. It makes me uneasy, and I don't like it. I hate that I have no control over this situation. And I hate that Ashton keeps showing up. "You look good."

Ew. "Thanks," I retort, grabbing the food and beginning to walk away. Ashton, the stupid prick, steps in front of me, blocking me from continuing to my seat.

Wonderful. Maybe he is stupid.

"Get out of my way, Ashton," I order. Ashton just laughs it off and shakes his head.

"No need to be so hostile, just having some friendly conversation," Ashton sneers. I scoff.

"Nothing about you is friendly. Now move," I demand again, hoping my voice doesn't sound as shaky as it feels.

Ashton reaches out to grab my arm, and Ellie's slushie almost falls to the ground before I catch it. I shoot a glare at him.

He can't do anything here, Gwen. We're in public. There are people all around us. He can't hurt you.

I keep repeating this to myself as his face falls into a deep scowl, and even though I'm wearing a coat, I can feel goosebumps rise on my skin.

"I'm sure you told your boyfriend about our chat the other day," he starts, "It wasn't smart of you to come down here alone," Ashton's voice lowers into a threatening tone. My body shivers involuntarily and I want to run.

I look back to the stands where my friends' eyes are locked to the guys, and then I look to the field to see if maybe by some miracle Ryker sees me. Not that he can do much since he's in the middle of a game.

Ashton's right. It was stupid of me to think I could come down here alone knowing he was out there with his threats. I guess I just assumed they were empty threats and that he wouldn't act on them.

He must have been really embarrassed about getting knocked on his ass, because he's taking this revenge thing a bit too far.

I silently give myself a pat on the back for refusing to sleep with him that night because who knows where I'd be now. Ashton is clearly a hot head with impulse control issues, and I can't imagine how he would have acted if we'd slept together.

"I can handle myself," I say with fake confidence. I can handle myself in most situations. But I've never been in this situation. I've gone my whole college career without getting into any trouble, and as soon as I meet Ryker Steele, my world's turned into something I don't recognize.

Not all of its bad, but this part? This is bad.

I feel my phone buzz in my pocket again. It's probably Lainey asking where I am with her food, but I can't reach it. I have to get out of here.

Moving my gaze from the field to Ashton's menacing brown eyes, I glare at him so hard I'm surprised lasers don't come out of my eyes.

"Touch me again, and you'll regret it," I threaten, taking some of the control back.

Ashton is twice my size, and I could never actually harm him myself, but I can't let him believe he has all the power. His eyebrow cocks.

"We'll see about that," his grip on my arm loosens and he takes a small step back, but not far enough.

Ashton plucks one of the cheese fries out of the tray and places it in his mouth, closing his eyes as he chews and moans.

"Delicious," he drawls, taking his thumb into his mouth and sucking it sensually.

I think it was supposed to have an effect on me, but the only thing it did was make me nauseous.

Why the hell am I here?

Chapter 40

RYKER

My lungs feel like they're on fire from exertion and the cold air. Now that I've been running around for a while, my body has warmed up, and a light sheen of sweat coats my back. My muscles are sore, and I'm pretty sure I may have tweaked my shoulder, but I can't even focus on the pain right now.

Pat and Holland have been on fire tonight, and as much as I hate to admit it, Ty Manning has been lethal tonight too.

This has definitely been the toughest game of the season, and it's all because of that jackass Walsh. He's got his whole team on a fucking war path, and they're coming for me.

Shaking all other thoughts out of my head, I focus on the play, my eyes locked on the ball as it moves swiftly through the hands of my teammates.

My adrenaline is at an all-time high and I've never been more ready to crush an opposing team. I turn to look over my shoulder and see Holland and Pat watching me. I nod, and they look away.

As we begin the play, my coach screams from the sidelines and the crowds screams drown out any other thoughts. When I look back in front of me, I catch a glimpse of a beautiful five four brunette. But she's not alone.

Fucking Davis has his hand on her arm and my jaw clenches so hard I think it might break. I have never felt so much rage in my body at one time. Not even when I'm dealing with my father. This kind of rage is all consuming. It feels like my heart is going to pound out of my fucking chest and I can't breathe.

He's touching her. His hand is on her. He threatened her.

The world around me blurs, and the only thing I can see through my tunnel vision is Ashton Davis's hand on *my* fucking girl.

My ears are ringing, and the shouts of my teammates grow distant. Gwen finally looks up as if she's scanning the field, and she finds me, locking her big blue eyes on mine.

"Steele, get your head in the game!" I hear someone yell.

"Watch out!" another voice calls. They sound far away, and I can't tell who they belong to.

A split second is all it takes. My focus snaps back to the field, but only for a second before a hulking mass of muscle, barrels into me. The impact slams me to the ground and I get the wind knocked out of me.

My eyes squeeze shut and the loud ringing in my ear makes it impossible for me to hear the commotion going on around me. I gasp, trying to get oxygen into my lungs but a sharp pain cuts me off. Fuck, I must have broken a rib.

Pain radiates through my body as I move to my side, clutching my torso. I can't even open my eyes the pain is so sharp. Coach's voice comes into focus, and then I feel multiple sets of hands on me.

"Ryker, can you walk?" Coach Shaw asks. I strain to sit up but it's no use. I shake my head no.

"Alright, son, hold on," he croons. Shit, this hurts. I've been tackled before, it comes with the territory, but never like this. This was deliberate. It had to be Walsh, but it happened so fast I didn't see what was happening.

I am going to kill that fucker. And when I'm done with him, I'm going to kill Davis too.

"Hold on, Steele. You're gonna be fine," I hear Pat's voice say, much softer than his usual tough guy tone.

His hand lands on my shoulder and gives it a light squeeze.

"We're all here, dude," Holland says. He must be on my other side.

"Oh my god, is he okay? Why won't he get up?" I'd recognize that sing-song voice anywhere. My girl. Gwen. She's okay. Davis didn't hurt her.

Relief washes over me, and I let out a big breath of air, forgetting that my ribs feel like they're searing into all of my organs.

"Ryker, are you okay? They're getting someone over here. You'll be alright," Gwen tells me, her voice laced with worry. I force my eyes open, just so I can see her face.

Concern is etched in her delicate features, and it makes my heart squeeze. She's worried about me. God, I can't remember the last time someone was worried about me.

I reach for her hand, ignoring the pain, and she grabs it, wrapping her tiny hands around me. I can feel my body shutting down, probably due to the pain radiating through me, and even though I want to fight to stay awake, the need to sleep feels stronger.

God damnit.

The sound of beeping rings in my ears, and a harsh light makes me squint as I try to open my eyes. I feel groggy and out of it, and I hate that feeling.

I'm in a hospital room. Perfect.

"Ryker? Honey? Are you awake?" my mother's voice breaks through the otherwise quiet room. Why is she here?

She rushes to my side and gives me a hug, a bit too hard. I wince, remembering what got me here in the first place. The game, Gwen, the hit.

"Yeah, mom. I'm awake," I reply hoarsely. She places a soft kiss on my forehead before backing away. Her brow is furrowed, and she looks like she'd been crying.

"I was so worried. You have a fractured rib, but you're going to be fine, thank God. I knew that rugby was dangerous, Ryker."

Great. I'll be hearing about how I should quit and find a new hobby for the foreseeable future, and I'll be benched for the next month because of that shit head, Walsh.

I pull myself up slowly, the pain a bit duller than before, probably due to the pain meds they're pumping into my veins.

That's when I see my father sitting in the corner of the room. I hadn't noticed him. Why would he be here? He doesn't give a shit about me.

"The coffee machine on this floor is broken, so I had to go downstairs," Logan strolls into the room with two coffee cups in his hand. He hands one to our mother and, she smiles at him sweetly.

Logan glances my way and nods once. Was he at the game? Did he see what happened?

"Holland, Pat, and Mason are here," Logan tells me.

The guys walk in, and I almost laugh at how similar their demeanours are. Pat's hands are tucked in his pockets, his face is pulled into a scowl. Holland looks just as serious, and of course, Mason is grinning ear to ear.

Mason strolls over to the side of the bed, his hand landing on my shoulder.

"You're alive, man," he chaffs. I shake my head, a hint of a smile crossing my lips.

"Shut up," I tell him.

Pat and Holland walk up next, Pat looking a bit uneasy.

"Glad to see you're still breathing, brother," Holland says. My lips purse and I nod.

"Yeah, hurt like a motherfucker. But I'm fine," I assure him, attempting to reassure everyone else in the room simultaneously. I am fine, but I'm fucking pissed.

Pat and I exchange a knowing glance.

"It was Walsh," Pat states what I already knew. The only fucker on that team that would have played that dirty was Walsh. He waited for his moment, and he took it. I can't really blame anyone but myself. I was too distracted by Ashton and Gwen.

I should have been paying attention to the game. I shouldn't have let that get in my head. But seeing him with her, yet again, it made me feel things I've never felt before.

Rage, jealousy, protectiveness, possessiveness, and defensiveness, all wrapped up in a tight little bow.

It's all new to me, feeling this way about someone, especially a woman. It's infuriating, and it's the last thing I need to be worrying about.

But I wouldn't change a thing, because I have Gwen.

"I know," I say pointedly. He nods, probably already thinking of ways to kill the bastard. This is why Pat is my best friend.

God, I hope Gwen isn't here. I would have liked to see her, but not while my father is here. I don't know how much he knows about her, if anything. I need to keep her away from him. I can't risk him getting too close to her and figuring out what she means to me.

He'd try to get rid of her. He'd try to remove anything he sees as an obstacle or a distraction, and I cannot have that happen.

"I think we should let Ryker rest, everyone," my mom suggests. I don't want to rest. I want to leave this hospital and go find Gwen. I want to hunt down Davis and Walsh.

"Good idea, honey," my father stands from his seat in the corner, placing his hand on the small of my mother's back, ushering everyone toward the door. He hasn't said one word this whole time, but of course he's opening his mouth when it's time to leave.

"We'll be back tomorrow when you're discharged, sweetie," mom tells me. Great, I have to spend the night here?

Mom gives me a quick kiss on my temple before smiling softly and leaving the room with Logan.

"See ya at home, bro. Bring home some of those grippy socks. Those things are so cool," Mason says with a grin, and Holland slaps him on the back of the head. "Shit, what the hell, Monroe?"

"You're an idiot," Holland tells him as they exit the room, leaving me alone with my father who for some reason is still standing at the end of my bed.

Suddenly, I want a nurse to come in and give me more meds to put me to sleep so I don't have to deal with whatever is about to come out of my father's mouth.

His brows are pulled together into a tight scowl as he looks down at me, no doubt thinking about what a terrible failure of a son I am.

"You're distracted," he says patently. "I've told you, you should be focusing on school and your grades, not some silly game," he spits. My jaw tenses as I bite back my response. I don't want to argue with him. I'm tired of having the same conversation over and over again.

"It's that girl, isn't it? That's why you're acting stupid and getting distracted at your games. You let some imbecile break your damn rib for some girl? Jesus, Ryker. When are you going to grow up?" his words sting, but I don't show any reaction. I can't let him know he's getting to me.

"It has nothing to do with a girl, father. I'm not distracted," I assure him, hoping he'll believe me and drop it. God, hope is a fucking bitch.

"Look at you. Broken, lying in a hospital. It's pathetic," he scoffs, shaking his head and looking to the ground before letting out a heavy breath of air.

"You will quit rugby. You will focus on classes, and you will graduate. Then, you'll take a job with the Steele Corporation and marry a woman of status. Not some little girl you've suddenly become infatuated with. Do you understand me?"

My blood boils and I'm surprised the beeping of the heart monitor hasn't sped up at all, because I feel like it's pounding as if I'd just run a marathon.

Gritting my teeth, I say the one thing I can to get him off my back about Gwen for the time being.

"There is no girl. There was a girl from my class that I used to help me pass an assignment, and now she's gone. She's no one. She's nothing," I lie, my heart constricting. Bile rises in my throat at the words I just uttered. I meant none of it, but my father seems to believe it.

"Good," he takes a step back, tugging at the end of his suit jacket. "Speak with your coach tomorrow, or I will."

He turns and walks out of the room without another word, leaving me alone with my rage and my thoughts.

How is this my life? Honestly, I know I've been a shitty person. I've treated people poorly due to my name and status, I've been cruel and unforgiving, but I blame it all on my father and my upbringing.

If I'd grown up with a father who actually cared about me, spent time with me, taught me how to be a decent man, maybe everything could have been different. My mother did her best, but a young boy needs a father, and mine was never around.

Okay, enough with the pity party.

I have to figure out what I'm going to do about Davis, and now Walsh.

Luckily, I have plenty of time to think while I'm stuck in this hospital.

Chapter 41

GUINEVERE

The past few days have been rough between going to class and Ryker being injured. I haven't been able to see him yet because I've been so busy, and that's killing me. I wanted to visit him in the hospital, but I decided it might be better if I let his family spend time with him.

Not to say I didn't try. I showed up at the hospital, but I ran into Ryker's brother Logan before I got to his room. Logan told me it was probably best if I wasn't there while his father was visiting. I didn't ask questions. I don't know anything about his family or their dynamic, and I wasn't about to make Logan explain.

I'll talk to Ryker about it when he's ready. Family can be a touchy subject, and if his reaction a few weeks ago to what I said about his life growing up was any indication as to how him and his family get along, there's probably a long story there.

Ryker missed our literary criticism class for the past two days, so I took the liberty of gathering all the notes and work he's missed so I can help him with it later.

I told Professor Whitely everything so she didn't think Ryker was just skipping class, and she of course already knew. His father must have called the dean to let him know. Or maybe Dean Ashby heard about the game the other night. Either way, everyone is aware of what's going on.

I haven't heard from Ashton since the game, thank God. When I saw Ryker get hit, the food in my hands fell to the ground, and I didn't even look back at Ashton as I took off running toward the field.

I'm pretty sure there were people yelling at me to get off, but I couldn't hear them. My ears were ringing, and my heart was pounding, the adrenaline in my body was higher than it had ever been.

All I saw out of my periphery was some guy, probably around the same size as Ryker, running straight for him and tackling him to the ground.

My head whipped around to see what had happened, and then I noticed Ryker on the ground, curled into a fetal position, his arm squeezing his torso. He wouldn't get up, and that made me panic.

I've never felt that kind of fear in my life. Watching Ryker get hurt made me feel things I didn't even know were possible.

In books, authors often write about how it feels like time stops when something traumatic happens, and that's exactly how it felt. It felt like time had frozen and everything else wasn't there. It was just me and Ryker.

I watched as some guys from the other team pulled the mammoth of a man away from Ryker and take him off the field. Ellington won the game by default, and Coach Shaw was pissed. He yelled at Weston U's coach for what seemed like forever.

When they brought the stretcher over to pick Ryker up and wheel him into the nearby ambulance, I just stood there, completely frozen. I vaguely remember Pat and Holland telling me it would be okay and to go back to my house and wait for news.

Obviously, I ignored them because I am not good at being told what to do.

As I work on an assignment for my elementary education class, my phone vibrates on the bed next to me. Ryker's name appears on the screen, and I swear to God my heart almost leaps out of my chest. I have never gotten this excited to see a guy's name on my phone.

Arrogant Asshole (Ryker Steele)

Arrogant Asshole (Ryker Steele)

Can I come over?

Me

Now?

Arrogant Asshole (Ryker Steele)

Yes.

I look at the time. It's a little past midnight. I don't even hesitate.

Me

Yes.

Shit. I haven't even showered, my hair is up on the top of my head in a mess of curls, and I have no makeup on my face. Why didn't I tell him to wait?

The butterflies in my stomach are going haywire as I think about seeing Ryker for the first time in three days. It's been agonizing not being able to touch him and be near him.

I don't know how I'm going to go all winter break without being with him when we're both back at home.

It occurs to me now that I have no idea where Ryker lives. We've spent so much time together, but I still know very little about him. He knows more about me than I do about him, and that makes me a bit uneasy.

Tossing my laptop to the side, I jump into action, immediately running to my bathroom and turning on the shower. Ryker will literally be here any minute, so I need to be quick.

After my five-minute shower, I wrap myself in a towel and leave the bathroom, my hair still in a bun.

My heart stops and I scream when I see Ryker already lying on my bed, looking as sexy as ever with his army green joggers and the black t-shirt hugging his muscles.

His black hair looks messy as if he's been lying down and hasn't brushed it, but he makes it look so fucking good. His green eyes move up and down my body as I stand there clutching the towel around me.

How the hell did he get in? As if reading my mind, Ryker moves his gaze from the hand grasping my towel to my face.

"Haley let me in," he explains, his voice low and hungry. "She was watching TV in the living room."

I thought everyone was in bed, but apparently not. I should have known Haley would still be up. I swear I don't know when that girl sleeps. She stays up for hours during the night, and I don't know how she does it. I practically fall asleep as soon as my head hits a pillow.

"Oh," I squeak, because apparently, I've lost the ability to say anything else.

"Come here," he orders in a gravelly voice that makes my clit pulse.

Taking a step toward him, he holds a hand up to stop me. I halt in my tracks, narrowing my eyebrows in confusion.

"Towel off," he demands. Oh my god. If I had panties on, they'd surely drop.

Letting go of my grasp on the towel, it falls to the ground, pooling around my feet. My arms instinctively wrap around my chest, feeling self-conscious about being on full display as I stare at the ground, my usual confidence gone out the window.

"No," Ryker's deep voice says. I look up to meet his scrutinizing gaze. His eyebrows are pulled together, and he looks disappointed. "Don't hide from me, Rebel."

Hesitantly, I unfold my arms, giving Ryker a full view of my breasts. My nipples pebble from the cold and from the starved look in Rykers eyes. Oh, I've missed him.

"Crawl to me," the seductive tone of his voice sends a tingle down my spine. I can't help the way my eyes widen at his command.

"What?" my voice is barely a whisper as I struggle to even come up with words. A small smirk plays on his lips as he watches my confused expression.

"Crawl to me, Guinevere. Get down on your hands and knees and crawl to me."

I blink. This is not how I was expecting this to go. I've never crawled to any man, ever. And if it were anyone else, I'd probably tell them to fuck right off. But my God, the way Ryker is looking at me right now, I'd do anything for him.

Slowly, I bend down and get to my hands and knees. I begin to move toward him, fully aware of my nakedness. This is so completely demeaning, but I can't even bring myself to care right now.

When I make it to the side of my bed, Ryker sits up, careful to not strain his injury, and throws his legs over the side, spreading them so I can fit between them.

I sit on my legs, kneeling in front of a fully clothed Ryker, waiting for his next demand. His hand reaches out and cups my chin gently, the features of his face softening.

"So fucking perfect," he mutters in a low, sexy tone. I'm so wet. I can already feel the slickness coating my inner thighs, and he hasn't even touched me yet

Putting some pressure under my chin, he forces me to stand, pulling me into him by my waist.

Ryker eyes my breasts before taking one into his mouth, nibbling and sucking on my already hard nipple. My head falls back and I let out a soft moan. I've missed him. I've missed this.

He releases it with a pop before lightly kissing the other one. Looking back up at my face, Ryker grins, and it makes my whole body tingle. He's gorgeous, and he knows it.

Pulling me onto his lap to straddle him, I can feel his hard erection through his joggers as it rubs against my naked flesh.

The friction alone makes me want to combust before we've even started.

"I missed you," he says, trailing light kisses across my collarbone and up my neck. My hands tangle in his hair as I lean my head to the side to give him better access.

Ryker pulls my face to his and within a moment, our lips are together, and my nerve endings are on fire. His warm tongue dips into my mouth and I didn't realize how much I was craving him. His taste, his smell, his touch.

He maneuvers us so that I am flat on my back, and he is on top of me.

"Ryker, your ribs. You shouldn't be lifting me," I tell him, worry laced in my otherwise soft tone. He really shouldn't be doing any strenuous activities while he's healing. It'll just make it worse.

Ryker chuckles lowly. "I'm fine, Rebel."

"Why do you call me that?" I ask, hoping he'll finally give me an answer this time instead of blowing off the question like he's done every time before.

He sighs, shaking his head, a small smile playing on his lips.

"Because…you're the only woman who's ever challenged me. You weren't afraid of me; you didn't run away. You never gave in to my demands, and you defied me at every turn," he explains, caressing my cheek with his thumb. "You, are my little Rebel," he leans in and leaves a soft kiss on my lips.

My heart pounds in my chest, and my lips purse as I try not to grin like a freaking idiot. I don't know what I was expecting, but it wasn't that.

He's right. I'm not like other girls.

"I thought you hated that about me," I say softly, my eyes searching his face.

He chuckles to himself. "I did, at first," he tucks a hair behind my ear. "But then I realized something."

"What?" I ask.

"It was sexy as fuck," he grins, before leaning down and capturing my mouth with his.

When he pulls back, he has a mischievous look on his face.

"Do you have any ice cream?" he asks, and I swear I didn't hear him right. Ice cream? Right now? I'm freaking naked. I thought he was about to fuck me and he's asking about ice cream? He can't be serious.

I blink a few times before replying.

"Um, I think so?"

Ryker doesn't say anything before he hops off the bed and heads for the door, leaving me fully naked on the bed.

"Ryker, what are you doing?" I ask, sitting up on my elbows and staring at him in bewilderment.

"Getting the ice cream," he says simply, as if this conversation isn't completely out of nowhere.

I begin to sit up, but he holds a hand up to stop me.

"Stay. I'll be right back."

He leaves the room, quietly shutting the door behind him, and I flop back onto the bed, extremely confused but a bit intrigued. I stare at the ceiling, my arms covering my bare chest as I wait, impatiently, for Ryker to return.

About two minutes later, Ryker strolls into the room with two bowls of ice cream and a shit eating grin on his face. God, for such a tough guy, he's adorable.

His eyes sparkle with mischief as he looks at me, setting the bowls on my nightstand.

"Mint chocolate chip, my favorite," he says, his voice deep and smooth like bourbon.

My stomach flutters. "Mine too," I tell him. "But can I get dressed before we eat it?"

Ryker's eyes go dark, and I can see the desire building in them.

"Well," he began, his voice husky, "I was thinking maybe we could find a use for the ice cream besides eating it."

Before I can ask what he means, he takes a spoonful of the cold treat and blows on it suggestively, taking a long lick off the spoon. I'm still not exactly sure what he intends to do with the ice cream, but I'm ready to find out.

Chapter 42

GUINEVERE

Ryker's been teasing me, and I can tell he enjoys seeing me squirm. I, however, am over it. I need him to touch me. I'm going to crazy if he takes any longer.

Ryker dips the spoon back into the ice cream, taking a big scoop, and bringing it to my mouth. I instinctively lick my lips as I take it in, tasting the sweet ice cream.

Without warning, he dips his fingers into the bowl and scoops up a generous amount of the cold, creamy dessert. My eyes widen in surprise as he traces a path of the ice cream down my chest, stopping to circle my nipples.

My breath hitches at the cold sensation, and my breathing becomes rapid. What is he doing?

I begin to squirm under his cold fingers, but he holds me down so I can't move.

"No moving. We wouldn't want to get ice cream all over your sheets, now would we?" Ryker asks in a teasing tone. I just stare at him because I'm honestly at a loss for words. I've never done anything like this, and I think I love it.

Ryker dips his spoon in the bowl and picks up another scoop and hovers it right between my breasts. I wait, my heart going wild.

Bringing the spoonful of ice cream down to my chest, I hiss when the cold touches my skin. Goosebumps rise all over my body as Ryker drags the ice cream down my belly, stopping at my bellybutton. He circles it with the spoon, the ice cream dripping into it. God, I'm going to be a sticky mess after this, but I can't even bring myself to care.

He uses his tongue to lick the ice cream off my naval before trailing his tongue all the way back up to my lips. I can taste the mint on his lips, and then on his tongue as he dips it into my mouth.

My back arches off the bed as I let out a soft whimper into Ryker's mouth.

I pout when he pulls away again, until he grabs another spoonful of ice cream and backs down my legs so he is kneeling between them. Bending them so my knees practically touch my stomach, he lowers the spoon down to my inner thigh, leaving a wet, cold trail up to my bare pussy. He does the same to the other side before leaning down and using his warm tongue to lick it up. Holy shit.

I can feel his hot breath as he gets closer to my pussy, and I want him to kiss me there. I need him to.

"Ryker, please," I plead. His green eyes peek at me from his space between my legs, and I swear I'm going to come just from the look in his eyes and the feeling of his breathing against my skin. He looks back up at me, a playful smirk on his face. He's going to make me say it.

"Please what?"

"Please eat my pussy. Make me come," I sound pathetic, but I don't care. The feral look on Ryker's face is worth it.

"My little Rebel, asking so nicely," he coos, nipping at my inner thigh. "Okay, baby. I'll make you come," he promises before diving down and taking my clit in his mouth.

I gasp as the feeling of his tongue circling my clit overtakes me. It feels so good, and I'm so desperate for release that I don't think this is going to take long at all.

He licks and sucks and my God, I'm going to come. My belly tightens and I can feel the heat spread in my body as my orgasm builds. Ryker must be able to tell I'm close because he grips my hips tightly and keeps me from wriggling underneath him.

"Ryker, I'm going to," I squeeze the sheets in my fists as my eyes close.

"Open your eyes, baby. I want you to watch me," he demands, my eyes popping open as I do as he says, watching him bring me to the edge.

This is so erotic, and it feels so good, and I can't hold back anymore.

My body tenses and I come hard on Ryker's tongue, letting out a loud moan and hurriedly covering my mouth with my hand, remembering my roommates are all sleeping.

Ryker groans. "Fuck, Gwen," he breaths, his eyes flickering with lust. "I fucking love tasting you."

I breath heavily, still coming down from my orgasm as I stare at Ryker who is wearing a cocky grin on his handsome face.

Sitting up to meet him, I reach for the hem of his shirt, pulling it over his head. My eyes move over the bandage covering the defined muscles of his torso. My fingers trace the material softly as I look back up to see his wary expression.

"Are you okay?" I ask, realizing now that what he just did may have hurt him. Ryker nods, grabbing my hand and linking his fingers with mine.

"Yes. I don't even feel it anymore," he assures me, but I think he's lying. I can tell he's still in some pain, but I don't push.

Pulling my hand from his, I drag it down to the waistband of his joggers.

"Lay down," I order. His eyes narrow as a smirk plays on his lips, doing as I say and laying down on his back. He winces a bit, and my heart squeezes. I hate that he's in pain.

I pull his pants down his legs, along with his boxers and watch as his large cock springs free. My mouth actually waters at the sight. Oh, how I've missed him.

Straddling him, I smile wickedly, grabbing a spoonful of ice cream and hovering over Ryker, sucking the sweet treat off with a loud, satisfied moan.

"Mmm, delicious," I taunt, my eyes never leaving his. Then, without warning, I lean down and drag the ice cream-coated spoon across his chest and up his neck, licking it up as I go.

I smile as his hands land on my waist, squeezing me tightly.

"Tease," he growls playfully, his eyes sparkling with desire.

I pout. "Me? A tease?" I ask in mock offense, and I'm honestly shocked at how sultry and seductive I sound. "You love it."

Ryker's breath quickens as I lean forward, my breasts grazing his chest as I trace the cold spoon along his neck again, drawing a shiver from him.

I giggle at his reaction and drag the icy metal down his chest, teasing his nipples and making them harden.

"You're so sensitive," I murmur with a grin. Ryker growls.

Dipping the spoon back into the ice cream, I bring it to Ryker's lips and watch as he takes the sweet offering into his mouth, his eyes closing in pleasure.

I withdraw the spoon slowly, catching a drop of ice cream that threatens to fall from his lip with my thumb, which I then suck into my own mouth, moaning at the taste.

"I understand now why you were enjoying this so much," I tell him. "This is fun," I say, my voice hoarse with desire.

I move the spoon lower, skipping over the large bandage that covers his ribs, and landing right above his cock. It twitches in anticipation, hard and throbbing as the cold metal draws closer. I deliberately take my time, teasing him mercilessly as I run the spoon along his inner thighs, eliciting delicious shudders from him.

Finally, I reach his cock, and with deliberate slowness, I coat the shaft with the cold, creamy treat, starting from the base and moving upwards. Ryker bucks his hips slightly, unable to control himself as the cold ice cream drips down his length.

"Mmm," I moan, my eyes sparkling with pleasure.

Scooping more ice cream onto the spoon, I hold it over Ryker's swollen member. I let a drop fall onto the engorged head, watching as it slowly slides down, creating a sticky trail.

I repeat this, covering his length with the dessert, before taking him in my hand and stroking him slowly.

Ryker groans, his eyes rolling back slightly as I pump up and down. I lean forward, my hair falling to the side as I lick off a stray drop of ice cream from his tip. I hum in satisfaction, making his cock twitch between my lips.

"Jesus, Gwen," he gasps, his hands sinking into my hair. "You're driving me crazy."

I smile against his length, relishing in the power I hold over him in this moment. Taking him deeper into my mouth, I suck and swirl my tongue, combining the taste of ice cream with the saltiness of his precum. My hand continues to stroke him in perfect rhythm, my fingers coated in the sticky sweetness.

Ryker's hips begin to move in time with my mouth, his breath coming in ragged gasps. I can tell he's close, so I slow my pace, determined to draw out his pleasure.

I sit up, smiling at him impishly. Ryker groans, his eyes full of desire and frustration.

"Not yet," I whisper, crawling back on top of him and lowering myself slowly, my eyes never leaving his as I slide down his cock. I gasp at the fullness and Ryker lets out a hiss.

Oh, fuck. This is exactly what I needed. How is it possible for him to feel this good?

I begin to move up and down slowly, getting used to his size. His hands grasp my hips, moving with me as I bounce and grind on his cock.

"You feel so fucking good," I pant, my hands landing on his chest. Ryker winces and I remember his ribs. "Shit, I'm sorry," I say, grimacing. He chuckles lowly.

"It's okay, Rebel," he says as he reaches up to cup my face, his eyes darkening with need. "Now keep fucking me."

I hadn't even realized I'd stopped moving.

As I begin to move again, Ryker groans and his hands find my hips again. My breasts bounce with each thrust, my juices coating his length as I ride him. Our bodies move in perfect rhythm.

I lean forward, this time setting my hands on his shoulders as I quicken my pace. Ryker thrusts upwards to meet me, our bodies slapping together in a rhythmic cadence. My whimpers are soft, mingling with his grunts of pleasure as we both chase our release.

"That's it, baby girl," Ryker growls, his voice rough with desire. "Ride me hard."

His words send tingles down my spine, and I ride him harder, ignoring the way my body feels like it's on fire.

"Ryker," I pant, my head falling back as I feel my core tighten.

"Tell me you're mine," he commands in a deep, breathy voice.

"I'm yours," I breathe, trying to concentrate on the feeling of pleasure at the base of my spine. His grip on me grows tighter, and a hand wraps around my neck, squeezing lightly. My eyes pop open and I meet his wild gaze.

"Only mine," he growls. "No one else's."

"Yes, yes. Only yours," I assure him.

Ryker thrusts into me hard. Once, twice, three times, and I'm about to lose it.

"And I'm yours…" he tells me, his voice softer than before. My heart skips a beat. He's mine. Ryker Steele, the man that has never been seen in a relationship is giving himself to me. And that feels better than anything I could have imagined.

"I want everyone on this campus to know that you, Guinevere Sharpe, are my girlfriend, and I'm your boyfriend," he thrusts again, and this time he hits spot that sends me over the fucking edge of the tallest cliff.

My pussy clenches around him, milking his cock as my orgasm rips through me. Ryker's hips snap up to meet me, his hands gripping my ass as he moves faster, harder.

"Yesss, baby," he hisses. "Come for me, Gwen. Show me how good it feels."

His words send bolts of electricity through me, and I cry out, my body shaking as my walls pulse around him. Ryker follows, his cock twitching as he releases himself deep inside me.

I fall forward, careful not to hit Ryker's chest too hard, laying my head on his shoulder. A light sheen of sweat covers us both as our heavy breathing slows down.

Ryker's chest rises and falls with his breathing as he leaves a light kiss on my temple.

I roll off of him, landing on my back beside him. Staring at the ceiling, I try to think of something to say, but there are literally no words to describe what just happened.

I have never in my life been so turned on, and I certainly never knew that sex could be this fun.

Chapter 43

GUINEVERE

Lying next to Ryker feels like home.

My head moves up and down with the rhythm of Ryker's slow breaths as I lay on his shoulder with my leg draped over his.

Even with the bandage on, he looks toned and sculpted, with little to no imperfections. I trace my finger over his collarbone and above his bandage. A reminder that he's not as invincible as he thinks he is.

Guilt seeps into my chest as I think about how I wasn't able to see him in the hospital. Does he think I didn't care enough to check on him?

"I tried to visit you…" I whisper softly. "In the hospital. I came, but your brother turned me away. He told me your parents were there and that it wasn't a good idea."

Ryker's body stiffens. For a moment, I wonder if it was the mention of his brother turning me away or the mention of his parents that made him react.

He doesn't reply, so I continue.

"Is there a reason it wasn't a good idea? Would your parents not approve of me?" I ask hesitantly. I may not be poor, but I'm certainly not Steele level rich. From what I know about the Elite's they usually have strict rules on who they can and cannot be with. Many still follow the archaic idea of arranged marriages.

I have a feeling I wouldn't be the girl Ryker's parents would pick for him. I have no title, no status in society. I am no one special.

Ryker clears his throat. "My father has this notion that I must marry a woman of status. Meaning, the daughter of a legacy

Elite, or someone from a high society family," he sighs. "It's ridiculous and obsolete, but it's what has been expected for generations."

My stupid heart skips at the prospect of marriage, not that I'm at all ready for that yet, but it does sound nice.

Leaning on my elbow, I hover over him. His eyes meet mine, and I smile. Ryker cocks an eyebrow and smirks.

"I didn't expect you to be smiling after I told you how ancient my father's thoughts are," he teases. I flip my hair behind my shoulder dramatically and pretend to examine my nails, my lips pursed.

I've never really told anyone this because it hasn't come up, and I don't think it matters much, because I am not a man.

"Gwen…" Ryker's voice is deep with warning.

"I may or may not be an Elite Legacy…" I tell him, biting the inside of my cheek. Ryker searches my face for a moment, his emerald eyes widening when he realizes I'm not kidding.

"Wait, seriously?" he asks in disbelief. I nod, biting my lip.

"My father was an Elite. Wade Sharpe. That's the only reason I'm at Ellington U. I grew up in Barrington," I explain, watching as Ryker's face contorts from confusion to shock.

"Wow. I grew up in East Greenwich."

My eyes widen. "No, you didn't. Seriously? That's only a thirty-minute drive away!" I squeal, a little too excited. Ryker chuckles.

"Yeah, I wasn't expecting that," he says.

"What?" I ask.

"Any of it," he shrugs.

We lay in comfortable silence for a few minutes before I decide to ask some more questions since I still don't know much about him. He's not an open book, and I can tell he doesn't like talking about his feelings.

I know his family is wealthy, I know his father owns a very prestigious security company, and I know their family donates a lot of money to this school. I know he has a younger brother, but I don't know how much they get along, or what their dynamic is like.

I haven't really seen them together much, but the few times I have, they've seemed standoffish. Not as close as Ellie and Holland are, and I don't know if that's normal or not. I didn't grow up with siblings, so I'm not completely sure how close you're supposed to be to your brother or sister.

"Do you and your family get along?" I ask cautiously. Ryker's hold on me tightens, and I know he's going to shut down. "Please, Ryker. I'd really like to know more about you."

I want him to open up to me. He's already given me more than he's ever given anyone else, and I'm so grateful for that. I want him to want to share with me. It would show that he trusts me.

Ryker lets out a long, deep breath, as if contemplating whether or not to share anything.

He stares up at the ceiling.

"My father and I have never gotten along. When I was younger, he was rarely ever home, and when he was, he'd be in his office all night. He never took me to baseball games or taught me how to throw a football. As I got older, he only spoke to me about The Steele Corporation and how I needed to be prepared to take over one day," Ryker chuckles under his breath.

"It's funny. I never wanted to take over the company. I wanted to branch out and do my own thing. I didn't want to be tethered to my family name. *His* last name. But now, I just know he's doing some shady shit. All he cares about is his money and his status in society."

My face falls as I take in everything he's just told me about his father. I can't say I grew up the same way since my father did actually spend time with me. It's only been the last few years that he's turned into a shitty dad.

I imagine a young Ryker sitting in his yard with a baseball in his hand, all alone, waiting for his father to play catch, but he never comes. My heart aches for him.

Ryker repositions himself so he's lying on his side, facing me. He grimaces slightly, then he tucks a piece of hair behind my ear. I smile at the sweet gesture.

"My mother was a good mom. She made sure we had everything we needed, tucked us in at night, and helped us with homework. She was a stay-at-home mom, so she spent a lot more time with us," his thumb gently rubs my cheek as he continues. "But she was a pushover. She'd do whatever my dad said, and she never tried to stop him when he'd…get physical with me. Logan never experienced what I did. He's only a year younger, but for some shitty reason, I got the brunt of it."

"Are you and Logan close?" I ask, already assuming the answer is no but wanting to hear him say it. Ryker laughs sardonically.

"Ha, no. We were never really close, not even as kids. We're polar opposites, and when I started to notice that dad was treating us differently, I began to distance myself. I turned cold and unforgiving. I blamed my mom for staying with my father and letting him treat me poorly. Logan never saw it that way, and it made things difficult between us."

God. I never realized how much he'd been through. Not that I would have; I didn't know who he was.

After I met him, I thought he was just another arrogant, rich asshole that thought the world owed him something. But hearing the story about his family and the way he grew up, it kind of makes sense. The tough guy persona, the dickhead façade, it was all a protective ruse he'd built up from his childhood.

Bringing my hand up to his cheek, I lean in and give him a feather light kiss on his lips.

"Thank you for sharing that with me. It means more than you know," I tell him, my voice thick with emotion.

"Anything for my girlfriend," he says as a wide grin spreads across his face. My stomach flutters as his words sink in.

"Girlfriend, huh?" I ask. "I think I like that," a grin that matches his taking over my features.

Good," he pulls me closer to him and kisses me, making time stop. "God, Rebel. You are intoxicating."

I pull back, narrowing my eyes.

"Now I need to give you a nickname," I pout. Something other than arrogant asshole, since I no longer believe that's the real him. The real Ryker is kind and passionate, he's possessive but caring, protective and loyal.

Ryker laughs. "What, no more asshole with more money than brains" he jokes, recalling what he'd overheard me tell Damian. My cheeks heat at the memory and I swat his arm playfully.

"No. What about…" I tap my index finger on my chin a few times. "Sour Patch Kid?"

Ryker's face twists with confusion. "Sour Patch Kid?"

I nod. "Yeah, you know. At first they're sour and then they turn sweet," I say with a shit eating grin. Ryker rolls his eyes.

"Next," he demands. I bite my lip as I think.

"Hmm…" I hum. And then it hits me. "Hot Shot."

His brows furrow. "Hot Shot. I like it," he winks.

"Hot Shot it is, then."

Packing has taken so much longer than I planned. I really don't have that much stuff to bring home, but I keep getting distracted when I find things I'd forgotten I had.

Luckily, Lainey, Ellie, Haley, and I will be living in this house until the end of the year in May when classes end. So I don't have to pack up everything I own and move it back home. All I need right now is some clothes, shoes, and obviously toiletries, but I won't pack those until this weekend.

I am leaving on Sunday to head home with Damian for Thanksgiving, and part of me can't wait to see my mom. I haven't seen her in months, and as much as we talk every day, I still miss her.

After Ryker left Thursday morning, Lainey and Ellie busted into my room demanding I tell them everything that had happened the night prior.

"Sounded like you two had a really nice time last night," Ellie had said with a wink.

"Trust me, there was no talking involved. They were definitely fucking all night long," Lainey chortled.

Then, Lainey informed me of a party at the Elite mansion tonight, and of course I'm being dragged. But now, I don't mind being dragged. I get to see Ryker, my boyfriend, my Hot Shot. My heart swells at the thought.

I have already begun to fall for him more than I ever planned to, and I know if this ends badly, it'll ruin me. Everything in me is telling me to run. To flee and never look back. But it's not possible. I can't bring myself to stay away from him.

Shaking away the negative thoughts, I head for the bathroom to take a quick shower after I've decided that packing can wait until tomorrow. I got most of it done anyway.

After I throw my wet hair into a bun and pull on an oversized tee, I check my phone. I have one text from Damian and two from Ryker. I decide to open Damian's first.

Damian Cole

Damian Cole

I'm coming over at nine. Tell Lainey not to be naked when I walk in this time please.

Me

When was she naked?!

Damian Cole

When I came over on Tues. You were at the library still. I swear I'm scarred for life.

Me

Omg!!

I make a mental note to ask Lainey about that later. I'm surprised she didn't tell me. I can imagine Lainey walking around naked and Damian walking in while she walks out of her room. She probably threw something at him. I kind of wish I was there to see it.

I pull up Ryker's texts next, and my face heats with surprise.

Hotshot

Hotshot

I am going to fuck you so hard tonight. Don't wear any panties, I'll just tear them off.

Me

Oh really? I'll make sure to wear my tightest jeans.

Hotshot

You just love to test me, don't you, Rebel? I think you deserve a smack on the ass for that comment.

Me

I look forward to it.

Hotshot

You're killing me, Gwen.

I toss my phone on the bed with a huge grin on my face. The result of talking to Ryker every single time.

Ryker has quickly become one of my favorite people, and I love talking to him. I love learning more about him and feeling like I can tell him things. What we have was unexpected to say the least, but it's also so incredibly strong.

A knock on my door interrupts my train of thought.

"Come in," I call. Two seconds later, Lainey strolls in looking like a fucking supermodel with her tight, short skirt, sequined halter top, and stiletto heels, her hair pulled into a half up half down look.

"Damn, Lainey. You look hot as fuck," I tell her, my jaw practically on the floor as I look her up and down. Lainey is insanely pretty, and she knows it. I've never met anyone more confident in themselves.

The thing about Lainey is that even though she knows she's attractive, she's not a total bitch about it. You know those girls that think they're hot shit, so they treat everyone else like peasants? Yeah, Lainey is not one of them.

I'm confident for the most part, and I typically don't give a shit what people think about me. But I'm nowhere near as confident as Lainey is.

Ellie is the opposite of us both. She's shy and reserved. She's quiet and doesn't draw attention to herself. The only time she's ever done something remotely out of her comfort zone was when she kissed that guy to piss off her brother.

She has no reason to be shy or self-conscious. She's gorgeous, and she's sweet. She's a catch, and I wish she could see it like everyone else can.

Lainey takes a look around my room and grimaces. "It's a mess in here! You were supposed to be packing, not throwing all of your shit on the ground," she lectures. Mom mode activated.

"Sorry, *mom*," I tease, rolling my eyes.

"What are you wearing tonight?" she asks, walking into my closet and pushing things around as she examines my clothes.

Finally, she pulls out a small blue dress with the tags still on that I'd completely forgotten about. I bought it last semester for the Fire and Ice dance, but I never went.

"This is perfect. This is what you're wearing," she directs, handing me the dress. "Get dressed. I'll do your hair and makeup."

With that, she walks out of my room, leaving me to change. I shake my head and chuckle to myself as I put the dress on.

Lainey did my makeup and curled my hair. When I look in my mirror, I don't even recognize myself. The light blue dress hugs my curves perfectly. The plunging neckline shows off my cleavage, and the hem of the skirt lands just under my ass cheeks.

I honestly might as well not be wearing anything at all. I don't know what I was thinking when I bought it. This is way out of my comfort zone.

But admittedly, I do look hot. The dark eyeliner and mascara make my blue eyes pop, my cheeks are a dark pink color, and my lips are a nice shade of red.

Walking out into the living room where Ellie and Lainey sit on the couch, and Damian sits in the corner in his normal chair, my face heats with embarrassment as they all turn to look at me.

"Wow, Gwenny. You look… wow," Damian says, his mouth practically hanging open. I look down my body and then back up.

"You think?" I ask shyly. I do think I look good, but it's always good to hear it from other people. Especially the people closest to you that you know won't lie just to make you feel good.

"I knew that dress was a good idea," Lainey squeals, patting herself on the back for her wardrobe choice.

Laughing, I agree with her. "Yeah, it was a good choice."

"Ryker is definitely going to be drooling tonight," Ellie teases with a wink. I roll my eyes.

"Oh, shut up," I tell her with a small smile because honestly, I like the thought of Ryker drooling over me.

Damian jumps up from his seat, clapping his hands together and heading for the front door.

"Alright, let's go party people!" he exclaims, opening the door and heading out with the three of us following right behind, and for the first time, I feel excited to be going to a party.

Chapter 44

GUINEVERE

The Elite mansion is full of rowdy, drunk kids and the vibes are unhinged. Everyone is excited to be leaving for winter break, and it shows. I've never seen the mansion this packed. It's like a can of sardines.

I've been looking for Ryker since I walked in, but I can't even see in front of me because of the bodies at all sides of me. I hold Lainey's hand as Ellie holds Lainey in a human chain as we weave through the people. Damian follows closely behind me. When I look back, he is scanning the room as if he's looking for someone, but I don't know who he'd be looking for.

When we finally make it to the kitchen, Ellie grabs us all some drinks. She hands Lainey and I seltzers and then gives Damian a beer. We clink our drinks together in the air.

"Cheers!" we say in unison.

Half an hour later, I still haven't been able to find Ryker, and I'm beginning to have a weird feeling in the pit of my stomach. Where is he?

I'm starting to feel a buzz, and I've only had two seltzers. Lainey is ahead of Ellie and I by at least three drinks, so she's having a blast as she dances with one of the Elite freshmen. I think his name is Teddy. He's sweet, and it doesn't seem like he's been totally corrupted by the Elite yet.

Teddy is handsome. He has dirty blonde, shaggy hair and warm brown eyes that made you feel safe and comfortable. I'm not worried about Lainey dancing with him, although I have feeling someone won't be happy about it if he sees her.

But Holland hasn't spotted us yet. He's too busy talking to Mason and Patrick. Where is Ryker?

Is he okay? Is he with another girl? Did he decide I wasn't what he wanted? Am I not good enough?

No, that can't be what it is. He was just texting me about wanting to fuck me. He wouldn't do that to me. Not after everything we've been through. Right?

I don't like where my thoughts are going. I hate feeling insecure and questioning myself. I promised myself I'd never let a guy make me feel like this again, and here I am, at a party that's supposed to be celebrating the end of the semester, worrying about Ryker and how he might be over me.

Taking a deep breath, I try to center myself. I take another sip of my seltzer and distract myself by watching Lainey and Teddy dance.

In my periphery, I watch Damian take a swig of his beer as he stares at something in the distance, or someone.

I follow his line of sight and land on Allie Moore, his partner from out literary criticism class. My eyes narrow as I look back at him.

"You like her, don't you?" I ask, knowing he'll most likely deny it. Damian hates talking about his feelings. He hasn't had a girlfriend since high school, since Mikayla DeSantis broke his heart.

Damian was completely in love with the girl, and they dated for a while, but one day she decided she wasn't ready for a serious relationship and broke up with him. The next day in school, she was walking hand and hand with Paul Hayes, the star of our high school's hockey team.

He's sworn off relationship since then, only having casual hookups and one-night stands. I've tried to tell him that not all relationships end up that way, but he didn't want to hear it.

But I haven't seen him look at a girl this way since Mikayla.

Damian scoffs. "No?"

I raise my eyebrows, trying to hide the smirk that's spreading on my lips.

"You totally do," I say, and even in the dimly lit room, I can see his face turn bright red. "Aw, Damian. You have a crush!" I playfully slap his arm as he shakes his head and looks at me.

"I do not like her," he lies through his teeth, causing me to roll my eyes. Why can't he just admit he has feelings for her?

"Dude, you've been watching her all night. When she danced with Eric Kastle, you looked like you wanted to murder him. You like her."

"Drop it, Gwen. Allie doesn't even see me that way," he says, and I swear he sounds disappointed. His shoulders stiffen and he stands up straighter.

"How do you know? Have you asked her?" I wonder.

"No, of course not. But she doesn't look at me like she wants to fuck, so I know she isn't interested," he explains, shrugging his broad shoulders. I want to hit him.

"Just because she doesn't look at you like she wants to jump your bones, doesn't mean she doesn't like you. Not everyone only thinks about sex, Damian. Go ask her out," I urge.

"Ask who out?" Ellie chimes in. I didn't even know she was listening. Damian sighs loudly, finishing off his beer.

I knew getting Damian to admit he has feelings for a girl would be like pulling teeth, but a small part of me was hoping that he'd break down a bit easier.

"He likes Allie Moore, but he won't do anything about it," I explain. Ellie jumps up and down with a squeal.

"Omg, I knew you had a heart. Go ask her. Allie is so sweet!" Ellie's smiling face looks from Damian to Allie, who is dancing with a group of her friends. Her auburn hair looks dark under the dim light of the room, and I can see why Damian would like her. She seems like fun.

Damian rolls his eyes, and I can tell he's breaking down. He looks back at me, his face softer and more vulnerable.

"Are you sure she'll like me?" he asks, and my heart squeezes. That bitch Mikayla really messed him up. I hate her. The thought makes me want to find her and punch her in the face. Damian is too good, too pure to think that he's not worth more than meaningless sex with random girls.

Placing my hands on both of his biceps, I look him right in the eye.

"Damian, you are by far one of the best guys I know, and you deserve someone just as amazing as you are. You deserve to be happy. If Allie doesn't see it, someone else will. But I think Allie will feel the same way you do," I assure him. "Just go ask her to dance. What's the worst that can happen? She says no?"

Damian lets out a sarcastic laugh. "Exactly. That's the worst thing that could happen. If she says no, I'll have to find the nearest cliff to fling myself off of. I'd have to transfer schools," he panics. I squeeze his arms.

"Stop. It'll be fine. She's not going to say no. Now go," I order, pushing him toward the dancefloor. He gives me a death glare before turning around and hesitantly walking to Allie.

When Damian approaches, Allie stops dancing and smiles at him. I don't hear what they say, but Allie must have said yes, because when the next song starts, they're dancing together. I melt when I see the smile on Damian's face.

"You go, bestie," I whisper to myself, a proud smile on my face. It falls when my stupid brain remembers Ryker hasn't come to find me yet. Damn you, brain. Damn you.

Out of the corner of my eye, I watch as Holland approaches Ellie and I, his eyes glued to Lainey and the guy she's dancing with. Here we go.

"What is she doing?" he seethes. Wow, subtle.

"Dancing," Ellie says pointedly. Holland's eyes narrow but don't move from Lainey as she grinds her ass against Teddy.

"I see that. Why is she dancing with him?" he asks menacingly. I shrug.

"He asked her. Teddy's nice."

"Yeah well, he just wants to get in her pants," he accuses. I stifle a laugh at his obvious jealousy.

"Why do you care?" Ellie questions her brother. His shoulders straighten and his face looks defensive.

"I just don't think she should be dancing with him," he goes back to watching and I watch him, seeing the exact moment he decides he's going to do something about it.

"Fuck this," he says, storming over to Lainey and pushing Teddy backwards. He grabs Lainey's arm and pulls her back toward us. Lainey's face is furious as she fights with Holland, trying to get out of his grasp.

"What the hell, Holland?" she hisses. He lets go of Lainey's arm, taking a step closer to her.

"You needed a break," he claims. Lainey's nostrils flare with anger. Yeah, she's pissed.

"Who says?"

"I do."

She takes a step forward until their faces are inches away from one another. Ellie and I exchange a wary look, waiting to see what Lainey's going to do. She doesn't take kindly to being told what to do, and Holland is on thin ice.

"Fuck you, Monroe."

Lainey disappears into the sea of people, leaving Holland standing here with an angry glare on his face. A minute later, Holland storms off in the opposite direction.

Man, I feel bad for them since they're going to have to put up with each other for another year.

Reality sets back in as I remember the fact that Ryker still has not made an appearance.

"You okay?" Ellie asks over the music. I nod, not wanting to explain the worry I'm feeling over not seeing Ryker yet.

"Yeah, just a bit warm. It's really hot in here," I lie. Ellie nods in understanding.

"It is. Do you want to step outside? I'll go with you," she offers, her eyes sincere.

"No, it's okay. I have to go to the bathroom," I tell her.

"Okay. I'll be here. Text me if you need anything," she smiles sweetly, and I glance over to Lainey and Damian one more time before heading for the stairs.

I don't have to pee, but I needed an excuse to go look for Ryker. Since I haven't seen him downstairs, maybe he's upstairs in his room or hanging out in the living room. But why wouldn't he text me to let me know.

The music pulsates through the walls, and the sound of the crowd dissipates as I make my way up the stairs. I walk into the living room to find it's empty. My shoulders slump and I let out a sigh.

Okay, so he's not there. Maybe he's in his room.

Walking down the hall, I find Ryker's room and open the door slowly. Peaking inside, I realize he's not there either. What the hell?

Anxiety ripples through me as I pull out my phone to send a text to Ryker.

Hotshot

Me

Where are you?

I shove my phone back into my pocket and begin to head for the bathroom to check myself. I'm sure I look like a mess since I've been sweating from the heat downstairs.

When I turn the corner, I bump into someone. God, I really do have a habit of running into people.

I'm surprised when I look up to see a girl I recognize.

I recognize her blonde hair and large hazel eyes framed by thick lashes as her lips twist in a mischievous smile. Jealousy surges through my veins as I remember her talking to Ryker in the library during our first session.

I don't really know what they were speaking about, but Ryker seemed really uninterested in the conversation, and she seemed butthurt over it.

"Oh, hi," the girl purrs, her voice low and smoky. "You must be Gwen."

My heart stutters. "Y-yes, I am. Do I know you?" I try my best to sound confident but I'm doing a shit job at it.

The girl laughs, and it's a sound that sends a shiver down my spine. "Not yet, but I certainly know you. Or at least, I know who you're looking for." Her gaze flicks over my shoulder, and her smile turns bitter. "Ryker, right?"

I feel a rush of embarrassment that this girl has seen right through me. Am I that obvious?

"Yeah… Do you know where he is?" I'm not sure why I'm even asking her. But she might know something about where Ryker is right now.

The girl steps closer, her perfume intoxicating, and goosebumps run down my arms as she whispers in my ear.

"Oh, I don't know where he is right now. But I do know where he was last night," she says ominously. My eyes narrow, and my heart picks up speed. What is she talking about? "He really likes it when you do this thing with your tongue while you, well, you know. I mean, you must know," she shrugs, and the bitter smile turns into the bitchiest smile I've ever seen.

My heart feels like it stops all together. I picture Ryker's face and his easy smile, remembering the way my pulse quickened whenever he was near.

I trusted him, and I'd allowed myself to hope that he felt the same way about me. Now, all I feel is the sting of betrayal, a bitter taste in my mouth.

The girl must see the effect her words have on me because she takes a step back, her expression transforming into one of false empathy.

"I'm sorry, I didn't mean to blindside you. I'm Amy, by the way. Ryker and I have been hooking up for a while. I think he might even want to make it official," she smiles, and I have a strong urge to slap her across her bitchy face.

I feel a rising sense of anger as I look into her hazel eyes.

"Why are you telling me this?"

Amy's eyes flash with a mixture of emotions, what looks like regret, resentment, and something like satisfaction.

"Because I've seen you two around campus together, and it looked like you were getting a little too comfortable, so I wanted you to know the truth. You seem like a good girl, and I wouldn't want to see you get crushed by a guy like Ryker," she explains, not sounding the least bit sincere.

My mind is reeling, and I feel nauseous. I let my guard down, I let myself feel, I let Ryker make me look like a fucking idiot. Why would he do this?

Amy's eyes darken. "Ryker likes to keep his options open. He always has, and you don't strike me as the kind of girl that likes to have casual relationships," she says, her eyes wandering down my body and back up to my face.

"Are you okay?" Amy asks, her voice turning soft as my ears begin to ring. "Look, I didn't come here to ruin your night. I just wanted you to know the truth. Ryker's a manwhore, and I didn't think it was fair for him to lead you on."

I know she doesn't actually give a shit about me or my feelings. She only wanted to rub it in my face that Ryker has also been sleeping with her. "Thanks," I say, barely audible as I turn and head down the steps, my heart heavy and my thoughts racing.

I need to get out of here, to escape the stifling air of deception that now seemed to permeate the party.

As I walk toward the front door, Lainey and Ellie find me, their eyes wide with concern.

"There you are!" Lainey exclaims. "We've been looking everywhere for you. Ellie said you went to the bathroom, but you've been gone a while."

I take a deep breath, steeling myself. "I want to leave," I state.

Lainey and Ellie exchange a confused glance. "Why? What happened?" Ellie asks.

I shake my head, not wanting to reiterate what just happened upstairs with Amy. I just want to go home and finish packing. I need to go home.

"Nothing, I just… I need to go. You guys stay, have fun," I tell them. Their expressions are a mix of worry and hesitation. "Seriously, go. I'm fine," I send them a fake smile before I turn around and head out of the Elite mansion without looking back.

How could I have been so stupid? I knew who Ryker was before getting involved with him. I knew he'd break my heart.

Why did I let him?

Chapter 45

RYKER

I received a text from my father around eight forty-five tonight asking Logan and I to meet him on campus at Whittaker Hall. Logan and I were preparing for the end of semester party at the mansion when our phones went off.

Father, Logan

Father

Meet me at Whittaker Hall asap.

My leg bounces rapidly as I sit in my father's campus office which he was given by Dean Ashby for his work with Ellington University and the Elite. My palms are sweaty against the wooden handles of the chair.

Logan sits next me, not looking nearly as agitated as I feel. But why would he be? He doesn't get the brunt of our father's disdain.

I feel his eyes on me as my leg continues to bob.

"Dude, calm down," Logan whispers, his eyes searching my face.

"Easy for you to say. He doesn't hate you," I grit out. Logan rolls his eyes.

"He doesn't hate you, Ryker. Don't be ridiculous," he hisses.

"He has a funny way of showing it," I scoff. My father has hated me since the moment I told him I didn't want to work for The Steele Corporation under his ruling. He thinks I'm disrespectful, unruly, and he can't stand someone going against him.

The door opens and shuts with a click as my father walks into the room and takes a seat across from us, the air turning instantly ten degrees cooler.

His black hair is slicked back, as always, the suit he's wearing is nicely pressed, and he's still sporting a mob mustache. The wrinkles under his eyes and on his forehead as he scowls make him look years older than his age of forty-five.

I realize now that I don't even recall a time I've seen my father smile. He's always had this perpetual scowl on his face. At least around me.

I can't imagine what he wanted to meet for that couldn't have waited until Logan and I came home in a few days. My hands grip the handles of the chair tight as my father begins to speak.

"Hello, boys. Thank you for coming so quickly. I needed to discuss some urgent matters with you," he says before tossing a manila folder in my direction. I can feel Logan's eyes on me as I pick up the folder and open it.

My jaw tightens as I study the pages in front of me. A picture of a man who looks like Gwen stares back at me. They have the same sapphire blue eyes.

My eyes scan the paper.

Wade Sharpe, class of 2001   *Birthday: April 7th, 1979*

Age: 45

Location: Los Angeles, CA

Active Elite Member from 1998 to 2001

Elite Status: Alumni   *Marital Status: Divorced*

Children: Guinevere Lane Sharpe

Appearance: Brunette, 6'0, blue eyes, Caucasian

Rae Quinn

My blood runs cold as I realize what this is. It's a file on Gwen's dad, on her family, on her.

I flip through the other pages, seeing a full file on Gwen's mother and on Gwen herself. I can't help myself from reading through Gwen's file.

Guinevere Lane Sharpe   *Birthday: October 31ˢᵗ, 2002*

Age: 22

Location: Barrington, RI & Essex, CT

Elite Status: Legacy   *Marital Status: Single*

Children: None

Appearance: Brunette, 5'4, blue eyes, Caucasian

I am about to explode as I wonder why my father has a file on Gwen and her family. Why he's showing it to me.

Closing the file, I look up at my father who is watching me expectantly.

"Why do you have these?" I ask, trying my best to sound nonchalant.

My father leans his elbows on his desk and steeples his fingers. "Dean Ashby informed me that your little girlfriend is a legacy," he tells me, his face unreadable. I already knew Gwen was a legacy since she'd told me a couple days ago, so this isn't groundbreaking news. But I suppose to my father, it is.

Logan looks over to me, shock clear on his face, but he doesn't say anything.

"I'm guessing you're still seeing her?" Father asks, cocking an eyebrow. Do I lie and tell him I have no idea what he's talking about, or do I tell him the truth? That Gwen and I are official. I decide on the truth, because I'm done giving a shit what he thinks.

"Yes."

Father leans back in his chair and straightens his suit. Without looking up at me, he says, "Good. Then you'll be getting married within the next six months, before you take your spot at the company."

My heart stops, and I'm pretty sure my jaw is on the floor. Logan's head whips from our father to me, waiting to see my reaction. I don't even have words.

Of course, I would marry Gwen tomorrow if I could. I know Gwen is going to be my wife one day. That is something I've known since the moment she showed me she wasn't like all the girls. Guinevere Sharpe is mine, and we will get married someday, but there's no way she'll agree to getting married in six months.

And what the hell does being married have to do with anything? I don't plan on working for the company anyway, so this is moot.

Steeling myself, I stand and lean over the desk.

"That's not happening," I tell him. "She'll never agree to that."

Father shrugs. "Then you'll have to make her agree. This is family tradition, Ryker. Your grandfather married before building the company, and he forced me to do the same before I began to work under him. Now, it's your turn. You're 22, the exact age your mother and I were married. It is what we do, and you *will* do it," he commands.

I swear my heart is beating so hard it's going to fly out of my chest.

"Father, I," Logan starts before father interrupts him.

"You will be doing the same next year. There is no debate or discussion. This is not only a Steele tradition, but an Elite tradition. As Elite's, you both have an obligation to the vow you took when being initiated in. This was always going to happen."

Logan's face turns red, and I've never seen him angry toward our father. He's never talked back or argued with his orders. He's always followed the rules and accepted whatever our father told him. But he looks fucking pissed.

"Do you know how crazy this is?" Logan shouts, standing from his chair abruptly. "There is no way in hell I am getting married next year. I don't even have a girlfriend. I'm sorry, father. But I'm not doing it."

I purse my lips, trying to hide a grin from taking over my face. I have never been so proud of my brother.

Logan walks to the door and reaches for the handle.

"Logan, we are not finished here," father says sternly.

"Yes, we are."

With that, Logan opens the door and storms out of the room, leaving me with our father who is practically foaming at the mouth. Logan has never had an outburst, and my father looks like he could have a heart attack from the interaction.

You go, little brother.

My father takes a deep breath before looking back at me, the displeasure on his face evident.

"See what you've done? You've corrupted your brother so much, he's beginning to become defiant," my father scoffs.

"Maybe he's just realized that your rules and traditions are stupid, and that he doesn't have to follow your every demand," I shrug.

"You will fix this. You will convince your brother to fall back in line, or so help me, God, I will take everything from you. Your inheritance, your home, your tuition, your car. Everything, Ryker. Do you understand me? You are not in charge here, son. I am."

I back away from his desk, staring down at him as I feel my phone vibrate in my pocket.

Fishing it out, I see a text from Gwen and my chest squeezes. I should be at the party with her. I should be dancing and drinking and kissing her. Not having this utterly ridiculous conversation with my father.

My Rebel

Me

Where are you?

Shit. I have to get out of here. I need to get home to her. When my father texted earlier, I didn't even think to tell Gwen. I just got Logan and drove to campus. My mind was racing with thoughts about what the meeting could be about and what mood my father was going to be in.

"I have to go," I state, not even acknowledging what he just said. He can threaten all he wants, but he wouldn't really do that, would he? At least, he couldn't legally take my inheritance, and I would get a lawyer if I needed to.

My father says he's in charge, but he won't be for long. Not when I find every little secret he's been burying since he became CEO of The Steele Corporation. I know there's something there, and I am determined to find it to get him out of my life for good.

Part of me feels guilty for wanting my own father out of my life because people like Gwen would do anything for their father to be in theirs, but Robert Steele is no father. He is a dictator. I will not allow him to run my life anymore.

He has another thing coming if he thinks I'll actually try to talk Logan into obeying his absurd rules. I don't even know why he'd ask that of me knowing I don't agree with him either.

Sorry, *father*. Not happening.

This ends now.

Chapter 46

RYKER

I find Logan leaning against my Escalade with his arms and legs crossed as he scrolls through his phone. His brown hair falls onto his forehead, and his face is pulled into a scow. It's eerily similar to our fathers, and I wonder if I too look like him when I'm angry.

The doors unlock with a click and Logan climbs into the passenger seat as I take my place behind the wheel. He doesn't say a word, and neither do I. There's nothing to say.

Pulling on to our street, cars line each side of the road, and people are milling about the lawn in front of the Elite mansion with cups and beer bottles in their hands.

As soon as my car is in park, I jump out, rushing for the front door. I have to find Gwen. I need to tell her where I've been and why I wasn't here. She's probably going to be pissed at me, but when I explain, she'll understand. She has to.

I spot Lainey, Ellie, and Damian in the corner of the room, drinks in their hands but concern laces in their expressions. Where is Gwen? Why isn't she with them? Why do they look worried?

I begin to make my way through the crowd, but I'm stopped by a dainty hand landing on my wrist. Whipping around, I see Amy standing in front of me with a small smile on her lips. Her eyes are soft, and she looks like she's been dancing all night, a light sheen of sweat coating her tan skin.

"Hey, where have you been? I've been looking for you," she says, a twinkle in her eye. Her voice irks me, and I want to get away so I can find Gwen.

"Around. I have to go," I tell her sternly, hoping she'll just walk away. But she doesn't. Instead, her face changes from the innocent girl to a more bitter expression. My spine straightens as her demeanor changes.

"I ran into your little girlfriend earlier. She seemed upset," she smiles mischievously. The blood in my veins runs cold at the thought of Amy speaking to Gwen. Who knows what she could have told her. Amy clearly isn't the kind of girl that gives up easily, despite how shy she'd acted when we'd first met.

My eyes narrow. "What did you do?"

Amy chuckles, shrugging before letting go of my wrist. I take a step closer to her, crowding her space. She doesn't even flinch.

"I just told her the truth," she says in a blasé tone, shrugging.

"What do you mean?" I grit out. Amy looks like she's proud of herself, and I know whatever she told Gwen was a blatant lie.

"That Ryker Steele isn't the kind of guy to settle down. That you need to keep your options open. That she's the type of girl that needs stability, and you aren't the kind of guy to give it to her," Amy says snidely. I can hear my heartbeat in my ears as my fists clench at my sides, my jaw tightening.

Don't hit a girl, Ryker. Don't hit a girl.

"Why would you tell her that?" I ask through clenched teeth. What is this crazy bitch's problem? She narrows her eyes questioningly.

"Isn't that what you want? Casual hookups and no commitment? Everyone knows Ryker Steele doesn't do relationships. I was doing you a favor," she explains as if she actually believes she was doing shit for me.

I shake my head and scoff in disbelief. My entire body feels like it's on fire, and my head is spinning. I was gone for a little over an hour. How did this happen?

"You don't know anything about me, or what I want. You're an insecure, jealous little bitch who for some reason, thinks she has a claim on me after I've repeatedly told you to leave me the fuck alone," I seethe. Amy has the decency to look a bit nervous, and a little offended. "You better pray I never see you again, because I will make your life at Ellington University hell."

I begin to walk away, feeling good about my threat when I remember one more thing I need to add. I turn back, meeting Amy's shocked expression.

"Oh, and if I ever see or hear of you talking to Gwen again, I'll make sure your time at Ellington comes to an end. Got it?" I ask with a tilt of my head. Amy nods, her eyes wide with fear. "Good. Now get the fuck out of my house."

With that, Amy scurries through the crowd, hopefully leaving the party, if she knows what's good for her.

Turning back around, I practically run to Lainey, Ellie, and Damian. When I arrive, they all look up, their expressions indifferent.

"Where have you been?" Lainey hisses. I take a deep breath before answering.

"I was in a meeting with my father. Where is Gwen?" I ask, trying to keep the panic I'm feeling out of my voice. Lainey rolls her eyes.

"She's been looking for you all night, asshole. She went to the bathroom, and when she came back, she looked like she saw a ghost."

Shit. "Where is she?" I ask again. I don't have time to be lectured. I need to find Gwen and tell her that Amy is a bitch, and she has no idea what she's talking about. I need Gwen to know that I want her, only her. I need her to know I love her.

Adrenaline pumps through me as I realize how deep I'm in this thing with Gwen. It's not just some hookup, it's not a fling. I love her. I'm in love with her.

The feeling is foreign, and my chest squeezes at the thought of losing her over some lie fucking Amy told her. This can't be it for us. She has to know that I would never hurt her.

"She left, man. She said she was going home," Damian tells me. Ellie and Lainey both hit his arm, and he brings his hand up to rub the spot. He grimaces.

"Ow! Why are people always hitting me?" he asks. Ellie glares at him.

"We don't know if Gwen wanted to see him, you idiot," Ellie sneers, rolling her eyes. I begin to leave, but a hand lands on my shoulder.

Lainey steps in front of me, her eyes narrowed. "If you hurt her, I will string you up by your balls. You got me?" she asks. For such a petite girl, she's really kind of frightening.

I nod before walking away and heading over to Gwen's house.

When I get to the front yard of Gwen's house, I notice her car isn't in the driveway. I run up to the front door and knock furiously, hoping she's in there. But when the door opens, it's not Gwen. It's Haley. My heart drops.

Haley's eyes move up and down my body before landing on my face, her face turning angry, but I don't have the time to care.

"Where's Gwen?" I ask.

"She left," Haley says spitefully. If all Amy told Gwen was that I'm not dating material, then why would Haley seem so mad at me?

"What do you mean she left? Where did she go?" Haley crosses her arms and scoffs.

"Really? So you fuck another girl and you want to know where Gwen is? Go screw yourself," she spits, and I feel like my world is crashing down around me. Fucked another girl? I didn't-

Fucking Amy. That conniving little skank.

I shake my head. "I didn't sleep with anyone other than Gwen. Tell me where she is so I can talk to her," I demand.

"Go home, Ryker. She's not here."

That's it.

I push past Haley, nearly knocking her over as I head for Gwen's room. She wouldn't have left without letting me explain first, would she?

Haley chases me, running into my back when I stop abruptly in front of Gwen's bedroom. Everything is neat, her bed is made, but the novels on her bookshelf are gone. I walk to her closet, opening the door and seeing that most of her clothes and shoes are missing.

Her bathroom is practically empty. Her toiletries and makeup are not in their usual spots.

She's gone. She really left.

Part of me is pissed at Amy for putting these ideas in Gwen's head, for telling her we slept together. Another part of me is angry with Gwen for even believing I could do that to her in the first place. And the final part of me is angry at myself for building this reputation up for so long that Gwen really has no reason not to believe I wouldn't do this to her.

I pull my phone out of my pocket and call her. It goes straight to voicemail. I call her again, and again, until I've called at least twenty times. Then I decide to text her.

My Rebel

Me

Answer your phone.

Me

Gwen, please let me explain.

Me

I can explain everything. Just answer.

Me

Come on, Rebel.

Me

Don't make me show up at your house. You know I will.

For crying out load, I sound insane, but I can't let her think I cheated on her. We were just getting to a good place. I finally let myself have actual feelings for her, and now she's gone, and I have to figure out a way to get her back.

There is no way I'm letting her leave me. Guinevere Sharpe is mine, and she's going to have to believe me, one way or another.

My phone vibrates and I swear I felt my heart leap out of my chest.

My Rebel

My Rebel

Leave me alone.

My blood boils. She's so damn stubborn, and I knew she wouldn't give in that easy but part of me was hoping she'd just let me explain.

Me

Not until you let me explain.

My Rebel

I don't want to hear it.

Me

Please. Just call me.

My Rebel

Don't contact me again.

I growl in frustration. How the hell am I supposed to explain that everything she was told is a lie if she won't even let me talk to her?

I try to call her one more time, but it beeps and hangs up immediately. She blocked me. She seriously blocked my number. She's really done with me.

For the first time in my life, I don't know what to do. I don't have a plan. I feel defeated, and a strange feeling overtakes my chest as I let reality sink in.

She's gone.

Chapter 47

GUINEVERE

The sound of my cell phone vibrating against my nightstand fills my ears as I sit at my desk in my childhood bedroom, staring out the window. I watch as snowflakes fall to the ground in a light flurry.

I've been ignoring everyone since I packed up my car and left Ellington three days ago. Damian is slightly pissed that I left without him, but he has a car, so I wasn't too worried about him getting home.

Lainey, Ellie, and Haley have been blowing up our group chat with questions about why I left without saying goodbye. They assume it had something to do with Ryker, which they'd be correct in their assumptions.

The night I got home, I'd received several phone calls and texts from Ryker. I ignored them until he threatened to show up at my house. I know he's not far, and I know he'd do it. So I answered him. I told him to leave me alone and to never talk to me again, and then I blocked his number.

I don't know what he wants to explain, but I don't want to hear it. I knew better. I did this to myself. I can't even blame him, really.

I knew what I was getting myself into. Ryker Steele doesn't do relationships. That's what everyone told me, and I chose to let myself believe I was the exception.

He'd opened up to me, telling me things about himself and his family that he'd never told anyone. I told him things about me that not many people knew. He said I could trust him, and I believed him. Stupid, naïve little girl.

Ryker betrayed me. He betrayed my trust, and that is something I don't give easily. And now, Ryker Steele is dead to me.

That bitch Amy knew what she was doing. She was trying to stake her claim, show me that I'm not capable of giving Ryker what he needs. And when she told me they'd slept together just the night before, it was like a slap in the face.

Just a night after what I'd considered the best sex I'd ever had, and Ryker went off and fucked someone else. God, I'm such an idiot. How could I think that I was any different than any other girl he's screwed?

His words were pretty, and the way held me made me feel like I was the only girl in his orbit. Meanwhile, he was laughing at me the whole time, probably thinking how easy I was to fool.

My eyes flood with another bout of tears, and I hate myself for crying. I'm pathetic, crying over a guy that clearly never cared about me at all.

Using the back of my hand, I wipe away the tears and take a deep, shaky breath. That's enough, Gwen. You are stronger than this.

Sammy, mom's new dog, pops up from his spot on my bed as my bedroom door flies open, Damian rushing through looking out of breath. I jump up from my seat, watching Damian bend over, setting his hands on his knees as he tries to calm himself down.

"What the hell, Damian! What are you doing?" I demand. He holds up a finger, indicating that he still needs a moment before he explains himself.

Finally, he straightens, still slightly out of breath. "Have you… looked at… your phone at all… in the past twenty-four hours?" he pants. I shake my head, walking over to my nightstand to grab my cell.

Over one hundred text messages from our group chat, and several missed calls and facetimes from Lainey and Ellie.

"Someone attacked Ashton Davis. He's in the hospital with a broken jaw and several other broken bones. He's in a coma," Damian rushes out.

"What?" I croak. My eyes widen and my heart leaps into my throat. He wouldn't.

Damian sits on my bed, petting Sammy on the head as he watches me.

"Lainey and Ellie think it was Ryker. He's the only one with motive."

There's no way Ryker would be that stupid. He may be an Elite, and they can get away with shit, but how is he going to get out of beating a man so badly he's in the hospital with multiple injuries?

My heart stutters. Is Ryker okay? Is he hurt? Is he in trouble?

"Is he…" I begin softly. "Did he get caught?" I shouldn't care. He's dead to you, remember?

Damian shakes his head before running a hand through his shaggy hair. "No. A couple of students found Ashton alone outside the gym. Apparently he was covered in blood and completely knocked out."

My breathing picks up as I begin to pace back and forth.

"Jesus," I say, exasperated.

"What happened between you two? Something must have really pissed him off for him to go off the deep end like that," Damian questions. Sammy rolls over on his back for Damian to rub his belly, and Damian does.

I stop pacing, recalling the night of the party and how everything I thought I knew went up in flames.

"If I'm going to tell you, I should probably loop Lainey, Ellie, and Haley in," I say, pressing the Facetime button on my phone to call the girls.

Lainey picks up first, unsurprisingly, followed by Haley, and then Ellie. Lainey looks more worried than I've ever seen her, and a twinge of guilt pinches in my chest. I tell my best friend everything, and I can imagine leaving without telling her why broke her heart.

"You better have a damn good explanation for completely falling off the face of the earth for three days straight," Lainey shouts through the phone, her anger palpable. I wince.

"Are you alright? Did something happen?" Ellie worries.

Haley stays silent. She already knows the gist of what happened since she was home when I came back to pack my stuff and get the hell out of there. She wouldn't let me leave until I told her why I was in such a hurry.

I exhale a deep breath I didn't even know I was holding before sitting on my bed next to Damian.

"I'm really sorry, guys. I didn't mean to scare you. It's just… something did happen… at the party" I hesitate. My friends aren't the kind of people to say, 'I told you so', but I know they'll be thinking it after I tell them the truth. I don't want them to think I'm stupid, even thought I am.

"Gwen?" Ellie urges. I pick at a string on my pajama shorts as I begin to explain everything.

"This girl, Amy, found me at the party. I recognized her. She was one of Ryker's prior hookups. She cornered me and basically told me that Ryker and I would never work because he isn't ready for a commitment. Then, she told me they hooked up," I explain. Lainey's brows furrow.

"So, he hooked up with a lot of girls before you," Lainey says.

"Lainey!" Ellie scolds. Lainey grimaces.

"Sorry, I didn't mean it like that. I just meant that you know he has a promiscuous past, but you can't let that bother you if you want a future with him."

"Except, it wasn't in the past…" I feel four sets of eyes on me as they all wait for me to explain further. "They slept together the night before the party. He cheated on me."

The words hurt to even say out loud. My heart feels like it's been yanked out and stomped on.

"Wait, what?" Lainey looks bemused.

"Oh, Gwen," Ellie coos.

I hear Damian exhale a breath and see him look down at the floor.

"Damnit, Gwen. I'm sorry. I wish you told us. We could have been here for you," Damian tells me, wrapping his arm around my shoulders and pulling me into his side.

"Why don't you look shocked, Hal?" Lainey asks, squinting her eyes. Haley shrugs casually.

"I already knew," she explains nonchalantly. Ellie, Lainey, and Damian's eyes go wide. It would be comedic if not for the situation at hand.

"What the hell? How?" Lainey shouts.

Haley chuckles. "Because I was home when she came back to pack. I told her she couldn't leave without giving me a good reason. I thought that was reason enough."

"And you didn't tell us?" Damian asks, sounding offended.

"Guys, it wasn't Haley's story to tell. It's Gwen's, and she told us when she was ready," Ellie says calmly. Oh Ellie, ever the levelheaded one.

"So now what?" Hayley asks, her picture shaking as she crawls into her car. I shrug.

"Nothing. Ryker and I are done. It's over," I say, feeling completely defeated. I don't want it to be over. I just want to go back in time to the other night when we laid in bed, sharing our feelings.

Ellie's face looks sad as she looks at me through the phone. Lainey looks like she wants to say something more, but she doesn't speak.

A loud sound comes from Ellie's end before a male voice booms in the background.

Ellie looks behind her before shouting, "Holland, get out of my room!"

"Is that Guinevere?" Holland asks, his voice deep and angry.

"None of your business, now get out!" Ellie demands.

There's a struggle as Holland seems to attempt to grab Ellie's phone out of her hand. Damian and I share a confused glance while Lainey looks like she wants to burst out laughing. Haley's connection gets lost as she appears to go under a tunnel.

Holland's face appears on my screen as I hear Ellie in the background cursing at him.

"What the hell happened between you and Steele?" Holland's deep voice demands.

"Don't talk to her like that," Lainey chides.

Holland rolls his eyes. "Shut it, Barkley. I'm not talking to you," he retorts.

"You're talking to my best friend, that means you're talking to me."

They really bicker like an old married couple. It's kind of adorable.

"I don't have time for your stupid comments, Barkley. Steele is out of his goddamn mind. I've never seen him like this. He's not eating, he's not sleeping, he's been drunk for the past three nights. He won't tell me anything," Holland runs a hand through his hair before rubbing the scruff on his chin. "I went to check on him today. He's in really rough shape. He almost killed that Ashton guy. I had to pull him off before he actually murdered him."

My chest becomes heavy as I take in Holland's words. Ryker hasn't gone home yet?

"Why didn't he go home? The Elite Mansion must be empty by now," I ask. Holland shakes his head.

"Logan's been trying to get him to leave, but he refuses. He says you won't talk to him. You won't let him explain. Explain what?" Holland asks. Ellie grabs the phone back, hitting Holland in the head.

"Leave her alone, Holland. She doesn't have to tell you shit."

I hear Holland growl before the slam of a door tells me he's left the room.

"I'm sorry about that. Holland never knows when to keep his nose out of anyone's business," Ellie shrugs. I force a soft chuckle out of my mouth.

"It's okay…" but nothing is really okay.

"Do you want us to come over? We can have a girl's night," Lainey suggests. Ellie and Lainey don't live far from me. In fact, they live in East Greenwich, the town that Ryker's from. Damian's hand flies to his chest, his mouth hanging open.

"Excuse the fuck out of you. I'll be there too," he says, his voice laced with offence. Lainey's eyes roll.

"Girl's night plus Damian," she groans. Lainey and Damian love each other, but they also butt heads often. Their friendship is funny that way. They can scream and yell at each other one minute and be best friends that next.

"Sure, that would be nice," and I think it would help take my mind off of everything.

Hearing how hurt Ryker is makes me want to drive back to Ellington just to hold him and tell him everything is going to be alright.

But he's the one that broke us. He's the one that cheated, and I shouldn't feel bad for standing up for myself and leaving.

He made his bed, now he can lie in it.

"Okay, be there in an hour," Lainey says, ending the Facetime call.

Sammy yawns loudly, and Damian and I look back at him as he pants, his long, pink tongue hanging out of his mouth.

He's a black lab mixed with something we can't quite identify. He really is adorable, and I'm glad he's been here to keep my mom company. As Damian pets him, I can see his eyes narrow in confusion.

"What?" I ask. Damian looks at me, then back down to Sammy.

"Who the hell's dog is this?" I bark out a laugh. How is he just realizing that he's been petting a dog on my bed when I've never owned a dog?

Chapter 48

RYKER

My phone has been blowing up for the past few days with calls from my mother, father, Logan, and the guys. Holland came to check on me last night, and I told him to fuck off. I don't want to talk to anyone or explain why I'm in such a shitty mood.

I haven't heard anything from Gwen, not that I really expected to since she told me to never contact her again. But a small part of me thought that maybe she just needed to cool down, and then she'd hear me out.

She thinks I slept with Amy. She believes I cheated on her, and it's killing me that she doesn't know the truth. Amy's a fucking bitch, and I should have her kicked out of Ellington just for messing with Gwen's head and causing her to hate me.

I've been so angry with myself and this situation, that I had to find some way to let go. To let some of this anger out before I exploded. So yesterday, I went to the campus gym and waited for Ashton to come out. When he did, I jumped him. I punched his face so hard my fingers bled, and I'm pretty sure one or two are broken. When he fell to the ground, I kicked him in the ribs multiple times until I was satisfied.

Then, I got in my car and drove home, burying myself so deep in alcohol that I couldn't even remember my own name. When Holland showed up, he helped me off the floor and forced me to take a shower. Blood stained my shirt and my face. My hand was also covered.

Holland, being the good friend he is, helped wrap it before helping me to my room and leaving me on my bed where I fell asleep not even ten minutes later.

Everyone in the mansion went home on either Sunday or Monday, including Mason, Pat, Holland, and Logan. I told them I'd be right behind them, but I could bring myself to get in the damn car. Not when I know Gwen is only a thirty-minute drive away from me.

If you go to Ellington, you either come from Rhode Island or live in Connecticut. Some come from New York, but it's not common.

Pat lives around the corner from me, Holland and Ellie live about ten minutes down the road, and Mason lives in the same town as Gwen. It's nice to be able to see each other outside of school, that way we can keep up with Elite business. Not that there's a ton since it's break.

Thanksgiving is tomorrow, and I know I have to be home for it, if only for my mother's sake. But I am dreading seeing my father. I know he'll try to order me to ask Gwen to marry me again, and at this point, I really don't see that happening unless I tie her up and force her somehow.

But that's not an option. I may be an ass, but I'm not going to force her into marrying me. My father will tell me that I have no choice. That I have to do exactly that, force Gwen to marry me whether she wants to or not. For an Elite, marriage isn't about love. It's about the title and power. They only want us married to reproduce the next generation of Elite's.

Many women don't care since they're marrying into money and status. They gladly hand themselves over to us just to say they are married to an Elite. But Gwen doesn't care about all that. She doesn't care that I'm an Elite. She doesn't care that I have money or authority.

That's one of the things I love most about her.

My phone continues to vibrate, and I'm about to chuck it across the room when I see Holland's name on the screen.

"What?" I growl.

"Dude, are you still wallowing?" he asks. My fist clenches around my phone.

"I'm not wallowing."

Holland laughs dryly. "Yeah, okay. Well, I talked to Gwen today," he tells me, and my mouth runs dry.

"What?" I ask, my voice low. I hear Holland's knowing chuckle on the other end, but I don't even care. How did he talk to Gwen? What did she say? Did she mention me?

God, I sound like a heartbroken teenage girl.

"She was on Facetime with El. She's really mad at you, bro," he says, as if I didn't already know this. I roll my eyes.

"Yeah, thanks. Did she say anything else? Like a reason or anything?" I ask, knowing the reason she's angry is because of the lies Amy told her, but I want to know if Holland knows.

"Not that I heard. But she did seem concerned when I told her you were at the mansion alone," he states, sending a spark of hope racing through my body. Maybe she doesn't hate me as much as I thought she did.

It's funny. We're back to exactly where we started months ago. Her hating me, and me being a desperate man, needing her to want me.

"I did hear them say they were having a girl's night tonight though," Holland's voice rips me out of my thoughts. "Are you ever going to tell me what happened?"

"Yeah. One day, but not now," I say, hanging up on him.

As I toss my phone on the couch, it lights up with a text. I groan when I see it's Logan texting me. Why can't everyone just leave me alone.

Logan

Logan

You need to get your ass home, like now.

Me

No thanks.

Logan

Mom is freaking out, and dad is pissed.

I can't help the sardonic laugh that escapes my lips.

Me

What's new?

Logan

It's not a joke, Ryker. I don't know what's going on with you, but you need to get your shit together, get in your damn car, and get home. NOW.

Fuck. Why does everyone have to be so goddamn annoying?

The last thing I want to do right now is drive home. It's ten, which means I won't even get home until around midnight. All I want to do right now is down a bottle of bourbon and go to bed.

I know going home is going to be a mistake. I know my father will say something to set me off and then I'll fight back, and mom will get upset that we're ruining the holiday. It happens every year. We're not the type of family that can sit around a table to eat Thanksgiving dinner and tell each other what we're thankful for. We're dysfunctional in the worst way possible.

But it looks like I don't have a choice.

———————————

I pull up to the gates of my family home, enter the passcode, and pull into our rounded driveway around twelve thirty to find that all of the lights are on in the main house.

The Steele Estate is a display of opulence and timeless elegance, set on a sprawling fifty-acre property that's been in my family for generations. The exterior of the estate is a testament to generations of refined taste and meticulous upkeep.

A grand wrought-iron gate with intricate detailing and the Elite crest stands as the formal entrance. The gate opens to a long, tree-lined driveway, where century-old oaks and elms form a natural canopy overhead. The cobblestone path is meticulously maintained, leading up to a circular courtyard paved with flagstones and adorned with a central fountain.

I'm actually surprised my egotistical father hasn't created a statue of himself to place in the fountain.

The main house is larger than any one family really needs, with a stone face and tall, elegant windows framed by classic white shutters. The symmetrical design is punctuated by a grand portico with towering Corinthian columns, leading to a set of double doors.

The property holds a large pool, and a fully equipped pool house with a bar, changing rooms, and a sauna, a tennis court, and a guest house.

One may think that this would be every kids dream, to grow up with all of this. But it wasn't mine. It was lonely, and cold. With my father rarely ever being home, and my mother trying her best to hide her depression, Logan and I were taken care of by our nanny and Tatia who made sure we were fed and well nourished.

I know my mother tried her best under the circumstances, but it wasn't enough for two young boys who needed their mom.

Putting my car in park, I turn off the engine, climb out of the car and grab my things, swinging my bag over my shoulder. I take a deep breath before entering into the large foyer.

Everything is exactly how I remember it. I haven't been home since Easter. I stayed at the Elite mansion over the summer and into the fall semester. My mom wasn't happy about my choice to stay away, but I think she understood. Logan came back often, so they kept her at bay.

A man greets me with a polite smile. "Good evening, Mr. Steele. Glad to have you home," he says. My face softens slightly as I give him a small nod.

"Anton," I acknowledge the man. Anton has been working for my family for years. He was here before I was born, and to my surprise, he hasn't left. He must be at least eighty now, but he refuses to retire, even though my mother has told him he can leave at any time.

For some reason I can't even begin to comprehend, he says he enjoys working for our family. He knew my grandfather and grandmother, he watched my father grow up, and then Logan and me. The poor guy deserves a break, but he just won't take one.

"Your father has requested your presence in his study," Anton tells me, a bit of what sounds like concern in his voice. Seriously? It's almost one in the morning. Why would he want to meet now?

Begrudgingly, I begin to walk toward the study, knowing this can only be about two thing, Gwen or Ashton. I knew my father would somehow hear about the incident in the campus gym parking lot. I didn't exactly make myself inconspicuous. I was too filled with rage to think of covering my tracks.

I made sure no one else was in the parking lot at the time, but I didn't think of the cameras on the outside of the building and lampposts. Dean Ashby was most likely made aware of what happened when Ashton was sent to the hospital. Then he must have looked through the security footage, saw it was me, and contacted my father.

Lucky me.

My heart races as I knock on the door to the study. My father's low, rough voice calls from the other side.

"Come in," he orders.

Inhaling deeply, I push the door open and enter the large room. My father sits behind his sizable mahogany desk, a glass full of what I'm guessing is bourbon in his hand as he stares down at a paper in front of him. His reading glasses are on the bridge of his nose, and he doesn't even lift his head to look at me.

Behind him is a floor to ceiling bookshelf that stretches from wall to wall, full of books I'm almost positive he's never even read, and no one had ever touched.

The bay window looks out into the front yard, so he must have watched me pull in. There is a leather chair in the corner of the room and next to it is a bar cart, fully stocked with glasses, ice, and the worlds finest liquor.

I've been in this office plenty of times, but it remains locked when my father is away. He forbid us all to go into his study without him. When I was younger, I thought nothing of it, but now? I'm pretty sure it's because there's something in there that he doesn't want anyone to find, which makes me all the more curious.

"Take a seat," my father commands in his deep voice, gesturing to one of the chairs that sits in front of his desk. I remain standing, because sitting means the conversation will last longer.

"I'd rather stand," I tell him. He finally looks up from whatever he's reading to scowl at me.

"It wasn't a request, son. Take a seat, *now*."

I refrain from rolling my eyes, doing as he says and taking a seat. I rub my sweaty palms against my jeans as my knee bobs nervously. This is what happened every time I see my father. How awful is that? That my own father makes me this fucked up.

He types something into his computer before turning it around for me to see. A surveillance video is pulled up showing the parking lot of the campus gym. Of course he has the video.

When I jumped Ashton, I wasn't exactly in my right mind. I'd been drinking all day, thinking about Gwen and how I'd win her back, and the rage that consumed me when I thought about Davis and the way he threatened my girl made me see red.

The video shows Ashton exit the building, his gym back slung over his shoulder and car keys in his hand. Then without warning, I come around the corner and ram into him, gripping the front of his shirt and pushing his back up against the building before landing punch after punch to his face. Ashton's head falls to the side, blood flowing from his nose and mouth as I let him go and watch him slump to the floor.

I stand over him, my fists clenched to my sides. There's no sound in the video, but I remember what I said to him.

"*Get near Gwen again, touch her again, or even think of her again and I will bury you somewhere no one will ever fucking find you.*"

I smirk at the reminder. I don't regret what I did. Ashton Davis is a piece of shit, and he got what he deserved. In fact, he's lucky I didn't do worse. He needed to get the message that I am in charge, not him. I'm the one with all the power. I could kill him and bury him, and no one would ever know because the Elite would have my back.

I don't think he'll be getting near Gwen again. Especially because I told him to pack his shit and drop out of Ellington. A little threat to him and his family did the trick.

The monitor goes black as the video ends. My father twists it back around to face him, laying his arms on top of the desk in front of him.

He clears his throat. "What the fuck was that?" he seethes. I shrug my shoulders, because what kind of question is that? He saw the video. It was pretty clear what that was.

"Just giving him what he deserved," I say, annoyance laced in my voice.

"I don't care what he did. You assaulted a man on campus. I don't give a shit what you do off campus, or even at the mansion. But on campus? This is the shit I'm talking about, Ryker. You are a child, and I'm done with it. You're lucky I have connections with the police, or your ass would be thrown in jail right now," he grits out between clenched teeth.

I stand abruptly, my hands slamming on the desk as I lean into him. "So let them throw me in jail, Father," I huff out an exaggerated scoff. "Oh, wait. You can't, because that would ruin your perfect image. Isn't that right, *Father?* Your appearance in society is the only thing you've ever cared about. You'd never do anything to tarnish it. And having your son tossed in prison wouldn't reflect well on you, would it?"

My father stands from his seat, slapping me across the face so hard I stumble back. Shit, that was unexpected. He's never hit me, but then again, I've never dared to speak to him like that. I was always too intimidated or scared. But not anymore.

I'm not that little boy anymore. I'm not afraid of him.

His face is red with anger, and if this were a cartoon, he'd have steam pouring out of his ears.

"Watch your mouth, *boy.* Don't forget that everything you have is because of me and my *image.* You'd be wise to show me some respect, because I can take it all away and you'll be left with nothing," he threatens. My eyes narrow as I glare at him in a mixture of anger and disgust.

I hate him. I hate him for never being around as a kid, I hate him for how he's treated my mother, I hate him for how he's treated me. I may not be as powerful as him right now, but I will be. And when I am, he will be obsolete. I will end him, and he won't even see it coming.

I don't even say anything to him. Instead, I turn on my heels, grab my bag off the floor, and storm out of the room, fuming.

Chapter 49

GUINEVERE

Girls' night was a little over a week ago, and it was a success. Ellie and Lainey showed up around ten with 5 tubs of different kinds of ice cream and wine, dubbing them the 'break up essentials.' I told them I didn't need it, but I ended up being really grateful for it as we started to watch sappy romance movies. Damian groaned at our choice of genre, but he wanted to stay, so he has to watch what we wanted.

We went through the classics like The Notebook, Ten Things I Hate About You, and A Walk to Remember. By the time the third movie ended, we'd gone through three bottles of wine, and a tub of ice cream each, and I was sobbing into the carton while my friends sat around me and rubbed my back, assuring me everything would be okay.

I was grateful that my mom was already asleep, because I don't think I could have explained everything again. I was trying to be strong, trying to not be affected by it all because it's my fault. I did this to myself, and now I have to deal with the consequences, no matter how shitty they are.

When my mom came downstairs the next morning, she was pretty confused when she saw us all asleep with empty wine bottles and ice cream cartons strewn about.

Of course, after they all left, my mom made me tell her everything anyway, which I did because I can't keep anything from her. She held me while I cried some more and wished more than anything that this wasn't my reality right now.

Thanksgiving dinner was exactly what I expected. It was just my mom and I with a turkey, some stuffing, and mashed potatoes. It was nice, and it gave my mom and I some time to catch up. My father actually called to wish us a happy Thanksgiving, but I refused to talk to him. I know I'm being immature, but I can't bring myself to even think about him let alone talk to him.

The December air is cold as I walk across the street from the parking lot to The Baked Bean, our local coffee shop which also happens to be a full bakery as well. Mom wanted me to pick up an apple pie because she's been craving one and she guilted me into getting it, saying she couldn't drive in the snow.

There really isn't that much snow on the ground right now, but I didn't mind going because I was beginning to go stir crazy sitting in my childhood home with my mother.

The man behind the counter greets me with a smile when I walk up to the counter. He looks familiar but I can't place where I know him from.

"Gwen? Wow, it's been a long time. How have you been?" the guy asks. I won't lie, he is really attractive. He has blonde shaggy hair and blue eyes mixed with a perfectly chiseled jaw covered in a thin layer of stubble. He's wearing a long sleeve shirt, his muscles visible under the thick material. The apron he's wearing sports The Baked Bean's logo in the middle.

When I look back at his eyes, it clicks. "Oh my god, Hayden? Holy shit, hi!" I grin as he comes around the counter, picking me up and twirling me around. I can't help the giggle that comes out of me as he sets me back down.

"Guinevere Sharpe, the one and only. How's that fancy college treatin' ya?" Hayden asks, and I roll my eyes. He attended Weston U, so he was at a 'fancy' college too.

"It's okay. How's your asshole of a brother?" I ask, not really caring how he is. Hayden Sawyer is the older brother of one Dawson Sawyer, the ex that broke up with me over text and never spoke to me again.

Hayden and I always got along. He's only a year older than Dawson, and he was always around when we were kids. Growing up, I always had a crush on Hayden. It's funny. I was attracted to Hayden way before I was attracted to Dawson. I think Hayden knew I liked him, but he also knew his brother had feelings for me, so he never said anything.

Or maybe he just thought I was some stupid little girl. Who knows. It was so long ago now that everything has begun to blur.

I do remember one night when I was fifteen and Hayden was sixteen.

We'd been fishing all day with Dawson in the little pond behind their house. Dawson went inside to change because Hayden had pushed him into the water. We all laughed about it, and Dawson was a good sport about it. He never really had a bad temper.

Hayden and I continued to fish as the sun set and it became darker outside. I'd casted my line toward the pond, but it wasn't going as far as I wanted, and I was growing frustrated. Hayden came up behind me, putting his arms around me and his hands on top of mine as he helped me cast the line again. This time it landed where I wanted, and a few seconds later, I was reeling in a small fish.

I squealed with excitement, jumping up and down as Hayden unhooked the fish for me to see. The grin on his face made my stomach flutter. He tossed the fish back into the pond, wiping his hands on his thighs before turning back to look at me.

When his eyes met mine, they seemed to darken as the grin on his face fell. His eyes darted down to my lips and back up to my eyes quickly. I wanted him to kiss me so badly. I was praying that he'd just grab my face and kiss me so hard I'd forget my own name. He took a step closer to me, and my legs almost gave out.

"Hayden," I said softly as he closed the distance between us. My heart pounded and my mind raced.

"Shhh. I just want to try something," he practically whispered as if he was talking to himself.

Before I could ask what he wanted to try, he grabbed my face and leaned in slowly, his soft lips touching mine and setting my nerve endings on fire.

When he pulled away, I pouted, afraid he was already regretting it. But his hands remained on either side of my face. His eyes searched mine before he spoke.

"Wow," he said in disbelief. "You're really good at that."

I grinned. "Thanks."

"Was that your first kiss?" he asked. I could feel my cheeks heat with embarrassment as I nodded.

"Yes," I told him. He shakes his head slightly.

"Mine too."

What? There's no way this was Hayden Sawyer's first kiss. He was handsome, and sweet, and girls must've been throwing themselves at him constantly. He wouldn't waste his first kiss on a girl like me.

"Seriously?" I asked. He nodded.

"Yeah."

"Why would you want your first kiss to be with me?" I asked, not sure if I wanted to know the answer or not. He chuckled, tucking a piece of my brown hair behind my ear as he looked me in my eyes.

"I've wanted to do that for so long," he told me. My heart skipped a beat, and I couldn't believe he was saying that to me.

"Why?" I didn't know why I was questioning it, but I wanted to know.

"You're just... you're beautiful."

I thought my heart was going to burst out of my chest at his words.

"Hey, what are you guys doing? Mom wants us to go in now," Dawson yelled from the deck on the back of the Sawyer house. It startled me, and I jumped back from Hayden.

We never spoke about that night again. Every time all three of us would hang out, there would be this tension in the room, we'd exchange longing glances, and sometimes we'd even flirt. But Dawson never seemed to notice.

Year's later, Hayden went off to college at Weston U and left Dawson and I behind at Kingston Preparatory School. To this day, I don't think Hayden ever mentioned it to Dawson, and I certainly never did.

Dawson wasn't a second a choice. I fell in love with him, and the memory of that night I spent with his brother faded every day.

I haven't seen Hayden since he left for Weston U, and honestly, I wasn't expecting to see him ever again. Our mom's stopped being friends after Dawson broke up with me.

The last I knew, Hayden went to Weston to be a lawyer. He'd always been into law and talked about becoming a big-time lawyer, moving to New York, and having his own firm one day. I was so proud of him for chasing his dreams, and I always hoped they'd come true for him.

But if he's here, working at the coffee shop, I have a feeling he never got there.

"He's still an asshole," Hayden says, bringing me back to the present.

I chuckle. "Yeah, well, some things never change," I tease, and Hayden smiles earnestly.

"Yeah, some things never do," he says softly as he looks over my body, landing on my face. My cheeks blush and my stomach flutters, reminding me of the way I used to feel around him all those years ago.

I don't know how to respond to that, so instead, I change the subject.

"I need a pie," I blurt out. Hayden smirks.

"Okay… what kind?"

"Apple," I tell him. "Please."

Oh, man. I sound like a total idiot. Why am I so nervous right now? My heart is going crazy in my chest, and I feel like I'm sweating. Get it together, Gwen.

"Apple pie it is," Hayden confirms, walking back around the counter and grabbing an apple pie from the stack of various pies in the bakery. He brings the pie over to the register as I walk up to the counter to pay.

The smirk is still on his lips as his blue eyes search my face. He can tell I'm nervous and I hate it. Why am I so damn obvious?

I haven't seen this man in years, and yet he still has that same effect on me as he did when we were kids.

I pull out my wallet, ready to pull out my card to pay, but Hayden holds his hand up to stop me.

"It's on the house, Sharpe," he says, and my stomach flutters. I used to love it when he'd call me that. He'd only do it when he was flirting, and it made my stomach flutter every time.

"What? Are you sure?" I ask hesitantly. He nods.

"Positive. Tell your mom to enjoy the pie," he says as he leans over the counter on his forearms. A piece of his blonde hair falls into his face, and he uses his hand to push it back. I watch the muscles under his sleeve as they contort when he moves his arm.

"How do you know it's not for me?" I ask, placing a hand on my hip. Hayden chuckles.

"You hate apples," he states. He remembers that? How does he remember that? It's such a miniscule detail, and he remembered.

I smile shyly, looking down at the floor because for some reason, I can't look him in the eye.

"You're in town for a couple weeks, right?" he asks, and I nod.

"Yes, I go back to campus after Christmas."

He stands straight, running a hand through his hair again. It must be a nervous gesture. "Okay…" he starts. "Can I take you to dinner?" his eyes meet mine, and they're full of hope.

Dinner? With Hayden Sawyer? My first crush, my first kiss, my ex's older brother. My mind races as I think of what to say. Part of me wants to say yes, but the other part of me thinks of Ryker. I don't feel the same way I do about Ryker with Hayden.

With Hayden, there's no longer a pang of longing. The memory of him is warm, like an old favorite song, but it doesn't stir me the way it once did. Hayden was my first taste of romantic feelings, a gentle introduction to the world of love and emotions.

But now, those feelings seemed almost childish, a naive prelude to what I now feel for Ryker. Ryker, with his crooked smile and the way he makes me feel seen and understood. The way I feel about him is deep and consuming. It's real, raw, and all-encompassing. But right now, all of that is overshadowed by a storm of anger and frustration.

My chest tightens as I think of the reason I'm mad at him. The sting of the thought cuts deep, and I think maybe I should give him a chance to explain. But what is there to explain? Amy was really convincing, and with Ryker's past, it's not hard to believe that I'm not enough for him.

Yet, despite the anger and betrayal I feel right now, I can't deny that I still have feelings for him. I think I might even love him.

I feel like this brought us right back to the beginning, when I couldn't stand him, and we only spoke about the project. Except, now I know what it's like to have him, to want him. I miss him. I miss the way his presence could calm me, the way his touch could make everything seem right. But I blocked him. I told him never to contact me again, and at the time it seemed like the right thing. But now I wish I could take it back.

As much as I thought I loved Hayden and Dawson, the way I feel about Ryker surpasses it all.

I just wish I could talk to him, tell him how I feel. In reality, I could, but I'm choosing not to because I don't know if I can handle hearing his voice.

"Gwen?" Hayden's voice brings me back to the present. I look up into his blue eyes as they search my face, waiting for me to answer his question.

"Sorry. I um… I'm kind of seeing someone," I half lie. Technically, Ryker and I aren't really together anymore, but I still feel connected to him. I still have these strong feelings for him, and I couldn't possibly start anything with anyone new right now.

Hayden's face falls slightly before he fixes it with a wistful smile. He nods, and I can tell that isn't the answer he was hoping for. It wouldn't be a good idea for us to go to dinner. Not after I dated his brother for three years. Everything's changed now, and even if I wanted him back then, I've moved on.

"Oh, well… that's good. Someone from school?" he asks.

"Yes."

"Do you love him?" he wonders, his question taking me off guard.

"It's complicated…" I tell him, because the truth is, yes, I do love him, but he doesn't know it.

Hayden tilts his head in question. "What do you mean?"

I sigh. "We're not exactly talking right now."

"Did something happen?" Hayden asks sincerely. I feel weird talking to him about this, but I like that he still cares.

"Sort of," I shrug. Hayden walks over to the coffee machine, pouring two cups of coffee, adding cream and sugar to one before coming around the counter to hand me one. He gestures to an empty table in the corner.

We take a seat and I look out the window, watching snowflakes fall to the ground like I'm in a life size snow globe.

"Tell me everything," Hayden orders, and I do. I tell him everything while I try to keep myself from crying because I am not allowing myself to cry in front of him. I'm not allowing myself to shed any more tears for Ryker.

"How do you know this Amy chick wasn't lying?" he asks once I'm finished filling him in.

I shrug. "I don't, but I-" he cuts me off.

"So, you don't know for sure that this guy even cheated on you? You're just taking the word of some girl who sounds like she's a jealous bitch?" he questions. Well, when you put it like that...

"I-"

"Listen, Gwen. It seems like you really care for this guy, and even though he sounds like kind of a douche, it seems like he cares about you too," he starts, grabbing my hand over the table and looking me in the eye. "I get where you're coming from, but you should let him tell you his side of the story. If not for him, do it for yourself. Maybe it'll help give you closure," Hayden's features soften, and it reminds me of the night he kissed me for the first time.

Hayden's always been a sweet guy, and it's nice to see nothing has changed. I'd been debating on whether or not to give Ryker the opportunity to explain, and I think this might've been the push I needed to do exactly that.

The problem is, how will I know if he's telling the truth?

"Thank you, Hayden, really. You've always been good with advice," I smile. Hayden looks pretty satisfied with himself.

"What can I say? I'm wise," he says, shrugging.

We stand and he gives me a hug. It feels warm and familiar. Pulling back, he leaves a gentle kiss on the top of my head.

"See you around, Sharpe," he says with a grin.

———

"See you around, Sawyer," I say back as I walk out of the coffee shop with my mother's apple pie in hand, feeling much lighter than I did when I first went in.

I don't know what's going to happen, but Hayden's right. I do need closure, and talking to Ryker is the only way to get it.

Chapter 50

RYKER

After the shit show that was Thanksgiving dinner, my mother begged me to stay for a few more days since my father left again to go back to New York for business. He's always leaving, and I can't imagine how lonely my mother must feel all alone in this big house with no one to talk to.

As much as I blame my mother for never being there for Logan and me as children, I don't like that she's so alone all of the time. That's why I agreed to stay.

It's easier to be here, now that my father isn't home. The house feels bigger, and I'm not walking on eggshells every time I leave my room.

With my father gone, it will give me some time to snoop around and see if I can find anything to use against him to get him out of The Steele Corporation. There has to be something in his office, I know it.

I think I'm so focused on it now to take my mind off of the feisty brunette I'm in love with. It's been hell, not seeing her and not being able to talk to her. Holland's been keeping me updated on her through eavesdropping on Ellie's conversations.

Since Mason lives in the same town, I've had him keep an eye on her. I've pretty much got eyes and ears on her at all times. There's no way I'm letting her leave me. She may think she's in charge here, and I'll continue to let her think that until I'm ready to show her that I'm the one holding all the cards.

Gwen is mine, and she will always be mine.

Mason informed me the other day that he saw her at a small coffee shop in their town. Apparently, it's right near a liquor store. I bring up the pictures he sent me of my Rebel talking to some douchebag at the counter, smiling and laughing. Then he sent me a picture of them sitting at a table, his hand holding hers, and then them hugging. My blood boils as I look over the pictures again.

I pull up her Instagram and see pictures of her, Lainey, Ellie, Haley, and Damian, some selfies, and then, pictures of her and the douchebag. She stands in between him and another guy who looks similar to the guy at the coffee shop. I assume they're brothers. Did she fuck them both? Hell, I don't even want to know.

She looks younger in the picture, so does the guy who I now know as Hayden Sawyer. Her hair isn't as long as it is now, and she looks innocent, almost pure.

A very large part of me wants to hunt this guy down and rip his fucking head off for touching what's mine. But I can't do that. Not if I don't want her to know I'm keeping an eye on her.

So instead, I make my way down the grand staircase and head straight for my father's office. Before he left, I watched him enter the passcode needed to enter, and I'm patting myself on the back for checking the lock the other day.

I peak around the corner to make sure I'm completely alone. We have staff working around the clock in this house, and the last thing I need is to get caught and for one of them to tell my father I'm snooping.

Entering the numbers into the padlock, I smile when I hear the telltale click of the door unlocking.

My heart pounds in my chest as the door creaks open. The office is dark, and it feels colder in here. It's weird being in here without the presence of my father looming over me.

I close the door behind me and quickly move to the large mahogany desk. My father is meticulous, and he'll know if anything is out of place. If he finds out I was in here, he'd kill me. The sad part about that is that I'm pretty sure he actually would.

I rifle through the drawers, my heart pounding faster thinking about what I could find in here. Pens, notebooks, and standard office supplies greet me, but nothing out of the ordinary.

Frustration bubbles in my chest as I slam the drawer shut. I run my hand through my hair, glancing around the room, my eyes landing on a locked safe on the bookshelf. How did I not notice that when I was in here the night I arrived home?

How the hell am I going to open a safe?

I try to enter the same passcode as the door, but it doesn't work. I try my mom's birthday, the day they got married, my birthday, Logan's birthday, and even his birthday. Nothing works, and I'm growing more agitated by the second. Of course it wouldn't be anything having to do with his family. Robert Steele doesn't have a family. He has himself, and that's all he's ever needed.

One more number pops into my head.

With shaky fingers, I enter the numbers two, zero, zero, one. The year he graduated from Ellington. After a few tense moments, the safe opens and I let out a sigh of relief.

Reaching inside, I pull out several folders, neatly labeled and organized. My father's neat handwriting marks each one. 'Financial Reports,' 'Client Contracts,' 'Legal Matters.' But one folder catches my eye. 'Confidential.'

I sift through the papers inside, all filled with legal terms and financial shit. As I continue the flip through, I find exactly what I'm looking for. There are records of tons of off-the-books transactions, shell companies, and payments to people whose names I recognize from the Elite, including Pat, Holland, and Mason's fathers.

Holy fucking shit.

This is what I need. Pulling my phone out, I snap a picture of the files, making sure they're clear enough to read. Then, I shove the papers back in the folder and place them all back in the safe, shutting and locking it.

I need to come up with a plan. I don't know if I should tell Logan yet, but Pat might know what to do. The guys should know their fathers are involved in this shit. This is even bigger than I thought.

———————————————

As I lay in bed staring at the ceiling, my mind runs over everything I found in the folder. I knew my father was into some shady shit, but I didn't think it was this bad. My father, the CEO of The Steele Corporation, has been involved in illegal shit for years. Embezzlement, bribery, fraud.

I bring up the group chat and send them a text.

The Elite Four

Me

Shit's about to hit the fan.

Patrick Samuelson

What?

Mason Howard

Hope you don't mean that literally.

Holland Monroe

I'm fully convinced we are not related.

Mason Howard

Fuck off.

Holland Monroe

What's going on, Steele?

Me

Sent an image.

This.

Holland Monroe

Shit.

Patrick Samuelson

Oh, shit.

Holland Monroe

Where did you find that?

Me

My father's office. Dumbass left a fucking paper trail.

Mason Howard

Wait. All our dad's names are on that.

Me

I need to know you guys are on my side with this. I'm not keeping this shit quiet.

Holland Monroe

Hell yeah. Dad's an asshole. I'm in.

Patrick Samuelson

We'll back you. Those fuckers deserve it.

Holland Monroe

Howard? You in?

Me

We've all gotta be on the same page here.

Mason Howard

I'm in. When are we doing this?

Me

Meet at the mansion asap.

I'm aware that it's almost one in the morning, but the guys will make it work. They always do.

I don't know how or when quite yet, but my father's reign as CEO of The Steele Corporation is about to be finished.

RYKER

It's four in the morning now as Pat, Mason, Holland, and I sit in the living room of the Elite mansion staring at the pictures of the files on our phones.

We've been trying to come up with a plan to expose our fathers and their corrupt businesses. Doing some more digging, we've found out that Holland and Mason's dads are involved in one of the most dangerous crime circles in New York. I knew they worked for the mafia.

Pat's father is into some questionable shit with a few strip clubs in the city, and my father, well, we already know his shit. He's been embezzling money from The Steele Corporation since he became CEO to fund his yacht, private jet, and who knows what else. He's also been giving money to the guy's dads for their businesses as well.

I should probably loop Logan in before I blow up our father's empire, but even though Logan's mad at our father right now, I think he'd still try to stop me from exposing him. I can't let him do that.

Robert Steele deserves to rot behind bars for the rest of his pathetic, miserable life, and I want to be the one to put him there.

"I say we just confront them," Mason suggests. Holland looks at his cousin, dumbfounded.

"I swear, did Aunt Mary drop you on your fucking head when you were a baby? Did all the Molly finally catch up to you and kill every single one of your brain cells?" Holland questions, rolling his eyes.

Mason slouches back down in his seat, crossing his arms over his chest and pouting like a child.

"That might not be the worst idea," Pat states, leaning forward and resting his elbows on his thighs.

Holland's head snaps over to Pat, followed by Mason who looks overjoyed with the fact that someone has finally agreed with one of his ideas.

"I'm sorry, what? Are you insane? That's a terrible idea," Holland chides.

"Confronting them all together might be the best way to do it. They're not going to do anything to us if we're all there. We could call a meeting at the Elite office in New York and do it in a meeting room. We bring all the evidence, and we each wear a mic to record what they say. Then we bring it to the cops for them to take care of," Pat explains. I don't hate the idea. But there is one big flaw with that plan.

"Have you forgotten that our fathers have connections with law enforcement? They probably have them all in their pockets. There's no way to tell who's on our side and who's working for them," I tell him. Pat nods, thinking. A thought hits me, and I grin.

"What the hell are you smiling at?" Holland asks, clearly agitated. He's really not good on no sleep. Turns into a real asshole really.

"What's something all four of the old men care about more than anything?" I inquire, hoping they'll understand what I'm asking.

"Money," Pat says.

"Power," Holland shrugs.

"Pussy," Mason chimes in. Pat, Holland, I turn to look at Mason who just shrugs. "What? It's true."

I shake my head. "Their status and image in society."

Pat and Holland nod in understanding.

"So we threaten to take it public," Pat grins.

"Exactly. We just have to wait for the right time," I state, and the guy's nod. "Who's ready to fuck some shit up?" I ask and I receive three mischievous grins that match mine.

I feel kind of guilty that I haven't said a word to my mother or Logan about our plan to expose our fathers shittiness, but I know they'll only try to talk me out of it. I'm not backing down now, not when I've gotten so close to ending this.

My father won't see it coming, and I can't wait to see his face when we walk in and burn everything to the ground.

It's been three and a half weeks since the meeting at the Elite mansion. We decided to wait until after Christmas to do anything so our families could have at least one more normal holiday. Now that it's over, we're more than ready to get this over with.

"We've already called the meeting. They think it's a standard Elite meeting," Holland tells us as he paces back and forth in our hotel room in the city. "We go in, show them the evidence, and demand they step down. If they refuse, we go public."

I stand from my spot on the bed and look at my friends. I really am lucky to have three brothers who would drop everything to be there for me.

"Thank you, guys. It means a lot that you're here," I say, not trying to get too sappy. They all look at me as if I'm crazy. Pat walks over to me, setting his hand on my shoulder.

"Dude, we're brothers for life. We'll always be there for you. Elite's take care of their own," he states, tapping my shoulder and giving me an honest grin.

I place my hand on his shoulder the same way he did mine. "Brothers for life," I confirm, and Pat nods.

"Brothers for life," Mason and Holland say in unison.

I shake my head. "Alright, enough of this sappy shit. Let's get this over with," I grunt.

When we enter the conference room at the Elite office building, the tension is palpable. Each of our fathers are already seated around the large table, their expressions a mix of curiosity and impatience. I should probably feel nervous, but I don't. I only feel anger and hatred toward the man that was supposed to be my dad.

Robert is the first to speak. "What's this all about, boys? We have to get back to work."

I step forward, not wanting to waste any time, and place the folder we've compiled of all the evidence on the table in front of them. They stare at it in curiosity and suspicion.

Holland's father's eyes narrow on the folder.

"What is this?" he asks. Daniel Monroe is cold and negligent. Much like my father, Holland and Ellie's father was never there. Except, they had it a bit worse because when he was there, he'd get drunk and abuse their mother right in front of them. But it was an arranged marriage by the Elite, and the Elite don't get divorces.

Holland steps up beside me, glaring at his father.

"We know what you've been doing. All of you."

There's a moment of stunned silence, and then my father's face twists into anger. "You have no idea what you're talking about."

Pat joins Holland and I closer to the table.

"So the embezzlement, the fraud, the bribery. You're really going to sit there and tell us we're wrong? The fucking files are all there," he seethes.

Our fathers don't look worried that we've figured out their secrets, except for my father who looks like he wants to strangle me.

"We're done being your little puppets. You're not going to ruin our lives and the lives of everyone we care about," Mason says.

Mason's father sneers. "Did you boys really think you could storm in here and threaten us?"

Holland, ever the calm one, looks at his uncle with disdain.

"We're not threatening you. We're giving you a choice. Step down quietly, let us take over, and we'll handle this internally. Refuse, and we'll take everything we have to the press," he shrugs.

The large conference room is thick with tension and animosity as the old men exchange glances. It's clear they hadn't expected us to find any of this information.

My father, still seething, finally breaks the silence. "And if we refuse?" he asks through gritted teeth.

I keep my voice calm and steady as I lean over the table to get in my father's face.

"Then we'll destroy everything you've built. We've already contacted our lawyers. You'll be finished. Your reputations that you've worked so hard for, the money, the power, it'll all disappear. You'll be nothing, no one," I grind out, shaking my head. "Grandfather would hate what you've done to this company and the family name."

My father lets out a bitter laugh. "Your grandfather was an idiot. He had no clue how to run an empire. The business was going under, and he was letting it. My father never did know how to do what it takes to survive," he leans forward so that I can see the fire in his eyes.

I fist his shirt, pulling him out of his seat and into me. I can see my brothers take a step closer, ready to pull me back if I go to far.

"Grandfather was a better man than you ever will be. You're pathetic," I spit. "You had a family, a wife, and all you care about is how much power you hold, and if you don't do as we say, you can kiss it all goodbye. That's a fucking promise."

I release his shirt, letting him fall back into his chair. He looks almost proud, but proud of what, I'm not sure.

The old men look at each other, the weight of the situation sinking in. They underestimated us, thinking we're too naive and loyal to ever challenge them. But what they didn't know is that we were biding our time until we could get rid of them.

After a tense pause, Pat's father finally speaks, his voice a mix of defeat and resignation. "What do you want us to do?"

Pat takes another step forward.

"First, you'll sign over your shares and step down from your positions. We take full control of the companies. Second, you cooperate fully with any internal investigations we conduct. We want to see exactly what's been going on behind closed doors. If you do this, we'll handle things quietly."

"You're still in college. How will you run a company while going to class and dealing with Elite matters?" Mason's father leans back in his chair, crossing his arms.

"We'll make it work," Holland tells him, his voice laced with conviction.

There's a long silence as our fathers seem to consider their options, which at this point, are very limited.

Pat's father looks up to us, his brows furrowed with anger. "Fine. We'll do it your way."

Pat tosses the folder we'd put together with all of the necessary legal documents for the old men to sign. We weren't completely sure this would work, and honestly, knowing some of the shit they're involved in, I wasn't sure we'd make it out alive.

But we had our lawyers draw up all the paperwork just in case everything went according to plan.

As our fathers sign the documents relinquishing control, I feel a sense of relief. I don't know how the four of us are going to make this work, but I know we'll figure it out.

Now, I just need to find a way to tell my mother and Logan. Logan has just as much pull in the company as I do, but I'm not sure he'll want to get involved. He's never really been interested in the business.

When they're finished signing the papers, Holland grabs the folders, and we start to head out. But before I make it to the door, I think of one more stipulation, this one being for my father only.

Turning around I face my father whose face is red and has his hands fisted on the glass table. A satisfied feeling runs through me, and I want to smile, but I hold it back.

"One more thing," I drawl, staring directly at my father.

"What?" he snaps.

"Leave mom. She keeps the house and gets her freedom."

My father barks out a laugh, and my fists clench at my sides.

"Who do you think you are?" he asks rhetorically.

"The one with all the power," I sneer, and my father stares at me with so much hatred, it's almost laughable.

"Fine."

With that, I head for the door again where Mason, Pat, and Holland stand waiting for me.

"Son," my father's rough voice calls. I stop but I don't look back at him. "You always were weak, controlled by your emotions. You will always be my greatest failure."

Rage fills my body, and I don't even have time to think before I'm jumping over the glass table and tackling my father to the ground.

I feel hands on my back and arms, attempting to pull me off, but they're useless. My fist pounds into my father's face repeatedly. All the years of pent-up rage and hatred for this man bubbles to the surface and I can't control myself.

Blood pours out of his nose and mouth as he lay unconscious under me. I should probably stop, but the anger is controlling me at this point.

"Fuck. You," I snarl before I'm lifted off of him by Pat and Holland.

"That's enough. It's over, let's go," Pat tries to calm me down, but the adrenaline in my veins is too much. My entire body is shaking, and I can feel my heart threatening to leap out of my chest. My ribs are sore because they still haven't healed fully from rugby, and my head is throbbing.

I yank out of Holland and Pat's grasp, angrily marching out of the conference room and out onto the cold streets of New York City.

We sit in silence on our way back to the mansion, and I'm still livid as I sit in the passenger seat while Pat drives.

I should be thrilled that the fathers agreed to our terms and have signed everything to us, but instead, I'm angry at the words my father spoke to me.

"You will always be my greatest failure."

What kind of a father says that to their own son? One that literally could not care about anyone but himself.

"You good?" Pat asks without taking his eyes off the road. I've had a while to cool down, but every time those words replay in my head, I get pissed off all over again.

I nod. "I'm fine," I lie.

"Bullshit," Holland calls from the backseat. "You almost beat your dad to death, Steele. You're not fine," he says.

My jaw tenses and I grind my teeth. "Drop it, Monroe."

"Why can't you just be honest and tell us what's going on in your head?"

"Fuck off," I seethe. I'm not doing this right now.

"Does this have to do with Gwen at all?" Holland inquires, and my fucking heart starts to beat rapidly again.

"What's going on with Gwen?" Pat asks, glancing over at me.

"She left him. Thinks he cheated on her the night before the end of semester party," Mason says. I never got around to telling Pat about what happened that night. The only reason Holland found out was because he saw me drunk and bloody after I beat up Davis. And the only reason Mason knows is because I have him keeping an eye on her.

"That's impossible. He was with me the night before the party. We went to Hillview for a meeting. We were there until after one," Pat tells him. "You didn't tell her?"

I glare at him. "I tried. She blocked my number and told me not to contact her again," I explain. Don't you think that would have been the first thing I tried to do?

Pat scoffs. "Since when do you take orders from a woman?"

Sighing, I stare out the window, watching the trees fly by and ignoring Pat's question.

"Shit," Holland murmurs.

"What?" Mason asks, looking up from his phone.

"He loves her," Holland explains, chuckling to himself.

Mason lets out a laugh. "Yeah, right. Steele in love? No way."

I can feel Pat's eyes burn into me as we pull into the driveway at the Elite Mansion. My friends know I've been notorious for sleeping around and never having any serious relationships with women. But Gwen is different.

Turning to look at Pat, he searches my face before a small smirk plays on his lips.

"I don't believe it," he says. "Our boy, fuckboy extraordinaire, has fallen in love," he teases. I punch him in the arm, and he grunts.

"No fucking way," Mason sits back in his seat and laughs.

"Fuck. Okay, yes. I love her. I'm in love with her, and she wants nothing to do with me. But I have a plan, I just need classes to start back up."

The guys look at me with curiosity, waiting for me to explain further.

This plan has to work. She's going to be mine, but I need her to want to be mine. I won't put her through what my mother's gone through. My mother didn't want to marry my father and look where that got her.

No, Gwen needs to want to be with me. And I'm going to do everything in my power to make that happen.

Chapter 52

GUINEVERE

My mom cries as she hugs me. I squeeze her back, trying not to laugh at the fact that she cries every single time I go back to campus as if I won't be back.

She pulls back, leaving her hands on my shoulders as her eyes look over my face. I give her a small smile.

"Mom, I'll be back in five months. And I'll come visit," I tell her. She tilts her head to side and scoffs.

"That's what you said last time."

She's not wrong. I did tell her before the Fall semester started that I'd come home every other weekend. But my classes got harder, and I had limited time to get things done, plus I didn't feel like driving the two hours home.

"I promise I will."

A knock on the door has us pulling away from one another before it flies open and Damian barges in. He's gotten a haircut since the last time I saw him so his blonde hair is no longer hanging in his face. Instead, the sides are shaved down, and the top is a bit longer. He looks good.

"Oh, Gwenny! Your ride is here. Are you ready to get back to the big El?" he shouts. I roll my eyes.

"I'm driving you," I deadpan as I grab my bags off the floor. I hear Sammy running down the hallway and he runs into Damian, almost knocking him over.

Since girls night, Sammy has fallen in love with Damian, and their relationship is actually pretty cute.

Damian leans down which gives Sammy the perfect opportunity to give him tons of kisses.

"I'm gonna miss you, buddy," Damian says before he stands.

My mom chuckles before turning back to me.

"Call me if you need anything, sweetie," mom squeezes my upper arms with a sad smile. I nod.

"I will, mom. Love you."

"I love you, Gwenny," she tells me as I walk to the front door, patting Sammy on the head before Damian and I head out.

———————

The drive back to campus wasn't as bad as I thought it would be. Winter break went by a lot quicker than anticipated, but part of me is happy to be back on campus.

Although everywhere I look reminds me of green eyes, dark hair, and the sexiest smile I've ever seen. I still haven't talked to him, even though I unblocked his number and have almost sent a hundred different texts before deciding against it and erasing the whole thing.

I'm being a coward. I know I should just reach out to him, but I can't handle being hurt by him again. If he confirms everything Amy told me, I don't think I'd survive.

But what if he tells me none of it was true? What if Amy was truly just a jealous bitch and told me they slept together to get me out of the picture? Would I take him back? Would he even want me back after I left him without an explanation and told him never to talk to me again?

What if I see him on campus, or on our way to classes? What if we have a class together? All the what ifs are driving me insane. I've been sitting in my room going through every single scenario possible and every one of them makes me question if I should just leave and go home. See if I can take the rest of my classes online or some shit.

But I'm not going to let him affect me that way. I'm going to suck it up, hold my head up high, and act like I'm not completely crushed by the only man I want.

I got an email from Professor Whitely this morning asking for me to come in to see her tomorrow morning before going to my first class. I'm not sure what she'd want me to come in for considering I'm not even her student anymore, but I can't say I didn't miss her. She's the only professor on this campus that I've ever actually liked.

"Bitch?" I hear a voice call from the hallway. I wide grin spreads across my face as I jump off my bed, tossing my phone to the side to run out into the hall.

Lainey stands there, her red hair now a shade of dark purple, wearing a black mini skirt and a bright pink crop top with a huge smile on her face to match mine.

"Bitch!" I run to her with my arms open, smashing into her, and we hold onto each other for a few minutes, squealing with excitement as if we hadn't seen each other at least five times during the break.

Lainey grabs a strand of her purple hair and twirls it around her finger. "Like the new hair?" she asks, batting her eyelashes flirtatiously. I reach up to run my fingers through it. The under part is darker than what's on top, and it makes for a nice contrast. It looks great on her, and I think it fits her personality so much better than the red.

"I love it. It's so you," I say, and her smile grows. I look out into the living room, but I don't see Ellie or Haley. "Where's Haley and El?" I know they drove together, so she has to be here somewhere.

"Hal texted the group chat and said she'd be coming tomorrow. She doesn't have classes tomorrow. And El is at the Elite mansion. Something about having to talk to Holland," Lainey shrugs. My heartbeat picks up and my skin crawls at the mention of the mansion. Ryker is probably already back, and the reality of seeing him makes me nauseous.

Fuck, this sucks.

"Speaking of the mansion, have you talked to Ryker yet?" she asks as she searches my face. I shake my head and she groans. "Gwen, you have to talk to him. You go to the same school. You live on the same road for Christ's sake. You'll run into him eventually, you know."

"I know, Lain. I just… I don't know what I'd even say at this point. It's been weeks since we've spoken and he probably hates me for leaving and not letting him explain himself," I whine. "Maybe I'll just drop out and move to Canada."

"You hate the snow, and Canada gets a lot of it," Lainey says pointedly. She has a point. "Just talk to him."

I groan exaggeratedly before walking into the living room and plopping down on the couch. Lainey follows and sits down next to me.

The front door swings open and Ellie walks through. We lock eyes and squeal before running into each other's arms.

"Hi!" Ellie's sweet voice chimes.

"Hi!" I grin. Seeing Ellie and Lainey has already made me feel so much better. They're like a breath of fresh air after weeks of drowning.

"I missed you," Ellie says. She's been stuck at home dealing with some family issues which she hasn't disclosed with the group yet, but we're not going to push her to tell us if she's not ready to share.

"I missed you too," I throw my arms around her shoulders in another hug, and she giggles.

My head peaks up to the open door behind her. My heart freezes in my chest and my throat tightens at the sight of Ellie's brother standing in my doorway. I haven't seen any of the guys since the end of semester party and I wasn't expecting to see them so soon.

"Hey," Holland says softly, as if we're friends. I pull away from Ellie giving her a wary expression. She gives me a sheepish smile. I look back at Lainey who just shrugs, clearly unaware of whatever is happening right now.

"El… why is he here?" I ask cautiously, gesturing to Holland who looks like he'd rather be anywhere but here.

Before Ellie can answer, Holland speaks up. "Inviting you ladies to a back-to-school party tonight at the Elite mansion," he says with a cocky grin. Hell to the no. I am not stepping foot in that house. Not after what happened last time.

"Absolutely not," I say, taking a step back as Holland invites himself in. He shakes his head knowingly as if he assumed that would be my answer.

"It's less of an invite and more of a demand," he says in a gruff tone. I cross my arms over my chest.

"A demand from whom?" I ask, although I already know the answer.

"Just be there. Ten p.m.," he orders, as if I'll listen to him.

"And if I'm not?" I challenge.

Hollands lips lift into a knowing smirk, and it makes chills run down my spine. "You will be."

With that, he moves past his sister and out the door, shutting it behind him.

My blood boils and I can feel the rage sinking in. Who does Ryker think he is? We haven't spoken in weeks and now he's demanding me to come to his house for a party? And he didn't even have the decency to ask me himself.

The freaking nerve.

He can't actually think that I'll show up. He's not that dense. Well, maybe he is.

My thoughts run back to the night of the end of semester party when Amy decided to blow up my life.

"I'm sorry, I didn't mean to blindside you. I'm Amy, by the way. Ryker and I have been hooking up for a while. I think he might even want to make it official."

"Ryker likes to keep his options open. He always has, and you don't strike me as the kind of girl that likes to have casual relationships."

My skin crawls at the memory and my eyes begin to water. Shit, I don't want to cry anymore.

Ellie walks over to me, setting her small hand on my arm.

"I'm sorry, Gwen. He didn't give me a choice. He just followed me over," she tells me, her voice genuine.

I nod. I know she wouldn't do anything on purpose, I'm just… I don't know, taken aback, I guess. I wasn't expecting Holland to be here, and I definitely wasn't expecting to be invited to a party where Ryker will be tonight.

Lainey hops up from the couch and head to where I stand. She reaches out and slams her hands down on my shoulders making me look at her. She gives me her best serious expression.

"We are going to that party, and you are going to look hot as fuck. Ryker is going to regret ever fucking with you," she assures me, but I'm not so sure about this plan, and Lainey can see that. "Trust me. Everything is going to fine. And if not, I'll kick him in the balls."

I giggle at the thought of Lainey kicking Ryker in the balls. I kind of feel like doing it too, but I won't.

"I don't think it's a good idea..." I say apprehensively. Ellie stands next to Lainey, and I feel like I'm being lectured.

"We've got you, Gwen. We always do," she tells me with a sweet smile.

I sigh heavily, knowing there is no way I'm getting out of this. "Fine. Okay, we'll go. But I'm not staying long. I just want to get a drink," I tell them in a serious tone, widening my eyes like a mother would do if they were scolding their child.

"Yay! Okay, we have two hours to get ready. Get your ass in the shower. I'll pick out the hottest outfit I can muster," Lainey orders like she's a drill sergeant. I laugh at the seriousness in her tone.

"Okay, okay," I say as I saunter off to my room feeling nervous and uneasy.

This is not going to end well; I just know it.

I adjusted my dress that Lainey picked out for me for what feels like the hundredth time, my fingers trembling slightly. Lainey and Ellie flanked me on either side, their supportive smiles doing little to calm the storm inside me.

The Elite mansion looks more intimidating than it's ever been as we stand and stare at it. I haven't been able to bring myself to go in yet, but Ellie and Lainey don't seem to mind.

Laughter and music spill out into the night, and already drunk partygoers stumble around the front yard.

"Are you ready?" Lainey asks, her voice gentle but I can hear the concern in it.

I take a deep breath, my heart pounding. "No, but I don't think I'll ever be. So let's get this over with," I say, putting on a brave face as I stand up taller and push out my chest.

The dress is a dark green color, with a plunging neckline that stops just above my belly button, and it's so short, I'm convinced my ass is hanging out of it. The black heels I wear have straps that go up my calf.

Lainey did a smokey eye look for my makeup and added some dark red lipstick to stand out. My hair is down in curls so it cascades over my shoulders and back.

I feel sexy, and I haven't felt sexy since… since I was with Ryker.

My chest tightens but Ellie squeezes my hand reassuringly. "We'll be right here with you the whole time, and we can leave whenever."

As we step inside, the strobe lights and smell of booze hits my nostrils, and the sea of familiar faces does little to ease my anxiety. I scan the room, looking for the man who summoned me here, but I don't see him yet. A wave of temporary relief washes over me.

"Let's get a drink," Ellie suggests loudly over the music, leading us to the kitchen. I nod numbly, trying to steady myself.

She stops abruptly in front of me causing me to run into her back.

"El? What's-" my voice drops off as I find what she's looking at.

Ryker stands in front of us, his black hair a bit longer than before, curling at the ends. He's in his signature black t-shirt and black jeans with combat boots.

He looks delicious, and my heart begins to feel like it's going to burst. I wasn't expecting to find him this soon. Did he see us walk in?

Ryker's eyes darken and I watch his hands clench into fists at his sides. A shiver runs down my spine and my pussy clenches at the way his green eyes look me up and down.

"You want us to stay?" she whispers in my ear. I swallow hard and take a deep breath before shaking my head. I need to do this alone. "Remember, the balls."

Lainey gives my hand another squeeze before grabbing Ellie and pulling her out of the kitchen.

There's a long silence between us and I can feel the tension building in the large kitchen. Before I know what's happening, Ryker is in front of me, grabbing my elbow firmly and pulling me away from the curious stares of the partygoers, and pushing me into a dimly lit room off of the kitchen.

The heavy oak doors swing shut behind us, cutting us off from the music and laughter of the party. My heart is on overdrive and the anxiety in my body is making my skin tingle. I don't even know how to feel right now, and it's beyond frustrating. He's beyond frustrating.

Ryker's breath is ragged, his eyes dark with a mix of emotions. I've seen him angry; I've seen him calm, but I don't think I've ever seen him like this.

"You left," he starts, and my eyes shoot to his. That's the first thing he chooses to say to me? "You left, and you didn't even give me the chance to explain," he grits out.

"What was there to explain, Ryker?" I snap back as anger begins to surpass the anxiety I was feeling just moments ago.

"I could have told you the goddamn truth!" he yells, frustration clear in his features. I scoff, shaking my head. "Do you really believe I'd cheat on you?"

I stand my ground as Ryker takes a few steps in my direction. "Why shouldn't I believe it? I knew I was never going to be enough for you. I was stupid to think you could want only me." I turn around to head for the door because this isn't going anywhere, but Ryker's large hand grabs my wrist, pulling me back.

"You know, I've never had to beg or grovel, but I'll be damned if I let you walk away without hearing me out,' he seethes before taking in a calming breath, his eyes softening just a touch. "I wouldn't do that to you, Gwen. You have to know that."

I don't know what to believe. I don't know what to say. This whole situation has been a huge fucking shitshow and I hate Amy for putting these thoughts in my head. I was fine. *We* were fine.

"How could I know that? Before me, you were known for one-night stands and hookups. Why would I be any different?" I ask, my vision becoming blurry as tears threaten to spill. I bite the inside of my cheek to keep them from falling.

His eyes flash with rage, his hands clenching and unclenching at his sides. "That's not fair. You can't use my past against me. You know I'm not that same guy you ran into months ago," he growls.

I cross my arms over my chest timidly. I know it's not fair for me to bring up the past. I know he's different now, but it's hard to trust that he won't miss that life one day.

"How do I know you won't get tired of me?" I ask, my eyes welling with fresh tears.

"Because I fucking love you!" he yells frustratedly. "I knew you were different from all the other girls because you didn't care about who I was or what I could do for you. You argued with me, you challenged me, you made me question everything I thought I knew, and I hated you for it. But it was never really hate," he moves closer to me and I flinch slightly before his warm hand lands on my cheek.

His face softens and my pulse races. Ryker loves me?

"I've loved you since the moment you showed me you wouldn't put up with my shit. And I can't stand the thought of you thinking I would ever do something to hurt you."

Ryker's eyes blaze with a fierce intensity as he walks me back until I'm pushed up against the wall. His hand reaches above my head as he uses it to hold himself up while his other hand still rests on my cheek.

"You want an explanation? Fine. But you're going to listen, and you're going to believe me, Gwen."

He knows I love it when he's demanding, and I don't want to be distracted right now. I'm still so confused and so hurt, but the way he's looking at me right now has me forgetting what I was even mad about.

"Amy and I fucked, yes. But it was way before I even knew you. She's been obsessed with me ever since, stalking me, and she must have seen us together. She lied to you, Gwen. I was with Pat at an Elite meeting the night before the party. I haven't been with anyone else since I met you. I have not and will not ever betray your trust like that."

He pushes his body flush against mine, and my breath hitches as I feel the rigid length of his arousal pressing against my stomach. Holy shit, I've missed that.

Amy lied. She was jealous and she lied to me to get me away from Ryker. I didn't even give him the benefit of the doubt. I just believed her and left. Oh my God, I'm a horrible person. How does Ryker not hate me right now?

"She… lied?" I ask, my voice shaky as I hold back tears. Ryker caresses my cheek softly, his features gentle as he nods.

"Yes, Rebel. She lied," he tells me, wiping away a tear that I hadn't realized had fallen. "Shh. Why are you crying?"

I try to look down so he doesn't see more tears spill out, but he holds my head in place, forcing me to look at him.

"Why are you crying, Gwen?" he asks again, this time more commanding.

"I'm just… I'm so sorry, Ryker," I say, giving up on trying to hold my tears. They stream down my cheeks as Ryker's face drops.

"What are you sorry for? You didn't do anything," he says.

"I left. I believed Amy and I left without giving you a chance to defend yourself. I hated you for weeks. I hated you because I thought you'd betrayed me. I hated that I loved you, even when I'd thought you'd cheated," my voice shakes, and I try to take a deep breath. "I'm sorry."

Ryker's head tilts slightly as his brow furrows. He searches my face before tucking a piece of hair behind my ear.

"Loved?" he asks. My lips turn up into a small smile.

"Love," I say, and a huge grin takes over Ryker's hard features. "I love you, Ryker."

Chapter 53

GUINEVERE

Ryker's mouth descends on mine, his kiss hungry and demanding. I can feel the raw power and urgency in his touch, his need to possess and dominate.

I can feel all of the anger, hurt, and betrayal begin to melt away as Ryker's kiss deepens. My hands find his shoulders, my fingers digging into his muscles as I respond to his touch. His tongue traces the contours of my mouth, tasting, exploring, demanding a response.

Breaking the kiss, he trails hot, open-mouthed kisses along my jawline, his breath hot against my skin. "Say you believe me, Gwen," he growls, his voice thick with desire. "Tell me you know I'd never hurt you like that."

My eyes flutter closed as I feel his teeth nip at my sensitive earlobe. "I believe you, Ryker," I whisper, my body already trembling for him.

Ryker's hands slide down to cup my ass, lifting me against him so I can feel every hard inch of his desire. "You're the only one, Gwen," he whispers in a deep, husky voice that makes my panties wet as his lips brush against my ear. "I've never wanted anyone else the way I want you. I ache for you, only you."

His words send a shiver down my spine, and I can feel the want for him building in my core.

Ryker's mouth finds mine again, his hands roaming over my body, mapping every curve as if to brand me as his own. My dress begins to slide down my shoulders, baring my soft, tan skin to him.

He leaves kisses down my neck, pausing to suck gently on the sensitive skin, leaving his mark.

I let out a soft moan as my head falls back to give him better access. His teeth graze my collarbone, his hands smoothing over my thighs, inching upwards.

"You have no idea what you do to me, Gwen," he mutters against my skin as I pant. "How much I need to be inside you."

My breath quickens as his fingers trace the edges of my lace panties. "Show me," I tell him, my voice thick with need.

He doesn't need to be told twice. His fingers hook into the waistband of my panties, sliding them down my legs. I step out of them, my body on fire with anticipation. Ryker's eyes darken with desire as his eyes move up and down my bare, willing body.

Lifting me into his arms, he kisses me as he walks over to the large desk that sits in the back of the room in front of a grand bookcase. He places me on the desk, spreading my legs to settle between them.

I gasp as I feel the cool wood against my back, my breasts heaving with each rapid breath. Ryker's hands caress my thighs, spreading me open to his hungry gaze.

"So fucking beautiful," he murmurs, his breath ghosting over my wetness. "And so fucking mine."

I whimper as I feel his hot breath on my sensitive core, my hips involuntarily lifting in invitation. Ryker obliges, his tongue sliding between my lips. He moans at the first lick, his hands gripping my thighs as he delves deeper, exploring me with slow, deliberate strokes.

My inhibitions have flown straight out the window. We should talk more. But I can't even think straight with his mouth on me.

Tangling my hands in his hair, I hold him to my pussy as waves of pleasure crash through me. Ryker licks and sucks, his tongue flicking over my swollen clit. I reach up to pinch one of my nipples, loving the way my senses are heightened.

I'm writhing beneath him, my body arching as an orgasm builds within me.

Ryker must sense my impending release, because he begins to flick his tongue faster, and he sticks two large fingers into my pussy making me cry out. My body tenses as my orgasm rips through me. Ryker doen't stop, his tongue relentless as he drives me towards another climax.

I'm panting and trying to catch my breath.

"Ryker...please..." I moan. "I need you inside me. Now."

"So needy, Rebel. So desperate for my cock," he pulls his fingers out and holds them in front of me. They glisten with my wetness, and when Ryker brings them to my lips, his hooded eyes darken. "Suck," he orders.

I open my mouth and shoves his fingers in. I suck his fingers, and my pussy clenches. This is the most erotic thing I've ever done, and I think I love it.

"You want me, baby?" he asks in his deep, smoky voice. I nod, because I've lost the ability to say words.

Ryker's eyes smolder as he rises to his feet, the outline of his erection evident through his jeans. He sheds his clothes slowly, sensually, revealing his chiseled body and thick, hard length. The bruises that once covered his side from his rugby accident are no longer visible.

He positions himself at my entrance, his breath ragged with lust and desire.

With a smooth, powerful thrust, he buries himself to the hilt, claiming me with a savage growl. I cry out at the feeling of fullness, my eyes rolling back in pleasure.

Ryker begins to move, his hips snapping as he drives into me again and again.

His fingers dig into my hips, holding me in place as he pounds into me with fierce possession. I meet his thrusts, my nails raking his back as I climb higher.

How did I go so long without this?

"Such a good girl. You take my cock so well," Ryker hisses through gritted teeth.

Ryker's body glistens with sweat, his muscles working as he thrusts deep, hitting the spot that drives me wild. My head falls back, and I let out a loud moan as another orgasm builds at the base of my spine.

"Come for me, baby girl," he growls, his voice hoarse with need. "Let me feel your greedy pussy tighten around my cock."

His demanding words send me spiraling over the edge once more. Crying out, my body convulses around him as pleasure overtakes me.

"Atta girl. Fuck, Rebel," Ryker groans.

With a few more powerful thrusts, Ryker stills inside me, and I can feel his dick pulsating as his body shudders with the force of his climax.

Collapsing onto me, he buries his face in my neck, his breath warm against my sweaty skin. My fingers stroke his hair as we let our heart rates slow. Ryker lifts his head, his eyes searching mine.

"Believe me now, Guinevere?" he asks, his voice soft but intense. Do I? Does this change anything? Can I trust him?

As he lay naked on top of me after fucking me and filling me with his come, I look into his green eyes, the black ring around them making them pop. I do. I do believe him.

That might make me stupid or naïve or whatever, but I believe that he loves me. I believe that everything Amy said was a lie. I believe that he would never purposely do anything to hurt me.

Reaching up, I push a few pieces of hair away from his face, keeping my hands on either side of his face as I look him in the eye. "I believe you."

Ryker's thumb brushes my swollen lower lip, his eyes moving from my lips to my eyes, a small grin forming on his lips. "Good."

When I left Ryker's last night, I felt like a weight had been lifted off my shoulders. When I got there, I was not expecting that we'd sleep together. In fact, I was planning on leaving there in tears, then sitting in my living room with a tub of ice cream as I sobbed while watching The Notebook because I love to torture myself.

He told me loves me. Ryker Steele loves me. If anyone would have told me that I, Guinevere Sharpe, would be in love with Ryker Steele and he in love with me when we first met, I would have laughed in their face. Like a full-on cackle.

There is no universe where I could have seen this happening. No psychic could have predicted it. It's truly one of those 'expect the unexpected' moments.

Campus is cold this morning, with the January weather in full swing. January is the worst month because it snows the most between now and the end February. You would think that the snowiest month would be December, but not in Connecticut.

The parking lot closest to Mallory Center was full, so I had to park at Whittaker Hall which is the furthest away from Mallory. It's like negative ten degrees out, okay, maybe that's an exaggeration. But it feels like it.

It should be a crime to have to walk around campus at this time of year. Trudging through the snow and cold is not something I enjoy doing, and if my mom didn't live in Rhode Island, I'd probably be moving somewhere warmer after graduation.

I wonder what Ryker will want to do after graduation. Will he want to stay in Connecticut or Rhode Island? Will he want to move somewhere completely different? Will he want me to come with him? I guess we have some things to talk about.

After what feels like eight years, I finally make it to Mallory and head upstairs to Professor Whitely's office. I still haven't been able to figure out what she'd want from me.

As I shake myself off and stomp my boots on the ground to get rid of the snow, I turn the corner to my old professor's office and bump into something hard. Looking down at the combat boots in front of me, my stomach flutters, knowing exactly who it is.

When I look up, I'm met with intense green eyes and a sexy smolder. My stupid heart skips a beat at the sight of him. Gorgeous and sexy as sin, as always.

"You make a habit of running into people?" Ryker asks, his lips twitching into a grin.

I set my hands on my hips. "Do you make a habit of standing in the middle of walkways?" I snap back, remembering having this exact conversation all those months ago.

"What are you doing here?" he questions, his eyes narrowing and his head tilting slightly to the side making his dark hair fall into his face. He brushes it back with his hand, and I imagine having that very hand wrapped around my neck as he pounds into me.

"I, um…" damnit, Gwen. Get a freaking grip. "Professor Whitely… she wanted to see me," I stutter like the dumbass I am. I internally scold myself for being so blatantly obvious as Ryker's lips turn into a knowing smirk. "Why are you here?"

Ryker shrugs. "Same."

My brows pull together as curiosity and suspicion course through me.

The door to Professor Whitely's office flies open, and our heads snap to the short woman with her signature black pencil skirt and blouse that shows off way too much cleavage for a college professor standing in the doorway with a wide grin.

"I thought I heard you two out here. Come in," she says, gesturing inside her office. We do as we're told, taking a seat in each of the chairs in front of her desk. I get a feeling of déjà vu as I watch Professor Whitely sit across from us.

She pushes her red rimmed glasses over the bridge of her nose before leaning forward and placing her forearms on her desk. She looks between both of us, and anticipation creeps in.

"So, you're probably wondering why you're both here. Well, let's get down to it," she says, clearing her throat before continuing. "I want you both to be my TA's this semester," she states. My eyes widen.

"What?" I ask, confused.

"Both of us?" Ryker muses. Professor Whitely nods.

"Both of you. You work so well together, and I think it would be more productive to have both of you instead of one or the other," she explains with a with a smile. "My classes get quite large, and I'd need you both to help grade, answer questions, and walk around during class to help students. Do you think you can do that?"

Ryker and I exchange a wary glance, but I know we're both thinking the same thing.

"Yes," we say in unison.

Professor Whitely smiles widely. "Wonderful! I'll send you both an email with all of the things you'll need, and you can start with my first class tomorrow morning. I made sure you both had no classes at that time, so you'll be all good to come."

She hands us each a binder full of papers and explains a bit more about what we'll be doing before dismissing us.

An hour later, Ryker and I lie on my bed. I'm cuddled up at his side as his finger gently traces over my back.

It's weird, all that anger and betrayal I felt just yesterday has completely faded away, and love and admiration have taken their place. I was fully prepared to start the semester off depressed and avoiding Ryker at all costs.

But here we are, naked and intertwined with each other.

"Are you ready to spend the rest of the semester with me?" Ryker probes, his voice hoarse and teasing. I pick my head up off of his chest to look him in the eyes.

"Definitely," I say in a sultry tone as I nip his earlobe. His hand moves into my hair, pulling me away from his neck. His eyes dance with warning, and my thighs clench.

"Don't start something you can't finish, little Rebel."

He did just make me come three times, and my body is spent, but I'd do anything for this man to make him feel good.

I move down his body slowly until my face is hovering above his dick, which is already hard. Peaking up at him through my lashes, I drag my tongue up his length slowly, swirling it around the head while I watch Ryker's head fall back with a groan. A smirk plays on my lips, knowing this is driving him wild.

Doing it again, I bring my hand down to cup his balls and squeeze lightly. He looks down at me with a dark expression.

"Don't be a brat, Guinevere. Suck my fucking cock like the good girl I know you can be," he demands in a deep, dominating tone. Shit, how does he do that? How can he make me wet without even touching me?

I begin to suck and twirl my tongue around him, his pants and grunts making me move faster. His hands weave into my hair as he moves my head, forcing me to watch him.

"Look at me while you take my dick in your mouth," he orders, and I do as he says, watching him as my head bobs up and down.

He begins to thrust into my mouth faster and harder, and within a few minutes, a hot stream of come slides down my throat. When he pulls out, he pulls me up, pressing his lips to mine.

"You are perfect, little Rebel," he tells me, his eyes searching mine. "I love you."

My heart flutters and I can't help the stupid grin that crosses my face. I don't think I'll ever get tired of hearing him tell me he loves me.

A few months ago, I wasn't sure if true love actually existed, no matter how much I wanted to believe it did.

I wanted a love like in the books I read. With men who love their woman unconditionally, irrevocably, completely. Men who look at them like they're the moon and the stars.

Real life isn't a romance novel. It's not love songs and perfection. Real life is raw, broken. It's imperfections and desperation.

I knew it had to be out there somewhere. That passionate, exciting, obsessive kind of love. The happily ever afters.

And I finally found it, with Ryker Steele.

"I love you," I whisper, and then, his lips are on mine again.

Epilogue

RYKER

The stands are full of proud parents, grandparents, and faculty, here to watch their students walk the stage for their college graduation.

The front lawn is packed with hundreds of chairs for the graduating students. I sit close to the back since my name starts with S, and the only good thing about that is that Gwen's does too, so she's only a row in front of me. Pat's in the same row as Gwen, with his last name being Samuelson.

She looks back at me, shooting me that drop dead gorgeous grin of hers that makes my chest squeeze. No one could have convinced me this would be my life by the end of my college career. Being the newly appointed CEO of The Steele corporation, having my brothers by my side, and being completely, head over heels in love with the most perfect woman on this planet.

The only thing that could make this day better is if our whole group was graduating today. Lainey, Ellie, Holland, and Logan still have a year to go, but I don't think it'll make much a difference since I know Gwen will be dragging me back here constantly to visit.

She was ecstatic for me when I told her the guys and I got our fathers to step down and hand over their titles to us. When I told her I'd have to travel to the city, she insisted we just move there together so we'd never have to be apart. I put a downpayment on a nice place in the Upper East Side the next day.

Logan and my mother were less than thrilled that I kept them in the dark about the takeover, but after the initial shock wore off, my mother was extremely thankful for what I did for her. She now has full control of The Steele Estate and will continue to get money from my father for the rest of her life. Logan told me he would have helped me with our plan, but it was better to keep him out of it. Now our father will only hate me, and not him.

The announcer's voice catches my attention when they call Gwen's name.

"Guinevere Lane Sharpe, Education Major."

My little Rebel walks up the stairs to the stage, her smile widening when Dean Ashby hands her her diploma.

Screams erupt behind me, and I know it's Lainey, Ellie, Haley, and her mother. Her father came up with some excuse not to come, but I think she expected that, so she wasn't too upset.

Gwen laughs and waves the diploma over her head before stepping off the stage.

I feel a sense of pride knowing that she's mine, and no one will ever have her again. No one can take her from me, and I will kill anyone who tries. I'm not losing her again.

———————————

As we stand around the big courtyard talking and laughing with our friends, I can't help but be thankful for everything I have. My life was a shitshow before I met Gwen, and now it's better than I could have ever imagined. And it's all due to her.

This feisty, strong, determined, resilient woman standing next to me, looking at me like I'm her whole world.

"I'm going to miss you so much," Lainey sobs into Gwen's shoulder. Gwen giggles. That sound has quickly become my favorite sound from her, other than her moaning my name.

"Lain, you live like thirty minutes away. And I'll be visiting Ellington as often as I can," she assures her.

"I know, but the house won't be the same without you," she whines. Ellie and Haley nod in agreement.

"Seriously, who am I going to complain to about Lainey's shitty cooking or Ellie's obsessive need to clean literally everything?" Haley teases. Lainey shoots her a glare.

"You said you liked my cooking," she says, looking offended. Gwen laughs again.

"You guys will be fine. And we'll talk every day. It'll be like nothing changed."

"I know it's impossible, but don't forget about me," Damian chimes in, Allie Moore by his side. According to Gwen, they hit it off at the end of semester party and have been together ever since.

Lainey rolls her eyes. "I'm going to try my hardest to forget about you," she teases before giving him a hug. I don't get their relationship.

"Hey, Barkley. You ready to spend another year with me?" Holland winks. Lainey's eyes narrow, shooting daggers at Holland's head no doubt.

"I'd rather step on Legos."

"Aw, come on, babe. Don't be like that," his hand flies to his chest in mock offense.

Lainey grimaces. "Don't call me babe."

"Would you rather me call you a bitch?" he muses, his eyes flickering with mischief. Lainey growls.

"Watch it, Monroe. I'm not afraid to knee you in the balls," she threatens, and Holland laughs. I'm pretty positive they're totally in love with each other and they don't want to admit it to themselves by the way they bicker.

"You know, I've never been into masochism, but if you wanna try it," Holland taunts, making Lainey shake with anger.

"Okayyy. As riveting as this little pissing contest is, we have more important things to talk about," Mason says as he steps in between them. "We're meeting back at the mansion, right?"

"Yeah. Teddy and Austin just got back with the kegs," Pat tells him. Mason shoots us a shit eating grin before throwing his hands in the air.

"Let's fucking party!" he shouts so everyone around us can hear him. Shaking my head, I lean down to kiss the top of Gwen's head before we follow Mason to the cars.

I hop in the driver's seat of my Escalade as Gwen climbs into the passenger side. She looks at me, her blue eyes sparkling with glee. I've never seen her so content.

"What?" I ask, reaching up to place my hand on the side of her hair. Her eyes search mine before replying.

"I didn't think it was possible to be this happy," she smiles.

I swipe my thumb over her cheek softly, thinking about how I got here and what I did to deserve this. Shifting in my seat, I face her, grabbing her hands in mine. She watches my face as I search hers.

"Gwen," I begin, my voice shaky. "I couldn't have imagined finding someone that I cared so deeply for, let alone finding someone that I want to spend the rest of my life with," my heart is racing and I've never felt this nervous in my life.

Taking a deep breath, I reach into my pocket to pull out a small, velvet box. Gwen's breath hitches when she sees what's in my hand and realizes what's happening. Her eyes well with tears as her hand covers her mouth.

I open the tiny box, revealing a stunning diamond. After we got back together, I knew I was never going to let her go again. I was positive she was it for me. So I had a family friend who owns a jewelry shop in the city make me a custom ring.

"Guinevere Lane Sharpe, my Rebel. From the moment I met you, my life changed in ways I never imagined possible. You brought this light into my world, you made me believe in love, and showed me what it truly means to care for someone," her tears flow a bit more now, and I wipe them away with my thumb before continuing.

"Before you, I never thought I would find someone who could understand me so completely, who could challenge me, and who could piss me off so much and make me hard at the same time," Gwen giggles. "You are the first person I've ever truly cared about, the first person who made me believe in a future filled with love and happiness. I can't imagine taking the next steps in my life without you by my side. It's not going to be easy, we'll have our challenges, but we'll be stronger for them. And I promise to love you, to cherish the ground you walk on. I love you so fucking much, and I want to spend the rest of my life showing you just how much," I take a deep breath as Gwen chews on the tips of her fingers nervously. I pull out the ring and hold it over her shaking hand. "Gwen, will you marry me?"

"Yes, yes. Oh my god, are you sure?" she giggles through her tears, and she's the prettiest goddamn girl I've ever laid my eyes on. I chuckle, placing the ring on her finger. She holds it in front of her, her face full of excitement, nervousness, and love.

"I've never been more sure about anything in my entire life. I love you, Rebel." Her grin grows wider as she throws her arms over my shoulders.

"I love you, Hotshot," she tells me before kissing me.

I am officially the luckiest man in the world, and I'm not going to let anything mess it up. Guinevere Sharpe, I'm never letting you go.

THE END

Authors Note

First, I'd like to thank you all for taking the time to join Guinevere and Ryker on their journey at Ellington University. I am so grateful to have you here.

I'd like to take a moment to acknowledge the people that have been so supportive and encouraging during this process. Writing is a crazy journey, and I'm so thankful for the people in my life that supported me every step of the way.

A special thank you to my parents for dealing with me as I asked them questions that I probably could have googled.

Thank you to my beta readers for your time and dedication to reading my story and helping me edit and helping me make it even better. I could have done this without you.

Lastly, to my readers, I wouldn't be here if it wasn't for you. Thank you for your continuous support and encouragement.

I love you all!

Love always,
Rae Quinn

About the Author

344

Rae Quinn is a romance author and screenwriter who lives in Upstate New York with her pup Layla. When she's not writing sappy romance novels, she's consuming way too much coffee, reading a book, and travelling.

Join Rae Quinn on social media to keep up to date on new releases, giveaways, and more!

Instagram: @authorraequinn_
Goodreads: Rae Quinn
Facebook: Rae Quinn – Author
Tiktok: _raequinn_